The Superwoman and
Other Writings

Portrait of Miss Miriam Michelson, *The World's Work* (1904).

[handwritten inscription] Deborah — Thanks for your support of women who break the mould — all the best, Michelson

The Superwoman and Other Writings by Miriam Michelson

ᴄᴗ

Edited with an Introduction
by Lori Harrison-Kahan

[handwritten inscription] To Deborah, Onward! Lori Harrison-Kahan

WAYNE STATE UNIVERSITY PRESS
DETROIT

ISBN 978-0-8143-4357-9; (paperback); ISBN 978-0-8143-4608-2 (printed case); ISBN 978-0-8143-4358-6 (ebook)

Library of Congress Control Number: 2018948422

Wayne State University Press
Leonard N. Simons Building
4809 Woodward Avenue
Detroit, Michigan 48201-1309

Visit us online at wsupress.wayne.edu

CONTENTS

Acknowledgments

"There is no such thing as a Superwoman," writes Chimamanda Ngozi Adichie in her book *Dear Ijeawele, or A Feminist Manifesto in Fifteen Suggestions*. Indeed, no woman can do it all alone, and it gives me great pleasure to acknowledge the individuals who contributed to transforming *The Superwoman and Other Writings by Miriam Michelson* from fantasy into reality.

This project would not have been possible without the support of Boston College's Undergraduate Research Fellowships. I want to acknowledge the talents and enthusiasm of the students who assisted me in recovering Michelson's work and editing this volume: Marena Cole, Marianna Sorensen, Grace Denny, Karen Choi, and Maggie McQuade. Thanks, too, to Arianna Unger, my research assistant during my semester as scholar-in-residence at the Hadassah-Brandeis Institute.

The interlibrary loan staff at Boston College also helped make this book possible. Thanks especially to Anne Kenny, Duane Farabaugh, and Shannon MacDowell, who put up with my barrage of requests. Staff at the Bancroft Library, the Houghton Library, the New York Public Library (especially Tal Nadan), the Lilly Library, the Library of Congress, and the University of Delaware Special Collections provided crucial assistance.

I was fortunate to have the opportunity to collaborate with Karen Skinazi on several articles and talks about Miriam Michelson while I was in the process of working on this book. When the task of recovering the work of such a prolific writer on my own seemed insurmountable, Karen's energy and shared passion for Michelson's writing buoyed me. A good deal of my thinking about Michelson took place through my collaboration with Karen, and I am indebted to her for the significant role she played in this book.

The members of my writing group, Kimberly Chabot Davis and Elif Armbruster, saw this book through from its proposal stage to the final edits. Thank you for helping me bring this "nasty woman" to the attention of a broader audience.

Joan Michelson, who wrote the foreword to this book, was one of its most enthusiastic supporters. Thank you for providing a living model of your great-great-aunt and for making me feel connected to the Michelson clan.

Many other friends and colleagues provided support and insight along the way, including Martha Cutter, Jennifer Tuttle, Desirée Henderson, Susan Tomlinson, Sari Edelstein, Mary Chapman, Mary Kelley, David Brauner, Axel Stähler, Michael Hoberman, Rachel Rubinstein, Caroline Luce, Shilpa Davé, Jean Lee Cole, Holly Jackson, Jacqueline Emery, Cristina Stanciu, Jean Marie Lutes, Christina Roberts, Cynthia Patterson, Ellen Gruber Garvey, Brooke Kroeger, Sharon Hamilton, Ilyon Woo, Joyce Antler, Sylvia Fishman, Shulamit Reinharz, Lisa Fishbayn Joffe, Josh Lambert, Jennifer Glaser, Sarah Casteel, Rachel Gordan, Chantal Ringuet, Kathryn Hellerstein, Jonathan Freedman, Donna Campbell, Jessica Lang, Betsy Klimasmith, Joe Kraus, Gary Totten, Luke Dietrich, Eli Bromberg, Jonathan Sarna, Amy Powell, Stephen Whitfield, Darren Gobert, Katherine Kendall, Jennifer Sartori, Barbara Cantalupo, Steven Zipperstein, Jacques Berlinerblau, Keren Hammerschlag, Adam Lewis, Chris Wilson, Rhonda Frederick, Min Song, Elizabeth Graver, Tina Klein, Allison Adair, Lynne Anderson, and Judith Wilt. For assistance with translations, thanks to Marena Cole, Karen Choi (and her parents), Father Jiang, and Yin Yuan. Special thanks to Boston College English Department chairs Suzanne Matson and Amy Boesky for supporting my research.

Audiences at the 2015 Society for the Study of American Women Writers conference, the Sixth International Charlotte Perkins Gilman Society conference, the 2016 Northeast Modern Language Association conference, the 2016 American Jewish Historical Society's Biennial Scholars' Conference, the 2017 MELUS conference, the 2017 Berkshire Conference of Women Historians, the 2017 American Literature Association conference, and Georgetown University's conference on "The Modern Jewess: Image and Text" provided useful feedback on papers about Michelson. Thanks to the Western Literature Association for awarding me and Karen the Don D. Walker Prize and demonstrating Michelson's importance to the field of Western American literature. Thanks to the staff and editors at *Tablet Magazine*, *MELUS*, *Legacy*, and *American Periodicals*, as well as George Anderson from the *Dictionary of Literary Biography*, for the role they played in bringing wider attention to Michelson and her work. I am grateful to Kathy Wildfong, the staff at Wayne

State University Press, and two anonymous reviewers for seeing the value in this collection of Michelson's writings.

Thanks to the Boston College undergraduates in the Introduction to American Studies and Scribbling Women and Suffragettes: Human Rights and American Women's Writing, 1850–1920 who read Michelson's work with me and showed me that her writing has much to teach students today. Thanks to my parents, siblings, and in-laws for their support, especially my father-in-law, Mort Kahan, for his faithful attendance at my HBI talks. And finally, with much love, I thank David, Cuyler, Amory, and Bailey for unwittingly allowing Miriam into the family.

FOREWORD

Though it may be interesting or even entertaining,
the foremost value of news is as a utility to empower
the informed.

American Press Institute

The *Superwoman and Other Writings by Miriam Michelson*, edited by Lori Harrison-Kahan, reveals fascinating, previously untold stories from a historic time in America: the decades-long fight for the passage of the Nineteenth Amendment, which gave women the right to vote in 1920. At once engaging and scholarly, this book describes that era through the prism of Miriam Michelson's reporting and her fiction, giving us an eyewitness account of the early women's movement. Aptly timed with the nation's commemoration of the Nineteenth Amendment's centennial, this book is also critical to our current moment when women's power and activism are surging anew.

You'll see in these pages that Michelson personally and persistently kept the women's suffrage movement and its key players front and center in the news of the day. I am proud to be her great-great-niece and to have followed in her footsteps as a journalist, and as one who features women and their advancement prominently in my own work.

Aunt Miriam's work and life choices address many of the issues we still face today: the power of the vote, women's role(s) in society, how we define "success," and the responsibilities of the media and journalists. She debated these issues and "new paradigms of femininity" (see p. 20 in this volume) out loud with her readers and editors in both her journalism and her fiction.

This book celebrates women's accomplishments and documents how far women have come. Yet, as I read Michelson's accounts, I kept thinking about how much things have *not* changed for women.

Yes, women now have the vote, but they still fight to be taken seriously, to be paid equally, and to advance their careers, especially into leadership roles—and continue to be blocked by gender discrimination and harassment. Although it was written over a century ago, Michelson's novella *The Superwoman*, which juxtaposes a matriarchal society with a patriarchal one, remains relevant to our current moment and will offer readers new perspectives about gender dynamics.

Michelson's body of work also reminds us that success comes in many forms, and it is up to each of us to define it for ourselves. Modern Western society tends to measure success in terms of status, power, fame, and fortune, but there are other choices. Michelson chose to measure her success in terms of making an impact, receiving her due (including financially), and living life her own way.

Journalism is a career that enables you to make an impact, and Michelson used it to its fullest. It requires courage, fearlessness, and commitment. It also requires enjoying writing alone, talking to complete strangers (often for hours), asking questions that risk making people uncomfortable, and listening to people of all stripes who sometimes push back.

A journalist needs thick skin, critical thinking skills (and fast ones), and the ability to communicate clearly and objectively with a dose of creativity. The art of journalism requires telling stories, and using wordcraft in ways that resonate with various people while also inspiring them to think anew. As these pages reveal, Miriam Michelson was a master.

I see so much of my own journalism, journey, and persona in my great-great Aunt Miriam's story—frankly, it's rather spooky—and much to live up to.

On behalf of women journalists, and all working women, I say, Thank you, Aunt Miriam. Thank you for your courage, for the power you helped us gain, and for the road you paved for us.

Thank you, Lori Harrison-Kahan, for bringing Miriam's story into present light in this fascinating and inspiring book—and for graciously inviting me to be a tiny part of it.

JOAN BRYNA MICHELSON
GREEN CONNECTIONS MEDIA
@JOANMICHELSON
WWW.GREENCONNECTIONSRADIO.COM

A Note on the Text

I n making editing decisions, I have prioritized readability and fidelity to the original texts. In some cases, I silently corrected obvious typographical and spelling errors; in other cases, where the error may have been intentional, I used "*sic.*" Peculiarities of punctuation were maintained unless they would create confusion for the reader. Capitalization is as it appears in the original texts except in the cases of newspaper headlines, subheadlines, and story titles, which were edited for consistency. I italicized foreign words when they were italicized in the original text and retained diacritical marks that appear in the original text. All notes are the editor's.

For those wishing to consult the original sources for the transcriptions, the *San Francisco Call* is available through the California Digital Newspaper Collection and *Arthur McEwen's Letter* is available through archive.org. The *Bulletin* (San Francisco), the *North American* (Philadelphia), the *Saturday Evening Post*, and *Ainslee's* are available on microfilm. Issues of the *Smart Set*, the *Black Cat*, and *Century Illustrated Monthly Magazine* containing the stories by Michelson herein are available on Google Books. The full text of *A Yellow Journalist* is also available on Google Books.

Although "In the Bishop's Carriage," "The Ancestry of Irene," and "The Pencil Will" were subsequently published as book chapters, the versions of these stories herein are transcribed from the periodicals in which the stories originally appeared. Most of the discrepancies between the periodical and book versions are minor (e.g., punctuation). When the book version corrected an obvious typographical or grammatical error, I silently made the emendation as well. In cases where a character's name was changed or there are significant or interesting differences in the content of the two versions, I have included a note so that readers can compare the two versions. Readers interested in further comparing differences between the versions can consult the book versions of *In the Bishop's Carriage*, *The Madigans*, and *A Yellow Journalist* on Google Books.

INTRODUCTION

Miriam Michelson, Frontier Feminist

W hile working as a reporter for the *San Francisco Bulletin*, Miriam Michelson published a review of *Women and Economics* (1898), Charlotte Perkins (Stetson) Gilman's sociological study of gender and power relations that became a manifesto for the first-wave women's movement. "CHARLOTTE PERKINS STETSON FLAYS HER OWN SEX ALIVE" announces the attention-grabbing headline on the top of the page. "She Says . . . That Women Are Not Entitled to Financial Support from Men," elaborates a subheadline beside a portrait of a stern-faced woman. The caption identifying the subject of the portrait as "CHARLOTTE PERKINS STETSON" appears nearly contiguous with the article's byline, "BY MIRIAM MICHELSON," visually suggesting that the names of the book's author and its reviewer would hold equal importance for readers. At a time when many newspaper articles and reviews were published unsigned, Michelson's name—printed in bold, all-capital letters—leaps off the page. The newspaper's layout affirms her status as a celebrity "girl reporter."

An independent, single woman who supported herself as a journalist, Michelson finds much to praise about *Women and Economics*, even as she warns her readers that the author's "radical views" about gender relations were likely to provoke outrage, especially among men. "The average man," Michelson predicts, "will . . . disapprove so strongly . . . that he'll refuse to read all that Mrs. Stetson has to say." In expressing agreement with the book's central tenets, Michelson's review attests to the ideological common ground she shares with Gilman, while also evincing significant stylistic differences between the two women writers. Quoting liberally from *Women and Economics* to support her claim, Michelson describes Gilman's prose as "thoughtful, candid . . . absolutely fearless, passionless." Michelson's writing, in contrast, reads as passionate and lively. Like her byline, it leaps off the page, its tone lighthearted, entertaining, and conversational, where Gilman's

1

is serious, erudite, and formal. Michelson cheekily declares, for instance, that Gilman has "out-Anthonyed Susan" and at one point familiarly refers to her subject as "the audacious Charlotte."[1]

Gilman was less than pleased with this endorsement of *Women and Economics* and did not reciprocate the other writer's admiration. According to Michelson, Gilman objected to the reporter's "flippant humor," "sensational quoting of forceful one-sided passages," and "italicizing of extraordinary statements that might destroy a symmetrical view of a book which she regards—and justly—as a big part of her life work."[2] About a year after the review appeared in the *Bulletin*, Gilman, who was visiting San Francisco from the East, reluctantly agreed to an interview with Michelson. Published in the *Bulletin* on December 12, 1899, the interview offers a glimpse into a one-sided rivalry between the two women. "I went to interview Mrs. Stetson this morning and was thoroughly and remorselessly interviewed for all my sins, journalistic and otherwise," Michelson reveals. "Mrs. Stetson interviewed me upon the Zionist movement, upon the pernicious effect of newspaper work, upon any symptoms of personal degeneration I had noticed, upon the probabilities of an obliging, versatile editorial writer being deprived of all journalistic virtue through sheer habitual mental depravity."[3] This attitude toward Michelson is not surprising in light of Gilman's antagonistic relationship with the yellow press. As scholars have shown, Gilman took issue with newspaper journalists' tendency to report on salacious details of her personal life.[4] In the case of the *Bulletin* review, Stetson's disdain is aimed at Michelson's playful manner of writing, which she associates with the sensationalizing tactics of West Coast journalism. She reminds her interviewer at least twice that "women in the East" accepted her book as "earnest work." Despite being the target of Gilman's displeasure, Michelson avoids going on the defensive. She continues to treat her subject respectfully, writing in the interview that "Mrs. Stetson talked herself brilliantly, forcefully and with that ease in expressing subtleties which marks the scientific mind."[5] In a 1900 editorial about Gilman's wedding to her cousin George Houghton Gilman, Michelson once again resisted what would be an easy opportunity for a counterattack; instead, she defended her fellow writer's second marriage against other journalists' charges that it was inconsistent with her feminist doctrine. Still, Michelson admitted that the new Mrs. Gilman "would be first to disown [her] championship."[6]

The differences in style and sensibility between these two women writers help to locate Michelson within American literary and cultural history. These differences, along with the similarities in Michelson's and Gilman's ideological visions, foreground two key phases in a larger narrative about American women's writing. The first phase encompasses the first-wave feminist movement and the ways that developments in print culture dovetailed with, and contributed to, changing ideas about womanhood (especially white, middle-class womanhood) in late nineteenth- and early twentieth-century America. This phase coincides with the boom in periodical culture, the entrance of women into the field of journalism, and the increasing recognition of women's commercial value in the literary marketplace as both producers and consumers. These developments in print and literary culture intersected with the emergence of Progressive Era political culture in which suffrage counted as one among many reform movements taken up by women writers in their fiction and nonfiction. In this phase, both Michelson and Gilman were central figures. While Gilman's influence as a writer and reformer has been well documented, Michelson's entertaining style and mass appeal allowed her to reach audiences who might have been put off by the suffrage leader's "radical views" and earnestness of purpose. This phase might be said to reach its peak in 1920, when women were granted the right to vote under the Nineteenth Amendment.

The second phase of the larger narrative about American women's writing picks up over fifty years later and takes as its backdrop the women's liberation movement. Influenced by second-wave feminist thought and practice, literary scholars of the 1970s set out to recover lost works by forgotten American women writers, expanding the canon and filling in gaps in literary history. In this phase, Gilman eclipsed Michelson. The early stages of recovery work solidified Gilman's status as a feminist forerunner deserving of sustained critical engagement. Today, her career as an activist and writer is the subject of countless works of scholarship, and her fiction and nonfiction are staples of undergraduate and graduate courses. Although later stages of feminist recovery demonstrated the importance of middlebrow writers and journalists, Michelson continued to escape notice. *The Superwoman and Other Writings* is the first edited collection of Michelson's fiction and journalism and the first book to draw attention to her formative role in feminist literary history and Progressive Era culture. This volume illuminates Michelson's career as a best-selling writer, popular contributor to mass circulation magazines, and pioneering journalist, whose writing and self-representation offered models of modern femininity that influenced the lives of ordinary women and men as well as the work of other women writers.

As the title piece of this collection, Michelson's novella *The Superwoman* simultaneously speaks to her place in and absence from feminist literary history. Published in 1912, the novella tells the story of a caddish male protagonist who finds himself washed ashore on an island inhabited by Amazonian women. In this "topsy-turvy" world, men are subservient, and women are omnipotent.[7] Despite his resistance to matriarchal rule, the protagonist falls in love with, and eventually marries, the powerful woman who saved his life. The plot will undoubtedly ring familiar to readers of Gilman's best-known work of full-length fiction, *Herland*, a feminist utopian novella originally printed in her self-published magazine, the *Forerunner*. But *Herland* was serialized in 1915, three years *after* Michelson's novella appeared as the lead story in the *Smart Set*, a popular literary magazine commonly viewed as a precursor to the *New Yorker*.[8] Given the high-profile publication of *The Superwoman*, Michelson's notoriety as a writer, and the fact that the two women occupied overlapping professional circles in mid-1890s San Francisco, it is likely that Gilman read and was inspired by Michelson's novella.[9] At the same time, the fiction and nonfiction that Michelson produced between 1895, when she began writing for newspapers, and 1929, when she published her last novel, *The Petticoat King*, bears the imprint of her engagement with Gilman and other contemporary feminist intellectuals. The recovery of *The Superwoman*, as well as of the other works of journalism and fiction in this collection, broadens our understanding of feminist literary history by offering a more collaborative, as opposed to individualistic, model of women's literary production. These works shed light on networks of mutual influence between women writers and the ways that various forms of Progressive Era print culture—newspapers, mass circulation magazines, novels—operated in conjunction with one another to expand women's participation in the public sphere.

In addition to enhancing our understanding of women's writing and Progressive Era culture, Michelson's recovery also fills gaps in ethnic and Jewish American literary history. When Gilman turned the tables on her interviewer during their 1899 encounter, "thoroughly and remorselessly interview[ing] [Michelson] for all [her] sins, journalistic and otherwise," she asked the *Bulletin* reporter not only about the degrading effects of her career as a newspaper journalist but also, strangely enough, about the Zionist movement. Given that Michelson had no obvious ties to Zionism, Gilman's question is presumably an allusion to Michelson's ethno-religious background as the child of Jewish immigrants.[10] Although Michelson only occasionally addresses Jewishness in her writing, this collection offers opportunities to consider how and why the formation of ethnic and Jewish American literary canons, like the process of feminist recovery, has embraced certain writers and kinds of narratives while neglecting others. In tune with ethnic literary study's emphasis on the marginalized experiences of the urban poor, scholarship on early Jewish American literature has focused on the New York–centric ghetto tale and the hardscrabble existence of immigrant writers and their characters, thus overlooking works by Western, first-generation, and middle-class writers. As an American-born writer who grew up on the western frontier and whose career was largely based in San Francisco, Michelson—whose work covers topics such as race (including whiteness), ethno-religious identity, nationalism and imperialism, and cross-ethnic relations—poses a significant challenge to well-established paradigms in ethnic studies. Her writing encourages consideration of the ways that writers from Jewish backgrounds engage with cultures, traditions, and histories other than their own—an aspect of Jewish American literature easily forgotten among the ghetto stories that dominate the turn-of-the-twentieth-century canon.

In this introduction, I offer a biographical overview of Michelson's life and career, considering her early experiences as the child of Jewish immigrants from Poland who became Gold Rush pioneers. Tracing the evolution of her career from San Francisco "girl reporter" to best-selling novelist, the introduction provides various contexts for reading the selections of her journalism and short fiction. I conclude with contexts for reading the title piece, the 1912 novella *The Superwoman*, within the larger tradition of feminist fantasy narratives. Because Michelson was a prolific writer in multiple genres and it is only possible to include a sample of her oeuvre here, I have included a bibliography of her work for further reading and research at the end of this volume.

An American (Jewish) Girlhood
on the Western Frontier

In 2015, Karen Skinazi and I published a scholarly introduction to Michelson and her work in the academic journal *MELUS: Multi-Ethnic Literature in the United States*, which was accompanied by a reprint of her short story "In Chy Fong's Restaurant" from her book *A Yellow Journalist* (1905). In this article, "Miriam Michelson's Yellow Journalism and the Multi-Ethnic West," we show that Michelson's attitudes toward gender, race, and class can be traced back to her upbringing as a Jewish girl on the nineteenth-century multiethnic western frontier.[11] As I further demonstrate here, Michelson's early environment—the legendary mining town of Virginia City, Nevada— shaped her career as a writer. By offering the rare perspective of a woman who was also an ethno-religious minority, her work contributes to Western literary history and compels revision of popular masculinist myths of the West.

Michelson was born in Calaveras County, California, in 1870, five years after Mark Twain's story "The Celebrated Jumping Frog of Calaveras County" put the region on the literary map. In 1854, her parents, Samuel and Rosalie (Pryzlubska) Michelson, immigrated to the United States to escape anti-Semitic persecution in Strzelno, Poland, briefly living in New York with their two oldest children. The Michelsons went on to chart an atypical course for nineteenth-century Jewish immigrants from eastern Europe. Lured by news of the Gold Rush, the family migrated westward, traveling by ship and mule wagon across the Isthmus of Panama and then up the coast, where they joined Samuel's sister and her husband at Murphy's Camp in Calaveras County, east of San Francisco. Formerly an Indian trading post, Murphy's had become a prosperous mining town, and the Michelsons made a living selling supplies to the miners. By 1867, the mines at Murphy's Camp were depleted, and the Michelsons moved their dry-goods business to the boomtown of Virginia City, Nevada, where they purchased a home for their growing family. The youngest of four sisters and three brothers, Miriam found playmates and co-conspirators among her siblings, who were to remain her closest family throughout her life. As an adult, for instance, she and her sister Julia, a single schoolteacher, lived together and worked side by side for suffrage and other causes.[12]

Miriam's youth in Virginia City coincided with the years of the so-called Big Bonanza, when new discoveries of gold and silver brought the mining town's population to its peak of 25,000 residents.[13] This period of Virginia City's history has become the stuff of literary legend. Authors Mark Twain, Bret Harte, and Dan DeQuille (the pen name of William Wright) began their careers writing for Virginia City's first newspaper, the *Territorial Enterprise*, under the tutelage of editor-owner Joseph T. Goodman, who later became a friend and mentor to Michelson as well.[14] Nonfiction works like Twain's *Roughing It* (1872) and DeQuille's *History of the Big Bonanza: An Authentic Account of the Discovery, History, and Working of the World Renowned Comstock Silver Lode of Nevada* (1876) mythologize the headiness of Virginia City's boom-to-bust economy. As Twain described the town following the discovery of the Comstock Lode: "Money was as plenty as dust; every individual considered himself wealthy, and a melancholy countenance was nowhere to be seen."[15]

In her own contribution to Comstock lore, her nonfiction book, *The Wonderlode of Silver and Gold* (1934), Michelson similarly captures the adventurous spirit of Virginia City. She does so, however, from the perspective of a woman for whom the western outpost offered opportunities for taking risks and exploring the outdoors, freeing her of the constraints of a traditional domestic girlhood. Throughout the book, for example, she catalogs the thrills that the mining town provided for her and her siblings: sledding downhill in winter into the main business district without street cars to "block . . . one's triumphant way"; dangerously commandeering an abandoned stagecoach; bearing witness to, and at times participating in, the scuffles of boy-gangs, named for the rival mines that determined their family's livelihood; and improvising rules for games of marbles "just as the law, like other things in new Nevada, had to be made up as they went along."[16] For Michelson, the newly settled West provided a space in which women, too, could make up rules and roles for themselves "as they went along," redefining, rather than rejecting, femininity, motherhood, sisterhood, domesticity, and women's work.

Explicitly invoking Charlotte Perkins Gilman's *Herland*, historian Susan Armitage in her classic essay "Through Women's Eyes: A New View of the West" describes the West as "Hisland." In "heroic tales . . . of adventure, exploration, and conflict," she explains, "women are either absent or incidental," relegated to stereotypes such as "the refined lady, the helpmate," or the prostitute.[17] Since then, historians and literary critics have offered correctives to the masculinist frontier myth, piecing together more complex stories that incorporate the ethno-racial diversity of a region where "women of color and numerous European immigrants mingled with native Paiutes and with Chinese women." Although the Comstock environment was "overwhelmingly male," as C. Elizabeth Raymond points out in *Comstock Women: The Making of a Mining Community*, women played a variety of roles in Virginia City during its heyday, "experienc[ing] the bustle in all its plenitude."[18]

Michelson's work is an important resource for ongoing scholarly attempts to document the diverse experiences of women in the nineteenth-century West. While some historians of the West cite her history of the Comstock region, *The Wonderlode of Silver and Gold*,[19] they have overlooked her fiction and journalism, which offer valuable insights into gender formation on the frontier. In the absence of extensive archival material, Michelson's autobiographical novel *The Madigans* (1904), for instance, provides an important glimpse into Michelson's own girlhood in Virginia City. Initially serialized in *Century* magazine as "Stories of the Nevada Madigans," the novel imagines Virginia City as a "Herland" of sorts. Centering on a family of six sisters who lay claim to the mining town as their playground, *The Madigans* revels in the tomboyish exploits of four-year-old Frances (known as Frank and named for their father, Francis); the twins Bessie and Florence (shortened to Bep and Fom); Irene, whose athletic feats earn her the nickname "Sprint"; Cecilia (Sissy), whose academic success fuels sibling rivalry with Irene; and fifteen-year-old Kate, who as the oldest, affects the "pretense of young ladyhood," mostly to antagonize her sisters.[20]

Left to their own devices after the death of their mother, the Madigan girls spend their time competing with one another and devising all manner of mischief. Historians and popular culture have depicted the Comstock as a hypermasculine, patriarchal environment; in Michelson's narrative, however, the girls dominate over their male classmates and evade their ineffectual father's weak attempts to impose order and discipline. In a 1907 interview for the *New York Times Saturday Review of Books*, Michelson named *The Madigans* her personal favorite among her novels, due in part to its autobiographical content. "Some of it did happen to me, and I always insist that I am Sissy, in spite of the fact that a friend of mine insists that she is," stated

Michelson, "I guess it is a good many childhoods."[21] Michelson may claim universal relevance for her novel, but in eliminating her brothers and transforming her real-life family into a sextet of sisters, she makes a deliberate decision to focus on the experiences of girls. The western setting creates an imaginative space in which Michelson, her characters, and her readers could experiment freely with alternatives to traditional gender roles.

The liveliness of Michelson's comic romp is on display in "The Ancestry of Irene," the story from *The Madigans* included in this volume. Although Michelson identified most closely with studious Sissy, fearless and fiercely independent Irene takes center stage in this story, and her friendship with the cross-dressing character of Jack Cody makes explicit the theme of gender reversal. *The Madigans* also illuminates the ethno-racial dimensions of Michelson's Virginia City childhood, with characters such as Indian Jim and Wong, the family's Chinese domestic servant, contributing local color. "The Ancestry of Irene" explores white racial appropriation, specifically the dynamics of "playing Indian," as Irene indulges a common childhood fantasy that allows her to try out different identities.[22] Deciding that she is not biological kin to her five sisters and that the "ordinary and humble" Mr. Madigan is, in fact, her foster father, Irene concocts a number of origin tales for herself, most notably that she is a lost Indian princess who will restore the land to her homeless tribe.[23] Mercurial Irene soon becomes disenchanted with the prospect of fighting white settlers to retrieve the millions they stole from the mines. She forsakes her imagined tribe for the fantasy that she is the daughter of one of the bonanza kings who discovered the Comstock Lode. The shifts in Irene's identity place Michelson's tale in dialogue with the history and literature of settler colonialism, indicating how European immigrant groups, despite a potential identification with ethno-racial difference, solidified their own whiteness by participating in the frontier myth.

Likely intended for an audience of young readers, *The Madigans* is the closest Michelson comes to addressing what it was like to be the child of Jewish immigrants on the frontier, and it is telling that she does so only indirectly. Just as she alters the gender makeup of her family for the purpose of her fictional account, she manipulates their ethno-religious identity by Irishizing her family's last name from "Michelson" to "Madigan." In the 1870s, Virginia City was dominated by Irish immigrants, who made up one-third of the population and had a strong sense of ethnic community. Jews, in contrast, were a small minority, their numbers never climbing above five hundred residents even at the height of the population boom.[24] Michelson's act of ethnic substitution may intimate identification between Jews and the Irish as European immigrants, but it also speaks to her conflicting allegiances and an interest in aligning herself with the dominant ethno-racial group. The individualistic impulse to downplay difference via a rejection of religious affiliation is an overarching motif in *The Madigans*. Leaving behind the Catholicism of his youth in Ireland, Mr. Madigan reinvents himself in America and becomes "an outspoken foe to religious exercise."[25] He passes on secular values to his daughters, declaring Christmas "nonsense," for example, and reading to them from Winwood Reade's *The Martyrdom of Man*, a book considered a "substitute Bible" for secular intellectuals.[26] In contrast to Jewish American narratives that associate assimilation with Christianization, Michelson constructs a narrative of secularization in which religion is cast aside in favor of the freedom of nonidentification and the fluidity of continual self-invention.

Demonstrating how the erasure of religious difference was a key component of ethnic assimilation, *The Madigans* resonates with Michelson's more direct statements about the role of Jewishness in her family history. In response to a question posed by her brother Albert's biographer, she stated: "Ours was [not] a religious family. I had no religious training whatever. Nor can I recall a religious discussion among us, nor a religious inhibition or compulsion. And I believe this unorthodox viewpoint would have been the case with both parents and children no matter what religious belief the former might have inherited."[27] In this revealing statement, Michelson disidentifies with Judaism by describing her parents not as themselves Jewish, but rather as born from Jewish parents. In distancing herself from her Jewish heritage, however, she is not simply conforming to societal norms. Instead, her characterization of her family's strict adherence to secularism as "unorthodox" affirms her view of herself as an iconoclast.[28]

Despite her claim that Jewishness played no role in her upbringing, Michelson's attitude toward race and ethnicity came in part from her own sense of difference as the child of Jewish immigrants, and her writing bears the influence of Virginia City's multiracial environment. Beginning with her earliest short stories, which are set in Nevada and feature Indian characters, "ethnic variety" became "a mainstay of her fiction."[29] Like her journalism, which often documents experiences of individuals living on the ethno-racial margins and communities subjected to white imperialism, her stories and novels incorporate black, Chinese, and Hawaiian characters, although her protagonists are usually ethnically indeterminate or nominally Irish. In *The Wonderlode of Silver and Gold*, Michelson describes the ethnic makeup of the Comstock community and acknowledges how this diversity produced animosities and divisions. The miners, she wrote, "weren't a body of men, they were individuals of twenty-eight different races, and of as strongly contrasted temperaments . . . Italians, Germans, French, Mexicans, Irishmen, Cornishmen, Americans, each with their own racial prejudices, customs, even a particular saloon to patronize."[30] The various migrant and immigrant groups were also in close contact with Paiute and Washoe people, who resided in camps at the outskirts of the city.[31]

Historians have shown that the residents of Virginia City tended to live and socialize in ethnic clusters. In *Jews in Nevada: A History*, John P. Marschall notes that while "Jews [were] spread through the Germanic-European section of town," several Jewish families, including the Michelsons, lived within close proximity to each other on A Street. Marschall is careful to point out, however, that the neighborhood "was not a ghetto."[32] In contrast to Chinese immigrants, who were confined to a segregated area and barred from working in the mines, Jewish merchants were well integrated into the community, with many of their children attending school alongside other Euro-Americans. That Chinese immigrants and Jews faced different degrees of popular prejudice is clear from Mary McNair Mathews's memoir *Ten Years in Nevada* (1880). Mathews dehumanizes Chinese immigrants, describing Virginia City's Chinatown as "a loathsome, filthy den . . . breed[ing] . . . pestilential disease" and "John Chinaman" as "truly the curse of the Pacific Coast." While she also harbors negative views of the town's Jewish shopkeepers, whom she depicts as greedy and untrustworthy, she admits to having "seen many" Jews whom she "thought were nice people."[33]

Even among the various races and nationalities that made up Comstock society, the Michelsons were singled out as different, and this difference tended to be associated more with their Jewishness than with their Polish background. In an oral history, one of Miriam's non-Jewish next-door neighbors, Alice Sauer, recalled the Michelsons as "foreigners" and one of the few Jewish families in town. She also noted, however, that Samuel and

Rosalie "were great friends of my parents," and that the Jews "didn't seem to have much of a society or organization, or anything like that."[34] Indeed, evidence suggests that the Michelson family earned the respect of Jews and non-Jews alike. In an 1869 letter to President Ulysses Grant supporting Miriam's brother Albert's appointment to the US Naval Academy, Congressman Thomas Fitch (R-Nevada) described their father, Samuel Michelson, as "a prominent and influential merchant of Virginia City, and a member of the Israelite persuasion." Fitch's esteem is openly motivated by politics. He goes on to note that Samuel "by his example and influence has largely contributed to the success of" the Republican Party and holds sway over "many of his co-religionists." Fitch advises Grant, who had previously alienated the Jewish community by passing an anti-Semitic order expelling Jews from the South during the Civil War, to support Albert's appointment as a means of securing Jewish votes and support.[35] As a result of the pressure from Fitch, Albert became the first Jew appointed to the Naval Academy, where he studied physics and went on to become the country's first Nobel Prize laureate in the sciences.[36]

As a mercantile family, the Michelsons faced the miners' class resentment, which was often mixed with prejudice against Jews. Still, historians have shown that anti-Semitism was much less of a factor for Jews in the West than in other regions of the country.[37] Due to the sparser population and the fact that pioneer families, by definition, did not have deeply established roots and traditions, frontier communities were fairly hospitable to Jews like the Michelsons. The popular imagination has constructed western Jews as outsiders who had the potential to become insiders.[38] A 1962 episode of the long-running television Western *Bonanza* titled "Look to the Stars" inserts Albert Michelson into the story of the Cartwright clan in order to teach a civil rights–era lesson about tolerance and bigotry. The episode is loosely based on facts. It depicts Albert as a young genius who causes trouble by conducting physics experiments in the streets of Virginia City. When Albert is expelled from school by an anti-Semitic teacher, who also tries to block his military appointment, the Cartwrights intervene, taking Albert under their wing and giving him free rein to test his scientific hypotheses on the Ponderosa Ranch. At the end of the episode, the Cartwrights publicly expose the teacher's bigotry, transforming Jews from victims of prejudice into patriotic citizens.[39]

By the time Miriam reached school age, Virginia City's historic Fourth Ward School had opened to meet the needs of the town's growing population. After attending the Fourth Ward School, Miriam briefly moved on to a faculty position; teaching at her alma mater from 1889 to 1890, she followed in the footsteps of her older sisters, Pauline and Julia, who had also worked as teachers at the school. Although the Michelson children had a reputation for brilliance and industriousness, with their mother emphasizing the value of education for daughters and sons alike, it appears that Albert may have been the only sibling to receive a formal education beyond high school.[40] Miriam's postsecondary education—like that of her journalist brother, Charles—primarily took place on the job, in her work as a newspaper reporter.

A Girl Reporter and the Progressive Era Press

In 1887, Pittsburgh native Elizabeth Jane Cochrane, known to readers as Nellie Bly, went undercover as a "crazy girl" from Cuba to write an exposé on the treatment of the mentally ill. By feigning a "little accent," speaking the occasional Spanish word, and alternately calling herself "Nellie Brown" and "Nellie Moreno," Bly performed insanity so convincingly that she was legally committed to Manhattan's notorious asylum for women at Blackwell's Island. Initially appearing as a series of articles in Joseph Pulitzer's *New York World*, Bly's account of her incarceration in "a human rat-trap" was later published in book form as *Ten Days in a Mad-house*.[41] An early example of immersion journalism, Bly's stunt ushered in the phenomenon of the "girl reporter." Making their bodies part of the sensational spectacle of the Progressive Era press, women broke into journalism by creating "models of self-reflexive authorship that involved not just reporting the news but *becoming* the news," as Jean Marie Lutes explains.[42] Bly's success bred imitation. In 1890, Winifred Black (Bonfils), who wrote under the pen name Annie Laurie, launched her career at the San Francisco *Examiner* by faking a fainting spell in order to investigate "how a woman unfortunate enough to be taken sick or injured on the public streets of San Francisco . . . is treated by those who are paid to care for the unfortunate and suffering." Laurie's sham illness gained her admittance to the city's Receiving Hospital, where her violent and callous treatment corroborated Bly's report from a "madhouse" on the opposite coast.[43]

It was against this backdrop that Michelson rose to fame as one of the West's leading "girl reporters" in the second half of the 1890s. Spanning the years 1895 to 1902 and culled from hundreds of articles that bear her byline, the selections of Michelson's journalism in this collection document her career writing for four papers: *Arthur McEwen's Letter*, a short-lived political weekly; the *San Francisco Call* and *San Francisco Bulletin*, two of the city's leading dailies; and the historic Philadelphia *North American*, which temporarily lured Michelson to the East. As these selections demonstrate, Michelson belongs to a rich and varied tradition of newspaperwomen who, until recently, were written out of American literary history. Uncovering the work of pioneer "ladies of the press" such as Bly, Laurie, Ada Patterson, Nixola Greeley-Smith, and Elizabeth Jordan, scholars Lutes and Alice Fahs have shown that female journalists—including several who, like Michelson, became fiction writers—played a crucial role in shaping literary and mass culture in the late nineteenth and early twentieth centuries. Unlike Bly and Laurie, Michelson did not change her name, go undercover, or manufacture elaborate stunts. Yet there was a performative quality to her journalism, a theatrical flair befitting her status as celebrity reporter and icon of modern American culture. Like her predecessors, Michelson engaged in "self-reflexive authorship," adopting the first-person persona of the "girl reporter" and making herself a central element of the stories she covered. Michelson's career lends further weight to Lutes's and Fahs's claims that women journalists, in playing up gender and the female perspective, created new paradigms of womanhood, which they publicized to readers on a daily basis through the pages of the newspaper.

Like the frontier of her childhood, journalism offered Michelson opportunities for adventure and a space in which she could operate outside the constraints of traditional femininity. She may have initially tried to chart a more conventional path by following her older sisters into school teaching, but she ultimately followed her male relatives into newspaper work. In the 1890s, her brother Charles and her brother-in-law Arthur McEwen made names for themselves as reporters and editors for William Randolph Hearst's newspaper syndicate. In his autobiography, *The Ghost Talks*, Charles described the allure of San Francisco newspaper life in the era of yellow journalism: "The old bonanza kings and railroad millionaires . . . were still alive. Their sons were figuring in all the fights and scandals that the community enjoyed.

The mines were still pouring in their millions, the ships from Australia and Hawaii and China were bringing in the romance of the Orient, the cattle ranchers were supplying their stint of picturesque news, and politics were raging furiously."[44] Journalism held additional allure for women seeking an outlet from middle-class Victorian femininity. As Skinazi and I explain, the semirespectable cover of newspaper work allowed independent women like Michelson to explore the space of the city and travel the country—and even the world—alone. Bly, for example, "solidified her status as feminist icon in 1889 when she published her account of her globe-trotting adventure, later titled *Around the World in 72 Days*, in the pages of the *New York World*."[45]

While this collection's documentation of Michelson's career provides feminist literary and cultural critics with new primary sources related to the emergence of female journalists, scholars of women's history will find equally rich material in the stories she covered. The articles she wrote on the women's movement comprise topics such as suffrage, dress reform, and temperance as well as debates about women's education, women working outside the home, single womanhood, matrimony, and divorce. Her interviews with prominent public figures such as Charlotte Perkins (Stetson) Gilman, Susan B. Anthony, Emma Goldman, and Carrie Nation are valuable for feminist scholarship. So, too, are her feature stories about everyday women's lives, like her investigation of women schoolteachers who are discharged for marrying (see "Does Matrimony Disqualify Working Women?") and her tribute to the "soul-marriage" of Eliza Babcock and Hannah Clapp, a lesbian couple responsible for establishing some of the first schools in the state of Nevada (see "Nevada's Feminine David and Jonathan: A Sketch from Life"). Articles about women and vice—a topic she tackled from different angles throughout her career—explore tensions between female victimhood (through exposés on human trafficking, for example) and agency (via prurient details of female thieves and murderers who saw criminality as a viable alternative to Victorian propriety and passivity). In addition to their often-sensational subject matter, Michelson's articles are notable for their vivid and entertaining writing style. "Miriam Michelson" may have appeared in bold bylines rather than in lights, but in the newspaper industry, hers was a marquee name that would attract readers and help sell papers.

From the beginning, Michelson's writing career was imbricated with the spectacles of popular entertainment and the mass media. A theater lover who confessed a "fleeting ambition to go on the stage," Michelson did some of her earliest work as a drama critic for the "Amusements" column of *Arthur McEwen's Letter*, a weekly edited by and named for her brother-in-law.[46] McEwen, who had married Miriam's sister Bessie in 1883, was responsible for coining the term "gee whiz journalism" to describe the sensationalist tactics of the yellow press. "Any issue the front page of which failed to elicit a 'Gee Whiz!' from its readers was a failure," famously stated McEwen, "whereas the second page ought to bring forth a 'Holy Moses!' and the third an astounded 'God Almighty!' "[47]

From 1894 to 1895, while covering plays and musical concerts for *Arthur McEwen's Letter*, Michelson also conducted a number of interviews with local and national celebrities, from music hall star Lottie Collins to suffrage leader Susan B. Anthony. The interviews reveal as much about Michelson's attitudes toward gender as they do about her subjects, supporting Lutes's claim that newspaperwomen implicated themselves in the stories they reported in order to publicize new models of womanhood. Interviewing Collins, for instance, Michelson barely touches on the performer's stage career; instead, she uses the opportunity to solicit Collins's opinions about whether women should ride bicycles and wear bloomers.[48] In "What Say Ye Women to This?," Michelson and Phoebe Couzins, one of the nation's first female lawyers, debate the merits of the "single life and an independent career." While fifty-two-year-old Couzins expresses some regret at pursuing the law at the expense of marriage and children, twenty-five-year-old Michelson opines that the "woman who remains single . . . may miss much joy, but she misses more unhappiness."[49] Michelson, who never married, held to this position throughout her life.

The first piece of newspaper journalism in this collection, "The New Woman Realized" (1895), which appeared in *Arthur McEwen's Letter*, exemplifies how Michelson's reporting provided opportunities to debate shifting gender roles and model new versions of womanhood. The contentious interview takes place in a San Francisco dime museum, where Michelson meets with Milton (née Louisa) Matson, a notorious cross-dresser whose story had been covered by the San Francisco press. Following his arrest in his fiancée's apartment for passing a bad check in January 1895, Matson was taken to jail, where he was revealed to be a biological woman who had lived as a man for twenty-six years.[50] Astonished to learn that Matson, despite claiming the male privilege of dress, opposes suffrage, Michelson argues the case of "advanced women," defending herself against Matson's "priggish" view that a woman "should stay at home and tend to her household duties."[51]

In an essay on cross-dressing in the nineteenth-century San Francisco press, Clare Sears analyzes newspaper accounts of the Matson case, arguing that, in keeping with "dominant ideologies and anxieties of the time," reporters crafted "an overarching narrative that characterized gender difference as intentional fraud and simultaneously expressed moral outrage and prurient fascination." Like other reporters, Michelson experiences what Sears calls "gender confusion" in her interview.[52] Although her interviewee clearly identifies as a man, she insists on referring to Matson as a woman, using "Miss" (even after Matson objects) as well as feminine pronouns. But she does not portray Matson's cross-dressing as an act of fraud, as other reporters do. Instead, she assumes that Matson's choice of masculinity could be aligned politically with the cause of women's rights. Michelson's "moral outrage" is not a response to the deceit of cross-dressing; rather, it is directed at Matson's conservative views about women and femininity. Michelson finds herself duped by Matson due to her own mistaken belief that cross-dresser and female journalist would be united in their challenge to gender norms. Although Matson's conservative statements and sartorial subversion fail to align with each other, Michelson manages to turn the interview into a form of gender protest. The article ends with the journalist raising her umbrella and going out into the street, which Matson had declared "no place for a woman," leaving the "man" behind to assume his "official pose" in the gloomy hall of the dime museum.[53]

The San Francisco newspapers' "prurient fascination" with cross-dressing serves as an example of the late nineteenth-century press's predilection for sensationalism. Yet, when it came to spectacles of gender, the very presence of a female reporter was often enough to elicit a "gee whiz!" response from readers. Newspapers took advantage of this, highlighting the novelty of the female reporter and using her as a vehicle for publicity. At the turn of the twentieth century, for example, women were more likely than men to receive bylines and to have their pictures appear alongside articles they wrote. These conventions textually and visually reinforced the embodied phenomenon of the "girl reporter." As Lutes writes, "Enacting a daily drama in a medium that was previously unthinkable," newspaperwomen "appeared both defiantly public and defensively feminine."[54] Newspaper work may have been viewed as a male profession, but a journalistic career did not obscure or neutralize women reporters' femininity. Instead, newspapers drew attention to their gender identity, making femaleness, and the female perspective, a significant part of the stories they reported.

During the three-year period (May 1895 to August 1898) that Michelson wrote for the *San Francisco Call*, the newspaper often capitalized on her identity as a female reporter. In addition to using a variety of techniques to highlight her name, the paper at times included her portrait with her articles, further amplifying her celebrity status. Rather than downplaying gender in her reporting, Michelson often used it to her advantage, entering spaces that would have been difficult for male reporters to access. For example, her article "Where Women Gamble" offers readers a rare glimpse inside San Francisco "poolrooms" that cater exclusively to members of "the fair sex" who wish to bet on the races.[55] Like Bly and other female reporters, Michelson inserted herself as a character in her stories, writing from a first-person point of view. While this nineteenth-century convention may unsettle contemporary readers trained to expect journalistic objectivity, Michelson's articles self-consciously offer a woman's perspective on a variety of issues—a perspective announced by the headline "VIEWED BY A WOMAN," which appeared above one of her earliest articles for the *Call*.

Michelson's first contribution to the *Call* was a four-part series on the second annual meeting of the Woman's Congress of the Pacific Coast, which took place in May 1895. The theme of this weeklong gathering of prominent female intellectuals and activists was "The Home," and speakers included national leaders of the women's movement, such as Susan B. Anthony, Rev. Anna H. Shaw, and Charlotte Perkins Stetson. The three pieces from that series that appear in this collection ("Viewed by a Woman," "Weeds and Flowers," and "The Real New Woman") introduce some of Michelson's signature rhetorical strategies. Both "Viewed by a Woman" and "The Real New Woman," for instance, exemplify a narrative mode I term "conversion journalism." These articles take the form of a conversion narrative in which a skeptic initially expresses doubt about the event being covered. Through the accumulation of facts and impressions, the skeptic confronts her misconceptions and is converted to a more modern and liberal point of view, becoming an ardent supporter of the progressive cause at hand.

"Viewed by a Woman" assigns the role of convert to a character known as the "Old Woman," whom Michelson first observes while riding the streetcar on her way to cover the congress. Described visually in washed-out tones such as "faded," "colorless," and "pale," the "Old Woman" is introduced as a counterpoint to the vibrant "new woman." Like Michelson, the "Old Woman" finds herself riveted by the bustling, self-confident new women traveling to the congress. When the congress attendees disembark, the "Old Woman" unexpectedly follows them. Losing sight of the "Old Woman" in the crowd, Michelson moves on to discuss the speeches and casual conversations she overhears at the congress. She presents the day's proceedings as a series of expectations happily proven false, expressing surprise, for example, at hearing "nothing at all of 'tyrant man'"; instead, she reports that the speakers treat men with "gentle, forbearing patience," hoping "to enlighten and ultimately to convert him." At the end of the article, Michelson returns to the larger frame of the conversion narrative when the "Old Woman" from the streetcar makes a sudden reappearance, rising and shouting "Amen" in response to a speech delivered by the congress president. Rather than simply transcribing the oratory of the congress, Michelson constructs a cause-and-effect narrative in which the "Old Woman," enlivened by the words of the speakers, is reborn as a "new woman" and accidental activist.[56]

Whether fact, fiction, or something in between, the "Old Woman" is a rhetorical device. Most often, however, Michelson cast herself as the protagonist of the conversion narrative, as exemplified by her fourth and final installment in the congress series, "The Real New Woman." The article begins with a series of statements in which the reporter catalogs her personal misgivings about "new womanhood." As Skinazi and I discuss in "The Girl Reporter in Fact and Fiction: Miriam Michelson's New Women and Periodical Culture in the Progressive Era," "Michelson uses the first person to create an identification with a skeptical audience, promising her readers that she is on their side."[57] By the end of the article, however, Michelson has replaced deleterious stereotypes of the new woman as professionally incompetent, mannishly unattractive, and shrewishly man-hating with a more accurate and nuanced portrait of the women's movement and its adherents.

The goal of the conversion journalism is, of course, persuasion; it aims to reproduce the experience of conversion in the reader by allowing him or her to follow along on the reporter's physical and mental journey. In taking the part of reluctant convert throughout her series on the Woman's Congress, Michelson uses the experiential first person to highlight her fair-mindedness and present herself as a reliable witness. In "Weeds and Flowers," for instance, she admits to finding both variety of flora at the congress, but rather than focusing on the "weeds" (women "who love notoriety for its own sake"), she gives most of her column inches over to the "flowers"—"those who have the brains and ability to think clearly and to act honestly and . . . to talk entertainingly." Michelson views this latter group as "the soul of new womanhood," declaring them "the best and strongest argument for woman suffrage."[58]

Through her self-reflexive style of reporting, Michelson emerges as a model of new womanhood and an "argument for woman suffrage." Newspaper readers get to see a single, independent, professional woman in action. In contrast to the heroines of nineteenth-century domestic fiction, who are typically moving in the direction of marriage, Michelson is the protagonist of a real-life urban adventure story, traversing the spaces of the city in search of new knowledge and experiences. By the time the Woman's Congress was done debating the relationship between the home and politics, Michelson's bold, first-person voice had already "CLEARED THE KITCHEN" (as the headline of her May twenty-fifth article announced), laying claim to the public sphere as a place for women.

Michelson's early journalism demonstrates how newspaperwomen mobilized Progressive Era print culture in support of women's rights and suffrage, modeling and publicizing new paradigms of femininity while simultaneously debunking negative stereotypes about "new women" that were especially prevalent in political cartoons.[59] Responding to caricatures of women's right activists, Michelson demonstrates in her writing on the congress that the "new woman" cannot be reduced to a single type. Instead, new womanhood produces variety—"all kinds and degrees of women," as Michelson writes, who are unified by the convention's "spirit of camaraderie."[60]

Michelson's newspaper journalism captures the diversity of women's experiences at a time when gender roles were radically shifting. From this collection's articles on Susan B. Anthony, Charlotte Perkins Gilman, Emma Goldman, and Carrie Nation emerge portraits of four very different personalities; as Michelson's profiles show, these reformers employed their own unique styles and strategies of activism and devoted themselves to different progressive causes. Addressing gender in relation to political, social, and economic forces, Michelson also wrote about women from all walks of life: actresses and educators, shopgirls and entrepreneurs, criminals and crusaders, single women and wives, slave girls and adventurers. Nor did she write only about white women. Her writing considers how her subjects' ethno-racial backgrounds, as well as class and sexual identities, intersect with gender difference.

Michelson may have established her career by offering a woman's viewpoint and writing about the growing presence of women in the political sphere, but she refused to be pigeonholed by the persona of the "girl reporter." Although much of her early work for the *Call* was limited to theater criticism, an area deemed more suitable for women, she quickly rose to the rank of dramatic editor and went on to break other gender barriers in the profession. Her fame as a journalist allowed her to branch out into new territory as a reporter, covering crime, politics, and sports—all areas considered the domain of men. As she worked her way from "girl reporter" to "front-page girl," popular periodical culture provided Michelson with a platform for a range of progressive issues beyond suffrage. In the following section, I offer context for reading her writings on race and imperialism and discuss how her journalistic work in these areas provided a springboard to her career as a fiction writer.

RACE AND IMPERIALISM IN MICHELSON'S JOURNALISM AND FICTION

On September 30, 1897, the *Call* devoted the first two pages of its broadsheet to an article about the United States' impending annexation of Hawaii. Heralded by the dramatic headline "Strangling Hands upon a Nation's Throat," the article is an impassioned plea for Hawaiian sovereignty, harsh in its condemnation of US foreign policy. Although the article makes a case against annexation from the point of view of native Hawaiians, readers would be left with no doubt as to its author. "Miriam Michelson Pens a Stirring Appeal on Behalf of the Islanders," a front-page subheadline announced. And on the second page, a caption beneath a sketch of a young woman sporting a pince-nez identified her as "MISS MIRIAM MICHELSON, Special Correspondent of 'The Call' at Honolulu."

Michelson's front-page story serves as an example of the genre of writing often referred to disparagingly as "yellow journalism" for its tendency to sensationalize the news with the goal of selling papers as well as promoting specific political and editorial agendas. The article's provocative message was made more so by the fact that a twenty-seven-year-old, unchaperoned "girl reporter" had sailed the Pacific to cover an international protest, the Hawaiian Patriotic League's petition against annexation by the US government. To American readers in the nineteenth century, the Hawaiian Islands were mostly the stuff of men's adventure tales, penned by writers such as Herman Melville and Mark Twain. (Jack London, who admired Michelson's writing in the San Francisco papers, was first to arrive in the islands almost a decade after her.)[61] Yet, as Fahs shows in *Out on Assignment*, Michelson was not the only newspaperwoman to undertake such a journey. Examining travel correspondence from Hawaii and other foreign outposts, Fahs demonstrates that, in addition to mapping "new territory for women in the public sphere," female journalists extended their influence to the larger project of late nineteenth-century American expansionism. In contrast to most of the travel writings Fahs analyzes, however, Michelson did not argue for "America's right to new territories and 'possessions.'"[62] Instead, she came across as a sharp critic of American expansionism, exposing it as part of the long history of racial imperialism at home and abroad and as a betrayal of the nation's democratic ideals. Michelson's correspondence from Hawaii illustrates how the rhetorical strategies she developed while covering women's issues enabled her to become a mediator across races and cultures—or, in the metaphor with which she described her reportorial presence among the native Hawaiians, "a sort of magical human telephone and phonograph combined."[63]

Made ephemeral by their publication in the yellow press, Michelson's newspaper writings employ narrative and stylistic techniques that today are more likely to be associated with the innovations of literary, or "new," journalism than the sensationalism of tabloid culture. Her career supports Karen Roggenkamp's findings in *Narrating the News: New Journalism and Literary Genre in Late Nineteenth-Century American Newspapers and Fiction*. Roggenkamp demonstrates that the literary aesthetic of "new journalism," which reached its apotheosis in the 1890s when Michelson was working as a reporter, was closely intertwined with the narrative and genre conventions of American fiction. As Roggenkamp explains, "The big business of urban newspapers . . . depended for its success on the reporters' narrative skills and their ability to mold information—sometimes factual and sometimes not—into dramatic and skillfully told tales."[64] To accomplish this goal, journalists used a variety of literary techniques more often associated with fiction and memoir than newspaper reporting. In "Strangling Hands upon a Nation's Throat," Michelson constructs scene and character, reproducing dialogue and deriving meaning from seemingly minor details. She structures her article not as a linear story, but as a series of distinct vignettes with pointed endings that together build to a powerful conclusion. As in her reporting on the women's movement, she also writes in the first person, simultaneously positioning herself as subjective narrator and neutral outsider.

"Strangling Hands upon a Nation's Throat" is one of many articles Michelson published that dealt with race and imperialism. At home, she often reported on situations and policies affecting racial minorities. Selections in this collection include an article on Indian boarding schools ("Changing a Bad Indian into a Good One") and an investigation of prejudices faced by black soldiers during the Philippine-American War ("A Military Matter in Black and White"). Her extensive coverage of immigrant communities in San Francisco's Chinatown is represented by "Where Waves the Dragon Flag," which is about Chinese New Year's celebrations that draw white visitors to Chinatown. A skillful interviewer at ease speaking with others regardless of race, class, gender, or fame, Michelson counted a powerful white police chief and a reclusive African American businesswoman among her informants. As Skinazi and I wrote in "Miriam Michelson's Yellow Journalism and the Multi-Ethnic West," "She was as adept at grilling congressmen and conducting jail cell interviews with murderers as she was discussing anarchism with Emma Goldman or racism with Emma and Walter Ngong Fong, an Anglo-Chinese couple whose taboo-defying marriage made national headlines."[65]

Even as Michelson opposes the nation's expansion beyond its borders in her correspondence from Hawaii, much of her writing romanticizes the transformative possibilities of the frontier, often extending its potential for Americanization to nonwhite populations. In writing about Indians, blacks, and Chinese immigrants, however, she also exposed a darker side of America's past and its present. This curious mix of racial discourses is heightened by the conventions of the Progressive Era press. Local color conventions, for

Miriam Michelson, "Strangling Hands upon a Nation's Throat," *San Francisco Call* (September 30, 1897). Michelson's front-page story on the annexation of Hawaii appeared in the *San Francisco Call* on September 30, 1897.

example, often contributed to exotic views of racial others, fixing them in place and time. Meanwhile, the journalistic practice of the interview gives her reporting a polyvocal quality, creating spaces for competing narratives. In functioning as a "magical human telephone and phonograph combined," Michelson transmits the words of people whose voices were excluded from the mainstream press. Whereas scholars have analyzed the ways that

A sketch of Michelson, "Special Correspondent of 'The Call' at Honolulu," accompanied the second page of the article. California Digital Newspaper Collection.

ethno-racial minorities have created counternarratives in the ethnic press, Michelson's journalism demonstrates how the mainstream press mediated between competing narratives and discourses, an act of mediation made possible by the figure of the "girl reporter" whose performance of nonthreatening white femininity allowed her access to people and places that were often off limits to male reporters.

"Changing a Bad Indian into a Good One" (1898), which appeared in the *Call* and is based on research Michelson conducted at the Government Training School in Carson, Nevada, exemplifies the contradictory racial ideologies that pervade her journalism. Compared to her trenchant critique of American imperialism abroad, here Michelson seems unable to reconcile her patriotism and assimilationist beliefs with her awareness of the nation's history of settler colonialism and continued violence to native people and culture in her present. She wavers between praising the school's civilizing mission, its ability to transform Indians into "real Americans," and questioning a government policy that forcibly removes Indian children from their homes and separates them from their parents. In the article's startling opening metaphor, she portrays "Uncle Sam" in savage terms of cannibalism by delineating his "recipe" for "changing a bad Indian into a good one." Readers may be left unsure whether to interpret Michelson's descriptions of catching "young and tender" Indians to "season" and "bake" before serving as grossly insensitive or sharply satirical.[66] While Michelson's interviews with Indian boarding school students suggest that most of them are grateful for the gifts of an American education, she also leaves important gaps in her article, noting, for example, that in one young boy's silence lies an untold story about unjust treatment by the American government. Because Michelson alludes to but does not fully record the boy's perspective on his cultural and physical dislocation, pieces like this one cannot stand alone; instead, they need to be read alongside Native writing on boarding schools and US assimilation policy, like Zitkála-Šá's autobiographical essay "The School Days of an Indian Girl," which was published in the *Atlantic Monthly* in 1900.[67]

Michelson's position on US racism and imperialism is unequivocal in "A Military Matter in Black and White," which focuses on the controversy over whether the military should allow white soldiers to withhold the salute from black soldiers of higher rank. Conducting interviews with regiments stationed in San Francisco during the military campaign for expansionism in the Pacific, Michelson juxtaposes the coarse racism of the white soldiers, who sneeringly refuse to "salute a nigger," with the magnanimity of the black soldiers, most of whom were willing to waive the salute for the sake of peace and country. At the end of the article, she bluntly confronts the irony of antiblack racism among US servicemen, expressing her own shame "that Uncle Sam, who is preaching the democratic doctrine of equality to brown-skinned men in the tropics (with the aid of military governors on one side and bullets on the other), doesn't practice it here in San Francisco."[68]

Michelson's writings about the Chinese population in the western United States represent her most sustained engagement with racial difference, an engagement that carried over from her journalism to her fiction. At the *Call*, Michelson had written about relations between whites and Asian Pacific Islanders, whether reporting on the annexation of Hawaii or the interracial marriage of Mr. and Mrs. Walter Ngong Fong. With her move from the *Call* to its rival, the *Bulletin*, in the summer of 1898, Michelson began to immerse herself more fully in San Francisco's Chinatown. Under the leadership of the *Bulletin*'s controversial managing editor Fremont Older, Michelson was part of a team of reporters who wielded the power of the press to expose rampant corruption in California, a state then under the control of the Southern Pacific Railroad.[69] While Michelson wrote about a wide range of topics for the *Bulletin*, she was often assigned to what she called "the Chinatown detail."[70] Since Chinatown was perceived as a cesspool of vice, municipal graft, and police corruption, the assignment offered opportunities to further her paper's mission by exposing one of the city's darkest underworlds. It would also shape her career in interesting ways as she began moving between journalism and fiction, contributing to the popular genre of the Chinatown tale.

Beginning in the 1860s with Mark Twain's sketches in the *Territorial Enterprise*, Chinatown literature became a popular feature of periodical culture. Bret Harte's poem "Plain Language from Truthful James," commonly known as "The Heathen Chinee," created a sensation when it appeared in the *Overland Monthly* in 1870, with some readers viewing it as a legitimization of anti-Chinese sentiments and others as a satire of Irish laborers' views of Chinese immigrants who competed for their jobs. As in his later short story "Wan Lee, the Pagan" (1876), Harte's attempts to offer sympathetic portraits of Chinese immigrants went awry because they were so infused with racial stereotypes that they ended up fueling sinophobia. In the 1890s, Frank Norris published stories set in Chinatown in the San Francisco journal the *Wave*. His most famous, "The Third Circle" (1897), was a sensational tale about a white woman kidnapped and enslaved by Chinese traffickers.[71]

Women writers also gravitated to the Chinatown genre, and like men, saw it as a chance to write about the titillating topic of sex slavery. Mary Austin, for instance, published "The Conversion of Aw Lew Sing" (1897), one of her first short stories, in the *Overland Monthly*. While Norris's plots revolve around white men rescuing white women from sexual enslavement by Chinese men, Austin's story features a poor Chinese vegetable gardener who rescues a beautiful Chinese woman from both the highbinders who enslave her and the missionaries who attempt to Christianize her, feigning his own conversion as a means of making her his legal wife. Other white women, like New York missionary Helen F. Clark, author of *The Lady of the Lily Feet and Other Stories of Chinatown* (1900), took conversion more seriously, writing Chinatown tales to promote the success of the missions in saving Chinese women.[72] Today, the best-known purveyor of the Chinatown tale is Edith Maude Eaton, who published as "Sui Sin Far" among other Chinese-sounding pen names. Born of an English father and a Chinese mother, Eaton, who lived in both Canada and the United States, is celebrated as the first Asian North American fictionist. Against the backdrop of the Chinese Exclusion Act of 1882, she published Chinatown journalism and short fiction in a variety of periodicals. As scholars have shown, Eaton adopted Orientalist motifs in her work and in her writing persona, but simultaneously deployed tricksterism and other subversive techniques to challenge anti-Chinese sentiment and traditional East-West binaries.[73]

Michelson's Chinatown writings share much in common with works by Eaton, who was also employed by San Francisco newspapers at the turn of the century. Both writers, for example, appeal to readers' fascination with exoticism and cultural difference while avoiding the condemnatory, moralizing tone prevalent in missionary writings about Chinese immigrants. If Eaton's Chinese persona lends her work the authenticating stamp of an insider, however, Michelson's "girl reporter" persona produces the touristic gaze of a white female outsider. These racial and gender dynamics are evident in "Where Waves the Dragon Flag" (1899), which appeared in the *Bulletin*. This piece of local color writing participates in exoticizing discourse through its detailed descriptions of place and demonstrates how popular representations of Chinatown are a product of the white imagination's fear of and desire for the East.

Interestingly, both Michelson and Eaton used fictional works to interrogate the San Francisco newspaper industry's practice of sending white reporters to Chinatown to dig up news stories. Eaton's short story "'Its

Wavering Image,'" which appeared in *Mrs. Spring Fragrance* in 1912, focuses on the doomed love affair between a white male reporter, Mark Carson, and a young, "half white, half Chinese" resident of Chinatown named Pan. Pan falls in love with Carson while serving as his guide to Chinatown, only to have him betray her trust when he publishes his article.[74] In Michelson's "The Fascination of Fan-Tan" and "In Chy Fong's Restaurant," two stories in her 1905 book *A Yellow Journalist*, the writer's fictional alter ego, "girl reporter" Rhoda Massey, similarly relies on a Chinese informant (this time an elderly woman named Gum Tai) when she goes undercover, disguising herself first as a Chinese boy and then as a Chinese slave girl, in order to investigate corruption in Chinatown. Perhaps because they were deemed too racy for the wholesome *Saturday Evening Post*, which serialized *A Yellow Journalist*, these stories were not printed in the magazine. Instead, they first appeared when *A Yellow Journalist* was published in book form. As exemplified by "In Chy Fong's Restaurant," which is included in this collection, these stories provoke ethical questions about tactics used by white reporters. A story whose plot depends on the heroine's donning of racial drag to go undercover, "In Chy Fong's Restaurant" offers valuable insight into Michelson's awareness of her own white privilege and the evolution of her career from journalist to fiction writer.[75]

In Michelson's three years at the *Bulletin*, she continued to experiment with journalistic form (going so far, in one instance, as to publish an article in verse) and found a home for some of her earliest published fiction. In March 1899, the paper reprinted "The Awakening of Zojas"; inspired by Edward Bellamy's *Looking Backward: 2000–1887* (1888), the science fiction tale was first published anonymously in *MacMillan's Magazine* of London under the title "A Strange Experiment, and What Came of It." On December 24, 1899, Michelson contributed a compendium of short pieces, "The Conversion of Choy Sing and Other Sketches," to the special Christmas issue of the *Bulletin*. Seemingly inspired by Austin's "The Conversion of Aw Lew Sing," the title sketch is a love story set in Chinatown, while another of the pieces, "The Road to Waikiki," indicates the hold Hawaii continued to exert over her imagination. The two earliest pieces of fiction that appear in this collection, "Ah Luey's Self" and "An Understudy for a Princess," are also set in Chinatown and Hawaii respectively. A tragic tale of a Chinese girl who aspires to the life of a prostitute, "Ah Luey's Self," which appeared in the *Bulletin* in 1901, reproduces Orientalist stereotypes, but it also evinces Michelson's concern with human trafficking and the lack of opportunities available to women of color—a topic she would return to in journalism (see, for example, this volume's "Two Little Slave Girls Owned in Philadelphia") and in fiction such as "In Chy Fong's Restaurant."

Orientalist motifs are similarly invoked and subverted in "An Understudy for a Princess" (1901), which appeared in the *Black Cat*, a literary magazine for amateur writers that published several of Michelson's early stories and is now best remembered for giving Jack London his start. In "An Understudy for a Princess," the controversy over expansionism that Michelson wrote about in her correspondence from Hawaii provides the backdrop for an interracial romance between a white adventurer and a Hawaiian woman who is impersonating the Crown Princess Ka'iulani. Hawaii also provided subject matter for what may have been Michelson's first attempt to publish a novel. Evidence of the novel, which was titled "Ululani of Hawaii," exists only in the form of a 1900 reader's report from publisher Houghton Mifflin, which rejected the manuscript as "a dull story of Hawaii a century ago, with Kamehameha for hero, told in a stiff, inverted style."[76] The Houghton Mifflin editor may have had legitimate reservations about Michelson's prose but almost certainly mischaracterized the plot of the manuscript. The title indicates that the book was not primarily about Kamehameha I, the founder of the Kingdom of Hawaii. Instead, the manuscript appears to have been a work of historical fiction centered on a remarkable *heroine*: the Hawaiian high chiefess, Ululani of Hilo (also known as "Ululani the Great"), whom Queen Lili'uokalani prized among her ancestors as the "most celebrated poetess in her day."[77]

Michelson's writings on race and colonialism in this collection will find a new audience today among Americanists interested in the literature of empire and the Pacific Rim. In her fascination with Hawaii's history of female leadership, we can also trace back the enduring feminist concerns that made her one of the nation's most popular fiction writers in the early years of the new century. Her forays into feminist historical fiction went unappreciated by publishers until the end of her career, when she published *The Petticoat King* (1929), a novel based on the life of Queen Elizabeth I.[78] But Michelson did have considerable success finding a contemporary audience when she translated her message of female empowerment into other genres, from the picaresque *In the Bishop's Carriage* and *A Yellow Journalist* to the utopian fantasy of *The Superwoman*, a story that takes place on an unnamed island inhabited by a civilization of women as brilliant and powerful as Ululani of Hawaii.

From Newspaper Journalism to Popular Magazine Fiction and a Best-Selling Novel

In 1901, Michelson's newspaper work took her to the East, where she spent two years writing for the Philadelphia *North American*, once again under the direction of her brother-in-law Arthur McEwen, who was then the paper's managing editor. Michelson's articles in the *North American* are somewhat different in tenor from her West Coast reportage. The journalism she produced at the *Call* and the *Bulletin* opens a historically significant window into a specific place and time; reading it, we are transported back to Old San Francisco at the height of the nation's westward expansion, a period of growth and progress that, for the city, would come to a temporary halt with the earthquake of 1906. Michelson's journalism creates a regionalist portrait of pre-earthquake San Francisco from the perspective of a woman who knew the ins and outs of her beloved home city and its surrounding areas, a perspective that she is unable to achieve during her brief stint in Philadelphia.[79]

Yet her work for the *North American* is significant for other reasons. In it, she continues to address women's issues through a variety of journalistic genres. Examples include an editorial rebuking the tactics employed by Susan B. Anthony's sister, Mary, who refused to pay taxes on her property until she was given the right to vote; a tongue-in-cheek marital advice column in which she counsels women on how to handle selfish husbands and whether they can be best friends with their exes' new wives; and an exposé of Martinique slave girls kept in the shadow of Philadelphia's Independence Hall. Being in the East also gained her access to women such as Nation and Goldman, whose profiles in this collection date from Michelson's time at the Philadelphia daily. Rounding out the journalism section of this collection is one of the last articles she wrote for the *North American*, "Motives of Women Who Commit Theft" (1902), which explores how "the widening of woman's scope as an economic factor has led to . . . women boldly tak[ing] the initiative in crimes which once they attempted only as subordinates."[80]

The topic of women and crime was to mark an important shift in Michelson's trajectory, ultimately leading her out of the newsroom and into a full-time career as a fiction writer.

At the same time that Michelson was working for the *North American*, her fiction had begun to gain traction in mass circulation magazines. By the end of the second decade of the twentieth century, she had published more than forty pieces of fiction in a range of magazines, including *Munsey's* and *McClure's*. While a few were aimed specifically at female audiences and published in the *Ladies' Home Journal* and the *Woman's Home Companion*, most of her stories, and especially those with strong heroines, held broad appeal for mainstream, rather than niche, audiences. In 1904–5, at the most productive point in her fiction-writing career, Michelson serialized novels in two of the era's iconic periodicals: *Century Illustrated Monthly Magazine*, which published "Stories of the Nevada Madigans," and the *Saturday Evening Post*, which published *A Yellow Journalist*. Two other popular literary magazines, *Ainslee's* and the *Smart Set*, consistently published Michelson's fiction throughout her career. Between 1903 and 1915, seven of her stories appeared in the middlebrow *Ainslee's*, which published prose by well-known writers such as O. Henry, Jack London, Stephen Crane, and Theodore Dreiser. Between 1900 and 1917, the highbrow *Smart Set* published seven pieces by Michelson, including two lead novellas (*Her Guard of Honor* in 1900 and *The Superwoman* in 1912); when she branched out into playwriting later her in career, it also printed two of her dramas, "The Curiosity of Kitty Cochraine" in 1912 and "Bygones" in 1917.

Michelson's career as a fiction writer coincided with a major boom in periodical culture that created a steady demand for stories. Beginning in the 1890s, thanks to technological developments in print and distribution and new business models that relied more on advertising than subscriptions, magazines became America's primary form of mass entertainment and a means of forging an imagined community across the vast nation. As David Sumner writes in *The Magazine Century: American Magazines since 1900*, magazines were "*the* national medium of communication and the only way to reach America's surging population with a message or a product." Sumner quotes Matthew Schneirov, author of *The Dream of a New Social Order: Popular Magazines in America, 1893–1914*, who describes magazines as "not only a regular form of entertainment, a source of pleasure for a national audience of readers, but a . . . powerful force in shaping the consciousness of millions of Americans."[81] Amid a culture of progressive reform, muckrakers like Ida Tarbell found a national audience for investigative journalism in mass circulation magazines. Despite her own reportorial training in the methods of Hearst and Pulitzer, Michelson took a different tack, turning her attention to magazine fiction. In a letter to an editor at *Century* describing her move from newspaper work to fiction, Michelson declared herself "reformed," alluding to the popular perception that women reporters who participated in "gutter journalism" were violating feminine codes of morality.[82]

But Michelson did not entirely leave her journalistic past behind. Instead, she drew on the rich repository of nonfiction stories she had covered as a reporter in order to compose entertaining fiction infused with the language and sensibility of modern womanhood. If Charles Dana Gibson had made the visual image of the modern girl part of the national consciousness through his magazine illustrations, Michelson's periodical fiction gave the "new woman" a voice. Sassy, slangy, and "as 'catchy' as ragtime" (to quote one reviewer), this voice helped propel America out of Victorianism and paved the way for the so-called middlebrow moderns.[83] The cadences of Michelson's first-person protagonists echo in the prose of her successors, writers such as Edna Ferber, Fannie Hurst, Dorothy Parker, and Anita Loos, who ushered the literary representation of the "new woman" from the ragtime era into and through the Jazz Age.

This collection exhibits Michelson's stylistic and thematic innovations with its reprint of "In the Bishop's Carriage," a short story that appeared in *Ainslee's* in 1903. Exemplifying Michelson's breezy tone and fast-paced plots, the story is a first-person monologue told from the point of view of a female thief named Nance Olden. The picaresque theme of female criminality has roots in Michelson's 1902 article "Motives of Women Who Commit Theft." By casting a woman as rogue, a role previously reserved for male characters, Michelson hit on a formula for pleasurably diverting readers while continuing to explore women's expanding place in the social and economic life of the nation.

A product of literary and theatrical intertextuality, as well as transatlantic cultural exchange, Michelson's unconventional heroine is in part the namesake of a real-life woman, actress Nance O'Neil, a California native who owed some of her fame to Michelson's glowing reviews and frequent comparisons to Sarah Bernhardt. According to Michelson's fawning interview with O'Neil in the *Bulletin*, she was born Gertrude Lamson, but took her stage name from the British actress Nance Oldfield.[84] Michelson's creation has a fictional namesake, too. As orphan Nance, reared on the poverty of Philadelphia's Irish alley, makes off with a gold watch and fur coat while conning a kindly bishop and wealthy matron into offering her protection from the police, readers will undoubtedly be reminded of the character of Nancy from Charles Dickens's *Oliver Twist* (1838). In Michelson's modern update, however, the girl pickpocket has thrown off her Victorian shackles. It is as if she has seized control of Dickens's narrative, transformed herself into the first-person protagonist of her own story, cleverly sidelined her Bill Sikes–like fiancé by landing him in jail, and exchanged her tragic fate for a triumphant happy ending.[85] The scandalous appeal of Michelson's streetwise narrator caught the attention of the Bobbs-Merrill Company, an Indianapolis-based firm known for publishing Mary Roberts Rinehart's mystery novels and other such popular fare. The press promised Michelson publication if she expanded "In the Bishop's Carriage" into a full-length novel. The result, also titled *In the Bishop's Carriage*, would define her career for years to come.

In 1904, *In the Bishop's Carriage* was a national bestseller. One of the most talked about novels of the year, it earned Michelson praise for her refreshing prose style, with many reviewers describing its plot and heroine as "unique."[86] The novel's ending generated significant debate. Some reviewers were pleased to find immoral Nance redeemed. With the support of the bishop (in whose carriage she took refuge in the book's first chapter), she leaves behind her life of crime, parlaying her talent as con artist into a successful stage career and trading up her felonious fiancé for a theatrical-manager husband. "Underlying all the story of vulgarity and sin is a ring of optimism," stated a *Literary News* reviewer, hopeful that the novel would influence criminals among its readers to reform as well.[87] For other reviewers, Nance was more compelling as crook than actress, and several critics noted that Michelson's predictable resolution threatened to undercut the novel's originality. "Why leave Nance Olden at the last in the shabby position of being just a prosaic conventionally respectable married woman like any other heroine?" asked one reviewer.[88] Almost every reader agreed about one aspect of the book: it was a page-turner. In an unusual endorsement, Speaker of the House of

Representatives Joseph Gurney Cannon described the experience of reading it thus: "I commenced reading it early in the morning and finished it that night and the coming morning and when I finished I drew a long breath and felt that I had forgotten everything else but the book and regretted that there was not more of it."[89]

In the Bishop's Carriage tapped into the zeitgeist of the new American century, establishing Michelson's reputation as a writer attuned to the sensibilities and desires of modern women. Although barely remembered today, Nance Olden was an American icon, a prototype for the flapper. Thanks to stage and screen adaptations, *In the Bishop's Carriage* had a long afterlife, becoming a fixture of popular culture for well over a decade. Shortly after the release of the book, playwright and director Channing Pollock purchased the dramatic rights in order to adapt it for the stage.[90] The play, with some of the most famous actresses of the day cast in the role of Nance, was performed around the United States for years, as well as in Canada and London. Its royalties provided regular income for Michelson, who accepted her story's continued success with humility. In 1909, in response to a note from her publisher expressing his regret that the theatrical run was coming to an end, she self-deprecatingly replied, "The marvel is . . . that the poor old Carriage should have run so long."[91] Michelson's publisher had, in fact, spoken too soon. Not only did the play continue to draw audiences, but also the emergent medium of moving pictures gave it new life. The 1913 screen adaptation made cinema history. Directed by Edwin S. Porter (of *Great Train Robbery* fame), *In the Bishop's Carriage* marked the full-length feature debut of silent film star and Hollywood legend Mary Pickford, who played Nance. Expecting a religious story based on the title, some viewers, including the star's grandmother, were shocked to see the sweet-faced young actress playing a girl thief and baring her legs on screen.[92] In 1920, a remake featuring actress Bebe Daniels circumvented such confusion by renaming the film *She Couldn't Help It*. Writing to her publisher in 1922 about a request she had received to transform the novel into an operetta, Michelson again expressed surprise at her story's longevity. "Just when it seemed that the antiquated and hard-working *Bishop's Carriage* had served every possible literary purpose, a new one has been suggested," she wrote.[93]

With *In the Bishop's Carriage* initiating Michelson's career as a novelist, the first decade of the twentieth century proved to be the most prolific period of

Silent film star Mary Pickford made her full-length feature debut as girl-thief Nance Olden in the 1913 film adaptation of *In the Bishop's Carriage*, based on Michelson's best-selling novel of 1904. The film was directed by Edwin S. Porter and produced by Famous Players Film Company. The Women Film Pioneers Project.

her fiction-writing career. In 1904, the Century Company brought out *The Madigans* in book form after serializing the episodic stories in its magazine. Following serialization in the *Saturday Evening Post*, *A Yellow Journalist* was released in 1905. By then, Michelson had a loyal fan base, and the book's publisher, D. Appleton and Company, reported significant advance sales for the full collection of Rhoda Massey stories. Doubleday, Page and Company published her next three books: another novel with a journalist-heroine, *Anthony Overman* (1906), which was based on Michelson's experiences covering the Esoteric Fraternity, a religious sect based in Applegate, California, for the *Bulletin*; *Michael Thwaites's Wife* (1909), a story about identical twin sisters that became the basis of a 1918 film titled *The Better Half*; and *The Awakening of Zojas* (1910), which reprinted her 1899 science fiction story as well as three new novellas.

This collection includes three of Michelson's "yellow journalist" stories, which have much to offer scholars and students interested in gender and race as well as the history of print culture. Published in the *Saturday Evening Post* in February 1905 and later collected as part of the book version of *A Yellow Journalist*, "The Pencil Will" shows its heroine using the resource of her gender to her advantage as she competes with male reporters for a big scoop. In its fictionalization of a real-life courtroom drama that was reported in the press in lurid detail, "The Pencil Will" allows readers to trace Michelson's moves between different forms of print culture: newspaper journalism, serial magazine fiction, and popular novels. The story further encourages consideration of Michelson's racial representations and brings into relief Rhoda's whiteness, through the character of "Mammy" Sinnott, who was based on Mary Ellen Pleasant, an enigmatic black abolitionist and entrepreneur who was labeled "Mammy" by the mainstream press. In newspaper articles such as "Dark-Skinned Lion-Tamer in the House of Mystery" (excerpts of which appear in this collection), Michelson contributed to the myth of Pleasant, who became a larger-than-life figure in the history of nineteenth-century San Francisco for her financial acumen, civil rights activism, and influence over wealthy white families. Other articles by Michelson reveal that Pleasant, who was caught up in a series of high-profile legal intrigues, became an informant for the reporter and that the two unconventional women developed a friendship. The narrative of a cross-racial alliance between strong women forms a subplot in "The Pencil Will." Rhoda and Sinnott end up aligned against the male reporters, who villainize the black woman, depicting her as an "evil genius."[94] Yet Michelson's own writing is guilty of perpetuating racial stereotypes; with her dialect-ridden speech and maternal devotion to her young white charge, Sinnott is, in many ways, a stock mammy character. The ambivalent representation of Mammy Sinnott and her relationship with the white reporter make the piece an interesting counterpart to Michelson's writings about Asian women, especially "In Chy Fong's Restaurant," in which Rhoda Massey goes undercover as a Chinese slave girl to investigate graft in Chinatown.

While Rhoda's Chinatown adventures appeared only in the book edition of *A Yellow Journalist*, presumably because they were not wholesome enough for the *Saturday Evening Post*, "The Milpitas Maiden," the final Rhoda Massey included here, appeared only as part of the magazine serialization. This story was published in the *Post* on June 24, 1905, but for unknown reasons, was not collected when *A Yellow Journalist* was published as a stand-alone book. The story, in which Rhoda is assigned to cover a national woman's suffrage convention, had its source in Michelson's coverage of the Woman's Congress of the Pacific Coast. As Skinazi and I argue in an article in *Legacy*, "The Milpitas Maiden" "add[s] to a rich and expanding archive of texts that fall under the rubric of 'suffrage literature.' "[95] Like all the stories in *A Yellow Journalist*, it offers readers a depiction of a successful professional woman who is rewarded rather than punished for being more committed to her job than she is to her beau, Ted Thompson, a male reporter at a rival paper. In one of the series' comic interludes, for example, Rhoda is so intent on chasing a story that she forgets a date she made with Ted to celebrate their engagement; apparently, the fact that she had finally agreed to marry Ted also slipped Rhoda's mind, and the episode ends with her leaving him behind as she elatedly rushes off to stop the presses with her "stunner" of a front-page story.[96] While Rhoda may be in a slightly more respectable line of work than the heroine of *In the Bishop's Carriage*, Michelson's girl-reporter protagonist shares Nance's dogged independence, slangy speech, and plucky persona. Rhoda's determination and pluck made her character an especially good fit for the *Saturday Evening Post*, a magazine that appealed to the "average American" by combining "nineteenth-century" virtues—especially the value of hard work—with "twentieth-century opportunities."[97]

Illuminating the interplay between commercial literary markets and changing conceptions of gender at the turn of the twentieth century, Michelson's writings are an important addition to American women's literature. The evolution of Michelson's career also speaks to the relationship between literature and reform in the Progressive Era. The fame and financial security that Michelson achieved as a writer allowed her to devote herself to other modes of civic reform and social activism. Increasingly, she turned her energy to politics. From 1908 to 1910, for example, she served as managing editor of the *Liberator*, a weekly journal published by San Francisco's Citizens' League for Justice; the journal took its name from William Lloyd Garrison's abolitionist newspaper, but its stated purpose was to liberate San Franciscans from the graft that held their city hostage during the reign of political boss Abe Ruef. Not surprisingly, Michelson also became a key player in the California campaign for suffrage, a cause she undertook with the belief that the woman's vote would redress not simply gender inequality but a host of other social ills as well.[98]

The Superwoman, Feminist Fantasy, and Suffrage Literature

I don't want to vote because it is unjust that I shouldn't, but because it is best—for the world and for me—that I should.

> —Miriam Michelson, inscription in autographed book shown at the Handcraft Exhibit for the College Equal Suffrage League of Northern California's Campaign of 1911[99]

On June 30, 1911, Michelson appeared before a group of more than three hundred young women gathered in San Francisco for the annual meeting of the College Equal Suffrage League. In a speech titled "The Reproach of Unladylike Behavior," Michelson "by her fun and irony warmed the audience into rippling good humor" as she made her case for suffrage.[100] Michelson's "witty and sarcastic" speech offered a historical perspective, demonstrating how the "fashions" of "ladyhood" have ebbed and flowed over time.[101] In the past, she noted, to achieve "real ladyhood," "we crippled our feet in China, we disfigured our bodies in America, and everywhere we hobbled our brains." But the definition of "ladylike" has since changed, she argued: "Now it is most ladylike to stand up, face things as they are, and accept them like a man; to be an athlete is possible, if not, a trained nurse or physician."[102] Four months after Michelson's speech, on October 10, 1911, voters in California passed Proposition 4, making the state the sixth in the union to grant suffrage to women. In light of California's successful suffrage campaign, Michelson's 1912 novella, *The Superwoman*, about a matrilineal society in which women rule by "mother right," reads as a celebration of newly acquired power. The fact that it is a work of speculative fiction, however, suggests that the battle was far from over and that gender equality still remained a future ideal.[103]

When Michelson published *The Superwoman*, she became part of a rich tradition of writers and activists who imaginatively evoked matriarchal societies of the past and the future as a means to advocate gender equality in the present. As Jill Lepore writes in *The Secret History of Wonder Woman*, stories about Amazonian societies had become "a stock feminist plot" among bohemian writers of the 1910s.[104] The examples Lepore cites—Max Eastman's 1913 poem "Child of the Amazons," Inez Haynes Gillmore's 1914 novel *Angel Island*, and, most famously, Charlotte Perkins Gilman's serialization of *Herland* in 1915—all postdate Michelson. But *The Superwoman* did, of course, have some notable predecessors. Elizabeth Cady Stanton often included stories of historical societies ruled by women in her public oratory. In 1891, for example, she gave a speech titled "The Matriarchate, or Mother-Age" at the first meeting of the National Council of Women of the United States in Washington, DC. In the speech, Stanton drew on anthropological studies of matriarchies to bolster her vision of a feminist utopian future, a "yet untried experiment of complete equality, when the united thought of man and woman will inaugurate a just government, a pure religion, a happy home, a civilization at last in which ignorance, poverty, and crime will exist no more."[105] Michelson may have known of Stanton's speech even if she was not present at the meeting. She was certainly present, however, at the Woman's Congress of the Pacific Coast in May 1895 when San Francisco activist Selina Solomons, who later authored the manual for suffragists *How We Won the Vote in California* (1912), gave a talk titled "The Matriarchate," in which she similarly cited evidence of past matriarchal civilizations and predicted that women would once again assume superiority over men.[106] Utopian versions of the trope appear in other nineteenth-century American works such as Lillie Devereux Blake's "A Divided Republic: An Allegory of the Future" (1885) and Mary E. Bradley Lane's novel *Mizora: A Prophecy* (1890). Nor was the fantasy of women's rule particular to the United States, as evidenced by British writer Elizabeth Burgoyne Corbett's *New Amazonia: A Foretaste of the Future* (1889) and Muslim feminist Rokeya Sakhawat Hossain's vision of "Ladyland" in *Sultana's Dream*, which appeared in the *Indian Ladies' Magazine* in 1905.[107]

This edition marks the first publication of *The Superwoman* since it appeared in the *Smart Set* in 1912. A highly readable text, *The Superwoman* holds great appeal for audiences today, inspiring new, and reviving old, debates about sexual politics, popular literature, and the uses of utopia. Opening up fresh possibilities for the study of feminist fantasy narratives, the novella's republication contributes to the work of literary scholars such as Mary Chapman, Angela Mills, and Leslie Petty, who have broadened our understanding of the suffrage movement beyond the polemics of first-wave orators, demonstrating that a range of writers, from experimental modernists to middlebrow moderns, helped women get the vote.

Promoting the publication of Michelson's *The Superwoman* as the lead novella in its August 1912 issue, the *Smart Set* played up the story's political angle. The editors promised readers that this "original and diverting" piece of fiction would "interest everyone and arouse wide discussion, especially among women, since the 'woman question' is so much in the foreground these days."[108] Opening in the realist tradition of Edith Wharton and Henry James, the third-person narrative introduces an arrogant bachelor, Hugh Ellinwood Welburn. As his last name suggests, Welburn is a man of the leisure class who prides himself on the wealth and status he inherited from his father. His initials, "H. E.," make him representative of the patriarchal everyman. Michelson's protagonist finds himself aboard a transatlantic ocean liner with both of the women he is courting: a beautiful ingenue and a sophisticated widow. Unable to make up his mind between the two women, Welburn considers flipping a coin—a capricious thought that suggests women's interchangeability and lack of agency on the marriage market while symbolically implying that his choice of wife is a matter of her monetary value. Before Welburn makes his choice, however, he is swept overboard, and the novella playfully switches genres, evolving into a fantasy narrative. Welburn awakes on a remote island ruled by Amazonian women who practice polyandry, using men primarily for reproductive and domestic purposes. In the world of *The Superwoman*, not only are traditional gender roles flipped, but also women are elevated to the status of deities, idolized for their wisdom, their physical strength, and their maternity.

Readers familiar with Gilman's *Herland* will mark many similarities. In both texts, for instance, male outsiders enter female-dominated societies that are guided by the religious principle of motherhood. Initially skeptical of the unfeminine women surrounding them, the men are schooled in the ways of the foreign land, come to see its utopian beauty, and find their place in the new social order through marriage. In the criticism on *Herland*, much has been made of the tunics that eliminate sex distinction and provide ease of movement for the women. *The Superwoman*, too, anticipates Michelson's and Gilman's polemics on dress reform.[109] Like *Herland*'s Terry, who complains that the men have been made into "neuters," Welburn views the toga-like garments worn by both sexes as a threat to his masculine identity.[110] Finally, Welburn's expulsion at the end of *The Superwoman* is echoed in *Herland*'s conclusion, which finds Terry on trial before the Over-mother for the attempted rape of his wife. Both men are exiled for violating the matriarchal laws of the land.

Yet the divergences between *The Superwoman* and *Herland* are more provocative than the similarities. Gilman was not simply imitating Michelson. Instead, the differences between these two texts demonstrate how Michelson and Gilman were playing with utopian conventions to engage in debate about feminist ideology. In contrast to Welburn's accidental sojourn, for example, *Herland*'s trio of male explorers actively searches for the "strange and terrible 'Woman's Land'" of legend, implying intertextuality with previous matriarchal narratives.[111] Gilman's story takes the form of a travelogue, narrated by sociologist Vandyck Jennings, the most open-minded of the men. This device allows Gilman to play Van's character off other male types: the chivalrous romantic, Jeff, and the chauvinistic cad, Terry (the character who most resembles Welburn). Unlike Michelson's nation of superwomen, Gilman's *Herland* does not invert gender roles; instead, it takes Michelson's utopian vision to its logical—or perhaps illogical—extreme, eliminating men and inventing the myth of parthenogenesis, which allows the Herlanders to reproduce. Mother love replaces heterosexual desire in *Herland*, yet the women welcome the male interlopers with an eye toward perfecting their civilization. If this "bisexual" society of the future were to maintain female superiority, it might resemble Michelson's matriarchal vision—a vision that looks forward and backward, evoking the ancient civilization of J. J. Bachofen's *Mother Right* (1861), a text that, not incidentally, Welburn recalls studying in college.[112]

As a comparison between *The Superwoman* and *Herland* suggests, Gilman did not give birth to her utopia parthenogenetically—and neither did Michelson. Their imaginations were fertilized by each other's writings and ideas and by their engagement with a range of other texts. Michelson's and Gilman's novellas provide evidence not of a monolithic utopian vision shared by all women, but of a dynamic dialogue about the ideals of gender equality and how best to achieve them—a dialogue not unlike the spirited debate of the 1895 Woman's Congress of the Pacific Coast, which first brought the two writers into each other's orbits and proved to be a breakthrough moment in both their careers. The republication of *The Superwoman* is not intended to topple Gilman's reign as "Mother Goddess" of feminist utopian fiction, or begin collecting her unpaid debt to Michelson. Rather, the novella, along with Michelson's other writings, exemplifies the need to consider women's literary history in terms of collaborative networks of exchange. Michelson's works encourage us to broaden the practice of feminist recovery—to widen the circle around success stories like Gilman's—in order to include writers and works who have been previously overlooked.

As a journalist and commercial fiction writer, Michelson had a significant, but unacknowledged, influence on women and men at a time when gender roles were undergoing radical change. Although it is a feminist classic today, Gilman's "lost" utopian novel *Herland* reached only a limited audience when it was originally published, appearing in a small, self-published magazine whose subscribers would have been predisposed to radical politics. Published in a popular mass circulation magazine known for its high literary standards, Michelson's *The Superwoman*, in contrast, was widely read in its time. Yet it has since languished unstudied for over a century.[113] Michelson and *The Superwoman* may very well have been neglected for so long due to the author's popularity, the perception that her work was, in the words of H. L. Mencken, no more than "a literary joy ride."[114] To women readers attuned to feminist undercurrents, however, Michelson's work was much more. In her autobiography, Edna Ferber noted the profound impact Michelson had on her life and career when she recalled reading the "yellow journalist" stories as they appeared in the *Saturday Evening Post*. "Those were fresh and racy newspaper stories all about a woman reporter and her dashing adventures on a big-town paper. There was the kind of newspaper woman I wanted to be. Immediately I dramatized myself as the Girl Reporter," wrote Ferber.[115] After she got her start as a journalist for a small-town newspaper, Ferber, too, went on to become a best-selling novelist and the first Jewish writer to win the Pulitzer Prize in fiction (for *So Big* in 1925). Her series about traveling saleswoman Emma McChesney, which was originally published in *American Magazine*, was modeled on Michelson's "Yellow Journalist" series, as was her debut novel, *Dawn O'Hara* (1911), which featured an Irish newspaperwoman as its protagonist. In the epic family sagas that followed, Ferber documented the diverse, multiethnic panorama of the United States. Crossing ethno-racial lines and flouting gender norms, Ferber's adventure-seeking, self-sufficient protagonists in novels such as *Show Boat* (1926), *Cimarron* (1930), *Saratoga Trunk* (1941), and *Giant* (1952) are the descendants of Michelson's heroines Nance Olden and Rhoda Massey.[116]

Michelson was never to equal the productivity and success she had in the years leading up to *The Superwoman*. "Let's just be grateful that there was a *Bishop's Carriage* and settle down to the fact that there isn't likely to be another," she wrote to newspaper editor Joseph Goodman, a friend from her Nevada days, "I'll keep on writing and sending books to you—not to make you miserable, but because of that precious, surely-tried, imperishable hope of yours in me."[117] Michelson not only kept writing but also continued to experiment with different genres. Eliding easy categorization, her wide-ranging oeuvre includes picaresque novels, science fiction, historical romance, parlor room melodrama, and literary journalism. Returning to her journalistic roots, she published nonfiction magazine essays on women's issues that complemented *The Superwoman* and shed light on her own life choices. "The Eternal Beggar" (1916), for instance, described how community property laws left women economically dependent on their husbands; implicit in this essay is an ideological explanation for her decision to devote herself to writing and politics rather than to marry and bear children. In 1934, Michelson published her last book, and only full-length work of nonfiction, *The Wonderlode of Silver and Gold*. A history of the Comstock region that draws on personal reminiscences of her youth in Virginia City, it is the closest she came to publishing an autobiography. When Michelson died on May 28, 1942, at age seventy-two, the *Oakland Tribune* memorialized her "varied life" as a "woman novelist," "pioneer feminist," and "early day politician."[118]

The journalism and fiction contained in this collection are at once a testament to Michelson's "varied life" and a chronicle of her times. Her writings allow readers direct access to the past in narrative form and through the eyes of an individual, admittedly undetached observer, who, as an independent woman and the child of Jewish immigrants, was at the forefront of major changes in American life during the Progressive Era. Through this edition's interplay between Michelson's fiction and journalism, readers can experience firsthand how Michelson's newspaper work fueled her imagination as a fiction writer and how she adapted narrative techniques from fiction to create a body of journalism that informs, provokes, and entertains its audience, even a century after it was written. Recent changes in journalism and the publishing industry due to the rise of digital culture make this collection of periodical writings especially timely for scholars of journalism and print history who are committed to exploring, restoring, and preserving print cultures of the past. Given Michelson's wide-ranging output, there are many opportunities for other scholars to build on the research I have begun here. My hope is that this collection models an approach to recovery that places literary and journalistic texts into conversation with each other and inspires future scholarship that delves not only into Michelson's work but also into the writings and careers of other forgotten women journalists and magazine writers.

NOTES

1. Miriam Michelson, "Charlotte Perkins Stetson Flays Her Own Sex Alive," *Bulletin*, December 10, 1898, 16.
2. Miriam Michelson, "Stetson Wedding," *Bulletin*, June 25, 1900, 21.
3. Miriam Michelson, "Mrs. Stetson Is in Town," *Bulletin*, December 12, 1899, 1.
4. See, for example, Sari Edelstein, *Between the Novel and the News: The Emergence of American Women's Writing* (Charlottesville: University of Virginia Press, 2014), 110–32; and Denise Knight, "Charlotte Perkins Gilman, William Randolph Hearst, and the Practice of Ethical Journalism," in *Charlotte Perkins Gilman and Her Contemporaries: Literary and Intellectual Contexts*, ed. Cynthia J. Davis and Denise D. Knight (Tuscaloosa: University of Alabama Press, 2004), 46–58.
5. Michelson, "Mrs. Stetson Is in Town," 1.
6. Michelson, "Stetson Wedding," 21.
7. Miriam Michelson, *The Superwoman*, Smart Set 37, no. 4 (August 1912): 16.
8. On the *Smart Set*, see, for example, Sharon Hamilton, "The First *New Yorker*? The *Smart Set* Magazine, 1900–1924," *Serials Librarian* 37, no. 2 (1999): 89–104.
9. Gilman tried to publish her own fiction in the *Smart Set* to no avail. She began her self-published magazine, the *Forerunner*, in 1909, shortly after receiving a rejection letter from the *Smart Set* for her story "The Housekeeper" and realizing that existing magazines were resistant to her writing. Michelson, in comparison, did not seem to have difficulty getting her work published in magazines despite ideological similarities. See the *Smart Set* to Charlotte Gilman, January 30, 1909, Charlotte Perkins Gilman Papers, Folder 133, Schlesinger Library, Radcliffe Institute, Harvard University.
10. The scholarship on Gilman's racism, anti-Semitism, and xenophobia is extensive. For an overview and thoughtful consideration of this trend in Gilman scholarship, see Judith Allen, *The Feminism of Charlotte Perkins Gilman: Sexualities, Histories, Progressivism* (Chicago: University of Chicago Press, 2009), 327–62.

11. See Lori Harrison-Kahan and Karen E. H. Skinazi, "Miriam Michelson's Yellow Journalism and the Multi-Ethnic West," *MELUS* 40, no. 2 (2015): 183–207.

12. The most complete account of the family's history can be found in Dorothy Livingston, *The Master of Light: A Biography of Albert A. Michelson* (Chicago: University of Chicago Press, 1973). It is worth noting that Miriam's sisters, Pauline, Bessie, and Julia, also led unconventional lives. While Julia and Miriam were unmarried, working women without children, their oldest sister, Pauline, married a well-known physician, Henry Bergstein, in 1880 and shortly after moved from Virginia City to Reno. After the couple's rancorous divorce in 1898, Pauline changed not only her last name back to Michelson but also the last names of their two children, whom she raised independently after her husband deserted the family; she and her children lived on the same street as Miriam and Julia. Miriam was close with both of Pauline's sons, one of whom, Marion Michelson, followed in his aunt's footsteps to become a reporter, first for the *San Francisco Bulletin* and later for New York periodicals such as the *World*. While Pauline was married by a rabbi in a traditional Jewish wedding, Bessie married a non-Jew, Arthur McEwen, a Scottish immigrant who became a legendary frontier journalist and editor. The McEwens eventually moved East, and Miriam visited them in New York for extended periods during the early 1900s, helping to care for Bessie who was in ill health. Bessie passed away in 1910, a few years after her husband, who died suddenly of heart failure on a trip to Bermuda in 1907.

13. Ronald M. James and Kenneth H. Fliess, "Women of the Mining West: Virginia City Revisited," in *Comstock Women: The Making of a Mining Community*, ed. Ronald M. James and C. Elizabeth Raymond (Reno: University of Nevada Press, 1998), 18.

14. For Michelson's correspondence with Goodman, see Joseph T. Goodman papers, [ca. 1891–1971], BANC MSS C-B 489, Bancroft Library, University of California, Berkeley.

15. Mark Twain, *Roughing It* (1872; New York: Signet, 2008), 225.

16. Miriam Michelson, *The Wonderlode of Silver and Gold* (Boston: Stratford, 1934), 52, 133.

17. Susan Armitage, "Through Women's Eyes: A New View of the West," in *The Women's West*, ed. Susan Armitage and Elizabeth Jameson (Norman: University of Oklahoma Press, 1997), 9, 10–12.

18. C. Elizabeth Raymond, "'I am Afraid We Will Lose All We Have Made': Women's Lives in a Nineteenth-Century Mining Town," in James and Raymond, *Comstock Women*, 4, 15.

19. On Michelson as an example of the "Real West" school of writing, see Andria Daley Taylor, "Girls of the Golden West," in James and Raymond, *Comstock Women,* 281.

20. Miriam Michelson, *The Madigans* (New York: Century, 1904), 299. An editor changed Irene's nickname from "Split" to "Sprint" in the *Century* version of "Stories of the Nevada Madigans" out of fear that Michelson's chosen name for her character would offend readers' sense of propriety. Michelson changed it back to "Split" in the book version of *The Madigans.*

21. Cited in Otis Notman, "Popular Writers from the Far West," *New York Times Saturday Review of Books* (June 1, 1907): BR356.

22. See Philip J. Deloria, *Playing Indian* (New Haven, CT: Yale University Press), 1998.

23. Michelson, *The Madigans,* 149.

24. On the Irish in Virginia City, see Raymond, "'I am Afraid We Will Lose All We Have Made,'" 12; and Ronald M. James, "Erin's Daughters on the Comstock: Building Community," in James and Raymond, *Comstock Women.* On Jews, see John P. Marschall, *Jews in Nevada: A History* (Reno : University of Nevada Press, 2008), 71.

25. Michelson, *The Madigans,* 28.

26. Michelson, *The Madigans,* 128; Warren Sylvester Smith, *The London Heretics, 1870–1914* (New York: Dodd, Mead, 1968), 5.

27. Robert A. Millikan, *Biographical Memoir of Albert A. Michelson, 1852–1931* (Washington, DC: National Academy of Sciences, 1938), 128–29. Miriam's experiences in Virginia City contrast significantly with those of her cousin Harriet Lane Levy (the daughter of Samuel's sister, Henrietta), whose family settled in San Francisco. Levy recounts her religious upbringing in her memoir, *920 O'Farrell Street: A Jewish Girlhood in Old San Francisco* (1947). The Michelsons were in close contact with their more observant cousins since Albert lived with the Levys while attending high school in San Francisco.

28. Michelson may have distanced herself from Jewishness, but as Skinazi and I note, "the secular press . . . took note of her ethno-religious background, and the Jewish press claimed her as one of their own." The *Washington Post,* for instance, described her as a "California Jewess who has succeeded with her pen," and she was similarly recognized as a famous Jewish woman writer by periodicals as wide-ranging as the *American Hebrew and Jewish Messenger,* the *American Israelite,* the *San Francisco Chronicle, Broadway Magazine,* and the *Arizona Republican.* See Harrison-Kahan and Skinazi, "Miriam Michelson's Yellow Journalism and the Multi-Ethnic West," 188. In a chapter of my manuscript-in-progress,

West of the Ghetto: Pioneering Women Writers, Progressive Era San Francisco, and Jewish Literary Culture, I discuss Michelson's Jewish background and disidentification from Jewishness at greater length, analyzing the sparse Jewish content of her writings and placing her work in relation to other San Francisco–based Jewish women writers of the period, including her cousin Harriet Lane Levy; the novelist Emma Wolf; and women's club leader and novelist Bettie Lowenberg.

29. Harrison-Kahan and Skinazi, "Miriam Michelson's Yellow Journalism and the Multi-Ethnic West," 188.

30. Michelson, *Wonderlode of Silver and Gold*, 170.

31. On Native American life in Virginia City, see Eugene M. Hattori, "'And Some of Them Swear Like Pirates': Acculturation of American Indian Women in Nineteenth-Century Virginia City," in James and Raymond, *Comstock Women*, 229–45.

32. Marschall, *Jews in Nevada*, 72.

33. Mary McNair Mathews, *Ten Years in Nevada* (Buffalo, NY: Baker, Jones, 1880), 249, 169, 53.

34. Mary Ellen Glass, "Alice E. Sauer: Reminiscences of Life in Virginia City and Washoe Valley, Nevada," *University of Nevada Oral History Archive* (University of Nevada Oral History Program, 1969), 9. Marschall's study of Jews in Nevada contradicts this to an extent. Although there were no Jewish congregations in Virginia City, there were two Jewish benevolent societies, including a B'nai B'rith Lodge, by the time Miriam was born.

35. Quoted in Livingston, *Master of Light*, 25. On Grant's anti-Semitism, see Jonathan Sarna, *When General Grant Expelled the Jews* (New York: Schocken, 2016).

36. Albert won the Nobel Prize in 1907 in recognition of his invention of the interferometer, a device that was used in experiments to measure the speed of light, among other discoveries.

37. In *A Kid on the Comstock*, for example, John Taylor Waldorf categorized the Michelsons as part of the "tony bunch." Waldorf's daughter relates an episode in which Albert Michelson's visit home from the East exacerbated tensions with children of miners, who further resented the siblings' scholastic achievements. See John Waldorf Bryant, *A Kid on the Comstock: Reminiscences of a Virginia City Childhood* (Palo Alto, CA: American West Publishing, 1970), 114. On anti-Semitism in the West, see Jeanne Abrams, *Jewish Women Pioneering the Frontier Trail: A History in the American West* (New York: New York University Press, 2006), 11; and Ellen Eisenberg, Ava F. Kahn, and William Toll, *Jews of the Pacific Coast: Reinventing Community on America's Edge* (Seattle: University of Washington Press, 2009), 7.

38. Edward Meeker's vaudeville song "I'm a Yiddish Cowboy" (1908), for example, derives its humor from the incongruity of Western life and Jewish identity but allows for the possibility that the "Yiddish cowboy" can become American, notably by creating a distinction between himself and Indians. In the chorus, "Tough Guy Levi" sings, "I don't care for Tomahawks or Cheyenne Indians, oi, oi / I'm a real live 'Diamond Dick' that shoots 'em till they die / I'll marry squaw or start a war, for I'm a fighting guy." See Rachel Rubinstein, *Members of the Tribe: Native America in the Jewish Imagination* (Detroit: Wayne State University Press, 2010), 21–58; and Alan Trachtenberg, *Shades of Hiawatha: Staging Indians, Making Americans, 1880–1930* (New York: Hill and Wang, 2004), 140–69.

39. The *Bonanza* episode may have contributed to the myth that Albert Michelson was a product of Nevada schools. In fact, because there was not yet a public school system in Virginia City, Albert was sent to San Francisco for his education. See Guy Rocha, "Myth #59: Shedding Light on Nevada's First Nobel Laureate," Nevada State Library, Archives and Public Records.

40. Dolores Waldorf Bryant, commentary in John Taylor Waldorf, *A Kid on the Comstock*, 118; Livingston, *Master of Light*, 17.

41. Nellie Bly, *Around the World in Seventy-Two Days and Other Writings* (New York: Penguin, 2014), 20, 31, 82.

42. Jean Marie Lutes, *Front-Page Girls: Women Journalists in American Culture and Fiction, 1880–1930* (Ithaca, NY: Cornell University Press, 2006), 5.

43. Annie Laurie, "A City's Disgrace," *San Francisco Examiner*, January 19, 1890, 11.

44. Charles Michelson, *The Ghost Talks* (New York: G. P. Putnam's Sons, 1944), 78.

45. Lori Harrison-Kahan and Karen E. H. Skinazi, "The Girl Reporter in Fact and Fiction: Miriam Michelson's New Women and Periodical Culture in the Progressive Era," *Legacy* 34, no. 2 (2017): 321–38.

46. Miriam Michelson, "What Say Ye Women to This?," *Arthur McEwen's Letter*, February 9, 1895, 5.

47. Quoted in Ben Procter, *William Randolph Hearst: The Later Years* (New York: Oxford University Press, 2007), 5.

48. Miriam Michelson, "Lottie Collins on Woman," *Arthur McEwen's Letter*, February 9, 1895, 5.

49. Michelson, "What Say Ye Women to This?," 5.

50. On Matson, see Clare Sears, *Arresting Dress: Cross-Dressing, Law, and Fascination in Nineteenth-Century San Francisco* (Durham, NC: Duke University Press, 2015); and Allan Bérubé, "Lesbian Masquerade," in his *My Desire for History: Essays in Gay, Community, and Labor History* (Chapel Hill: University of North Carolina Press, 2011), 41–53.

51. Miriam Michelson, "The New Woman Realized," *Arthur McEwen's Letter*, February 16, 1895, 9.

52. Clare Sears, "'A Tremendous Sensation?': Cross-Dressing in the Nineteenth-Century San Francisco Press," in *News and Sexuality: Media Portraits of Diversity*, ed. Laura Castañeda and Shannon B. Campbell (Thousand Oaks, CA: Sage, 2006), 1, 15.

53. Miriam Michelson, "The New Woman Realized," *Arthur McEwen's Letter*, February 16, 1895, 9. Although some of Michelson's reviews in *Arthur McEwen's Letter* were signed "M.M.," disguising her gender identity, here she signs her full name, Miriam Michelson, so that the signature, which ends rather than begins the article, reads as a rebuke to Matson.

54. Lutes, *Front-Page Girls*, 4.

55. Miriam Michelson, "Where Women Gamble," *San Francisco Call*, March 18, 1898, 16.

56. Miriam Michelson, "Viewed by a Woman," *San Francisco Call*, May 21, 1895, 4. While the term "New Woman" is often capitalized, I am following Michelson's convention of using lowercase in the newspaper article; interestingly, she does capitalize "Old Woman."

57. Harrison-Kahan and Skinazi, "Girl Reporter in Fact and Fiction," 321–38.

58. Miriam Michelson, "Weeds and Flowers," *San Francisco Call*, May 24, 1895, 8.

59. For more on suffrage print culture, see Mary Chapman, *Making Noise, Making News: Suffrage Print Culture and U.S. Modernism* (Oxford: Oxford University Press, 2014).

60. Michelson, "Viewed by a Woman," 4.

61. See, for example, Jack London to Cloudesley Johns, May 18, 1899, in *The Letters of Jack London: Volume 1*, ed. Earle Labor, Robert C. Leitz III, and I. Milo Shepard (Stanford, CA: Stanford University Press, 1988), 76. In subsequent years, London and Michelson often published in the same magazines, and in 1904, London's famous story "The Sea-Wolf" was serialized alongside Michelson's "Stories of the Nevada Madigans" in *Century*.

62. Alice Fahs, *Out on Assignment: Newspaper Women and the Making of Modern Public Space* (Chapel Hill: University of North Carolina Press, 2014), 233.

63. Miriam Michelson, "Strangling Hands upon a Nation's Throat," *San Francisco Call*, September 30, 1897, 1.

64. Karen Roggenkamp, *Narrating the News: New Journalism and Literary Genre in Late Nineteenth-Century American Newspapers and Fiction* (Kent, OH: Kent State University Press, 2005), xiv.

65. Harrison-Kahan and Skinazi, "Miriam Michelson's Yellow Journalism and the Multi-Ethnic West," 190.

66. Miriam Michelson, "Changing a Bad Indian into a Good One," *San Francisco Call*, April 24, 1898, 25.

67. For a history of Indian boarding schools, see David W. Adams, *Education for Extinction: American Indians and the Boarding School Experience* (Lawrence: University Press of Kansas, 1995).

68. Miriam Michelson, "A Military Matter in Black and White," *Bulletin*, December 3, 1899, 9.

69. "There never was a better newspaper fight than the *Bulletin*'s," Michelson wrote to Older years later. Miriam Michelson to Fremont Older, undated, Fremont Older papers, 1907–41, Box 1, BANC MSS C-B 376. Courtesy of the Bancroft Library, University of California, Berkeley.

70. Miriam Michelson, *A Yellow Journalist* (New York: D. Appleton, 1905), 93.

71. See Karen A. Keeley, "Sexual Slavery in San Francisco's Chinatown: 'Yellow Peril' and 'White Slavery' in Frank Norris's Early Fiction," *Studies in American Naturalism* 2, no. 2 (2007): 129–49.

72. See Helen F. Clark, *The Lady of the Lily Feet and Other Stories of Chinatown* (Philadelphia: Griffith and Rowland Press, 1900).

73. See, for example, Dominika Ferens, *Edith and Winnifred Eaton: Chinatown Missions and Japanese Romances* (Urbana: University of Illinois Press, 2002).

74. Sui Sin Far, "'Its Wavering Image,'" in *Mrs. Spring Fragrance and Other Writings*, ed. Amy Ling and Annette White-Parks (Urbana: University of Illinois Press, 1995), 61–66. For a story about a female reporter working in Chinatown, see also Sui Sin Far, "The Success of a Mistake," *Westerner* 8, no. 3 (1908): 18–21, reprinted in *Legacy* 29, no. 2 (2012): 270–79.

75. For a detailed reading of these stories, see Harrison-Kahan and Skinazi, "Miriam Michelson's Yellow Journalism and the Multi-Ethnic West."

76. Miriam Michelson. Category: Fiction; received: Mar. 6, 1900; sent to editor: Mar. 7, 1900; decision: Mar. 11, 1900; letter sent: Mar. 12, 1900. Houghton Mifflin Company reader reports on manuscripts submitted for publication, MS Am 2516, (7915)–(8279), (8043). Houghton Library, Harvard College Library.

77. Queen Liliuokalani, *Hawaii's Story by Hawaii's Queen* (Boston: Lothrop, Lee, and Shepard, 1898), 399.

78. In 1913, Houghton Mifflin again rejected a manuscript for a feminist piece of historical fiction by Michelson titled "The Duchess of Suds: A Romance" and based on her moderately successful 1911 play of the same name. The heroine

is the mistress of King Charles I of Spain and the mother of Don Juan. The reader's report described the manuscript as "a not more than medium historical novel by a writer who made a success years ago but has never equaled it since." See Miriam Michelson. Category: Fiction; received: June 26, 1913. Houghton Mifflin Company reader reports on manuscripts submitted for publication, MS Am 2516, (A8451)–(A8820), (A8569). Houghton Library, Harvard College Library.

79. For Michelson's reporting on the aftermath of the 1906 earthquake, see Miriam Michelson, "The Destruction of San Francisco," *Harper's Weekly* 50, no. 2576 (1906): 623–24.

80. Miriam Michelson, "Motives of Women Who Commit Theft," *North American*, May 6, 1902, 8.

81. David E. Sumner, *The Magazine Century: American Magazines since 1900* (New York: Peter Lang, 2010), 16. See also Richard M. Ohmann, *Selling Culture: Magazines, Markets, and Class at the Turn of the Century* (New York: Verso, 1996).

82. Miriam Michelson to Robert Underwood Johnson, March 17, 1904, Century Company records, Manuscripts and Archives Divison, the New York Public Library, Astor, Lenox, and Tilden Foundations; Haryot Holt Cahoon, "Women in Gutter Journalism," *Arena* 17 (1896–97): 568–74.

83. Mary Moss, "Notes on New Novels," *Atlantic Monthly* 97, no. 2 (1906): 47. On "middlebrow moderns," see Lisa Botshon and Meredith Goldsmith, eds., *Middlebrow Moderns: Popular American Women Writers of the 1920s* (Boston: Northeastern University Press), 2003.

84. Miriam Michelson, "Nance O'Neill [*sic*] Will Some Day Wear Sarah Bernhardt's Crown," *Bulletin*, March 5, 1899, 9. For more on O'Neil, see David Beasley, *McKee Rankin and the Heyday of the American Theater* (Ontario: Wilfrid Laurier University Press, 2002), 279–82 and 285–416.

85. *In the Bishop's Carriage* is thus an interesting precursor to Sarah Waters's 2002 novel *Fingersmith*, which rewrites *Oliver Twist* from a queer, female perspective.

86. See, for example, "Madame Raffles the First," *Chicago Tribune* [no date], Bobbs-Merrill MSS, Courtesy, The Lilly Library, Indiana University, Bloomington, Indiana.

87. Review of *In the Bishop's Carriage, Literary News* (April 1904): 52, Bobbs-Merrill MSS, Courtesy, The Lilly Library, Indiana University, Bloomington, Indiana.

88. Untitled, undated, and unattributed review in Bobbs-Merrill MSS, Courtesy, The Lilly Library, Indiana University, Bloomington, Indiana.

89. J. G. Cannon to the Bobbs-Merrill Company, June 8, 1904, Bobbs-Merrill MSS, Courtesy, The Lilly Library, Indiana University, Bloomington, Indiana.

90. In his autobiography, *Harvest of My Years* (1943), Pollock confessed that he wrote the play without having read Michelson's novel because he "never had time" and "success in dramatizing a novel depended on not knowing too much about it." The fact that Pollock knew the story of *In the Bishop's Carriage* well enough to adapt it without reading the book speaks to the popularity of the novel and how the plot and characters were very much part of general cultural knowledge at the time. See Channing Pollock, *Harvest of My Years* (Indianapolis: Bobbs-Merrill, 1943), 169.

91. Miriam Michelson to H. H. Howland, September 1, 1909, Bobbs-Merrill MSS, Courtesy, The Lilly Library, Indiana University, Bloomington, Indiana.

92. Kevin Brownlow, *Mary Pickford Rediscovered: Rare Pictures of a Hollywood Legend* (New York: Harry Abrams, 1999), 83.

93. Miriam Michelson to Mr. Julian Bobbs, September 18, 1922, Bobbs-Merrill MSS, Courtesy, The Lilly Library, Indiana University, Bloomington, Indiana.

94. Miriam Michelson, "The Pencil Will," *Saturday Evening Post* 177, no. 5 (1905): 9–11, 40.

95. Harrison-Kahan and Skinazi, "Girl Reporter in Fact and Fiction," 324.

96. Miriam Michelson, *A Yellow Journalist*, 169.

97. Jan Cohn, *Creating America: George Horace Latimer and the* Saturday Evening Post (Pittsburgh: University of Pittsburgh Press, 1989), 28.

98. See Miriam Michelson, "Vice and the Woman's Vote," *Sunset Magazine* (April 1913): 345–48.

99. Quoted in *Winning Equal Suffrage in California* (College Equal Suffrage League, 1913), 134.

100. *Winning Equal Suffrage in California*, 57.

101. Mary Ashe Miller, "Crowds Flock to Hear Lights of Literature," *San Francisco Call*, July 1, 1911, 11.

102. "A Bargain Counter of Intellect," *Pacific* 61 (August 14, 1911): 6–7.

103. On Michelson and suffrage, see also Harrison-Kahan and Skinazi, "Girl Reporter in Fact and Fiction."

104. Jill Lepore, *The Secret History of Wonder Woman* (New York: Vintage, 2015), 87.

105. Elizabeth Cady Stanton, "The Matriarchate, or Mother-Age," in *Elizabeth Cady Stanton, Feminist as Thinker*, ed. Ellen Carol DuBois and Richard Candida Smith (New York: New York University Press, 2007), 274.

106. "The Morning Session," *San Francisco Call*, May 26, 1895, 8.

107. There were male influences as well. Michelson and Gilman were both influenced by Edward Bellamy's *Looking Backward, 2000–1887* (1888), while the title of Michelson's text suggests she had in mind both Friedrich Nietzsche's

theory of the *Übermensch* from *Thus Spake Zarathustra* (1883) and George Bernard Shaw's *Man and Superman* (1903). For more on feminist appropriations and the term "superwoman," see Lucy Delap, *The Feminist Avant-Garde: Transatlantic Encounters of the Early Twentieth Century* (Cambridge: Cambridge University Press, 2007), 249–91.

108. "The August *Smart Set*: A Foretaste," *Smart Set* 37, no. 3 (July 1912): n.p.

109. Michelson's article "The Terrible Consequences of Clothing with Women Inside of It" was published in *Sunset Magazine* in February 1915, followed by Gilman's *The Dress of Women*, which was published in the *Forerunner* a few months later.

110. Charlotte Perkins Gilman, *Herland and Related Writings* (Buffalo, NY: Broadview, 2013), 151.

111. Gilman, *Herland*, 34.

112. Gilman, *Herland*, 81.

113. The circulation of the *Forerunner* was about 1,500 subscribers. Under the editorship of George Nathan and H. L. Mencken, the *Smart Set* published writers such as James Joyce and F. Scott Fitzgerald, helping to bring modernism to the masses. It had 165,000 subscribers at its peak.

114. H. L. Mencken, "The Last of the Victorians," *Smart Set* (October 1, 1909): 156.

115. Edna Ferber, *A Peculiar Treasure* (New York: Doubleday, Doran, 1939), 115.

116. For more on Ferber's career, see Lori Harrison-Kahan, *The White Negress: Literature, Minstrelsy, and the Black-Jewish Imaginary* (New Brunswick, NJ: Rutgers University Press, 2011), 58–95; and Eliza McGraw, *Edna Ferber's America* (Baton Rouge: Louisiana State University Press, 2014).

117. Miriam Michelson to Joseph Goodman, n.d., Joseph T. Goodman papers, [ca. 1891–1971], BANC MSS C-B 489. Courtesy of The Bancroft Library, University of California, Berkeley.

118. "Miss Michelson Had Varied Life," *Oakland Tribune*, May 31, 1942, 9.

1

THE SUPERWOMAN

Smart Set 37, no. 4 (1912): 1–48

I T was a curious chance that had brought the three together aboard the same ship—a most disagreeable chance, Welburn declared it, when he and Millicent Bourn met Mrs. Finlayson face to face at the foot of the main stairway.

He and Millicent, with Mrs. Bourn of course behind them, were coming up from the saloon. Mrs. Finlayson was coming down. And a superb descent hers was! She was in black, a black of elegance, of distinction, in which the poise of her exquisite figure was apparent—in fact, just apparent enough. And the black hat—despite its exaggeration of smartness, its ultra-long, wide plumes and almost grotesque size—became on that wonderfully placed head and throat the fitting crown to a face whose radiant charm challenged the roses she carried.

They were his roses; Welburn noted this with satisfaction, even in the vexed moment in which he recognized the difficulties of the situation. He had selected those gorgeous American Beauties himself, and he thrilled now to see how perfectly the young widow became them. He had not known what boat she was taking across; he had left it to Seldner, his man, to find that out and to see that the flowers reached her.

And now here they were together, the three of them, he and the two women, one of whom he intended to marry.

Welburn did not like it; in fact, he distinctly disliked it. He had taken passage on the boat the Bourns had chosen with the determination to give five days to his fancy for Millicent Bourn and to see what came of it. If in the close consecutive companionship of ship life she should still seem to him the delightfully girlish, tender, docile, well bred, properly schooled and exquisitely pretty little thing he had known her, why, then he would marry her.

He had said it to himself, and he meant it, though he sighed as he said it, thinking regretfully of the *diablerie* that was Paula Finlayson, the fearless sophistication of her, the wit and worldly wisdom—all aside from her beauty. Ah, the man that married Paula would never be bored for a moment, would never curse the sodden futility of life, the worthless inadequacy of accomplishment, the ennui of inaction!

And Welburn had been so bored all his life, all his life! Oh, how he had wished with a fever of desire that there had been something to wish for! To crave, to want, to hunger for something—anything! To will with passion to have; to fight, to struggle; to care enough to struggle! To live! For what is life but to want and to get, or even fail to get? And he had merely got all his life without wishing first, as his father had before him, and his father, too. Welburn's was a heritage of distinction as well as of caste.

Therefore what could he want? How could one want whose millions slipped ever before him superserviceably anticipating, quenching desire; whose childhood had been a succession of unwished-for toys, of unearned diversions; whose manhood's talents had never tested themselves, for all those eager, golden fingers that officiously fitted keys to every lock before he could even long to break one open?

But he had decided to marry because—well, merely because. There were subsidiary reasons, such as disgust at the temporary substitutes for a mate which a multimillionaire might find, but it was not this that really determined him; nor was it because of the dignity of the married state, nor the prestige of family appanage,[1] nor the feebleness and incongruity of old bachelorhood. To be honest, and he was honest with himself—a man of great wealth could afford to be, he had often said—the reason that he was marrying was because that was the next thing to do.

And he was marrying either little Millicent Bourn or Paula Finlayson; either of them, he said with a grin to himself, because both being of his caste and to be won only on the terms of a man's complete surrender, he could not wed both.

---

1. Appanage: inheritance.

And now here they were together on board. He might not even, having the presence of the one, learn to long for the other. Both were here. Both were willing.

Ah, didn't he know it? Didn't Millicent show it, in every unconscious turn of her girlish body, that felt his presence as naïvely as a flower feels the sun, as a petted dog quivers in anticipation of its master's touch? Didn't Paula show it, by every artful grace she could not but exhibit before him, by every clever intuition, by her tact and her social skill, by her very garments, by the daring suggestion her eyes made to his?

And here they stood within his hand's reach, the flower of the women of his class, the two perfect blossoms shaped by wealth and culture and caste. In all the garden where his kind was privileged to rove, there was nothing to equal them. If ever women were worth the price a man has to pay for such as these, the two who stood—one behind and below him on the stairway, the other just above—these two spelled value received for a man's liberty and the perquisites of the wedding ring.

Perhaps, he said whimsically to himself, all in the moment before speech that they stood here, perhaps he might take one, and so at last come to know what it was to want—to want the other.

BUT WHICH ONE, AND which should be the other, Welburn had not decided when evening came—nor when the second evening came—nor the third. But he had determined to make his decision before the boat landed. If he did not, then he must toss up for it.

Therefore on the fourth night he did not sleep; in fact, he did not go to his suite at all, but told his man to turn in and not to wait for him. Snug in his fur-lined burberry, though a high wind was on and the sea wild with a driving rainstorm, he walked the deck as long as he could keep his feet, walked and pondered and let fancy picture the future for him, first with Millicent for his wife and then with Paula Finlayson.

And then suddenly, as he was standing clinging to the railing, so deep in thought as to be half unconscious of the madness of the storm and of the gigantic battle between the great ship and the furious sea, a mighty wave broke over the struggling vessel, and, receding, swept Welburn off his feet and away with it.

II

WELBURN could swim. At college, after a tremendous water feat, they had christened him the "Twentieth Century Leander."

"Leander!" he had repeated then, folding his dripping arms and standing a moment in his trunks facing his admirers. "Leander—bah! Show me the Hero worth swimming for, the girl that won't meet a fellow half—no three-quarters—of the way!"[2]

Tonight, after the first submerging and the resenting reaction of his body against the indignity of force—a body that had been guarded and trained and ministered to since babyhood by experts in the cult of the flesh—he came to the surface, struggled from his coat and struck out manfully. Then, lifting himself high in the water, he shouted for help.

Again he shouted. And again.

The steamer, a high, black mass a-twinkle with lights, nosing doggedly into the black storm ahead, passed with the rush of a limited train. And he went down again into the boiling whirlpool she left behind her.

When once more he came to the surface and cleared his lungs, he shouted again for help. And again. And then, though he could no longer see the steamer's outline, nor hear for the buffeting of the waves, he called again.

The feebleness of his cry in that roar of the elements was absurd, even to Welburn. He unfastened his shoes when he could and kicked them from him, swam a few strokes, rested, and then relieved himself of his coat and waistcoat and swam on again.

Where? In what direction? Wherefore?

Never once in that struggle in the cold, wet blackness did the questions come to him. He swam because he could swim. He swam ahead because that was his route so far as he knew, the route he would have taken had he been lying aboard ship snug in his cabin *de luxe* with its perfectly appointed bath, its private dining room and drawing rooms.

"I'd have done better," he said to himself as he buffeted his way along, "to

---

2. Leander: a figure from Greek mythology who would swim across a strait to see his lover, Hero. Their romance ends in tragedy when Leander drowns in a storm, leading to Hero's suicide.

have tossed up for it—heads, Millicent; tails, Paula—and gone to bed and to sleep on it."

He felt himself shivering with the cold of that black night water. He struck out then with a swift, long over-head stroke that set his heart to beating hotly.

"Wonder which it would have been?" he mused—or rather, something in him, independent of him, mused. "Heads or tails?"

His eyes began to become accustomed to the darkness; he could see now the white gleam of foam at the edge of the rushing waves when they broke. He threw himself upon his back and looked up into the black heavens, but the sharp rain cut his face, and, because he was weakened probably, he did not protect himself and the waves swept the salt water into his lungs.

He was still weaker when he had cleared his lungs and, turning on his side again, swept forward. But even then he, or some part of him, muttered: "All for love or the world well lost!"[3] and his strained, salt-frozen features stiffened into a cynical grin.

And all the while he swam—swam as though ahead of him, a mile maybe, or two, or even five or ten or twenty, lay land and life and common, ordinary things.

"If only it had been love," he said once in that unreasoning, hindered, buffeted passage onward through nothingness to nothingness—"if only it had been, it might—have been—worth while."

It was not only his words that came in gasps now; his thought, too, hesitated. In time he was capable of no thought further than the reflections that had come to him since he struck the water. All else he forgot; but over these he went again and again mechanically, hardly knowing that the thought, each time it presented itself, was not new.

He knew cold and darkness and the strangling taste of salt water; and, too, his body began to know utter weariness, the fatigue of superhuman, impotent effort. But all this was physical. Behind the senses thought slumbered or was drowned, only now and then coming to the surface with a mechanical iteration that was robbed now of meaning. He knew always that he was swimming for his life. But the only words that were left to him at the last were the foolish words in which he had couched a foolish thought.

---

3. *All for Love; or, the World Well Lost* is the title of a 1677 play by John Dryden.

So he muttered, "Heads, Millicent; tails, Paula," without the slightest concurrence between expression and will.

And so he swam and lost consciousness, but swam still and found it again; and found himself measuring his futile strokes, beating them futilely against the tireless waves to the rhythm of his folly: "Heads, Millicent; tails, Paula."

III

WHEN he woke to life and felt the rise and fall of a vessel's deck under him—though he had no idea how he had come there, nor whether the last sinking he remembered had indeed been the last—the rhythm of that senseless tune he had chanted so long still twisted his blue, shivering lips.

"Heads, Millicent," he whispered through his agony of living again, to somebody whose arm he felt uplifting his frozen, stiffened body. "Tails, Paula."

And then, under the illusion that he had unburdened himself of a communication of tremendous significance, he fell back again into the blackness of unconsciousness, and revived, not knowing how many hours and days had passed in the interval, to mumble feebly: "Was it heads—or—or was it tails?"

There was no answer. And this time Welburn was himself enough to resent it.

"Heads—or tails?" he demanded authoritatively.

It was all the ideas he had. Apart from physical sensations—and these were all torture now—it was the only consciousness of life he possessed. Obscurely to some blind instinct that was fighting for his reason the thought was of value, merely because it was all he had. It seemed to him a vital necessity to cling to this, therefore, to insist upon it.

"Heads or tails?" he mumbled again, and, his will dragging consciousness with it as one might drag a dead weight to light against almost overmastering forces, with such an effort his groping hand found his pocket and sought there for a coin to toss.

That was the limit, though, of his endeavor. He knew that he had failed; he knew that he was no longer in the sea—though in dreams for months after he beat his way nightly through mountains of water—but he did not know when he was taken off the boat that had rescued him, nor where he was, nor the sort of people into whose hands he had fallen. Although he must at times, during the days when he was being nursed back to life, have lifted his eyes to the strange faces that bent over him while he drank from the cup held to his lips, he never afterward remembered seeing anyone between the time he had been swept overboard and the day that Gurtha stood before him.

She stood in the doorway of the little house, a heroic figure, looking curiously down upon him as he lay outstretched, large, statuesque, deep-bodied, wide-breasted, clear-eyed. And he knew there was only curiosity in those eyes of hers in almost the same moment that he knew she was there. The heavy braids of her brown hair were wreathed about her haughty head and low across her forehead; he noted this unconsciously, and that her wide parted lips showed teeth square, strong and white. The folds of the single garment wrapped about her left bare an arm and shoulder massively strong yet shapely, legs sinewy and to him unbeautiful, and sandaled feet large, compact and perfectly proportioned.

He supposed it was his illness, his weakness that made the sight of her unpleasant to him. He turned from her in distaste; she was too big for a woman, too calm, too arrogantly poised. She made him feel weak, effeminate—doubtless, he reminded himself, because he was ill. But he closed his eyes to shut her out.

Then suddenly as he did so he had a vision of what memory had shut in behind those lowered lids. He saw Millicent Bourn as he had seen her last—blonde, petite, childlike, exquisitely, softly, fragilely pretty in the delicate fabric of her girlish white embroidered frock. And he saw Paula in her sapphires and emeralds, her trailing peacock blue chiffon with the shimmering of iridescent net that caught and held it, clinging to that lithe, sinuous body of hers as though it loved it.

Ah! He caught his breath. Now he wanted—with all his soul he wanted something. And that something was civilization.

It was a suddenly perceived want that told this to his mind, though his body, for all the days that he had lain there sick and suffering and beaten, had craved, dumbly craved, for the comforts of that very civilization he had not known he lacked—till he saw Gurtha.

Quickly he opened his eyes and saw her again. The unbleached linen sort of chiton that clothed her had slipped aside as she bent for a moment to enter below the low lintel, and her left breast showed full and round and firm, set high upon her broad chest and strongly uppointed.

Welburn's features twisted into a quick grimace. His world knew him as anything but an anchorite, but just now there was to him something grossly distasteful about the figure that came toward him, something he would have called almost indecent in this half-clad, boldly erect young woman, whose stride in its long, wonderful lines was like a man's—no, like some animal's—a panther's, perhaps. And yet some ungainly animal's, he added to himself, for his mind's eye was filled with the petticoated grace of cultured girlhood in Millicent Bourn, the grace of artful maturity in Paula Finlayson.

Oh, to hear the sound of silks as women move! In memory it came to Welburn, a music of the spheres. At the thought, suddenly his eyes lit with laughter. Whose skirts? What woman's? He asked himself the question, and decided then and there to let chance solve the riddle.

Again his hand sought his pocket; and as he made the gesture it seemed to him—so long he had lain unconscious, so complete was the gap he had not bridged—but the consummation of the thought that had come to him aboard the boat that rescued him.

But he had no pockets, he discovered. He was clothed in a long, loose, sleeveless tunic, the color and texture of that worn by this strapping young woman who now bent over him.

"I want to flip a coin," he said peremptorily, irritated by his pocketless, pajamaless condition. "Where are my trousers?"

She paid not the slightest attention. Putting his hands aside and holding them with a placid strength that astonished him, she felt with wise, experienced fingers of his ribs on the left side and then on the right; and under that strong, knowing pressure, so skillfully directed, he felt pain.

"Rib smashed, eh?" he said, and discovered that it was difficult to draw a full breath.

She did not answer. She bent her head. "By Jove, what braids!" Welburn exclaimed to himself. Her ear over his left lung, she listened carefully to his breathing.

Then she tested the rib again, just where Welburn knew now the hurt lay, watching him attentively to see when he winced, till he cried out angrily and shook himself free of those strong, merciless hands.

"Yes, you've struck it all right," he snarled. "Suppose you take a hammer now and make sure!"

She looked down upon him a moment reflectively, and Welburn said to himself that he hated gray eyes in a woman, particularly that dark, greenish gray without a hint of blue in it; and then she turned without a word and walked out of the place.

IV

HE pulled himself up with difficulty and lifted his head to look after her.

Perhaps she was dumb. But even so, she certainly was not deaf, or she could have had no reason to listen to his breathing. Having her hearing then, she had heard him speak and had calmly ignored everything he had said.

He was obliged to lie down quickly; he found that he was very weak.

His pillow annoyed him. It wasn't a pillow really, but a small, hard cylinder that fitted into the nape of the neck. Oh, for a pillow, the full, freshly laundered, fine, linen-covered down ones smelling faintly of lavender which Seldner used to place with almost reverential care one behind the other when he opened his master's bed at night and laid out the silk pajamas on the chair and the slippers beside it.

Welburn took the cylinder from beneath his head and hurled it as far as his strength would permit. It went clear across the room and, banging forcibly against a shelf whereon stood a row of jugs and plates of a deep red pottery, sent them crashing to the floor. With a sigh of content Welburn settled back on his bed.

A little old man came running in. He looked bewildered from the broken pottery upon the floor to Welburn upon the bed and back again. And his amazement was so great and so genuine that Welburn laughed aloud.

The man looked up from his task—he was picking up the pieces of pottery from the floor—and, the pillow in his hands, came trotting over to Welburn. Welburn took the pillow from him and, instead of placing it under his head as the old fellow evidently expected, sent it flying again to the shelf upon which the pottery had stood. A light of comprehension dawned in the little man's eyes.

"Exactly," said Welburn drily. "You can see through a hole in a millstone yourself, evidently. Perspicacious old party, you are."

The old man turned from contemplation of the shelf upon which Welburn's pillow now rested and, at first hesitatingly, as though distrusting Welburn's sanity and his capacity to reply reasonably, and then more rapidly and eagerly as he saw the stranger's eye fixed lucidly upon him, burst into speech—in a tongue which Welburn had never heard.

Welburn listened eagerly. His ear drank in the uncomprehended words, for he had not heard human speech for ages, it seemed to him—ages ago when Paula Finlayson—the last to leave the deck late that last night on the steamer—had looked up at him, in her dark, deep eyes the light whose significance he had thrilled to as she herself was thrilled. He knew that by the rise and fall of her breast beneath the chiffon that exquisitely revealed its contour.

"Good night," she had said in her sweet, warm contralto. "Good night, dear old boy." She put a hand on his arm, warm and white and blazing with jewels. "There was an ass—Balaam's,[4] the Scriptures say," she whispered, "who knew not how to take the gifts the gods provided. Good night." And she had danced away, blowing back to him a kiss from the ends of her fingers whose pressure he still felt upon his arm.

Ah, what an ass he had been, indeed!

He looked up at the little old man in front of him, still chanting in his syncopated speech, still marking every phrase with a rising inflection that plainly demanded an answer.

"Foolish question number nine hundred and ninety-nine!" said Welburn when at last he paused. "I suppose you want to know what there is in it for you if you restore one Hugh Ellinwood Welburn to the bosom of his family, to his friends, to little old New York and the world in general, eh?"

A torrent of speech broke from the old man. It was accompanied by much gesture, out toward the open door where Welburn heard now the surging of the sea, out toward the glassless window through which came the sound of many soft, sandaled footsteps, up toward the open roof and even down to the floor. And here was a gesture that Welburn thought he comprehended, the gruesome pantomime of burial, the universal, common process of entombment the old man was sketching with his gnarled, trembling hands.

"Yes, yes, you mean you thought you'd have to do that same kind office for yours truly," interrupted Welburn with a shiver. "Thanks, awfully. But now what's more to the purpose is: Where am I? Who the devil are you people? Is there cable connection in this God-forsaken Somewhere? After you found

---

4. Balaam's ass: a biblical reference to Balaam's talking ass in Numbers 22.

me and hauled me into your boat, where did you take me? Where's my belt with my money and papers? I'll settle with you all right. Can't you send me the chief, if you've got one? Any old high muck-a-muck will do. I want to get into communication with New York. Are there any Americans or English here? I want—oh, hell, I want everything! I want to get out o' this. I want a doctor, d'ye hear? And I want to know what right that female who poses for the almost altogether has to jab me in the ribs where they seem cracked, and what she found out by laying her dear head so confidingly upon this manly breast—and, incidentally, where she got her manners."

To this outburst the old man joyfully responded. It gave him pleasure evidently to know his charge a talking and a rational being, however incomprehensible. And as he talked, more slowly now and carefully, it seemed to Welburn that, though his meaning was altogether beyond him, he caught a word now and then that was familiar, a German word, he fancied, in a maze of unfamiliar sound, a sort of old High German of the Dark Ages, it might have been, he surmised, with a remote likeness to the Suabian[5] dialect. Welburn, who had been educated abroad, had spent some time on classical linguistic philology, and felt himself upon not entirely unfamiliar ground.

"Undoubtedly, my dear sir," he said at length with a sneer. "I don't know what the deuce you're saying, and you are evidently a benighted being that never heard of English, or Volapuk,[6] either, I'll bet. I wonder if I might try you in Dutch or—or Lord knows what!" He was depressed by the knowledge that communication between himself and his rescuers was impossible. He realized the futility of speech on his part, as on theirs; besides, he was very weary now, and weak, too. "All that you say is beautifully expressed and shows perfect judgment," he added with a wry grin. "In other words, you can spiel to beat the band; the only difficulty is you don't say anything. Consequently, this talk-fest of ours may just as well quit right here. Gee, I'm tired!" Wearily he closed his eyes.

The situation was worse than he had expected. If there was no one among these queer folk that he could make understand, his return to comfort, to his

---

5. Suabian (or Swabian): adjectival form of Swabia, historical region of southwestern Germany.
6. Volapük: created by Johann Martin Schleyer, a German cleric, in 1880 to be spoken as an international second language.

people, to Manhattan in short, might be postponed for some time. And he wanted—more intensely than he had ever wanted in his life—he wanted his own—now, this moment. He wanted care. He wanted comfort. He wanted consideration, subservience—the everyday things he had had ever since he had known himself and his world. He was wretchedly weak, and there was a curious hollow sort of agony somewhere under one of his left ribs. It seemed to him he was so tired that a world of lifetimes could not rest him. And he lay upon a narrow pallet of boughs on an earthen floor among a beastly lot of—of dagoes, he growled to himself for want of a better word.[7] And you never could have made him believe that, even among savages, there could be so unfeeling a creature as that one who had poked and prodded him and found out—he knew she had—what was the trouble with him, and then walked off unconcernedly without a word, even a word in her own tongue. And he could not make himself understood. And he was helpless and sick and stripped of his clothes. And—and—He pulled himself together. Suppose so! One needn't behave like a woman about it.

The situation was temporary, though horribly disagreeable. Other fellows, of course, had had unpleasant adventures, and had described them afterward as though they were the greatest jokes imaginable. He should have much sport relating it all when he got back. What a stir it would create! He could imagine the newspaper accounts.

And yet there were tears of utter weakness in his eyes when after some minutes he felt an arm slip under his head and, looking up, saw the little old man bending over him. He held a bowl in his hand of that same dark red pottery which Welburn had destroyed so enjoyingly.

Welburn was so weak and indifferent now that he wondered at and envied himself even the wrathful desire for expression that had moved him. Now he could only drink from the bowl. Its contents were strange to his eye, and their taste not such as to provoke an Epicurean palate.[8] But the stuff was hot and soothing and satisfying.

He drank it all with the old man's encouragement and help. Then he settled down upon his cot, and soon he slept.

---

7. Dagoes: usually used as an ethnic slur to refer to people of Italian, Spanish, or Portuguese descent.
8. Epicurean palate: predisposed to luxurious tastes.

V

IN the days that followed Welburn learned much. He learned patience, for one thing, and gratitude. For the old man's care was incessant. A sharp pneumonia had developed in Welburn's left lung, due he supposed to its being pierced by the broken rib; and he was, of course, weakened by exposure and handicapped by the lack of comforts to which his body was accustomed.

He learned to know what longing is. But the things he longed for would have made him shout with derisive mirth, if there had been either mirth or derision left in him. He lay long days thinking; he dreamed at night of doctors, of doctors and nurses and clean, comfortable hospital beds and medicine bottles and—yes, the odor of hospital disinfectants. He wanted so much, he had so little. Oh, for the frock-coated, suave, deferential man of medicine with the flattering seriousness with which he regards a millionaire's ailments, the capable hands of him, the scientific gravity, the artful eye, the manner of weight, of purpose, of power! How curative, how blessedly curative the whole civilized hocus-pocus of his practice! Fevered, in pain, in doubt as to the effect of the curious treatment to which he was subjected, his morale weakened by isolation from all that was familiar, by bodily helplessness and mental imprisonment due to ignorance of the strange tongue this people spoke—Welburn thirsted for the pathological priest of civilization with a fervor that had its pathos as well as its absurdity.

He waked often with a word on his lips to a white-capped, white-robed nurse of whom he had dreamed, and his voice (which the old man who tended him had never heard save authoritatively, in irritated resentment at lack of comprehension, at lack of comfort, at pain) was melodious now with satisfaction, with consideration.

If at this stage of his illness Welburn could have been asked what was in his estimation the crowning glory of twentieth century civilization, he would probably have answered—starch! Starched skirts, starched cuffs and collar, and a fever chart—and a clinical thermometer. He wanted nurses, many of them, a whole hospital staff if he could have telephoned for them, all white-robed, all quick-footed and soft-voiced, all experienced, attentive, eager, devoted, as millionaires' nurses should be.

And he had so little. Only a wrinkled, mild-eyed little old man whose name, so far as Welburn could judge from its frequent repetition accompanied by a gnarled finger pointing at himself, was Ainu. This, and the smell of something like eucalyptus oil vaporized, and the odor of its burning leaves.

He learned, as his disease ran its course and his vitality went down under the virulence of it, to feed his imagination deliberately as a morphine fiend might on dreams, whose fatuity was mercifully not apparent to one so weakened as himself; dreams of how delightful it would have been to be thus ill at Ellinwood Towers, his newest country place, or on the yacht, or abroad, for the flutter the illness of H. E. Welburn would cause among European medical savants. But he found himself, after luxurious contemplation of each of these blissful possibilities, fixing upon New York as the place of all places in the world where he wished to be and to be ill in. Oh, the many, many doctors there, and the nurses, and the hospitals! In imagination he saw himself lying in turn in every one of them, with the whole hospital staff concerned about him, with every nurse upon the *qui vive* for his comfort, with the city's administration even so wrought up about him that the streets upon which the hospital abutted were withdrawn from traffic and covered with tanbark.

And the newspapers—oh, the columns and columns of printed hopes and fears of the effect of such a death upon the nation's finances; the photographs of himself and his mills and his forests and his factories, his corporation presidencies and directorships, his country places, his city residences, his philanthropic fads, and feats social, erotic and athletic! Oh, the gluttonous delights of disease under such conditions! To be ill in New York!

In the critical hours of his illness, shut in upon himself, without companionship, without hope, he never wished himself well; he had not strength enough for that. To be ill and cared for in modern scientific fashion, this was the acme of desire to the multimillionaire, H. E. Welburn. And he felt that one might even die content, if twentieth century American doctors and nurses could not save one.

Imagine the funeral. The mighty men of dollars who would mourn, and sincerely, for many a house of finance would go down in wreck, many a fortune be offered up on the funeral pyre of a Welburn. And the priests of high politics that would be affected, and the social blight on all his many connections, and the flags at half-mast, and the massive buildings draped in black, and the long, long lines of silent marching men, his men, his workmen, whose industrial lives and fortunes he held in the hollow of his hand, tramping, tramping solemnly through the hushed, cleared streets behind his prone, quiet body.

A tear—a tear of self-pity, of weakness, of sorrowing resignation—slid from beneath his closed, fluttering eyelids and ran down his cheek.

That tear and the wet path it traced before it was lost under his unpillowed head shocked and astonished Welburn. He opened his eyes full of protest at his own incredible sentimentality.

They fell upon Gurtha.

VI

A FLUSH of shame, of intolerable indignity, swept over Welburn's body. A woman had seen him weep. At that unbearable thought he could have wept again—with rage. How he hated this woman—hated her with that burning hate the proud spirit has for the one who beholds it humiliated!

His eyes, still tear-suffused, sought hers defiantly.

She met them for a moment incuriously, almost abstractedly; there was no surprise in her own calm gaze, and no sympathy.

Welburn winced. There was something even worse than being caught sniffling by a woman. What if the woman were utterly unmoved by and uninterested in the fact?

He caught his breath and his fists tightened.

"Oh, you ministering angel!" he said aloud—as loud as he could, which was a weak whisper, devoid of strength as well as humor, a mere gasp of wrathful sarcasm. "You sweet and tender creature! You—you everlasting womanly near-divinity! I—I'd like to wring your neck!"

She listened, not to the words evidently, but to the querulous, febrile quality of his voice. Then she turned and gave a quick order to Ainu, and the obsequious little man obediently hurried away.

She bent over him then intently, her strong hands hurrying over the examination, her ear listening at his breast, her probing eyes upon his drawn cheek, his fever-tightened mouth, his shining, raging, sullen eyes. Once she even lifted him, and sitting there beside him bracing his body with hers, she held him upright while she listened between his shoulders to his labored breathing.

He let her do with him what she would; he was too weak to resist, to care. He longed for only one thing—to speak her tongue, of which he could but stammer a few bare substantives, that he might tell her what he thought of her, sexless, unpitying savage that she was!

Oh, how Millicent Bourn would have behaved under such circumstances! How solicitous her sweet face would have been! How she would have pitied him!

A hysterical gasp shook him. Instantly Gurtha's eyes were upon him.

He ground his teeth. He would die before he should sob outright in this woman's presence.

He turned from her. It was an instinctive movement of repulsion, but he could not bear the pain it cost him to lie upon his left side. With a sigh of utter surrender he fell back and lay prone.

Ainu came back, not alone. Behind him walked four sturdy, sandaled men, clad like him in the linen tunic, and bearing a litter. Upon this, at a command from Gurtha, they laid him; and he moaned, despite himself, at the pain the mere moving cost him. The bearers looked curiously down upon him then, curiously and a bit contemptuously.

Then Gurtha covered him with a great fine cloak of feathers, and walking beside him as the litter was carried out of the house, kept it close about him.

What were they doing? Where were they taking him? Welburn did not know. He thought he did not care, so weak and wretched he felt.

When they stopped to put the litter down he was unconscious. And he waked to find himself lying naked in the ground, in an open, shallow trench of hot, muddy earth, near which he could see a small geyser steaming.

He fought them in despair, in rage, in terror. Was this what they had rescued him for, to bury him alive? He cried out, and struggled and sweated and swore.

In vain. Quietly Gurtha gave orders, touching his face now and then as though to feel the temperature of the skin. The hotter he got the better she seemed satisfied. And the bearers piled the hot, moist earth about him stolidly, quickly, till presently he lay buried indeed, but only to his chin.

In utter exhaustion he closed his eyes and lay there motionless. And as he lay, to his pain-stupefied brain suddenly, even as though someone had spoken it, the word "death" came.

He knew the word in this people's tongue. He had learned it from Ainu the week before when a spider, crushed beneath the old man's foot, writhed for a moment and then stiffened and lay still. Welburn, idly lying there, had watched, and when the thing lay quiet his questioning eyes had met the other's. The old man muttered a word that evidently signified death.

And Welburn, repeating the word after him, had stiffened his own body, thrown back his head and closed his eyes in simulation of death. When he opened them, the little old man was nodding vigorously. Welburn had learned one of his first lessons in the new tongue.

Was he, Welburn asked himself now, going to die? They were evidently not going to bury him alive, since they had left his eyes and nose and mouth uncovered. But was he going to die? Oh, it was not fair that such a question be put only to oneself! Was he going to die? He must know. Someone must tell him.

He opened his eyes and stared at Gurtha. She still stood over him considering him gravely.

"Death?" He put the question in her own language.

Quickly she bent down to him, her face alight.

"Death," he whispered, not questioningly this time, but gravely, almost resignedly.

"Death!" she cried then, and her voice rang out vibrant, sonorous, as though his weak whisper had set a great bell clanging. "Death?" She shook her head superbly and smiled.

It was wonderful to see her smile. In the very crisis of his emotion, the rebirth of hope for life that her confident voice begot in him, Welburn could but look at her. She was so splendid as she stood there with that smile of battle on her lips, in her shining eyes.

"Death!" she said again disdainfully, and smiling, shook her head. "Gurtha!" And again, tapping her own breast, "Gurtha."

She was promising it to him, promising him life. Who could doubt that superb assurance?

Welburn closed his eyes.

Soon, all through his relaxed body, a welcome warmth diffused. Soon his laboring lungs felt the balm of a curative oil, for they had placed a sort of cage about his head in which, from a purring kettle swung over a tiny heap of coals, a thin stream of vapor expanded. A fine perspiration broke out all over him; he felt a heavenly fatigue, an exquisite, painless, infinitely gentle drowsiness.

VII

"WHEN I return to my country," Welburn was saying to Gurtha, speaking slowly for the difficulties the new tongue presented, "I shall buy a steamer, fit it out and come back here to bring you many things which we have that you have not."

"You have learned quickly to speak our tongue," she said irrelevantly, looking at him with a sort of impersonal speculation which he had found particularly trying.

"Thank you," he said drily. "At college they used to tell me I had a genius for dialects."

"Yes?" she commented idly.

"Yes," he said curtly.

He had never met anyone so unresponsive to sarcasm; it was as though this woman was tone deaf to the vocal inflections which, he realized now, supplied a second language in his world, finer, more subtle than the first.

But who would think of subtlety and Gurtha in the same breath? He looked over at her with his old feeling of distaste, and met her eyes calmly regarding him. She was so deplorably unfeminine. How did the women of her world—the quizzical thought came unbidden to him—contrive to get husbands, if they were like her, so destitute of charm, of that fascinating coquetry of indirection, for instance, that ever present suggestion of flight which so spicily stimulates pursuit, that Paula Finlayson evoked in him, in every man who knew her?

He sighed heavily.

Gurtha made a quick movement of attention, of effort.

"Why—why did you not become a teacher?" she asked in the tone of one who renews an uninteresting conversation through sheer kindness.

Welburn winced, her intention was so apparent. It was as though she treated him like a sick, peevish child whose nonsense one pretends to listen to. And Welburn was not accustomed to women's regarding his conversation in that light.

"Because," he snarled, "a Welburn is altogether too valuable to the world to be turned into a mere animated dictionary."

To his surprise she turned animatedly toward him. Her face as fine, he could not help noting, when she was interested.

"Valuable!" she cried. "Useful, you mean? Splendid! Tell me, what great place is yours in the world?"

He laughed. She looked almost like the women of his world, women he had known, though modeled more largely, as she bent forward, her great eyes fixed upon him. Not in costume—he glanced deprecatingly at the uncolored linen folds that draped her—but in that natural, feminine attitude of being impressed, of desiring information about himself, so to speak, of hanging upon his words.

"My father, you know," he said lazily, "was John J. Welburn."

He said the mighty name half apologetically, as he was used to saying it to strangers, for really it was too tremendous a club to use on mere ignorance.

She waited.

He laughed again, this time with vexation. He had forgotten that, by a superlative irony of fate, he was now upon one of those few spots on the whole globe where John J. Welburn's name was not talismanic. Actually, a name like that! And this queer woman had never heard of it, did not know what it implied.

A sudden determination came to him: he would make her know.

"My father was the richest man in the world," he said baldly, partly because his command of words in the new speech was not great, partly because of the necessity of crudely expressing himself to this crude nature, but mainly because he needed to say it once this way; it almost atoned for the deprivations, the humiliations he had suffered. "This island upon which you live, the whole island kingdom, in fact, he could have bought, with all that there is on it, if he cared to, and sunk it—as he probably would—without feeling one ten-millionth as poor as you would if you lost that bronze buckle that holds your dress."

He pointed to it. Her eyes fell to her hip where the buckle was clasped, then lifted again to his face.

Welburn was pale. His illness had been long and convalescence slow, and even yet at times he felt that hollow pain in his left lung. But now a deep flush mounted to his very eyes. Oh, the braggart that he was, that circumstances, that this woman made him be!

"I beg your pardon," he said quickly. "I—I don't know exactly how otherwise to phrase it, to make it clear to you. You see, my—my father was the biggest money king on earth. He owned ships, railroads, whole territories if his land could have been put together. A man like that holds European kings and princes in his hand, sets them flying at each other's throats or keeps them at peace. In America he fixes the tax—really he does—though indirectly—he fixes the tax the world shall pay him on supplies—food, clothing, fuel, that sort of thing. He owns the Senate, for all practical purposes—a working majority; he makes Presidents. He brings about panics, says when the earth shall wax fat and when it shall be lean; when men shall prosper and reproduce their kind and when they shall starve and die childless. He limits production as he sees fit, and plays God to men's hopes. He lifts up his friends and crushes his enemies. He—well, in short, he's the system; he's It. And since my father's death, why, of course," he concluded lamely, "I am all that he was."

So! He had said it. He had had to say it, vulgar as it was; there was no one to say it for him. How else were these dense people to understand his position, his requirements, his rights, now that he had been temporarily stripped of everything, who owed the very garment that covered him at that moment to the charity of these outlanders?

Could he lie there sick, weak, stripped, and let them think him a beggar—he—H. E. Welburn?

He waited a moment. She did not speak. Then he added deliberately, biting out his words with that disposition to thoroughness which marked him: "I have more money—which means more power—than almost any other man on earth."

Thoughtfully she shifted her position.

Piqued, astonished, Welburn looked curiously at her.

Could it be that he had overshot his mark? In his desire to make her—herself and her people—comprehend, had he put the facts into terms too great for her comprehension? Were riches such as his conceivable to such a mind, or—a growing, intolerable, incredible thought tortured him—did she merely believe him to be a liar, a bragging liar striving to attain consequence in her eyes?

"Good God!" he exclaimed in English, pulling himself up on his couch, sweating in agony and staring at her, his eyes demanding at once belief, accession, apology.

She took a step toward him and drew up over his chest the unbleached wool coverlet he had displaced.

"What did your mother do?" she asked in an unimpressed voice.

"My mother!" he repeated harshly.

He had a bewildered feeling that he had made a cad of himself to no purpose. What he had said he had said. And she calmly asked such a question!

"Yes,"—she nodded slowly—"your own mother, what did she do?"

He laughed a short, angry, contemptuous laugh. "My father does not interest you evidently," he said.

She shook her head. "Who can say," she asked simply, "what man is one's father?"

"What!" He gave a long, low whistle of astonishment.

"But the mother is different," she added.

"I should say so!" he gasped. "*My* mother was an Ellinwood."

"Yes?"

It was merely a vocal punctuation, but Welburn felt the question. In his exasperation he chose not to answer it.

"What, in your country, is an Ellinwood?" she asked interestedly.

He looked at her wrathfully, and looked away and looked again; in doubt, in irritation.

"An Ellinwood—" he began, and then stopped, smiling, restored to good humor by the very absurdity of the thing.

How explain to a mind like this, incapable of conceiving a John J. Welburn, what an Ellinwood is—an Ellinwood, the daughter of an Ellinwood, the flower of a fine, inbred race, the perfection of family culture, the exquisite crown of femininity, of grace, of purity?

She looked over at him, waiting eagerly.

"It interests me so much to know about her," she said with a quickening breath and that wonderful look of animation in her face that transformed it.

"What did she do?"

A smile and a sneer lit up Welburn's eyes. It was such an old dodge, and so badly done this time; so many pretty women had tried it and thought it fetching—that interest in your mother for the sake of her son.

He fell back lazily.

"Embroidery," he mocked deliberately. "She had the loveliest hands I ever saw."

She looked at him quite evidently amazed, and then from him to her own hands, browned and long and close knit, and then to his, lying weakly on the cover, white against it.

"I don't believe you understand," she said patiently. "The word you have used is wrong, I think. It means in our tongue not weaving or spinning or making cloth in any shape, but merely a sort of playing with colors and thread or coloring earth—designing, in a sense."

He nodded. "The sort of thing," he suggested lazily, "that your mother does."

She sprang to her feet.

"*My* mother!" she exclaimed. "I am Gurtha Wynchild—Gurtha, daughter of Wyn, the Mother, whose mother is with the Mother Goddess."

"Ah!" He was unenlightened, so he added deprecatingly: "It was to other mothers, other women, that I alluded."

"And in your country do 'other women' do embroidery?" she demanded disdainfully.

"Surely." He knitted his brows perplexed.

"And you are the son of such a mother?"

"Yes." His lips twitched with amusement. "But won't you pity my ignorance and tell me what sort of embroidery does Madame Wyn do?" he asked with lazy patronage.

"Such *embroidery* as is fit for women's hands to do," she cried with significant emphasis, facing him now with uplifted head and flashing eye. "The weaving of cloth for naked bodies, the seeding of earth for hungry mouths, the building of shelter for unprotected heads, the making of laws for the timid and the weak, the sending up of prayer to the Mother Goddess of us all!"

He looked up at her amazed. She was a different being. Her sonorous voice echoed in his ears like a call to battle, and her haughty head and boldly chiseled features, her whole attitude, called to something in him, instinctive, hidden, buried under ages, a call to memory, race memory that stirred now as he gazed at her and lived again in its reincarnation—poetry.

"An Amazon!"[9] he said to himself, his eyes dwelling with sensuous pleasure upon her statuesque pose. "A Valkyrie![10] A Theodolinda![11] With the

---

9. Amazon: in Greek mythology, a race of female warriors.
10. Valkyrie: in Norse mythology, a maiden who makes decisions about who gets to live and die on the battlefield.
11. Theodolinda (ca. AD 568–628): queen of Lombardy.

goddess's winged helmet—all that glorious hair unbound—jeweled bosses upon those superb, impudent breasts!"

And to himself he hummed a bar or two of the inspired chorus that is the beating of mounting wings upon the air. He forgot in that moment that it was with Millicent Bourn he had last heard the marvelous strain, with little Millicent the night of her introduction to the world that sat about in that glittering horseshoe of light and talked of the opera and of each other; and half the talk that night had been of him and whether he would marry her.

But all this Welburn had forgotten; he was looking up at Gurtha, a new light in his eye.

"Won't you please forgive me and be seated?" he begged with charming deference. "It was half a joke and all a misunderstanding. Your mother is— some princess doubtless. How should I know? Or—of course, I should have known." Pleadingly he held out his hand.

She did not take it. Was that a custom of which she was ignorant? Were there others, even more pleasing, that he might teach her?

"You will forgive me?" he begged.

She looked down upon him, obviously puzzled. His voice, now so soft and silken, the voice of allurement, the spoken song of the pursuing civilized male, till this moment had been that of the master to an inferior, querulous, sharp, imperious, commanding, patronizing or laden with the hidden significance of sarcasm.

"Yes," she said at length. "For you are merely ignorant."

Again, he held out his hand, smiling as a man smiles at penances inflicted by feminine hands.

"There is a pretty custom among us," he said. "When a woman forgives a man who has offended, she gives him her hand in token of it."

She smiled as at some childish whim and put her hand in his; and he lifted it to his lips with as much gallantry as though it was Paula Finlayson's white, tiny, perfumed hand he kissed.

She drew it from him, but slowly, as though amazed, looking from it to him in wonder and disgust.

Then without a word she left him.

Welburn voiced his bewilderment at her action to Ainu when the old man came in.

"Why, old fellow, in my country," he concluded, "the girl whose hand is kissed may box your ears if she's a prude or far above you in station, but even then—I say, tell me, what do you do here when you meet a girl you want to make love to?"

"You want to make love to a girl?" The little old man looked at him in astonishment. "Before she has made love to you?" he demanded incredulously.

"Wh—what!" Welburn pushed aside the bowl from which he had been drinking. "You can't mean—Look here, did you never—Hold on; I guess we're not talking of the same thing. Do you mean to say—Oh, nonsense! Did you wait for the girl to—"

"Of course," said Ainu simply. "I am still—waiting."

"Well, I'll be—" Welburn burst into laughter so hearty that the pain in his lung caught him till he choked. "And you'll die an old maid, eh? Oh, what a country! Say, Ainu—"

But the gentle little old man would hear no more. With dignity he set the bowl down beside Welburn's couch.

"You will drink when you have finished your cruel laughing," he said with a trembling voice, and went to the door. But there a second thought halted him. "You are strong enough to be taken to Wyn, the Mother, tomorrow. She will see you then," he said, and closed the door behind him.

Welburn looked after him, tears of laughter and pain in his eyes.

"Hugh, my boy," he said to himself, "you have evidently got yourself beautifully disliked by the only two people you know in this blessed paradise for females."

VIII

AMONG the experiences to which Welburn never alluded when he got back to the world was his first meeting with the Mother of all the tribe.

He knew her as soon as his eye lighted upon her for a person of consequence; he had lived too full a life, his experience was too wide and varied for him not to recognize position and caste and dignity, even in such surroundings. And there was all of these in the manner of the woman who remained seated when all present rose to receive him.

She was not old, a woman of fifty, possibly more, of great virility and height, dressed as Gurtha had been, as all the women present were, but crowned—as they were not—by a coronet of graying braids.

Welburn looked for Gurtha, but she was not there. No young woman was present. At the head of a long table of a sort of grass fiber wound upon wood sat Wyn; about her were a dozen women approximately her age. At a smaller table to the left were half a dozen men.

"You have learned to speak our tongue, I am told," the Mother said when Ainu had led him to a couch and left him. She spoke very slowly and sat directly facing him.

"After a fashion—yes," said Welburn.

"Then you may tell where you come from, what is your place, who is your mother, how you came to be struggling in the water when the Captain of the Boats found you."

Welburn sat up.

"That's all very well," he said deliberately, "but I think I am entitled to know first where I am, who you are, you people, how soon I can have a ship to take me to America—above all, where my clothes are, particularly my belt, that I wore under my shirt filled with valuables and papers."

An indignant murmur arose. To his surprise, Welburn, watching the men at the table on the left, saw that their dissatisfaction was even greater than the women's.

But the Mother's voice stilled it.

"You are entitled—if you understand the use of the word you have spoken—to nothing," she said gravely to Welburn, but without anger. "You are thrown naked upon our bounty, our mercy. You are, besides, a man; and we have already too many men."

Welburn turned in amazement from her to the men at the small table. But all he could read in their faces was approval of the speech he had heard, that and a curious grudging resentment of himself. "Do you mean to say," he demanded, turning again to Wyn, "that I'd be more welcome if I were a woman?"

"Of the last hundred babies born to the clans, seventy-nine are male children," she said severely.

"More than three-quarters, eh? I congratulate you," Welburn remarked easily.

They stared at him, amazement in every eye. And he smiled back politely, as one might who questioned the relevancy of such statistics to his own case, but was ready to be interested in them, nevertheless.

"Let us understand each other." The Mother leaned forward in her great chair and spoke very distinctly. "Do you mean to imply that in the country from which you come such a proportion of male births would be cause for congratulation?"

"I have never in my life heard of an unwelcome boy baby," laughed Welburn. "But what has that to do with me?"

Authoritatively the Mother rose to her feet. With a gesture she dismissed the men at the side table; and they withdrew without a word, though now upon their faces was a look of wistful doubt and delight, the look of a child as it listens to a fairy tale.

"Surely," Welburn interposed, a secret something in him responding to the look in every one of their faces, "surely I may speak before men as well as—"

"What have men to do with counseling?" interrupted the Mother harshly. "Concerning war—yes. Concerning hunting expeditions—yes, or the sailing of the boats. But what have men to say about management of the clans?"

"I—I guess I don't exactly understand your language," stammered Welburn, bewildered.

"We shall see," she said briefly. The men having departed, with another gesture she bade the women be seated, then seated herself and faced Welburn.

"I am Mother of all the tribe," she said with dignity. "These"—she indicated the women about her—"are mothers of the clans. You may speak—openly. Why is the birth of a male child cause for congratulation among your people?"

"Why? Why? Why, it's obvious," he said impatiently, baffled by the puerility of the topic and her determination to pursue it. "If a boy has ten chances to a girl's one to make a living; if he has a hundred chances to a girl's one to distinguish himself—in business, in the professions, as a statesman, an artist, anything; if he has a thousand to her one to get the mate he wants and liberty to—to enjoy himself besides, would you want your child to be a girl or a boy?"

She did not answer. Evidently she could not. She and the women about her were staring at him as though he were mad. It compelled him to further expression.

"It seems," he began tentatively, stumbling over the words and trying to make himself clear, "it seems to be somewhat difficult for you to credit. But it's true, I assure you. In fact, I don't see how it could be otherwise. It's natural and it's right. Who could imagine a world where the rulers, big and little, in family and in state, were not men—the real rulers, I mean, however the *title* of royalty may be vested? We give our women a chance, a very fair chance. But the prizes of the world belong to the men, of course. How else could it be?"

"How else!" The Mother spoke threateningly; her breast heaved and her somber eyes shone with displeasure. "How else! We shall teach you how else." In insulted dignity she faced him.

"Hush—hush!" The woman closest to her put a hand upon hers. "See—do not be angered, Mother. A wise woman is never angered by a fool, nor a truthful one by her who tells lies."

"True, true. Thank you, Brida." The Mother turned from her and faced Welburn calmly. "What is your name?" she asked. "Son of what mother? Or would you pretend that in your topsy-turvy country descent is through the father? Does the man there bear the child?" And leaning back in her chair she laughed heartily, while the women about her gave way to immoderate laughter.

A dull red burned in Welburn's pallid face. He had lost his sense of humor. Never in his life had he been so laughed at. He had been defied, he had been vilified, he had fought the bloodless, bitter, merciless battles of civilization, but he had not known ridicule, nor heard his word doubted. He set his teeth and braced his body against the raised back of his chair, and caught his breath with the pain that pierced his chest at the quick motion.

"I decline to answer your questions," he declared deliberately, "or to speak further with you. I don't know just how savage you and your people are. You can kill me if you want, I suppose, but you shall not insult me."

Defiantly he rose and faced her.

For a moment then her eyes, glowing with vengefulness, met his. But only for a moment. She had sat, a finger on her lip, as though meditating upon his fate. Now she leaned forward, and threw out her hands with an ample gesture.

"It is as well," she said slowly. "It is as well; keep silence. Keep silence among the clans. They'll not believe. Who would? And fear not for your life. The Earth Mother bears males as well as females. You have no right among us. You have no welcome from us. But live, if you desire, and learn that the great Mother Goddess of us all decreed the woman clan and the mother right."

She rose, and, followed by the women, left him. And he sank back upon his chair, angry, weak and helpless, and raging at his helplessness.

He started to go and then sank back, remembering he must wait for Ainu; and so he sat there, his face buried in his hands.

Gurtha came out to him, a gracious motherliness in her face now, softened by the sight of his helplessness.

"Here, this is yours," she said, and laid upon the chair beside him a little heap of shrunken clothing and his oilskin belt. "My mother bids me tell you you shall have all that is yours, and more."

Eagerly he caught up the belt and ripped it open. Its contents were intact. He drew a long sigh of relief. With the touch of these new bills in his hands he was himself again; he held the magic that was his power; and with that touch the incident of his adventure became transitory, trivial, too trivial for emotion, too transitory for impatience.

He drew out two five-hundred-dollar bills and held them toward her.

"I must beg your mother's pardon," he said courteously, "for my display of temper just now. I owe you much—much more than I can ever repay. But the material debt to you personally for your services you will permit me to discharge at least."

She took the bills from him and examined them curiously.

"An excellently strong, tough weave of paper," she said critically. "More durable and finer, I think, than our own."

He smiled at her *naïveté* and at her knowledge, both so queer to him.

"That money," he said, seeking for an equivalent that should impress her, "would buy twenty thousand loaves of bread in my country, or a thousand garments such as you wear. It would feed and clothe a family for a year comfortably."

"Yes?" she said indulgently, and tore the bills in half. "Here, you know, it is useless, except as a model for better paper weaving." And she bent interestedly over the edge of the fragment she held, examining closely its composition. "Of what is it made?" she asked intently.

Welburn eyed her angrily.

"I'm sure I don't know," he said curtly. His money was money to him. All his life it had been a real thing, a tangible thing, the most precious of things. It angered him to see it destroyed. It angered him to hear her call it useless. "Your mother says I am to have all that is mine," he added, with no modulation to his embittered voice. "Does she include in that the right to be sent back to civilization?"

"To be sent away to your country?" she repeated. "Oh, surely; we have too many men. I wish you had been a girl," she added softly.

There came a hysterical catch in Welburn's throat, born of the desire to laugh at her folly, and to cry, to cry for joy at the prospect of getting back to the world.

"But when?" he asked huskily, eagerly. "When?"

"We do not know where your world is," she said gently. "The best we can do is to send you out to sea when the boats go, to where Captain Than picked you up, and there to abandon you in a boat. Would you dare?"

"Dare!" He laughed aloud. "Dare!"

"You must like your world, to take such a risk," she said wistfully.

"A man's world! Ah, it's a man's world!" he cried.

She nodded. "I have heard," she said, and eyed him indulgently.

"And when do the ships go?" he demanded, so content he could not even find fault with the doubt in her accent.

"Every spring," she said, "to the north to get shark oil."

"Every spring!" Welburn's face was ghastly. "Only once a year? My God!" he exclaimed. "A year! A whole year!"

IX

A CRUSHING depression fell upon Welburn, an inhibited mental state in which he could neither face the future nor bear the present. It was impossible, he said to himself again and again, to live a year in such an environment; it was impossible to get away from it.

Everything in him revolted at his position; by temperament, by training he was the last man fit to cope with such a problem in readjustment; his nature was unpliable, rigid. "The Welburns never change," had been a shibboleth in the family; he had heard it first when he was too young to understand its significance. And that hereditary tenacity of opinions, beliefs, instincts had bred a race of unyielding, strong-willed men and stubborn, if apparently docile, women.

And yet unceasingly reason impressed it upon him now that he must fit himself into this new life; that he must adjust his point of view, at least temporarily while he should be among them, to that of the strange people with whom he found himself.

But what was that point of view? His habit of mind turned away, repelled from contemplation of it, from an attempt to conceive it. How could Hugh Welburn face a situation in which everything that had been a cause of congratulation to his family for the twenty-eight years of his life—his wealth, his power, his standing, his personality, his very sex—had, by a curious miracle of reversion, become a disadvantage, a positive hindrance?

He found himself brooding continually upon a phrase the Tribe Mother had used—the words "mother right." What did that phrase mean? What half-remembered curious social corollary did it carry with it?

Somehow it sent his groping mind back to his early days at college. The solution, he felt sure, was there, away back there, somehow. Every time he said the phrase to himself in his search for enlightenment, some odd association of ideas brought before him the campus and the old hall of archeology. What had these things to do, these very sources of wisdom and culture, with the curious social customs of the people among whom he found himself, a people that spoke of "mother right"?

Mother right! Mother right!

The campus of a summer night, sweet with scents of evening; the old hall ivy—overgrown, and within—within, on the platform, the famous old German archeologist from across the seas, who spoke to the students in his own language of—of— Of what did he speak? And what was the obscure connection between that night's lecture and this strange adventure of his into the unknown?

Mother right[12]—yes, the lecturer must have said the words, and in the same tongue which Wyn had used with a different accent. Mother right and—and—Welburn could see despite the lapse of years, despite the fact that he had not been consciously so impressed, he could see the grin upon the face of the lad next to him, and all along the bench whereon his particu-

---

12. Swiss anthropologist and sociologist Johann Jakob Bachofen published *Das Mutterrecht* (*Mother Right*) in 1861. In it, he argued that motherhood was the foundational element of many ancient civilizations.

lar group had sat that night years ago; a grin of crude amusement, of boyish speculation and derision.

But at what had they, and he, smiled at that particular time? What could have been funny in a dry lecture on archeology? What was there amusing about—about—yes, he remembered—about long quotations from Caesar concerning the Ancient Britons and Strabo's Arabia Felix?[13]

Mother right—yes. Mother right and—and—*the matriarchate!*

He cried the word aloud. It was that—it was that—the rule, the supremacy of women. No wonder the fellows grinned.

He had dug the memory out of the past. It all came back to him now; the old, old primitive supremacy of women had been the lecturer's theme; a rebuilding in fancy for the benefit of the students of that ancient absurdity, that race blunder, as though the world stumbled in its evolution upward into civilization; the sex-superiority of women; its tribal and family and individual supremacy.

No wonder the fellows grinned.

As Welburn sat in his cottage thinking the thing out, a smile of amusement, of derision, came over his face—the same smile of mocking speculation that he and his fellows had worn that night years ago when the old German archeologist and author had pictured forth that primitive time in the world's history of its peoples.

But as he sat, slowly, slowly the smile faded from his lips; in his eyes there grew an expression, affronted, incredulous, the look of one whose intelligence is insulted. The matriarchate was dead these thousands of years. Was he asked to credit one instance of survival of the system in this isolated island state; a survival inexplicable, unscientific, anachronistic as that of birdlike mammals, mere links in evolution's chain, which persist in obscure and out-of-the-way corners of the world, having strangely outlived their contemporaries?

He was still sitting with this amaze upon his face, in his eyes the refusal to believe what one fears is true, when old Ainu came in to him.

"Ainu," he asked quickly, "how long has Wyn, the Mother, ruled here?"

"I was a man of fifty when she came to rule," answered the little old man.

---

13. Strabo (ca. 64 BCE–after 21 CE): a Greek geographer. Arabia Felix (Happy or Flourishing Arabia): the fertile region in southwestern and southern Arabia.

"And—and Ainu"—Welburn's voice was tentative, hesitating, a hesitancy that made him indignant at himself—"did her father rule before her?"

"Her father!" Ainu looked at him curiously. "No. How could that be?"

"Who? Who then?" Welburn demanded with quickening breath.

"Why—the mother, the mother of Wyn, who is mother to Gurtha, who shall one day be the Mother if she lives and strengthens the tribe."

Welburn looked at him in dismay, and the kindly little old man met that look and puzzled over it.

"How should it be otherwise?" he asked patiently. "What child shall know its father for certain? Surely descent is through the mother. What have you of the father but his belief—his mere belief—in his own paternity?"

"In—in families of chiefs, of rulers?" asked Welburn. It was a forlorn hope.

Old Ainu lost patience. "In all families. How else?" he demanded with rare self-assertion. "Is there any way of tracing, of proving the father's connection with the child?"

Hopelessly Welburn looked at him and looked away. He had more questions. They surged within him; they crowded to his lips. But he could not ask them, so sure he was what the answer would be.

"See then," old Ainu said soothingly as he bent himself over his tasks over the stone hearth, "what foolish questions a man may ask. From the Mother Earth comes all life. From the mother woman comes human life. She is the creator. She is ruler, head of the tribe, of the clan, of the family. She makes the laws for her children and her children's children, and, by reason of their common motherhood, communes with the Mother Goddess over all. She chooses her mates and strengthens the tribe with that source of strength— girl children—if the Mother Goddess be favorable. She presides in council, being wise and experienced in ruling her own family. She decides vexed questions for the good of the people, having mother love in her heart of course. She fixes the fishing season, being a good housewife, portions the fields, cures the ailing, prays for the dead."

"And—and man?"

"Man!" Again Ainu bent that curious, doubting look upon him, as though questioning his sanity. "What of man? What is left for *him*?"

Old Ainu turned his back indignantly and busied himself with his pots.

"What does man do?" repeated Welburn. "Tell me."

The old man turned upon him, pot in hand, stirring its contents while he talked. "Behold," he said with simple dignity, "what man does."

"He cooks!" exclaimed Welburn.

"Aye, cooks and sews and nurses, if he be weak and old. If he be young and strong, he builds houses and ships which the architects plan, plows fields, makes roads, spending his great strength as a docile animal might, or a great machine, under the direction of one not so strong always in muscles but greater in wisdom and authority."

"A woman?"

"A woman."

"Ye Gods!" Welburn dropped his head into his hands. It was impossible but it was true. The old, centuries old, discarded mode of living, the curious system which the old archeologist had insisted was merely a *Vermittelspunkt*, a thoroughfare for the race in its progress, its education in living, this, this feminist system was the rule among the people into whose hands he had fallen! Its men had never known any other; its women believed he lied when he spoke of any other!

How was he, H. E. Welburn, the most masculine of men, the most devout believer in male primacy, to live a year of his life in such an atmosphere as this? He sighed, and thought enviously of adventurous predecessors who had merely fallen into the hands of cannibals; here was he, caught in an eddy, as it were, of time, where social customs only whirled about instead of progressing. He thought of that old German professor, dry, systematic, destitute of humor, profoundly learned, with a leatherlike complexion, a still, expressionless face, shortsighted eyes and a queer, nervous affection of the facial muscles that kept his eyebrows dancing. And he had an irrelevant longing to do that scientific gentleman bodily harm.

Gurtha found him in an attitude of extreme depression when she came to him that evening.

Solicitously she regarded him. "Let me listen," she said, and bent her head to put her ear at his chest.

"Pshaw!" he exclaimed, reddening and drawing away. "There's nothing the matter with me."

"Why do you sit then looking as though you were in pain?" she demanded.

"Because—because," he cried angrily, "I want to get away. I want to get back to my own kind. I can't live here among—" His tongue stumbled; after all, one couldn't say what was in one's mind. "I can't live among people who don't live my way. I must get away. Look here. I will pay any price, anything you ask, for a ship. But now—now—tomorrow morning! Anything you ask I'll pay."

"In what?" she asked.

"In—why, in money."

"This?" She drew from a flap in her gown the torn bills he had given her.

He buried his face in his hands. Oh, the mockery of it—to hold in his hands unlimited purchasing power and not to be able to buy a thing!

She came over to him and laid her hand upon his shoulders.

"Don't be discouraged," she said, and her full voice was low and very pleasing.

"Perhaps you can work and earn enough to pay for men and boats. You are not strong as our men are. You cannot hunt, nor make your own weapons, I fear, nor do the work the women do upon the farms. But in your country you must have had your place. Tell me what can you do? Can you make clothes?"

"Clothes! Do I look like a tailor?" He bit out the words ill-temperedly.

She looked at him as though a bit puzzled by his accent. "I don't know. Can you prepare food?" she asked.

"Good Lord! A cook! What next?"

"I don't understand," she said slowly. "What did you do in your own country?"

His eyes met hers, indignant, outraged.

"I did nothing," he said deliberately.

"Nothing!" She repeated the word doubtfully.

"Absolutely nothing."

She stared at him.

"You would call it nothing," he added in defiant explanation. "I mean, nothing except to amuse and interest myself. I traveled and entertained, sailed my yacht, ran my automobile, was learning how to fly, gave orders to the managers about the mines, the mills, and attended a few—mighty few—directors' meetings. But a gentleman, you must understand, does nothing—what you would call nothing."

There was a silence. She stood quite still regarding him, and despite himself he grew uncomfortable in that silence.

"You seem," she said at length hesitatingly, "not ashamed of it." She pushed aside a chair that stood in her way. There was contempt in her eyes and in her poise. "Either you are lying again," she said slowly, "or you have no shame. In either case—"

"Look here!" cried Welburn, springing to his feet. "Don't you dare to speak to me like that!"

Her amazed eyes met his calmly.

"Dare!" she repeated. "Why not? What could you, a weak, blemished man, do to me?" And she fronted him, calm in her strength, her astonished eyes level with his.

Disgusted, he turned from her. "Gentlemen," he said bitterly, "do not lay hands on women."

"No?" she commented interestedly. "What did you mean then?"

He opened his lips to reply, then with a glance of scorn turned impatiently from her.

"Perhaps you did not mean anything," she said placidly, "and I misunderstood. But, as I was saying, you must work. The men begrudge your being here, as it is. They will not feed and clothe you. Think, if you can, of something you might do, if you would live with us till the boats sail in the spring."

And with this she left him.

X

WHEN Welburn became reconciled to the inevitableness of his sojourn among these strange people, he began to interest himself in their origin, in the peculiar reversal of their social customs, in the sociological problem they presented, in their beliefs, their myths, the degree of their ignorance of the world, his world.

He learned that the Teutonic hint in the structure of their language was confirmed by certain traits in physiognomy and in tribal customs. They knew that another world existed, for the waters of the sea had from time to time laid at their feet evidences of a civilization unlike their own. But it never occurred to them to go out and seek that other world, nor could they conceive of a race life differing profoundly from theirs. Gurtha once told him of a myth that interested him—of two, a man and a woman, who, centuries before, had revolted against the customs of their tribe and had put off to sea, enduring incredible hardships and, coming at last to these islands, had founded here a new home.

But all these inquiries of Welburn's came much later. At first, for days and weeks and months, he would not let his curiosity awaken; he would not permit himself to wonder how it was that these people had escaped discovery by the sea searchers, nor where on the round world these islands were located. He would not let his mind occupy itself with any solution of his fate but one—how to get away, how to reach civilization and the twentieth century. For he had come to believe that he was dwelling in an archaism, that he had been thrown back in time as well as in ways of living.

He shut himself up in himself. He asked no questions, cared for no explanation of anything he saw or heard, did not trouble himself to justify himself, was indifferent as to whether the delicacy of his left lung, resulting from his illness, was to be permanent or not, and met each new curious pair of eyes that came to gaze upon him with disdain, with defiance and cold, hard, incurious contempt.

He ate what Ainu set before him. He listened with such evident boredom when the old man chatted that at last communication between them became limited to the essentials.

There was one thing, though, in which, even at this time, he was keenly interested, and he used to tell of it, when recounting his adventures after he got back to his world, as a curious psychological trait in human nature.

"You'll laugh at it at first; you'll think it mighty funny," he used to say when with the cigars came after-dinner confidences he had for a few of his friends, "but my trousers were the one thing in all that topsy-turvy madhouse that kept me sane and a man. There, laugh! I knew you would. And now listen, and perhaps you'll understand how I came to feel that there is nothing inherently humorous about what the common or garden American calls plain 'pants.' But there is something psychologically potential about the dress that to a man means sex, something altogether disproportionate, I'll admit, but none the less powerfully effective.

"I would not dress as those people did—the men and women almost alike. I swore I would not. In my heart I think I was afraid of what the dress and the feminist customs together might make of me. I feared, if you must know it, for my manhood. Yes, laugh! But remember that ever since I had known myself and my sex, I had known myself as differentiated in clothing from women; and without that differentiation, absurd as it may seem to you who have never been outside of a masculine world, I could not be myself.

"And those water-soaked, shrunken, torn, bedraggled breeches were all I had that was of value to me, since real money had none.

"So I set myself to tailor another pair, if you please. Oh, yes, it's funny," he would admit, at the guffaw this statement was warranted to provoke, "and you may laugh if you choose at the tongue-tied, scowling-faced, intent-eyed, blundering wretch whose fingers were all thumbs, who sat there for days after he had ripped up his only pair of trousers, trying to fashion a duplicate out of the unbleached linen that was the clothing of this people.

"Poor devil, poor fool of an amateur tailor! Can't you see him? He was always in a vile temper—which *is* funny, though he was joke-proof; his fingers were sore from blundering needle pricks, his heart was sore and hopeless, his pride, his sex vanity was trailed in the dust.

"The first pair, boys, was of a shape, a cut, never seen on sea or land. Besides, they shrank when I went out in the rain. But I didn't know how bad they were till one day Gurtha saw them on me. Then—well, then I'd have given every cent I had in the world for a marked-down pair made of shoddy from a Fourteenth Street show window.

"Do you wonder that I went straight to a factory in New Jersey when I landed? With my first breath I demanded to know how the damned things were put together.

"Well, I made others. And the disheartening thing about it was that in all that time I lived among those people and obstinately, determinedly, un-humorously was a scarecrow in handmade, homemade, personally conducted breeches, I never knew whether or not I had made a successful pair. For of course I was the joke of the place. You can't conceive, naturally, in a country like ours, where, in a sense, variety is the style, the effect of one breeched individual upon a skirted people uniformly clad. They never got used to me. I never could get a man among them to put 'em on, even for a minute, to let me see how they looked. They would not dress in tubes, they said, and upon each new arrival from the other islands or the mountains or the boats off at sea, the effect of me was a thing for entire clans to joy in. When Than first saw me—well, I won't speak of Than. There are reasons. I won't let myself think of him."

WELBURN WAS WEARING HIS last pair of summer trousers that year when he discovered that fate had another blow in store for him. The weather was changing. It was growing cooler. The linen trousers were uncomfortably light. He felt shabby, cold, too; but that was nothing compared to the humiliation of finding himself insufficiently, unseasonably clothed.

He remembered a scantily clad shopgirl he had seen on Fifth Avenue once as he came out of his club. It was autumn, but a sharp hint of winter was in the air, and this silly chit had on thin worn pumps, torn openwork stockings and a scant, faded wash skirt that drew tightly about her thin legs as she turned the windy corner. He understood now that proud, lying look of defiance and denial in her eyes as they met his before he stepped, buttoning his fur coat up to his chin, into his limousine.

He knew there was exactly that same expression in his own eyes now when Gurtha met him one clear cold day in his flapping linen trousers; a winter Gurtha, all in warm red wool, of that same dark, deep red that dyed the pottery.

"Let us walk together," she said. He fell in by her side, and they walked long, past the waterfront where the boats were being mended, through the village where the mills were grinding, into the hills where men were hammering stone. (This was one reason why he never afterward cared to walk with women when he got back to America; he could not again fit his stride to theirs after walking with Gurtha.)

It was on this walk, though, that he thought he hated her more than ever for what happened, for what continually happened, forming a sardonic, running commentary upon his helplessness; for showing him to her so terribly at a disadvantage, here where he was as much out of his element as the fish just then escaping from the broken meshes of the long seine the folk were pulling in.

"Your nets," he said on the spur of the moment to the fisherwomen, "are so foolishly made, so soft and perishable. Surely they might be improved. Why, in my country, even in the most primitive villages, the twine is strong, much more durable than this."

He spoke as he would if he had come across incompetency and wastefulness in his own machine shops; contemptuously he shredded the soft fiber into bits and cast it from him.

"Yes?" Greyl, the head fisherwoman, came eagerly forward, while all the workers listened closely. "How do they make it? Tell me. Of what is it made?"

"How do they make it?" Welburn repeated the questions, lightly disdainful. "I'm sure I haven't the faintest idea."

And he turned away, joined Gurtha, and they walked on.

It was at the quarry that the scene was repeated. But here Rohn, the mighty quarryman, the sweat on his reddened brow, the muscles of his great naked arms shining with sweat in the sun, listened to Welburn's criticism of his rude axe and his scornful comparison of it with the mighty engines of his world.

"Ha!" he said. "Then tell us how. Tell us how 'tis done in that wonderful world of yours."

"Tell you how! D'ye think I'm a stone breaker?" Welburn demanded, turning haughtily away.

And then behind him a mighty shout of laughter arose, of laughter and derision and unbelief.

"He knows!" Rohn cried after him. "He knows, but he won't tell! Oh, no! But sure he knows and tells the truth!"

At the village they stopped and watched Freydal and her husband, just married, building their new house in her mother's yard.

"Oh, for a hammer and nails," Welburn said to Gurtha—"an American workman's box of tools! It makes one's fingers itch to do the thing right."

"Oh, do it then," she cried, her rich voice warm with emotion. "Make us one," she added wistfully. "Show us how."

He laughed.

"If we are blundering on," she urged, "if we are doing weakly and ill what can be done well and easily, how can you resist showing us the way?"

He looked with some surprise into her eyes, wet now with unshed tears.

"My dear Gurtha," he said with some patronage—she was so feminine at this moment—"for a very simple reason: I don't know how."

"You don't know!"

"Of course not. How should I? Men in my position don't concern themselves with that sort of thing. These tools are turned out by the tens of thousands in factories. Do you suppose I ever inquired how it was done?"

"Then"—she hesitated and stopped for a moment, but began to speak again, a mocking, incredulous note in her voice—"then you wish me to think that everything we do here, all we know, all we are, is wrong and foolish and feeble; that your people know a better way, but that you cannot help us in one single instance! You have seen, but you do not know; you are wise, but you cannot help. How then are you going to live?"

"To live!" he repeated.

"Yes—even here, among us whom you despise. Of what use are you? What I know I know. When I suggest betterment it is because I can help to a better way. But you—will you make tubes for our men to wear—who will not wear them?"

Welburn looked down at his trousers and bit his lip with vexation.

"Well," she said, "tell me: what work can you do?"

Oh, that he might answer! Oh, that he might just once meet her upon his own ground, that he might show her what he was, what he really was with all his money back of him! Or even—yes, there were times—and this was one of them—when he said to himself if ever he should get back to civilization he would go into his own shipbuilding yard, or his steel foundry, or some friend's factory merely to learn how to do the things he had told these unbelieving people could be done; merely to come back and quench the mocking light in Gurtha's eyes and prove his veracity. Then, content, he'd sail home again.

But meanwhile?

Meanwhile Gurtha waited. More, the vital question waited. What could he do? He must answer that, and answer it with the means at hand; he must, but how?

"I have thought," he said at length slowly, angrily, curtly, "that I might give you and your people other designs for weaving patterns or ornamentation."

"For ornamentation?" She repeated his words in a low voice.

"Yes. I have, or used to have, some artistic skill. The artists—impecunious, gifted, foolish fellows—used to flatter me, they thought, by saying a good artist had been spoiled in making me a millionaire."

She did not speak.

He looked at her with some impatience. She might know, if she had any imagination, he said to himself, how hard it was for a fellow so completely out of his *milieu* to place himself. She might, at least, be sympathetic.

"I do think I can work at that," he continued with an effort. "At any rate, I'll try my hand at it."

"It—it's a child's work, you know, with us," she said slowly. "The boys amuse themselves with it."

He flushed an angry red.

"Among us, on the contrary, the artist is honored," he retorted.

"Then why do you speak of them with contempt?"

"I do not," he said stiffly.

"There was contempt in your tone. 'Gifted, foolish fellows,' you said."

He looked at her curiously. "You did not always understand my tone," he said significantly.

"I have learned. You say more in tone than in words."

"Ah!" He looked at her quizzically, even a bit fatuously.

"Yes, you say much," she repeated. "But you do nothing."

It was as though, awaiting a compliment, he had been boxed on the ears.

"Don't you think," he demanded wrathfully, "that you would find it a little difficult to fit yourself into *our* civilization if called upon suddenly? Don't you think it might be a bit difficult for *you* to earn your salt?"

She faced him quickly, stretching out a strong arm and laying her hand, not lightly, on his shoulder.

"Make no mistake," she said sternly. "If set in any world anywhere, Gurtha Wynchild could alone build her home, could make her clothes, could find her food. Would that your man's world, as you call it, had done as much for you!"

She stood there superb in her strength and in her confidence. But he, as he looked at her, had a swift vision of this strong, confident creature set adrift in his world of paved streets and skyscrapers, of workmen and workingwomen stripped by a new economic system and by crippling specialization of their tools, their opportunity, their very access to earth itself.

How would even such a non-interdependent as this fare in such conditions? How gallant might be her struggle against them—but how futile!

Welburn looked at her, and there was more pity than admiration in his eye. He felt a sudden, strong tug at his heart as in imagination he saw her taken at her word by fate and transported into a twentieth century environment. He felt the desire to protect, to help, to shelter. And in that moment, for the first time, their relationship was reversed.

But no comprehension of this could come to her. She dropped her hand and walked ahead.

"Come," she said; "you shall teach the children new designs."

XI

ON a raised platform Welburn stood drawing enlarged designs upon the slate wall that faced the children. He was giving them new patterns.

This that he was drawing now was his recollection of the mosaic in his bathroom at Ellinwood Towers; he had sent an artist to Pompeii to copy it for him.[14] The one above was a fret that had been worked out in marble in the balustrade of his famous staircase in town. A third was something he had seen in the Forum.[15] Another came from a Navajo blanket, and another was part of the decorative detail of the Colonne Vendôme.[16]

He had not been sure that he could do this work; he had tried and failed once. Now that he found himself acquiring skill and ingenuity, he felt the need for better tools. He turned to Aldar, the young brother of the Captain of the Boats, who superintended the design class, and explained to him the necessity for a blackboard and crayons.

"Yes?" the young fellow agreed quickly; he was a pleasant, ruddy-faced, sweet-tempered chap, with an ingenuous boyishness whose charm even Welburn felt. "Yes, that sounds possible. Listen, lads." He turned to the class. "Welburn says that in the schools of his country they don't have walls of thin slate like ours, but great, low blackboards all about the room, on which they draw designs with white crayon. Tell us how it's done," he added to Welburn, "and we'll make one like that."

There was a hush among the students; in a moment a hundred boys' eyes were fixed upon Welburn. They were not all inquiring—Welburn saw that; most of them were slyly mocking. In an instant he regretted his suggestion. And in that instant he saw Gurtha stop at the open doorway. She had heard. There was expectancy in her face; hope struggled there with apprehension.

"I—I wish I could tell you," Welburn stammered, a note of passionate regret in his voice, for he saw shame in Gurtha's face now at his admission—shame

---

14. Pompeii: ancient Roman city that was destroyed when Mount Vesuvius erupted in AD 79.
15. Refers to the Roman Forum.
16. Colonne Vendôme (Vendôme Column): a monument erected in Paris by Napoleon to commemorate the Battle of Austerlitz. It was an obelisk modeled on Trajan's Column in Rome.

for him in his humiliation. "I'm sorry, but I never inquired what the process is. I wish I did know how blackboards are made."

A shout of boyish laughter went up, the amused laugh of children who have been told of an absurdity and find it come true.

Welburn understood the malice in that laugh. These boys had heard of him as a liar and a boaster who inevitably failed when put to the test. But, oddly, it did not pain nor anger him. He was hurt too deeply, touched too emotionally by that look of pain in Gurtha's face, that look of sympathetic suffering which he had not conceived those clear, confident eyes could wear.

Like a child then he yearned for power to make her proud of him; like a child he longed to display prowess, to compel her admiration, to fight and win before her, to make her heart beat with fear for him and delight in him. It was as crude and powerful a desire to "show off" as he had felt long ago, when, a boy of ten, he had waked to puppy love and it had driven him to make a fool of himself. But before Welburn could have yielded to it she was gone; she had passed the door and was out of sight.

Young Aldar, whose quick eyes had seen her, too, ran quickly after her.

Welburn threw down the roughly shaped piece of soft slate with which he had been drawing. The children were bending again over their work, with only a sly wink now and then at each other to betray them. Welburn stepped to the open door, drawn irresistibly to the spot where Gurtha had stood.

He was helpless, poor—poor in strength, in power, in skill, in repute, in influence—poor in everything, even opportunity. What chance was there for him to do the deed that should challenge her admiration? In this primitive and perverse feministic environment, what room was there for masculine achievement?

He stood and gazed helplessly before him. His was an unseeing eye, for its vision was turned searchingly within. Yet almost subconsciously he beheld Korin, the farmer, overseeing her men slaves out in the fields to the east, and turned away only to become aware of the architect, Jefa, standing before a half-finished structure, patiently explaining details to her husband, Thoy, the carpenter; while from in front of the barracks came the voice of masterful Joliffe, Captain of the Army, berating her men for clumsy inefficiency.

With a sigh and a curse—though Welburn was not ordinarily a profane man—he turned to reënter the classroom. As he did so, Gurtha and Aldar passed down along a tree-shaded lane together. Welburn could not see her face now, but her arm was about the lad's shoulders, and in Aldar's boyish face there was a wakened glow of delight, a sudden putting forth of attraction, that brought to Welburn a quick memory of Millicent Bourn the first time her wise mother had left them alone together.

"Faugh!" exclaimed Welburn, and reëntered the schoolroom in disgust. It was disgust, Welburn repeated to himself as mechanically he stood with his back to the children drawing design after design, and all alike. It was disgust. But, oh, there was something else in it, a personal hurt, a longing, a desire for strength, for prowess. He had nothing, not even beauty like this boy's—a young, half-grown lad of color and gentle, pearly-eyed timidity and puppy prayer for affection that was wonderfully appealing.

"Faugh!"

Welburn recoiled from his own thought. He was conscious of a subtle, insidious attack upon his morale. Was it possible that he could harbor weak, traitorous doubts of himself and his masculine primacy? Was he, despite all his training, despite his proud sex heredity and an uncompromisingly male temperament, was he yielding to the steady, confident, established assurance of his environment?

He dropped his drawing pencil and faced his class.

There had come to him an overmastering determination to assert himself, to assert *himself*, his sex, to make the protest of rightful male supremacy. That such a protest could have but one result in such an environment was no concern of his; that it must mean misapprehension and further obloquy for himself could not now be a consideration to influence him. He had the martyr's one-idea insensibility to atmosphere, to effect; he had the proselytizer's indifference to futility. He must speak. He must protest. Above all, he must make his protest to these boys, the youth of his sex, so strangely denied their birthright.

"Boys," he cried breathlessly, ardently, "stop your work. Listen to me. I want to tell you something, something that concerns you, that touches upon your inner selves, your manhood. Listen!"

Curiously the eyes of the lads were lifted to him; the feeling in his voice was an imperative demand for audience. They shoved aside their slates and, looking up to him, fell into attention.

"You must know, you've got to know and I've got to tell you," Welburn went on, so in the thrall of his subject as to be unconscious of the slight interval that had elapsed since he began to speak. "I've got to tell you what it means to be a boy, to be male, to be a man. You can't know, of course—you can't conceive, trained as you are to subserviency; it isn't your fault. But do you know, can you realize that there is a land, a great, great world, infinitely greater than this petty island matriarchate, where everything is as it is not here; where sex—your sex—is supreme; where every earthly advantage is masculine; where men are masters and rulers and makers of conditions; where to be a man is to have every door of opportunity and experience and achievement open to you; where all the traditions are of male accomplishments; where all future hopes are based on masculinity of brain and masculine strength and masculine genius? There to be a woman is to be a thing of dependence, of limitations, of sufferance, of magnanimous and kindly forbearance, of pity and negligible consequence; a thing that lives by subterfuge and coquetry and indirection; that has no given name even, but a contemptuous feminization of some man's, her father's or her husband's; that holds all she has as the generous gift of man; that submits her mind, her heart, her soul, her body and sometimes life itself to the pleasure of man—her teacher, her lord, her benefactor, her master!"

A hush fell upon the little assembly, a silence of awe, of doubt, of uncertainty, even of palpitating, guilty hope.

Could such things be? Could such things be and be accepted, be right? With the ardor of youth's perennial belief in the ideal, in the impossible, these boys faced this new creed of sex. However incredible such a condition might seem to lads born to reverence of the mother right and a deprecating admission of the disadvantages of masculinity, there was no doubting the sincerity in their teacher's voice.

It was sincere, so sincere that for the moment they were blind to the incongruity of Welburn's present helplessness and inferiority in their world, in the light of his claim to male primacy; blind to the reality of his personality's conflict with the ideal he preached to them; blind to the absurdity of himself in his present situation as an apostle of the doctrine of manhood triumphant, of the sardonic commentary he was himself upon his own apotheosis of masculinity.

So they listened. So he talked. Talked? He sang the saga of sex, the glory of the male, the earth heaven which he had seen with his own eyes where the lowly of the matriarchate were lifted up into might, into power; where, this breeched Ezekiel[17] proclaimed, man's Man God had exalted him that was low and abased her that was high; where, in short, man had come into his kingdom.

It was inevitable, of course, under the circumstances, that Welburn should in this outpouring forget all else. In a sense, his tongue was rehabilitating him. Shorn of all artificial aids which the accretions of civilization had built up for him, weakened in body by the hardships he had undergone, thrown naked into another world, it was the only weapon he had. And it fought, it battled for his self-esteem, for his auditors' recognition of his worth, for sex privileges worn so long through the ages that the memory of man had forgotten their origin.

And then—was it suddenly or gradually?—something happened. He became aware that he was not alone with his disciples, that the *entente* between him and them had been broken, that a disturbing element had entered.

Swiftly he turned, and stood face to face with Than—Than, Captain of the Boats, the sea still in his throat, in his nostrils; Than, a sailor, just home from his semi-annual voyage south; bearded Than, bronzed, mighty, with a laugh of incredulous delight now in his childlike eyes, derision twisting his bearded lips and bursting chuckling from his throat.

"Look, lads, look!" His deep bass shook still with laughter as he pressed forward facing the class and pointing delightedly at Welburn. "Look at the mighty thing a man is in that man world, that—that *pa*triarchate where the male is supreme! Look—look at this specimen! Don't you ache to go to his world, to be like him? I say, don't you? Wouldn't you like to look like him? Wouldn't you like to brag like him? Wouldn't you like to lie yourself big like him?" And, doubling over, he roared with laughter, in which the boys joined.

Welburn was white—with rage, with impotence, but with another emotion that held him dumb, that paralyzed him for the moment.

All at once, in the shout of amusement that went up from the class, in the broad-mouthed grin on every face, he saw himself as they saw him. He saw his body in its unnatural, inharmonious tubular costume, still unskillfully constructed, set against Than's; his pain-weakened, civilization-sapped, soft body contrasted with the towering height and breadth of Than. He saw his personality, weak, emotional—as, when warring with its environment weak-

---

17. Ezekiel: a Hebrew prophet.

ness always is—discredited, weakly attempting and failing, relying upon the weak weapons of speech, of argument, of vocal contention, appealing weakly to the ideal, to fancy, to the imagination; while Than merely stood and laughed and was himself.

When Welburn saw Gurtha standing with Aldar behind the mighty bulk of Than's body, the binding force of that self-revelation snapped. With a snarl then he sprang at the sailor's throat.

But she stepped between them with the gentle, good-natured fearlessness of strength.

"Than," she said, "I'll not have him hurt. He's not strong yet."

"By heaven"—the words burst from between Welburn's clenched teeth; he had borne too much—"I'll not be protected by you!"

Than looked quickly, incredulously from him to Gurtha.

"The thing I pulled out of the water," he said contemptuously, turning his back on Welburn. "It can live—for all I care."

But Gurtha did not listen. Folding her arm within Welburn's, she half led, half urged him away.

"Am I so unpleasant to you?" she said to him in a low voice.

XII

WHEN, one warm day of the late Indian summer, Welburn received a summons from Wyn, the Mother, he thought he was at last to be called to account for what he had said to his class. His effort had failed, it was true, but such as it was, it had been incitement to rebellion and disobedience of the Mother's commands.

To his surprise he found her gracious, though Than was with her.

"You two have met?" she asked, when she had welcomed Welburn.

Welburn flushed.

"Twice," said Than. "Once in the open sea far to the northwest. My boat was fighting in unknown waters, waters I had never dared before, when there drifted toward me a thing pale, water-wrenched, water-bruised and beaten, so near dead it seemed hardly worth my while to fight the water for it."

"Oh—I—thank you!" Welburn's words came with difficulty. The gracious multimillionaire, men had called him, but his tongue stumbled now when he had to give thanks for his very life. "I have never thanked you," he added. "I did not know it was you. I do thank you now. If ever I can repay—"

"And once," Than proceeded imperturbably, "when the creature I'd dragged back to life, nursed by my clan, healed by the Mother's daughter, sprang at my throat."

"You said I lied," cried Welburn. "The life you saved is not worth living if saving warrants insult."

"You fought?" The Mother looked up quickly.

A smile played about Than's bearded lips and lingered in his eyes.

"Gurtha separated us," he said.

A silence came upon them. And in that silence, from nowhere, for no reason he could name even to himself, suddenly Welburn realized a change of position, sensed an attitude toward himself that was wary and watchful, that took him into account as one to be reckoned with.

"Tell him, Than," Wyn said, "of your discovery."

The Captain turned toward him. "At sea," his deep voice began, "that night I found you, I was far, far out of the beaten track. In all the history of our tribe no boat had ventured thus far out. But mine, my own boat, has a sort of outrigger I have learned to fashion that steadies me in the high seas. The night I caught you then from the crest of a black wave you had been dashed against the outrigger, but I caught you and passed you back to the men to see if there was any life in you; for myself, I went forward and stood in the boat's high prow, and there I saw a thing I never saw before, nor no man of our tribe."

Welburn leaned forward. "Tell me," he said.

"I cannot describe it exactly." The Captain knitted his heavy brows. "So strange a sight! It was as though a mighty shape passed me in the dark, passed me swiftly and far off with no sound louder than the angry waters, yet exciting them, it seemed to me, by its very passage."

"How large?"

The Captain shook his head. "Large as the world from sea to sky, and shining through the dark as though starred from base to topmost point."

A trembling came upon Welburn. His knees went weak and his heart beat fast. "The ship!" he gasped.

"You know—you recognize the thing?" demanded Than.

Welburn nodded. His heart seemed held by an unyielding hand. "My ship," he stammered. "The ship I was on."

"Ah!" It was the Mother's voice. She spoke in a gratified tone, as one whose calculations turn out well. "That makes you catch your breath!"

Welburn nodded; he could not speak.

"And yet," she went on easily, "it may mean joy to you—not regret."

"Joy!" Welburn repeated.

She nodded brightly. "Where Than, the Captain of the Boats, has gone, there Than can go again, and take you with him, and wait for the miracle to pass again."

Welburn started. Suddenly the hand that had seemed to hold his heart loosed its clutch; suddenly it went beating madly out of time.

"So that when the spring comes you may be sent to your home once more," Wyn said, and watched him closely.

"Thank you."

He looked out through the vine-enclosed doorway. Beyond the sea glowed, and, glistening from her bath, Gurtha stood erect, fresh from the sea.

"Or—or even sooner," she added, "perhaps."

He turned to see the Mother's deep, searching eyes upon him.

"Sooner!" he repeated. "I thought that could not be."

"And yet it can," she said deliberately. "Eh, Than?"

"If you wish," the sailor said simply.

Again Welburn's eyes turned to the strip of creamy sand without. Upon it Gurtha sat in her loose red robe drying the long wind-blown strands of her brown hair.

"Well?" said the Mother.

"Thank you," Welburn said again.

"It shall be when you wish," she said.

He could not speak. Something had caught him by the throat, an emotion so strong that the whole world seemed dead and dark and dull except for a shining blaze of strand by the sea, upon which a young woman sat and dried her hair.

He rose unsteadily. He was drunk with exhilaration, with satisfaction, with vainglorious delight.

He might go! He might be sent back in spring, or "sooner," or "when he wished." And why? Why should it be when he wished? Why should Captain Than get out his boats unseasonably and court danger for a stranger's sake, and the Mother concern herself to make so remarkable an exception to the tribe's rule of living? Why, if not for one sole reason?

And that reason?

They feared the thing he had not dared to hope.

Welburn went out to see if his suspicion was well founded—out to where the sun shone on the warm red of Gurtha's robe.

She looked up when he came. But the sun beat upon her golden lashes and half blinded her; it sought the gold in the soft brown of her wet unbound hair and dazzled him.

"Come," he said, "we must talk."

She looked down upon her bare feet in the sand, bare and strong and finely formed. He got down on his knees and took them between his palms and dusted the creamy sand from them; they were cool from the salt of the sea. Then he fastened on her sandals, and when he rose she put out a hand that he might help her to her feet.

He loved her for that. It seemed to him if he had not loved her for anything else he must have loved her for that, for once having played the woman, his sort of woman, to his man. His glad eyes sought hers to tell her of it, to thank her for it, but she walked beside him, clouded in her hair, like some super-womanly saint of old, he said to himself, and only the fine, strong, straight profile was presented to him.

He did not care to talk till they were beyond observation. When they had reached a sheltered inlet where a narrow stream sought the sea, he turned to her.

"I may go home," he said slowly, his hungry eyes watching her. "I may go before spring. Captain Than will take me when I wish. The Mother has consented."

She looked at him in silence, gravely, consideringly; she was like a statue of womankind, he thought, as she stood and listened and looked. Yet her very stillness drew him; there was such concentration of passion in her intense, brooding face.

"Do you care?" he stammered, catching at her hand.

Her breast rose and fell as she stood there, her great eyes deepening as they gazed upon him.

"Gurtha," he cried, "will you care when I'm gone?"

"No," she said slowly. "No, for you will not go."

"Only one thing will keep me." He held out his arms. She came to him, and with a cry he folded his arms about her.

"A moment," she said, and bent her head till it lay on his breast.

His lips sought hers, but she put up her hand. "The lung is still weak," she said thoughtfully, listening at his breast as she had done that first day months ago in Ainu's cottage.

"But, Gurtha—" he began passionately.

She listened a moment longer. "It has improved, though," she said cheerfully. "Who knows—in time it may be entirely cured!"

His arms dropped from her. "I love you," he said angrily, not tenderly. "Do you understand? I love you! Damn lungs and pathology generally! I love you—I love you—I want you!"

"Why, yes," she said, smiling into his enraged, longing eyes. "And I hope soon you will be a strong, full-bodied man fit to be father to a child of mine. Then I shall marry you."

Bewildered, he looked at her. "And if not?" he demanded. "If I'm to be a—a sort of one-lunger?"

Quickly she turned upon him. "Do you think," she cried wrathfully—"do you dare think a blemished man could be father to a daughter of Gurtha, daughter of Wyn, daughter of the daughters of the Mother Goddess? Ah," with disgust she added, "what sort of people do you come from?" And she hurried from him.

"Gurtha," he cried, running after her, "wait, wait!" and he caught her hand and held her. "Listen. I will wait, and I *will* get strong. I know I will, for I want you so. But you—will you wait for me? Can you?"

"I should marry soon," she answered thoughtfully. "No woman has a right, where women are few and men are many, to refuse to do her duty by the tribe."

"Indeed!" His voice rang wrathfully. "And whom should you marry, pray?"

She looked at him, open-eyed. "What does it matter?" she asked. "Than or Aldar or Jief the hunter or the councilor Namur."

He met her gaze and laughed for very rage. "You'll drive me mad," he said in low, tense tones. "What sort of woman are you, and what do you think I am? It sets me frantic! I could murder you when I see you with young Aldar!"

"He's such a pretty boy," she said, and added regretfully: "If you think it unkind, if it vexes you, I'll not put my arm about his neck."

"If it vexes me!" He stood dumbfounded, gazing at her. "See, Gurtha," he said slowly, carefully choosing his words, "it is not a matter of what your world calls right and mine calls wrong. It is something that lies just between us two. Do you love me? Tell me, do you love me?" he implored.

"Hush—hush!" she said, yet smiled upon him. "I should blush with shame for you if anyone heard us."

"But *do* you love me?" he cried.

"Hush," she said again; "a man must not be so forward."

An exclamation of wrath and impatience burst from him.

"Well, then," she added softly, resignedly. "But be forward only when we are alone."

He looked at her unheeding, throwing out his arms as though to dissipate intangible obstacles. "Listen," he said impetuously. "Would you burn with hate and jealousy and passion if I were to fondle Jola, Jefa's daughter, as you do Aldar—if I were to love her and you, too?"

She caught her hands from him and faced him now with horror.

"Go!" she said with repulsion. "Go back to your world where such an iniquity is possible! But I won't believe it. No, I *don't* believe it. It is not possible!"

Utterly bewildered, he looked at her. "But, child," he said, "can't you see how iniquitous your people's way seems to me?"

"That is because," she said earnestly, "you have not been taught the true way, the right way of life; because there is something fundamentally impure, wicked about your way of living. I do not know that you even worship the Mother Goddess. What belief is yours?"

"What is yours? Just what is it you believe first? Tell it to me."

"In the beginning there lived only Avah, the Mother Goddess. Alone she dwelt in all the world of sea and sky and land, and nothing lived save her. And as she dwelt through all the long, lonely centuries she came to long and long for companionship; till so mighty became her godly longing that alone and a virgin she conceived and created life. She bore a daughter, Hora, sister goddess to all maidens, and then sons whose names are of no consequence. And from these are descended all that live."

She finished. She had spoken solemnly, slowly, reverentially. Now she looked challengingly at him.

"What an absurd little myth!" he said gently.

She broke angrily from him.

"It's pretty," he said, "and in a small way is related to our belief. Will you let me teach you our belief, our ways?" he begged.

"No; I will teach you mine," she said, and put her two hands upon his shoulders, swaying toward him.

He caught her to him and kissed her again and again till he was breathless.

"You are mine!" he cried. "Mine! Mine! Do you hear? Mine, I tell you. There is only one thing we two can teach each other. I want you. God, I want you so, I'll—I'll—Oh, nothing matters—nothing! I can live your way—live any way except without you!"

She held his face between her palms and drew him close.

"Even according to our laws?" she demanded, her eyes in his, her lips on his.

GURTHA AND WELBURN STOOD side by side; the little finger of his right hand was bound to that of her left. He looked down upon the slender thong that bound them and, so strong was his sense of their unity of emotion, of passion, that he could hardly conceive so small a thing held them physically together.

They drank the contents of a single beaker.

To Gurtha old Ainu gave the whip, gave it in his capacity of bridegroom's friend, since Welburn had no mother here, as a symbol of man's subserviency. She took it and smiled; and Welburn smiled back at her, drunk with the light in her eyes.

He had carried fire to Gurtha's hearthstone, there in the place of her mother's house, where they should live and be part of her clan.

And then Wyn, standing before them, dipped the branch of a flowering eucalyptus in the basin of water Aldar held before her and sprinkled it lightly upon their faces, calling the name of Avah.

Then she turned to Gurtha.

"Will you not cast away your husband?" she asked.

"No."

It was Gurtha's voice, and it sang like an organ to Welburn.

The Mother turned to Welburn. "Will you not cast away your wife?" she asked.

He met her gaze, but he did not see her. He listened to the words, but he did not hear them. For though his body was here in the place of the Mother's house, his spirit was far off. He saw the great Gothic church across the sea. February it would be now, with snow lingering on the crowded city streets where the people would be gathered. Within, too, it would be crowded, the organ throbbing. There was the odor of hothouse flowers, of perfumes, of finely clad human bodies. A man in black was walking down the carpeted aisle. A woman in shimmering white walked beside him. He could smell the roses in her bouquet, feel the texture of her satin gown as it brushed against him. He could hear Grieg's "Wedding March."

"Will you not cast away your wife?" Wyn repeated, looking searchingly at him.

Welburn laughed aloud. "No—no!" he cried, and laughed again.

"Happy will it be if thus with you two," said Wyn solemnly, and turned away.

"Come," said Gurtha, holding out her hand, which trembled. "We will build our house."

XIII

"OH, if it only be a girl!"

"But, Gurtha!" Welburn exclaimed.

"A girl! A girl!" she cried, putting her hands upon his shoulders and pressing his face to hers. "Oh, love," she added despairingly, "if it be not a girl!"

He took her face between his palms, a face exquisitely humanized now, and looked adoringly into her eyes; they were welling with tears.

"How you care!" he said softly.

"Care! Care!" she repeated fervently.

"Why—" But she had no words to tell how she cared.

"Yes," he said, "how women do care! I have heard the women of my world speak with just that passionate prayer in their voice for a boy—a son."

"Oh!" She lifted herself from his arms and sat a moment amazedly regarding him. "Not truly? But only as a sweet second to a husband's wish, you mean?"

"Why not truly?" He laughed and drew her back to him. "If a boy be born to all the best and biggest life holds?"

She smiled patiently; she was always forgetting those curious, inverted customs of his world.

"So, in my world, shall my daughter be born to all the best and biggest our life holds. You do—you do hope my baby will be a girl?"

He looked at her and only smiled. The year of love, of communion, of loving enlightenment, had softened, had disciplined Welburn; he knew now, he thought, the few essentials there are in life; for him the one great requisite was this he held in his arms; he was content.

"You don't care!" she charged, and shook him by the shoulder with loving petulance. "Ah, but it will—it will be a girl," she sighed happily, and settled down again within his arms.

"How do you know?" He laughed and brushed her lips with his.

"Because—because—why, everything favors it," she whispered. "For one thing, don't you know that to seek your mate without the tribe is to increase your chance of a daughter?"

"Nonsense!" he said.

"Oh, truly," she insisted, opening wide eyes upon him. "That is old tribal lore. Oh, if it is, if it is a daughter, I shall owe her to you! How I shall love you!" she cried, and pressed her lips passionately to his.

"And if not?" he retorted. "How you will hate me!"

"Nonsense!" she said in her turn, and sat and thought for a moment in silence. "Had I married Than," she said then with conviction, "my firstborn might have been a boy."

Welburn's arms fell from her.

"Gurtha," he said firmly, "I have given up my world and come into yours. I have taken my place in your mother's family and become a son of her clan. I have forgotten much and learned much. I know now that happiness is independent of custom, of place, of people. But there is one thing to which not even your love can reconcile me—or, rather, that for very love of you I shall never endure. And this I swear."

Her eyes were on his face as he spoke, tender, patient, prescient eyes, with a hint of apprehension in them of coming sorrow.

She rose and put her hands in loving caress upon his hair, upon his face, and in silent, loving sympathy she bent and laid her cheek upon his.

"I shall go now," she said with an effort. "You will let me go alone for an hour?"

He held her for a moment, all his tenderness awakened by the new, soft gentleness of her manner. She smiled again at him, a loving, maternal glance of tender gratitude, and then she left him.

Welburn's eyes followed her as she walked slowly with effort toward the house, and then, passing a moment from sight, out again, this time toward the forest.

There was something in that lagging step that tugged at his heart. She had been so free—her gait had been that of a wild animal, he remembered having thought when he first saw her, so silken-muscled, so lithe and strong in its grace and power. And now she was caught, the wild, free thing in the trap of the world, in that trap whose lure is love, whose springs are mighty with passion, from whose bars, when they close upon its victim, there is no escape save through death or agony—the agony of maternity.

A hush came upon Welburn's soul, the hush of humility and awe that man knows when the realization of womanhood comes home to him.

As he had said, Welburn had learned much in the year, a year of new life of the senses, of original and firsthand experience, of thought unhampered by precedent and bodily fitness working itself out in terms of a new environment, pitting itself against new conditions and conquering them.

And—economically—he had forgotten more. He had all that sophistry of his civilization which makes men content to measure the height of their social accomplishment from the false base of what other men have done for them. He had forgotten the old terms of the artificial logic which shut its eyes to the pretense of the rich man's standing on stilts, the stilts of other men's labor. He had passed beyond pride in his wealth—the wealth others had amassed for him; he had passed beyond pride in position—the position others had achieved for him. He knew himself to be wealthy now for the first time in the independence Gurtha had taught him, an independence of every other human being in attaining a livelihood.

As he sat, his thoughts went back now to the spring nearly a year ago, when the boats sailed out to sea.

He was alone with Gurtha then on an obscure little island of almost primeval wildness. Here they lived alone while she taught him all she knew of living close to and wrestling with nature. Here he learned the universal and primitive joys of success, of meeting and conquering alone and unaided by civilization the primal facts of life. Here he felt that he had learned self-respect and become a man who had earned the right to live.

On the day the boats had sailed they two had swum far out to sea to watch them. But not till they were beyond the furthermost point of the island did they see the long line of boats stretching out toward the horizon, their sails like a flock of drifting birds.

"Are you sorry?" she asked, as she swam with long, strong strokes beside him. "Do you regret?"

He smiled back at her and shook his head. He could not then swim as easily as she. Now he could outdistance her.

She came over closer, and, throwing herself upon her back, floated beside him, her face upturned to his.

"Listen," she said, "don't speak, for we are far out and you will need your breath should we go farther. But if you regret, if in your heart there is the smallest hurt or longing now, now when the boats are sailing toward your world, just lay your hand on my shoulder and let me swim after them. Just that. I can call, and they will hear and wait. I can carry you to them easily."

"And come with me, come along home with me?" he asked, a catch in his breath.

She shook her head. "Do you see me," she asked gently, "in that world of yours? Would you have me live the life of woman as you have told it to me?"

XIV

BACK through the forest Gurtha came.

Even before she had passed the long alley of tall, bare-trunked eucalyptus, Welburn saw her and began to run toward her. She walked hesitatingly, slowly, as though walking were a new art scarce learned, as though never again would she walk as she had the day he first saw her. Her head, which she was wont to carry as a sunflower stalk carries its yellow crown, was bent, and in her whole pose there was a hovering, brooding something that caught at Welburn's heart and made it flutter as he ran.

When he came nearer he saw what it was; and she stood waiting, her shoulder pressed against a tree, while he flew to her.

"I have brought you our daughter," she said faintly, and held out the infant in her arms.

He did not speak; he could not for the emotion that held him. She, too, was content with silence; content, too, to lean heavily upon his arm, panting as they walked slowly home together. And for the exquisite joy of upbearing her, of feeling her soft weight upon his arm, he thanked her in his heart.

It was only when they had reached the cottage and she sank down upon the couch and he moved out to the open door that she spoke.

"I did not cry out," she whispered proudly to him, "nor even moan. Our child shall have no coward for mother. She shall be strong and brave and bear her children, when they come, bravely."

Wyn, the Mother, came to her, and she greeted her with, "He has given me a daughter, Mother. Look, she has his eyes."

And the Mother, grasping Welburn's hand for the first time in friendship, said gravely:

"From now on it is the tribe that is in your debt. You owe us nothing. You have overpaid."

He laughed. What fuss about a girl baby! There came into his mind curiously at this moment the memory of the day he had told Gurtha of certain Chinese customs to restrict population, and she had run from him as from one who knows things that are too horrible to conceive, remaining away the whole day and all that night till he had gone in search of her and brought her back.

"And any service you may demand," Wyn's deep voice went on smoothly, "is yours of right—even to that greatest one which means the loss of you."

Welburn started and looked quickly, searchingly at her.

She met his gaze quietly.

"Whenever you shall decide to return to your world, at any season, at any hour, the boats are yours," she said. "They shall seek the ocean course where you were found, and do all that can be done to deliver you safely to your own people. And the trial to find that path you left and put you on it shall be made as many times as we have sailors' lives to give. To this I pledge myself."

"Thank you," Welburn said lightly. "I would thank you more enthusiastically if I had any idea of accepting your offer."

Gravely she regarded him. "You believe you never will accept that offer?" she asked.

"I know I never will," he said slowly.

"Strange! What holds you from your world where, you have often said, you are privileged by sex and position and wealth?" she demanded.

"This," he answered, and looked down upon the baby hand which had curled tendril-like about his finger. "It is the real bond, of which the thong you bound about my finger and Gurtha's on our marriage day was the symbol."

"Let her name be Ninnith," Wyn said, rising to depart, and then, laying her hand lightly on the child's fair head: "Ninnith shall be your name—Ninnith, mother of many daughters," she said solemnly—"Ninnith Gurthachild."

That moment brought to Welburn a quick, hot pang of revolt, like those old bitter, raging, unreconciled thoughts that used to stir him at the ways that were not his. He felt a fierce passion of ownership in this child, a passion that would have seemed incredible to him two years, a year, even a month before. But the tiny thing had crept about his heart as its tiny fingers twisted about his finger. It was his, his! If he could at that moment, he would have torn it even from Gurtha's breast and fled with it to have it wholly to himself.

And it did not even bear his name!

When the Mother was gone he turned to Gurtha. "Are you satisfied to have our child so named?" he asked.

Her great, placid eyes turned questioningly to him. "If it had been a boy," she said, smiling gently, "you should have named him yourself. The Mother names no men children."

For a moment he did not speak. Her rich, full voice, so perfect in his happiness, quieted him. He would not agitate her.

"What would you have called him?" she asked.

He put an arm close about her, holding the two within its circle.

"What would *you?*"

"Hugh," she said, and kissed him. "Hugh—your name, your dear, strange, blessed name."

"Another Hugh Welburn?" he said, his heart beating at her tenderness.

She sat up startled.

"Why, no; how could it be? It would be Hugh Gurthachild," she said simply, as though so self-evident a matter required no explanation, "my daughter's brother. Hugh Gurthachild." She said it again and repeated it, each repetition a caress. "I love it. Shall we," she whispered, lifting her arm to pull his head close to hers—"shall we have a son, too?"

"I don't know," he said, and looked past her out at the sea.

A son, a son of his body and not of his name! A son Hugh, his very other self, his future self who should live after he was dead, with a name that was not his!

She put out her hand to him. He had gone far from her. She knew that. Love and life with him had taught her.

She took the sleeping child from her breast, loosed from his finger the clinging baby fingers that, at separation, gave a start and eager clutch at the air, and laid it along her knees.

"Ninnith," she said softly, and her tone was a prayer. "Ah, surely you love that name! Ninnith, my baby! Isn't it like her? Ninnith, the one who is true. Hugh, have I never told you the myth of Ninnith?"

He shook his head.

"It is not part of our religion, you know," she explained in a low voice that the child might not be waked. "It could not be that, for the great Mother Goddess in proportioning the sexes as she did decreed our life. But yet it is an ideal, and she was Hora's child, Hora, daughter of Avah. You're not listening," she broke off.

He threw off his abstraction. She was too lovely, sitting there, the long braids hanging down over the loose robe that fell about her great beautiful body like the drapery of a sculptured goddess, with the sleeping child across her knees, and the Madonna look, that had mysteriously grown upon her, shining out from behind the open simplicity of her face.

"Tell me," he said, and smiled and listened.

"Ninnith, the daughter of Hora," she began slowly, "was the last of all the Goddess's children. And while her many sisters and brothers grew up and mated and bore daughters and sons, she alone held away from them. It was thought she never would know love and life. And her mother, Avah's daughter, was angry with her and cursed her for one who would not do her duty by the world, a world of few women and many men, even as our own. And Hora sent her out of Paradise. But one day Ninnith, who had wandered sadly away from all her people, met a man unlike the men she had known. And suddenly—suddenly it happened. She loved. And he loved. And together they went their way. And she bore him children, many daughters whom Hora welcomed into Paradise, but never could Ninnith herself reënter there."

A silence fell upon her concluding phrase. Welburn, who had been listening idly, more to her voice than to her tale, waited for an explanation.

"But why?" he asked at length.

She looked doubtfully at him.

"Haven't I told you? Her very name tells it. Ninnith, true to one. Those two never loved but each other; never before they had met, nor after, nor when he died and left her alone. It's pretty, isn't it, even if it is impossible?"

"Impossible!"

"Isn't it?" she asked innocently. "Have you such a pretty myth in your world?"

"It isn't a myth," he said thickly. "It's our ideal—it's our belief, our—"

"Oh," she interrupted, bending eagerly forward, "is it? In your world are all women Ninniths, and all men like Ninnith's man?"

"All our women are Ninniths," he began proudly, "or rather, all the women in my clan, so to speak—that is, all except—"

"Yes?" she asked eagerly.

"It is not a myth with us," he said again, but impatiently. "Our men—"

"Yes?" she said again.

There was a pause.

"Oh, you would not understand," he said at length irritably. "Our women, our men, have but one husband or wife."

"All their lives? From the beginning to the end but one mate?"

He hesitated. Her crystal gray eyes were watching his face, which she had learned so well to read.

"Oh," she said slowly, "I see. How like our worlds are after all, yours and mine!"

Welburn rose and left her.

He did not look back to see her sitting there with the baby Ninnith across her knees. He hurried off into the forest and climbed the hill, pushing off sharply toward the bare headland, whose prow seemed set toward the sea. And there he stood and faced northwest and looked in the direction the boats had gone in the spring, the way toward home.

And here he met Than, like him, looking out to sea.

"An early spring it looks to be," the Captain said. "Shall we sail earlier this year?"

"Earlier!" Welburn repeated at a loss.

"You are Captain of the Boats," Than said stiffly. "In effect you are that, not I, for the Mother has commanded me to take orders from you."

"Oh! Yes." Welburn stood still again gazing out beyond. Then suddenly he turned to Than.

"Did you see," he began eagerly, "last spring did you see anything like you saw before—the great ship all alight?"

The Captain shook his head. "I did not go so far north," he said. "It was a stormy spring. I knew 'twould be."

"Yes?" Welburn questioned. "And can you tell? Then what of the coming spring?"

The sailor's eyes narrowed; he caught his beard between his fingers and tweaked it roughly.

"Why should you care?" he demanded savagely. "Are not my orders to take you hence when you wish, to bring you back if we should fail, and every spring to try again—if that shall be your wish?"

Welburn met his eyes, not childlike now but clouded with jealous hate. And as he looked he learned one thing: if ever he should try that journey with Than, the Captain of the Boats, he might reach home, but never might he come back again to Gurtha and the child.

XV

THE child Ninnith was swimming at Welburn's side, and as she swam he kept his arm outstretched beneath her ready for an emergency; kept it till the little thing noticed it and darted off, affronted, so that he had to turn and swim after and capture the little naked satin body, that slipped in his wet hands, to Ninnith's glee.

It was wonderful to watch the baby. Welburn found himself trying to remember other babies he had seen in the days when babies did not interest him; but he could only call to mind pallid little faces smothered in laces and furs in the baby carriages along the Drive or in the Park, and fretful baby cries and uncertain imbecile-like baby gestures.

Whereas this little thing that grew so close to his heart was deft and sure in every motion; had learned to swim before she could walk; had learned trust in him and had never had to learn self-confidence.

He had never heard her cry, and when he commented upon this to Gurtha, she asked him haughtily whether the child's mother was a weakling and a coward, or was he. And her laugh, that chuckling baby laugh of Ninnith's, was such music to his ears he could not hear it without smiling sympathetically.

He loved to listen to her chatter, and often exclaimed to Gurtha at the child's precocity.

"Of course," then Gurtha said superbly; "a girl talks early."

"Of course," Welburn grimly agreed, with the inferential masculine irony that accepts and accounts for the female's early development linguistically. "They even do with us. But not so early as this."

"You forget," Gurtha had reminded him gravely, "a Wynchild is of the priests; the Mother Goddess speaks through her. She must quicken under that touch. She must be bigger, finer, nobler than other daughters of women."

"Yes, yes, I see," he had said, smiling.

Today, as was his custom, he swam back to shore with Ninnith astride his shoulders, a baby Nereid[18] holding him fast by the ears, her rosy heels beneath his chin, while she crowed commands for speed, her happy face upturned, the tiny gold curls clustering wet upon her forehead, her lashes glistening and her eyes alight.

On the shore waiting for them sat Gurtha. From far off Welburn could see her; his eyes seemed to have gained in power and far-seeing by these years in the open, just as his body had developed and strengthened and broadened, till he was stout and sturdy almost as Than himself.

It seemed to him that he had made the comparison mechanically, but as he shot toward shore he became aware that it was Than who was lying at Gurtha's feet; Welburn's mind had anticipated his eyes in seeing the Captain of the Boats there with her.

And why?

As he swam, Welburn put the question to himself. Why should he have known Than would be there? And despite himself, despite his deep desire and his determination not to admit it, he heard the answer as clearly as though it had been spoken: because Than was always there, Than and his young shadow, Aldar. And it was Aldar he saw now, standing within a few feet, his eyes bent upon Gurtha and Than.

It was a beautiful boy figure, this Aldar's, strong and straight and white, with the bloom of adolescence upon it, with its young, godlike head, its childlike eyes and happy, laughing mouth.

At the consciousness of that beauty, Welburn's temper suddenly snapped. He gave himself over, as he had not in years, to a comparison of the situation

---

18. Nereid: in Greek mythology, a sea nymph who helped sailors on difficult voyages.

with a similar situation in his world. He let himself think how it would be with him and his wife, how he would deal with this sort of thing under other customs in another country. He had learned—with difficulty and slowly— that to live at all in this fantastic feministic environment he must put aside his old opinions, his ingrained ideas of sex morality, his unshaken belief in male superiority, in masculine prerogative in matters of sex. He had found that for him under existing conditions there was nothing more futile than idle comparisons, than emotional longings, than raging, passionate resentment against things as they were here.

But what he had learned, what reconcilement and adaptability he had conquered by shutting the door of his thoughts, held good, not for his own intimate life, but for that of the community. Gurtha's people might follow their ways of living—thus far he had come—without outward criticism from him. But for Gurtha and himself it was different. Tenaciously he held to the belief that the teachings of centuries had bred in him, had made inherent, as much part of himself as the blood that beat now at his temples, that was hot with hate of Than, of Aldar; that iterated and reiterated that this woman was taboo because she was his.

But was she his?

Suddenly, incongruously, almost crippling his body, which was making for Gurtha and Than, impelled by a murderous rage, as it did for the time paralyze his purpose, came a memory five years old. It was the memory of his own sister who had married a titled French libertine, semi-royal in descent; who had lived abroad ever since and poured her millions into her husband's hands; who had come face to face with just such a situation as this, sexes being reversed, a situation, though, which was not merely threat but fulfillment; and who had made herself the laughing stock of her new environment by her futile public protests against the unwritten laws of license which obtained in her husband's set.

"Gertrude"—Welburn could hear his own voice through the lapse of years, remonstrating impatiently with her—"as a woman of the world you must behave like a woman of the world, not like a stupid little country girl whose ignorance may make her demand impossibilities. How can you be guilty of such a *bêtise*?[19] You know how men live. If you don't, you'd better find out

---

19. French for "foolishness."

quickly and quit stirring up a scandal that only puts you in a ridiculous light. And me, too. If you could change things it would be different. But you can't. And you're not so silly as to cut off your nose with a divorce shears to spite your face. If your masculine ideal is that of *bourgeois* faithfulness to one woman, you should have married, not a descendant of Louis Quatorze, but a small shopkeeper of the Middle West, who would be true to you—provided he never met with temptation to be otherwise. Oh, you little fool, you poor, dear little fool! And I thought my sister knew life!"

By the time Welburn's feet touched shore he was comparatively calm, not reconciled. There was a deep ridge between his eyes that foreshadowed strife, a latent, if postponed, determination and preoccupation whose grim influence little Ninnith felt, for she, who was always loth to leave him, ran readily from him to her mother. He walked ahead slowly, intent on his effort at self-control. He was telling himself that he could not be ridiculous; he would not be futile; he must not be impotent and absurd.

And he kept tensely repeating this while Than lifted himself from the sands at his coming and with a nod walked away, while Aldar, with a short, swift run, hurled his young body into the sea and swam superbly out—a spectacle of beauty and strength and skill at which Gurtha's eyes widened in appreciation.

It was still the foremost thought in his mind, the only one he yet dared formulate, while he watched Gurtha take the little girl in her arms, rub her body dry with soft, warm sand, dust off the satin skin with light, loving strokes, tie the pretty sandals on those perfect feet, rub the golden head till it crinkled into shining curls, and slip over it the single garment, the sleeveless, slit tunic.

Welburn fancied his thoughts were all turned within to where rage and impotence festered in his heart, yet he could not, he could not now, he never could watch this pretty ritual of mother service without a softening at his heart and a smile upon his lips.

"That's better," Gurtha said, her eyes upon him. "I cannot bear to see that ugly angry ridge between your eyes. I cannot bear to know you at strife with things."

He did not answer directly. He was not ready yet to say what he should do. He was compelled to indirection by his very helplessness and indecision.

"Ah, but we are fine," he said to Ninnith, who stood now dressed regarding him curiously.

He drew her to him. "Coral beads on our pretty frock," he said, lifting the edge of her skirt. "And a coral necklace here." He pressed his lips to the baby neck, firm and cool from the sea. "And coral ornaments even at our sandal tips!"

He lifted both little feet lovingly, and she stood erect and strong in his hands and crowed with delight.

"Why is she so fine today?" he asked and turned to Gurtha.

"Jola marries today," she said reluctantly. "We shall go to the wedding."

"Jola!" Welburn exclaimed. "Jola, the wife of Nol?"

Assenting, Gurtha met his eyes; her own were patient, kindly, forbearing.

"She married Nol six months after our marriage," he said harshly. "Her boy is younger than Ninnith."

She nodded slowly, keeping grave, tender eyes upon him.

"She takes a second husband, Hedon, eldest of the three great brothers, sons of Brida, the Mother's closest councilor. It is a strong addition to Brida's clan; it makes hers the strongest clan in fighting men of all the tribe."

Welburn set the child upon the sand and rose to his feet.

"But Hedon," Gurtha added slowly, "can never be chief husband while Nol lives. He must even serve Nol, if Nol so wishes, and all the children that be born shall be Nol's children, and his authority over them only less than Jola's, the mother."

Welburn looked at her a moment without speaking. Then he turned and walked away. In her wisdom, she let him go without another word.

XVI

"BUT what would you have?" asked Ainu.

"Decency," cried Welburn.

"Decency!" The little old man repeated the word thoughtfully. "I have pondered on all you have told me of your world, but—forgive me—I cannot think it decent. Perhaps," he added humbly, "it is because my father and his father before him and his, back to the beginning, thought differently. Do you know"—he glanced timidly at Welburn striding up and down the forest aisle—"I sometimes believe man cannot think of such things but as his ancestors thought; it is not you and I thinking, but your dead father and mine thinking in us."

Welburn stopped in his restless walk and looked down at him. Welburn had left the court of the Mother's house, where he and Gurtha lived, to wander off by himself and try to come to some conclusion about the menace he felt threatening his peace. He had been alone out in the woods for days. Since he had learned forest lore from Gurtha, he could easily find his food in the wilds and build a shelter.

He had thought that far away in the undisturbed silence of the forest he could reason the thing out and come to the peace of decision. But the days passed and still he saw no way out. Around his heart twined the tendrils of his love for his child, a passion of which he could not have believed himself capable in the old days in another world, a love, it seemed to him, greater than Gurtha's, than even his for Gurtha, now that the customs of her people were forcing them asunder.

Could he cut through that tender bond—could he free himself and go back alone to civilization and the man's world to which he belonged? Could he do without Ninnith? Could he learn to forget her, the closest thing to him here, to whom he had whispered English words, words he himself had learned from his own mother, from the very beginning? Could he leave her, the brave, happy little thing, so quick to learn, so eager to please him, so appealing in her consciousness of the sweet secret they two shared in the English speech they two alone knew? Could he give up this child that made his heart beat with pride in her and love and tenderness?

And would Gurtha give her up? Perhaps, for sheer love and pity for him, if the child had been a boy. But her girl child, her daughter!

Welburn flung himself upon the ground with a groan and covered his face with his hands. It was at this point in his bitter musings that he heard a man's sandal tread upon the crackling underbrush, heard it even when it was faint, with the new keenness of the senses that he had acquired; and presently Ainu stood before him.

The gentle little old man looked frail and old; his soft eyes regarded Welburn gravely, kindly.

"Listen," he said sitting down beside Welburn, "and take heed, I implore you. When Jefa's husband Ferl stayed long away from her house without her permission, he came back to find the house doorway which had always faced east, now open toward the west."

Welburn looked up at him. He liked the little old man whose care of him when he was cast upon his mercy he realized now. But he liked him, too, for the sweet and gentle philosophy that was characteristic of him. Among the men of the tribe, even of the clan, Welburn still was a stranger; they disliked, resented him. But in Ainu Welburn felt a disinterested, generous affection.

"It's good of you, Ainu," he said, and rose hospitably to offer the old man refreshment. "I don't understand what you mean by Jefa's peregrinating doorway, or what a funny thing like that has to do with me, but I'm glad you came."

Old Ainu laid a detaining hand upon him.

"The doorway had not moved of itself," he said slowly. "Jefa had divorced him."

Welburn laughed. He could not help grinning at the discomfiture of the shut-out husband. He was thinking, too, whimsically, of the many-doored residences some families of his acquaintance might have needed if this custom were borrowed by his world.

"Ferl understood," the old man's gentle voice went on, "when no way was there where he had been accustomed to enter, that never might he enter again. Don't *you* understand?"

The grin left Welburn's lips. He stood in silence, comprehending now the significance in the old man's eyes. He had a vision of Ninnith—Ninnith climbing up into his lap to lay her head upon his breast and in a baby whisper repeat the words of his native tongue that bound him and her so secretly, so strongly.

"It is the mother right," said Ainu simply.

"He had children?" asked Welburn after a pause.

"Two sons. He never saw them again."

Slowly Welburn let himself down beside him. Silently he sat gazing before him. Silently, for a time, Ainu sat beside him.

"See," the old man said at length, "there are but two ways to live—to bear, or not to bear. He who does either has the people's respect. He who does both has neither the people's respect nor his own. If you could change things it would be different," Ainu's mild voice continued; and Welburn recognized with a bitter grin the echo of his own advice to his sister. "But man does not change things. Things change man."

Welburn nodded.

"You yourself are changed since you came," said Ainu gently.

In spite of himself a laugh burst from Welburn. At odd moments he could look at his plight and see the humor of it, but not for long.

"Who the devil wouldn't change," he growled, "alone, in a topsy-turvy world like this? You might as well expect a sane man to get a madhouse full of lunatics to listen to reason."

Ainu drew back. "This is our way," he said stiffly. "Make it your way or—"

" 'Or'!" repeated Welburn with bitter irony. "That's the deuce of it!" And he thought of Ninnith and lapsed into silence.

"I think it strange," said Ainu, puzzled, "that you hesitate. If you *are* privileged in your world, if it is true that you are favored there because of your sex, your position, your wealth, why should you hesitate to return there? Why do you stay? How can you stay? It—it almost makes one doubt you."

A laugh, an angry laugh, broke from Welburn's lips.

"There spoke the Mother," he snarled. "But—one cannot blame her. It does seem strange. So, she sent you?"

Ainu did not reply directly. "On earth," he said slowly, as though he were repeating a religious lesson, "are few women and many men. If there were many women and few men, what would happen? Upon your heart now!"

"Why—Brigham Young,"[20] admitted Welburn with a wry smile, and added an explanation.

"Exactly," said Ainu with some satisfaction. "It is perhaps not wise to say as much in public. The Mother is stern about such things. But alone in the forest two men together may be honest. If—now as honestly, man to man, alone in the forest—if every man were mated to a woman except yourself, and no single woman remained—"

An exclamation of wrath interrupted him. "I won't assume indecencies," cried Welburn.

"Indecencies! Why, you speak with disgust of customs among your own people with regard to a certain class of women. Yet you say these things must be. Ah, you have no respect for women! I wonder the Mother Goddess lets you live."

---

20. Brigham Young (1801–1877): leader of the Mormons and believer in plural marriage.

"No respect for women! Why, it is for our very reverence for women that things are as they are among us. We would not have them bear the burden put upon them here."

Ainu looked up puzzled. "Ah! Then no woman works among you, no woman toils?"

"No woman of my class—my clan, if you will."

"But other clans?"

A desire to shock the old man came to Welburn, born of his own impatience with the situation. "My dear Ainu," he said lightly, "we have women shoeblacks and women plowhorses and women hodcarriers and even, in some out-of-the-way coal mines, we have women who draw the coal up in buckets on their heads, lug it up on their hands and knees."

"Hush—hush!" interrupted Ainu. "The Mother Goddess may hear you!"

With dignity he rose. "I had hoped," he said coldly, "that you were big-minded and honest enough to put yourself in another's place. If Than were Welburn and married to Gurtha, and Welburn—"

But Welburn would listen to no more. He left the old man where he was, and literally taking to his heels, he ran from him—ran as if he felt that, though those feeble footsteps could not overtake him, the faltering words might. He ran long, through the mighty aisles of the forest, ran from Ainu's words and his own thoughts. Then he turned sharply and climbed to the high west headland.

And here, when he could go no further, his thoughts caught up to him. So he threw himself down, panting, his fevered face set out toward the sea, toward his own world, his own ways. And he lay there and weighed and pondered and battled and despaired and hoped, and came to his decision.

Then he turned his face back toward the village.

On the way down from the headland he met Than.

"What of the spring, Captain?" he asked.

"'Twill be early." Than's words were curt ; he kept his eyes out to sea.

"And the sailing?"

"That, too, will be early."

"How early?"

Brusquely the Captain turned and looked at him. "As early as you wish. What is your pleasure?"

"To sail the day, the hour it becomes possible."

A light leaped to Than's eye. Welburn saw it and laughed in his heart at the fellow's simplicity.

"The boats will be ready in a day and a night," the Captain said quickly. "The second day at daybreak then. I'll go and make things ready." And with a loose, free stride he tore down the hill, like one whom good news makes fleet of foot and light of heart.

Welburn followed more slowly. In Wyn's courtyard he entered and went straight to Gurtha's house. The doorway, he remarked with a cynical grin, was still open toward the east, and there Gurtha sat fashioning a tunic for Ninnith, who slept in a bough-built cradle among the leaves of the spreading tree that shaded the court. A bright cord fastened to the boughs and to Gurtha's wrist kept the light cradle swaying. She stitched, and, every now and then, like a deep note beating time to a gay measure, slowly, languidly she pulled the cord and the cradle rocked.

Gurtha looked up. "Oh, I am glad!" she said. "I am glad!"

"Glad whatever it is that brings me back to you?" Welburn demanded.

She put down the little frock, loosed the cord and stood up to meet him.

"Nothing has come between us," she said in her thrilling voice, "but your own thoughts. Do you regret our life together? Is there regret in your heart?"

He opened his arms. "Come," he said, "and see if there is."

She came to him and he folded his arms about her. Half-mechanically then, half-roguishly, she put her ear to his breast.

"Ah!" she sighed happily. "Your breathing is strong and steady and sure. How well you are! But apart from that, and that is well, we are today as we were that day long ago, that day I listened," she added softly.

"Yes," he said, and looked full into her eyes, "we are today, but how about tomorrow?"

She met his significant gaze fairly a moment, then her lids trembled and fell.

"Ah, why won't you—" she began.

But he closed her mouth, his lips on hers.

"Gurtha," he said quickly, "that thing cannot be said between us. Only one thing can now, this: If you love me, come with me and bring Ninnith. Come with me to a world where I can live with you both and be happy. The boats sail day after tomorrow. Come!"

Startled, she stepped out of the circle of his arms, and stood, breathing quickly, looking at him. She looked long, her eyes reading his face, reading the trouble, the struggle, the emotion written there in deep lines.

"See," she said slowly, "you know our world now. If things were changed and I with you in your home—if it had come about that way, our meeting—should I make such an appeal to you, what would be your answer?"

"I'd come," he cried, and thought he spoke the truth, so quickly he spoke, so ardent was his desire. "I could not but come, if you loved the child as I love her, and the alternative was separation for you from her forever. For pity, for love, oh, Gurtha, I'd come!"

"Then so will I," she said, and gave her hand.

XVII

THEY were like lovers again, and that night Welburn talked of all he could do for her, all that he could give to her in gratitude, in payment. She had never seemed to him so sweet, so feminine, as now in this new role of renunciation for the sake of the man she loved.

But in the morning she waked with a question on her lips.

"I have been thinking," she said slowly, "in my sleep. Or else I dreamed. You must tell me—what of Ninnith there? See, I have learned to love you more tenderly, it seems to me, than ever a woman of our tribe loved before. I am weak through love of you; so I would even go with you. But what of her?" she asked again, pointing to the cradle where Ninnith lay. "My own birthright is mine to throw away, if I choose, for the one I love. But hers is neither mine nor yours. What of Ninnith there?"

He laughed and caught her to him. Ah, Ninnith, he said, should live such a life as Gurtha could not even fancy, so sweet, so full, so fine, so fair it should be. She should be tended by the wisest, most experienced nurses; she should be educated by the greatest experts of the age. She should have her horses, her servants, her establishment such as a royal princess might envy. She should be watched and shielded and cultivated as flowers were in the conservatory at Ellinwood Towers. She should be clothed in such finery as only the daughter of an American money prince might wear. She should travel and be courted by the great ones of earth. She should have everything, great or small, she wanted; there was nothing in the world he could not buy for her. She should be the star of his life, the pride of his days, his special, sweet solace on earth, no matter how many children, how many sons even, might come to them.

Gurtha listened. She had never heard him so eloquent as now with the hope of home ahead. She had never heard that patronizing, condescending, masterful tone to his voice. She listened. But she did not speak, and he began again.

"Oh, I shall be the proud and happy daddy!" he chuckled. "The world will ring with the praises of the beautiful Miss Welburn, the artistic Miss Welburn, the wealthy, philanthropic Miss Welburn, the athletic, merry Miss Welburn, the—oh, the adorable Miss Welburn! I declare I'm dead in love with her already. We'll call her Nina, though Ninnith is pretty, and I'll sit back—you and I, Gurtha—and I'll do the smug papa act, and challenge the world to produce her peer."

Still Gurtha did not speak. And Welburn lay a while lost in thought. He was building, in fancy, the nursery at Ellinwood Towers. A court of flowers, of course, and a splashing fountain, an artificial lake warmed for bathing, and an open air sleeping porch that—

"Will my daughter learn to clothe herself?" Gurtha's voice broke in upon him.

"Hardly," said Welburn from the depths of his dream of content. "Paris'll do that."

"Will she learn to find her food and build her home?"

"Not on your life!" he declared with energy. "There'll be a thousand men and women to do it for her."

"She will be of the dominant class?"

"Oh, surely. Being her father's daughter, and most likely because of her husband's position."

"But not through herself?"

"Not if she works," he answered slyly, enjoyingly.

"Then only those among you may rule who do not work?" she asked, troubled.

"With their hands, yes, or as the mental servants of others. Oh, it'll be all right—all right, Gurtha. Trust me for Ninnith's future!"

"Will she know to heal the sick, to—"

"No," he interrupted. "There's where I put my foot down. No woman doctors in the Welburn family!"

"To make wise laws?"

"Oh, Gurtha, be reasonable. Wait till you see a Tammany[21] boss and the members of a State legislature before you put my daughter in such a gallery as that!"

"Shall she be tall and strong, so strong no one may wrestle with her?"

"I sincerely hope not. Nix on the female Sandow,[22] if you please."

She looked puzzled, and it did not occur to him to enlighten her. It was not altogether his words though; she was familiar with the curious locutions that had always made his speech different from her own, and which seemed to multiply now that his thoughts were hurrying home.

"On the contrary," he added, "her environment will, of course, moderate her. Her governesses will see that she becomes soft, gentle, obedient, ladylike."

"Ladylike!"

"Yes," he said contentedly. "Quiet in manner, with delicate hands and pretty feet, a soft voice and a charming diffidence in expressing herself, a pure little heart and a nicely cultivated mind, and—just the right shade of deference to her father's opinions or her husband's."

"You are—serious?" she asked.

"Never more so."

"Will she—will she cultivate the fields?"

"Not in a million years!"

"Will she choose her husbands as a free woman should? Shall she have any man she desires?"

Welburn made a wry face. "'Husband,' Gurtha—singular," he said in an irritated voice. "And in America girls—er—don't do the choosing."

"Shall her daughters bear her name?"

Curiously now Welburn waked, became conscious of the trembling wrath in Gurtha's voice. He put out his arm to draw her to him. But she sprang up.

"Why should I rob my daughter?" she demanded. "What sort of tribe mother am I to cheat her of her freedom and give her baubles instead? What

---

21. Tammany Hall: a New York City political organization founded in 1789 and associated with corruption due to charges against bosses such as William M. Tweed.

22. Eugen Sandow (1867–1925): German bodybuilder.

sort of father are you to conspire against his child? Go back! Go back! Ninnith, daughter of Gurtha, daughter of Wyn, daughter of the daughters of the Mother Goddess, stays here!"

And catching up her gown, she stormed out to her bath in the sea.

A while Welburn lay and thought it over. What a bungler he had been! If he had only waited to do these things for Ninnith, not tell of them beforehand! Yet how could one lie to Gurtha? And now—what to do, what to do? How undo what he had done?

If he had had the power he would have taken her by force, the force a man rightly uses to compel his wife to the right. If he could but seize her, have her carried on board ship, bring her to his home, conquer her there by love and devotion and patient, unswerving determination; bring her to see the proper relationship of the sexes and the justice of masculine supremacy as the world has ordained them; teach her and love her and pet her, as is a magnanimous man's joy with his wife; shower upon her all the gifts that generosity delights in for the loved one's sake—till, finally, after long, loving years together, bound close by the many children of a great and enduring love, and disciplined by years, by public opinion, by her husband's wisdom and good sense and patience, she should come at last to look at things in the right way; to know purity and chastity, refinement and delicacy, those jewels in the crown of womanhood; and to thank him—to thank him for realization of these, as well as for emancipation from labor and responsibility; to be grateful for the little, protected, make-believe kingdom whose queen she should be, for being screened from contact with the base and rude and cruel facts of life, for the poetry of existence which should be hers, if—if only—

Ah, if he only could!

Welburn drew a long sigh, a sigh of relinquishment, of realization, and turned his back upon dreams; turned it, too, upon the bitter futilities of regret. He would not let himself dream again of what life with her might be; neither would he let himself think of what her life without him would be.

In that sigh he gave her up. She would not live his way; he could not live hers. His soul divorced her. He closed the doorway of his heart to her. Never again might she enter there.

But go he must. He might have stayed yesterday—who knows?—if she had said no to his plea and there was no way but the dangerous one he now had to choose. Today he could not stay. He had projected himself so strongly into that life he knew, that life of strength and privilege and power, that he could not again live without it, could not go back to subserviency and shame.

He would go. Without Gurtha, since he could not change her, but not alone. The child was his as much as hers. She would keep Ninnith by force. By force then or by guile he would take her.

That day he made his plans, saw Than and worked with him to get the boats in readiness.

He was a genial Than now, cordial and kind and willing, with the old childlike look in his eyes, the smiling lips and the mighty muscles at the disposal of everyone. He seemed like one who had been bewildered by a denial which he could not comprehend; who now became his trustful, happy self, since once more the world had become normal, a world of reason, of promise, of hope.

They worked together like men who had but one goal; and since that irrevocable spiritual divorce which Welburn had pronounced in his heart, which now sundered him and Gurtha, he could work with Than, and could even appreciate the sailor's simple strength and courage, his brave, childlike, gentle nature.

That night—or rather, almost morning, for the stars were paling—Welburn stole into the mother's courtyard and to the tree where, in her leafy cradle, Ninnith slept. He had her in his arms and out beyond the enclosure before she even stirred, so swiftly and silently his sandaled feet had borne him.

Then when she opened sleepy, startled eyes, he lifted her till his lips were at her tiny ear.

"Say 'Daddy,' Ninnith," he whispered in English.

"Daddy," she murmured lovingly.

"Say 'Love,' sweetheart."

"Love," she echoed.

"Now say it all—say it all, Ninnith."

"Daddy—love—Ninnith," she cooed, and then laughed out triumphantly.

He caught her to him, hushing her against his breast.

"Now say—say 'Home,' my baby. Say, 'Home with Daddy.'"

"Home," she crowed.

"Yes," he said, holding her close, "with Daddy."

"With Daddy," she whispered, and put her lips up to be kissed, and soon slept again.

With that tender weight hidden close to his heart under his big cloak, he hurried down to the boats.

He had read long ago—he remembered it now with a pang of sympathy for dead and gone parents, situated as he was this morning—of savage mothers, wives of polygamous husbands, who had killed their babies and themselves when the new wife came. He thought the solution, now that he could understand, an inevitable one, if there were no other outlet. But there was—for him there was, there was! For out yonder—he saw it as he came closer—pale and mysterious and potent, softly breathing and purring as the tide lifted, under the haggard stars stretched the sea. Down there on the sands, all ready and waiting, were Than and his men. And beyond—civilization!

"You have no fear?" Than greeted him, his eyes shining in the dawn.

"Of what?" Welburn demanded.

"Of the unknown. Of failure perhaps and—even death."

With a confident laugh Welburn shook his head.

"At dawn like this one fears," the sailor said simply. "All that Than can do I'll do for you—it is the Mother's will and my own desire. But there will come a morning like this, quiet and terrible and lonely as this, when you'll be alone in your boat, seeking your home alone. Do you realize it?"

Again Welburn laughed. "I shall not be alone," he said. "I have a talisman," and he pressed the sweet bundle he carried closer to him. "Besides, it is not the first time I have been alone with death. Last time I battled with the sea I had no boat, I knew no direction. 'Twas black night, not morning. And I was a weakling, a child, compared to the man I am today."

"You are indeed a man," he said. "That much—vigor and strength and endurance—that much our life has given you."

"Yes," agreed Welburn, taking his place in Than's high galley and laying the sleeping child carefully down beside him, "and more. Cast off."

The Captain turned to give the order, then hesitated.

"On sailing the Mother comes to watch us off, to ask the Mother Goddess to hold her men safe and bring them home again to her and the tribe."

Welburn glanced at the sailor, whose clear, light eyes were full of faith unquestioning.

"She'll not come today," he said. "I have given out that we sail an hour later than we do."

Perplexed, Than bent toward him. "And Gurtha—" he began.

But at that name upon those lips, in spite of all his philosophy and all his civilization, something in Welburn broke loose; something primitive and fierce and bloody that dated back, back even before the child came to the mother, and with its coming brought marriage, the family, the clan, mother right and the matriarchate.

Cursing in that strange tongue Than had not heard since the night three years ago when he drew this stranger from the sea, Welburn sprang at the Captain's throat. His eyes were fierce and bloodshot, and he saw as through a bloody haze.

And in that moment Ninnith stirred, waked by all the clamor, and gave a cry, a baby cry of fright in seeing that face, which she had known only as a hovering sky of love and infinite tenderness, contorted now with jealous agony.

That cry stayed Welburn's arm.

"Ah," said Than; "now I see."

"Daddy!" sobbed the baby.

It wrung Welburn's heart. That his fearless baby should tremble, should sob with terror! He turned and took her in his arms and soothed and caressed her, murmuring lovingly, pleadingly to her under his breath in the tongue they alone knew.

To Than the Captain he spoke but two words. "Cast off," he commanded.

The Captain shook his head.

"Cast off!" repeated Welburn. "You have said I am Captain of the Boats. Obey my order then. Cast off!"

"You shall not steal the child," said Than, his clear eyes troubled. "If it were a boy—But you are taking the strength of the tribe—its very source of strength. It is unholy, a sacrilege."

Welburn looked at him, sat a moment considering and looked at him again in silence, measuringly. Then he spoke quietly, tensely, deliberately.

"Choose," he said. "Cast off, or put us both on shore."

A second Than stood wavering, then turned to his men.

"Cast off!" he cried. To Welburn he added, striding off as from something unclean: "The outraged Mother Goddess will punish you."

XVIII

IF there were no sea and no mountains, no sky and no desert, all men would be atheists, Welburn was fond of saying in his old age, when he had unlearned the cynicism of his youth and his time, built a great church at Ellinwood Towers, and gone back to the faith of his fathers.

His was not the sort of temperament to tremble at mention of a divinity—and a woman divinity at that. He never became abject in his belief, even in later life. But in the awing dawn of morning that fateful day, with the sphinxlike mystery of the sea facing him, and at his back a strange, impossible, outlived situation, with nothing that was friendly about him, but enmity in the very land slowly receding behind him, in that moment he shivered at Than's words.

"Oh, it's all very well for you fellows," he would say to the few to whom he could talk of the past. "You can smile ironically and please your conceit by feeling patronizing and critical. *You* wouldn't have permitted yourselves a superstitious thought—not you! You would have been wholly at ease, devilishly sarcastic and tremendously up-to-date. Oh, yes, you would. And so would I—*here*, with my feet upon my own hearth, with my chequebook at hand, my servants about me, the police at the end of an electric button, two Senators I'd made at my elbow.

"Here, you know, you'd be right and you'd have the consciousness of right. You'd be right legally and morally. You'd have all the law, man-made and divine, backing you.

"Out yonder—out yonder you'd be wrong, and you'd feel it and shiver at the knowledge of it. And you'd have all the law and a woman divinity against you, God help you!"

WHEN A CRY WENT up from the sailors at the oars, and Welburn's eyes, following theirs, saw Gurtha swimming with great strokes after them, he did not shiver, nor feel a paralyzing consciousness of wrong; he braced himself for battle.

That strong, white body was being propelled through the water with tremendous force and rapidity; yet once in its onward push it halted, while over the waters came a call, a sonorous mother call, vibrant and agonized and imperative:

"Nin—nith! Nin—nith!"

The little one stirred within the circle of Welburn's arm.

"Mother!" she cried gaily, and leaned far forward to watch.

The silent oars were lifted from the sea; the boats stood still. Again that great call sounded over the water, a solemn chant, moving, commanding.

"Nin—nith! Nin—nith!"

The little one trembled, struggled a moment, almost physically, for expression. Then memory of a profound religious impression stirred subconsciously in that baby breast, the memory of the First Year ceremony in the templed forest, where a girl child is consecrated to her mother's clan.

"Ninnith," she cried in her baby treble, reverently as though again taking part in that solemn antiphonal chant of the creed of her mother—"Ninnith, daughter of Gurtha, daughter of Wyn, the Mother, daughter of the daughters of the Mother Goddess!"

Welburn frowned. He had been indignant when the little one learned the words. He had resented the task put upon his baby, as well as the ritual of that impressive ceremony in which his fatherhood had had no recognition.

He caught the baby to him. "Say 'Daddy loves Ninnith,' sweetheart," he begged.

The child's lips trembled, and silently formed the words he wished. But the mother tongue was with her strongly at that moment, the words so solemnly impressed upon her, repeated to her over and over and over again. She could not so quickly think in her father's language.

Resolutely then Welburn turned. He stood the baby upon the lifting taff-rail of the boat, his arm firm about her, and together they faced Gurtha swimming now close to the outrigger.

He would appeal to her. He would implore her in pity to come, to come with him and the child.

He had gone far in twenty-four hours, had unlearned more, it seemed to him, under stress of strong emotion, and in facing the inevitability to which he thought he had been reconciled, than even in the years he had spent in Gurtha's house in her mother's courtyard. He could not now have spoken as he did that morning only a day old. His passionate tenderness for the child had taught him too much—too much of mother love, of mother right.

So now, now he would promise anything she demanded, and he would do his utmost to fulfill that promise, so far as his world would let him, but so far that she must see his good faith, must know him true to his word. She should teach her child what she would; she should make of her what she would, if only both would come with him, if only both would try the other world, his world, with him!

Thus far his thought had gone no further. He had not even faced an alternative, so sure he was that his passionate plea must prevail.

Then suddenly it happened. Did the boat lurch? Did someone of the sailors—Aldar standing there behind, eager for his first cruise—actually push the child?

Welburn always insisted that not even that mother call of Gurtha's could have loosened the little one's hold from his neck, could have made her plunge to her into the sea. Besides, he would argue—and those who knew him well were so fond of him they would not question the thing he loved to believe—the baby went into the water feet foremost with a cry—not as a fearless creature would who lived half her days in the ocean.

Gurtha caught her to her and turned without a word, and, holding her close, swept past them, her face turned straight toward shore.

It was many days later that Welburn was put into a boat, provided with water and food, and set adrift. Even at the last he and Than did not strike hands. For when Welburn had started to leap overboard after Ninnith, the Captain and his young brother had, in a second's time, intercepted him, overpowered him, bound him fast.

"Cast off!" then cried Than. "Cast off!"

And the boats beat their way to the north.

When they had sailed a thousand miles, Welburn was freed and lowered into the boat provided for him. "Cast off!"

Than's command to his men as they rowed away were the last words Welburn heard in that strange tongue. Often though, old as he is, and though the muffling years have piled silence upon silence between that time and now, he hears Than's voice again in dreams. He dreams of mighty battle in the boats; he feels the thongs that bound him while Gurtha shot with Ninnith through the sea; he rips them with the herculean strength of dreams; he fights a swift and bloody battle, and plunging into the ocean, swims after them.

2

Newspaper Journalism, 1895 to 1902

Introduction to Part 2

Between 1895 and 1902, Miriam Michelson published hundreds of newspaper articles under her byline. This volume gathers together twenty of those articles in order to offer readers an overview of her career as a journalist. Written mostly in the first person, these articles draw attention to Michelson's carefully constructed persona as a newspaperwoman. Through Michelson's active stance as witness, participant, and storyteller, these writings illuminate the late nineteenth-century phenomenon of the "girl reporter" and bring to life a decade in which increasing numbers of women combined grit and femininity to make their mark on the field of journalism. As historical and cultural documents, Michelson's newspaper writings also shed light on many key episodes in the Progressive Era and on the role that journalism played in shaping the course of history. I have chosen these articles for their historical value and vivid narrative style as well as their relevance to current scholarship in the fields of American studies, women's and gender studies, race and ethnic studies, and the history of the American West.

Michelson's early articles from *Arthur McEwen's Letter* and the *San Francisco Call* demonstrate her lifelong engagement with gender issues, providing important context for her later fictional works like *The Superwoman*. The first article in this section, "The New Woman Realized," offers a rare glimpse into the nineteenth-century transgender experience. Focusing on the 1895 Woman's Congress of the Pacific Coast, the articles that follow—"Viewed by a Woman," "Weeds and Flowers," "The Real Susan B. Anthony," and "The

Real New Woman"—paint a portrait of the first-wave feminist movement and its leaders.

By 1897, Michelson had expanded beyond women and gender to address issues of race, immigration, and imperialism, taking an approach that today would be identified as "intersectional." In "Strangling Hands upon a Nation's Throat," she reports on the US attempt to annex Hawaii from the perspective of the islands' native women who organized a coalition against annexation. Like Michelson's correspondence from Hawaii, "Dark-Skinned Lion-Tamer in the House of Mystery" retrieves women of color from the margins, centering on an overlooked historical figure, black abolitionist and entrepreneur Mary Ellen Pleasant. "Turning a Bad Indian into a Good One" details the government's attempt to educate and assimilate Native American children by establishing Indian boarding schools; it is one of Michelson's many investigations into the effects of US colonialist policy on people of color at home and abroad.

Themes from Michelson's *Call* articles resurface in her reporting for the *San Francisco Bulletin*. "Where Waves the Dragon Flag" represents a series of articles Michelson published about immigrant life and white-Chinese relations in Chinatown, while "A Military Matter in Black and White," which focuses on the experiences of black soldiers during the Philippine-American War, contains another pointed critique of US racism and imperialism. Combining elements of feature stories and investigative reporting, these writings can be read productively alongside a later article Michelson wrote for the Philadelphia *North American*, "Two Little Slave Girls Owned in Philadelphia." In this piece, Michelson's attention to gender, race, class, colonialism, and immigration converges in an exposé of human trafficking—and, by extension, of the nation's hypocrisy when it comes to extending its freedoms and protections to women of color.

While the articles collected here have, in many ways, withstood the test of time, it is important to keep in mind that Michelson's work was a product of her historical and cultural moment. Her writing was shaped by the socially progressive ideologies of her era, but these pieces also contain outdated views and language that expose her positionality as a middle-class white woman whose relative privilege at once enabled and circumscribed her encounters with people of color. These pieces should not be read and studied *in spite of* such limitations; instead, Michelson's biases and blind spots tell us much about white women's mediating roles in the mainstream press and the newspaper industry's investment in widening its readership by appealing to white female audiences.

At the *Bulletin* and the *North American*, Michelson continued to explore women's increasing presence in the public sphere. In asking "Does Matrimony Disqualify Working Women?," Michelson addresses the tension between women's paid labor and domestic duties, raising questions about gender and work that remain salient today. "Nevada's Feminine David and Jonathan," which functions as an obituary of educator Eliza Babcock and a memorial to her relationship with partner Hannah Clapp, similarly profiles the lives of working women; it simultaneously documents the experience of a same-sex couple, drawing back the curtain on what historian Carroll Smith-Rosenberg famously described as the nineteenth-century "female world of love and ritual." While many of these pieces illuminate the lives of ordinary and little-known women, a number of them offer new perspectives on the most prominent reformers of the late nineteenth century and early twentieth century. The articles on women's rights leader Charlotte Perkins (Stetson) Gilman, temperance crusader Carrie Nation, and radical activist Emma Goldman read as lively and incisive dialogues about politics and activism, documenting Michelson's relationship to, and with, other influential women of her time.

In selecting these samples of Michelson's newspaper writings and placing them after *The Superwoman*, but before the short stories collected in Part 3, I aim to highlight the symbiosis between Michelson's journalism and fiction. The articles on Gilman ("Charlotte Perkins Stetson Flays Her Own Sex Alive," "Mrs. Stetson Is in Town," and "Stetson Wedding"), for example, offer context for the feminist themes of Michelson's fiction and allow readers to draw connections between *The Superwoman* and Gilman's utopian novella *Herland* (1915). The final newspaper article included here, "Motives of Women Who Commit Theft," which treats female criminality as a by-product of greater independence, can be read productively alongside Michelson's short story "In the Bishop's Carriage," which is told from the point of view of a female thief.

Given the formulaic conventions of contemporary news reporting, with its emphasis on factuality and objectivity, readers today may be surprised to discover that Michelson's distinctive voice—with its jaunty, conversational, and often comic tone—defines her journalism as much as it does her fiction. Even as she reported on some of the most serious topics of her day, Michelson endeavored to keep her readers entertained and engrossed. We should refrain from writing off her style as no more than attention-grabbing sensationalism, however. Instead, her work needs to be considered as part of a larger tradition of literary journalism and narrative nonfiction experimentation that was popularized by realist and naturalist writers like Mark Twain, Stephen Crane, Theodore Dreiser, and William Dean Howells and that flourished with the postmodern innovations of "New Journalists" like Tom Wolfe and Joan Didion. Precisely because they are composed in Michelson's signature style, these newspaper articles provide rich source material for journalism historians and for scholars and students of print culture working at the nexus of historical and textual analysis.

Stylistically and thematically, the newspaper writings in this collection are representative of Michelson's most compelling work, but they also comprise only a small portion of her total output. For a fuller view of Michelson's journalistic career, readers should consult the bibliography herein to seek out additional newspaper publications. These uncollected articles range from an impressive trove of theater criticism to coverage of college and professional athletics that places Michelson among the nation's first women sports writers. It is likely that Michelson wrote many more newspaper articles beyond the ones I have identified. Although my research turned up references to Michelson writing for the Virginia City *Territorial Enterprise* and the *San Francisco Chronicle*, I was unable to verify these claims, due to the fact that turn-of-the-twentieth-century newspapers usually did not include bylines. Presumably, some of Michelson's unattributed writings also appeared in the *Call*, the *Bulletin*, and the *North American*. While I took note of news articles without bylines that bore the imprint of her style and interests, it was not possible to ascertain whether she was the writer. For the purposes of introducing her to a new generation of readers, I focused on the articles that explicitly credit her. Opening a window into Michelson's life and times, these pieces are intended to provoke further interest in this pioneering newspaperwoman as well as future scholarship that builds on my research and uncovers a vaster archive of her writing.

THE NEW WOMAN REALIZED

But Miss Matson Doesn't Believe in the
New Woman We All Talk About

Arthur McEwen's Letter, January 15, 1895, 9

Either the sights at Wonderland[1] are very marvelous, or the kinds of people who go there have vivid imaginations, and can dispense with such paltry accessories as scenery, costumes—atmosphere, in short. The hall is large and bare; there are no seats, and the light is such as the skies, clear or cloudy, may send. At one end of the hall, facing the windows, is a high platform, with a chair and a small table upon it. Here Miss Matson[2]— who has been a man for twenty-six years—in a rather loosely fitting dress suit, a tall silk hat, immaculate linen, and spectacles, sits and reads—or pretends to read, for I don't believe she's as indifferent to the curious gaze and comments of the public as she'd like to be. She wears men's clothes easily, with no affectation of coquetry, and her broad, large, florid face is impassive; but her eyes are not steady, and her hands are restless.

I believe she's honest when she says notoriety is very distasteful to her.

"I accepted this position at the museum because it is a very lucrative one. But I see no reason why people should be interested in me, for I am no more extraordinary"—she pronounces it as if it had but five syllables, and she hurries over the end of the word—"no more extraordinary than that chair."

Miss Matson's speech is brusque, short, and decided. She uses no slang, and no contractions. But her voice, though deep, is not a man's voice. Dress

---

1. Wonderland: a San Francisco dime museum.
2. Milton (née Louisa) Matson: a cross-dresser whose biological sex was discovered when he was arrested for passing a bad check in San Francisco in 1895. Matson subsequently agreed to exhibit himself at a dime museum.

Miss Matson in any dark, sober gown, and she'd be the stout, stolid, middle-aged, comfort-loving Englishwoman we've all seen—and don't admire.

Comfort-loving—that, I think, is one clue to the puzzle of this queer woman's character. I once knew an Englishwoman who, I think, would form a link between us ordinary women and the Miss Matsons. She, too, had sacrificed vanity to her comfort. Her hair was short and iron-gray, like Miss Matson's. She wouldn't hear of a corset. Her skirt was scant, and came just to her shoe-tops. And when these same shoes, thick and broad and ugly as a man's, needed polishing, she sturdily mounted a bootblack's stand, and sat calmly, reading the paper, till the work was done. And she, too, walked off feeling that she had done nothing "extraordinary"; and doubtless she had the same sort of scorn for, and impatience of, people's stupid curiosity.

"My life has been a very uneventful one," Miss Matson surprised me by saying. "I do not know why an opinion of mine should be particularly interesting. But if you wish my ideas, as you would ask those of any person of intelligence, very well. I will have no more of the 'Miss Matson' matter. I will not discuss my private affairs nor answer personal questions." She threw one leg over the other and looked very decided.

"Oh, very well," I said. "Tell me, please, do you approve of woman suffrage?"

"Of women voting? No; not I. The street is no place for a woman, nor are politics her affair. She should stay at home and tend to her household duties."

This was tempting, and I yearned to say: "Why, then"—but I didn't.

"You know," I went on, "one of the arguments in favor of the ballot for women is that their presence and influence at the polls would purify politics."

She laughed at this, tossing her head as though she hadn't much faith in woman's ability to cleanse the political Augean stables.[3]

"The thought of voting," she said, "is utterly foreign to my idea of woman's position. I am very conservative in that respect, and I dislike all this publicity and talk about women. I disapprove of advanced women. I altogether disapprove of them."

"Have you ever met any of them?" I asked.

---

3. Augean stables: in Greek mythology, Hercules's fifth labor was to clean the stables of King Augeas. The term is used to refer to tasks that require heroic efforts of cleaning, or reforming, due to excessive filth that has accumulated over a long period of time.

"I have not been so unfortunate," she answered, stiffly. "I should certainly not care to know a woman of that kind."

"Well, we women are going to vote." The pertness of my tone was the natural result of her priggishness.

"I shouldn't be surprised at anything American women might do," she said, contemptuously.

"Are English women so much nicer?" I asked, sweetly.

"English women are more reserved, more dignified, more domestic. They do not court notoriety."

"Oh, they don't. Don't they? Then why have you"—It was what I thought only. What I said was:

"Then you'd have a woman possess all the conventional virtues, enough for herself and her husband, too, I suppose. She should stay at home?"

Miss Matson nodded her close-cropped, big gray head,

"She should mind the babies?"

She smiled assent. But Miss Matson's smile is not genial.

"She should go to church?"

"No. I don't believe in humbug."

"Well, but all of us," I said piteously, "can't get married. Some are doomed to be old maids, and not all are fortunate enough to have some one to support them."

"Why don't you make a move to turn out these big things from behind the counters in your shops? Let the women have their places, and set them to shoveling—doing men's work."

"Then you'd have us all shop girls?"

"Or school teachers, or seamstresses, or milliners." She waved a large, fat hand vaguely.

"A doctor, now," I said hopefully. "Don't you think there ought to be women physicians to treat women?"

"I do not."

"Nor lawyers?"

Miss Matson looked almost shocked, and quite disgusted.

"No."

"And clergymen—or, rather clergywomen?"

Miss Matson's disdainful shrug was like a man's, lifting not only the shoulders, but the whole chest.

"If you had a daughter"—I began.

"My dear madam," she interrupted, hastily, "I can't imagine such a possibility!"

"Well, your sister, then. You'd wish her to live a perfectly conventional life, to marry, and all the rest of it?"

"I certainly should."

I wished there was something stronger than an interest in an imaginary sister that I might appeal to.

"Don't you think that women sometimes choose the wrong path in their youth, and then are carried on just by the momentum of their first enthusiasm?"

"That may be." She pursed up her mouth and lifted her light eyebrows. "Sarah Bernhardt[4] said to me about eighteen months ago, 'My life—one bungle!'"

It was funny to see her unconscious attempt at imitation of the Bernhardt—the most female of feminines. Any man could have done it better.

"Do you think," I asked, "that Bernhardt actually regrets her life?"

"She is a bad woman, you know, a very bad woman."

"And is she finding out the wisdom of the old maxims we used to write in our copybooks, and see nothing in them but the height of the 't's' and the up-curve and down-slant? 'Virtue is its own reward,' is it?"

"I—suppose so."

It was one o'clock and the hall had begun to fill. The band was playing furiously outside. A one-legged man hobbled in, a group of Swedes with their blunt, stolid faces, boys—not nice boys—and a very few women.

The manager appeared, an elegant being in a dress suit himself, and a wide shirt-front in which glittered a large diamond, clear as glass.

Miss Matson settled herself in her official pose—"to work hard all day," as she calls it. I gathered up my muddy skirts with a glance at her polished boots and prepared to leave.

"All the same," I said, affected perhaps by the environment, "things are changing. Women will vote, and if they must earn their living, they'll become doctors, and lawyers, and journalists, and lecturers."

---

4. Of French and Jewish origin, Sarah Bernhardt (1844–1923) was the most famous actress of the nineteenth century.

"I hope I shall not be on earth to see such a state of affairs," Miss Matson remarked.

"Ladies and gentlemen," began the manager, and I went down the dark, wide staircase and out into the rain.

"Here's a woman," I thought as I raised my umbrella, "who has out-heroded Herod.[5] Compared to her, the most rabid female suffragist is a timid, shrinking, prudish, conventional creature. And yet Miss Matson couldn't be more illiberal, more bigoted, if she'd been a man all her life instead of only three-quarters of it."

---

5. Herod the Great: the Roman-appointed king of Judea from 37 to 4 BCE.

VIEWED BY A WOMAN

Miriam Michelson Gives Her Impression
of the Congress

San Francisco Call, May 21, 1895, 4

W/hen I stepped into a Sutter-street car Monday morning there was a woman seated in the corner opposite me. Her hair was a faded, grayish red, her face was lined and rather colorless, and her prominent pale blue eyes were tearful and melancholy. But she was really more mindless than miserable, and her sorrowful appearance, it seemed to me, was due more to weakness than to woe. More women entered the car on its way downtown, a mother with her two daughters, a gray-haired woman and others. Their faces were just the ordinary, preoccupied faces of women who haven't much time or wish for thought or action other than the duties which are typically feminine.

At Larkin street a crowd of women came in. They were on their way to the Women's Congress. You would have known it by the important-looking little documents they carried, by the fuss and flutter of their conversation, by the demure, business-like style of their clothes, but most of all by an awakened sexless intelligence in their faces and the self-confidence in their brisk movements. The women already in the car looked them over from toe to bonnet; then their faces subsided into indifference and self-absorption—all but the woman in the corner. She seemed fascinated by the new woman. She stared at her, she knit her light brows feebly, and positively forgot her troubles in watching this new kind of female. When the car stopped at the corner and with a bustling dignity the new woman alighted, suddenly the old woman rose too in a dazed, uncertain way and followed the crowd. She passed into the hall and I lost sight of her.

Women, women! All kinds and degrees of women. They filled hall and balcony; they stood against the walls, and, standing, filled the aisles. They were enthusiastic and hopeful and full of excitement.

"I do hope they'll begin on time. Women never do, you know," said an excitable, well-dressed young matron.

"Perhaps they're waiting for some man. A man's name is first on the programme—or rather program," chuckled a bright-faced woman with short dark hair streaked with gray.

The other smiled appreciatively, then she said, "Well, you know, punctuality isn't one of woman's virtues."

"I don't know about that," said the other stoutly. "I'm always on time and so are you."

"Yes, but we both were business women. Besides, you know, men make such fun of us about that."

The short-haired woman sniffed rather scornfully.

"This morning," she said, "coming over on the boat there was just the homeliest woman I ever saw. A regular fright. John said, 'I bet she's going to the Woman's Congress.' 'I bet a nickel she isn't.' I said. So we watched her, and when she got off at Kearny street I collected my bet. But I got more than a nickel's worth of satisfaction out of it."

There was triumph in every woman's eye when half-past ten arrived, and with it the president and principal members of the congress. So much for man's accepted ideas of woman. But although there is a tendency in some of the speakers to attribute all the ills that flesh and morals are heir to to the political slavery of women, I heard nothing at all of "tyrant man." On the contrary, a gentle, forbearing patience was manifest in most of the allusions to him. He is unhappily in the wrong, but that is his misfortune, not his fault, and with time and feminine remedies they hope to enlighten and ultimately to convert him. I discovered, too, that although the new woman insists upon sharing man's political and business life, she intends that he shall be compensated by increased responsibility as husband and father.

"Every mother owes it to her child that he be well-born," read an essayist yesterday.

"And so does every father," she added in one of those significant asides, which characterize women's speeches.

But the most striking thing about this woman's convention is the spirit of camaraderie it fosters. At Golden Gate Hall women are actually so interested in things that they put aside forms. Introductions are unnecessary. If you can tell your neighbor that that shy, sunburned, dark-haired girl is Beatrice Harraden;[6] that this woman with the intellectual oval face is Charlotte Perkins Stetson,[7] that that one who wears her hair in a gray mane down her back is Laura de Force Gordon;[8] that the bust is of Lucretia Mott;[9] if you know which is Susan B. Anthony[10] and the Rev. Anna Shaw;[11] if you know who is the woman in the swell gown and the one that looks like a guy, the woman next to you will not hesitate to make use of you. I saw a young woman rise and offer her chair in a very gentlemanly manner to an older woman she did not know, saying simply, "I should have liked to give you a seat before, but the crowd is so great I couldn't get out."

These congress women seem to have lost some feminine vices and gained some masculine virtues. Their self-possession is not the assertive arrogance of small-minded, notoriety-seeking females. Their conviction is tempered with dignity and charity. They are not shrewish, and they deliver their message in a frank, good-natured way. They have learned how to disagree without quarreling, and they are willing to admit that there are two sides to a question and an infinite number of points of view. I don't know that this makes them more admirable to men, but it makes them more women's women. The audience yesterday certainly showed great enthusiasm; they indulged in that feminine kind of applause known as the Chautauqua salute,[12] and the speakers were quite old-womanly in their allusions to "Dear Aunt Susan," "Saint Susan B. Anthony," "That martyr, Lucretia Mott," and "Our dear Elizabeth Cady Stanton." But there is an accent of sincerity and

---

6. Beatrice Harraden (1864–1936): British writer and suffragist.

7. Charlotte Perkins Stetson (1860–1935): American writer and women's rights activist.

8. Laura de Force Gordon (1838–1907): California lawyer, editor, and social reformer.

9. Lucretia Mott (1793–1880): American women's rights activist and abolitionist.

10. Susan B. Anthony (1820–1906): founder of the National Woman Suffrage Association along with Elizabeth Cady Stanton.

11. Rev. Anna Shaw (1847–1919): first female minister in the Methodist Protestant Church, temperance leader, and suffragist.

12. Chautauqua salute: applause that consists of waving handkerchiefs instead of clapping hands.

evidence of unusual friendship among women in the accounts of those old days "when our ideas were not received with applause, nor ourselves overwhelmed with flowers," as Miss Anthony gently expresses it.

The congress woman is evidently deeply religious. "Orthodox of the orthodox," said Rev. Anna Shaw. Miss Shaw tells a story well. She is the most manly, not mannish, woman in the congress. Her voice is deep and full. She speaks clearly and can be heard all over the hall. She tells with a chuckle of Miss Anthony's wish to impress an Eastern audience with the propriety of their religious views, and of the unfortunate figure of speech she used when she introduced Miss Shaw as her "right bower." "But," gleefully adds the Rev. Anna Shaw, "every man in that orthodox community knew what a right bower is."

"The religion," said Mrs. Cooper in her opening address, "which is all for the next world and none for this, is good for neither."

"Amen to that!" came in hysterical, quavering tones from the back part of the hall.

Everybody turned around. It was the Old Woman with the faded red hair, who had sat in the corner of the car. Her pale eyes were bright with excitement, there were two red spots on her high cheek bones, and her hat was a little awry. But she was quite unconscious of people's attention. The chair upon which she sat had been to her a penitent's bench, she had suddenly come to a realization of new womanhood, and when the next speaker said in tones of conviction: "The new woman has come to stay," another heartfelt "Amen!" from the back of the hall attested the Old Woman's conversion.

WEEDS AND FLOWERS

Miriam Michelson Finds Both of Them
in the Woman's Congress

San Francisco Call, May 24, 1895, 8

O ne of the cleverest women in the congress said a very true thing the day it opened.

"The new woman," said Eliza Tupper Wilkes,[13] "has come, and with her her caricatures; the exaggerations, the cranks who accompany every movement and italicize it."

The speakers of the congress, of course, are the flowers of this strange new plant which has grown up in the United States. That there should also be weeds and wild varieties of the same species is not surprising.

The women who are talking to thousands of people every day at the First Congregational Church are of three kinds: those who are actuated only by conviction, those who love notoriety for its own sake and those who have the brains and ability to think clearly and to act honestly and sincerely and to talk entertainingly.

The first class embraces those well-meaning followers, whose tactless enthusiasm is a cross which all reformers must bear; the second comprises those to whom insignificance is worse than death, and the third is the soul of new womanhood, the model which others will see and copy, the fittest which will survive, the best and strongest argument for woman suffrage.

Miss Anthony has convictions so strong that they have outlived and triumphed over ridicule, failure, vituperation and old age. She has seen the world grow up to her ideas, and now she occupies a unique position in

---

13. Eliza Tupper Wilkes (1844–1917): one of the first female ministers in the United States.

women's affections. Miss Anthony is a woman of strong intelligence, of enduring friendships, of wide experience. Like other veterans she loves to tell of the battle she has won, but this is done so impersonally, so modestly and with such honest feeling, that even he who does not approve of the victory must needs applaud the victor.

Miss Anthony has talked on various subjects in the congress, but for her all roads must lead to the one destination. In her opinion woman suffrage is vital, is imminent, is the step which must be taken before further traveling is possible. Miss Anthony's style of address is not at all elegant. It is unmistakably sincere; it is destitute of pretentious airs and graces; it is thoroughly self-unconscious. She deals with practical things in a homely way. If she is at a loss for a word she is not at all ashamed to ask for it; if she loses the thread of her argument she acknowledges it; if the phrases and fashions of modern topics are strange to her she uses her own good sense to make principles of her own. She never quotes from a book or an author. She tells you what this man said to her, what that woman said about her and she has not spared the women of the congress the history of their early heresy.

She has something to say and says it forcibly and simply. But she is an actor, not a talker—a woman of sense rather than a woman of brains.

The Rev. Anna Shaw has both sense and brains. She is an impulsive, enthusiastic speaker; her voice is full and very pleasant. Miss Shaw must be very good-natured and quite as quick-tempered. She is impatient of shams, of cowardice and of the patent, stereotyped objections to woman suffrage. She has no particular reverence for man's opinion simply because it is man's. She speaks quickly and clearly, using vigorous words, deadly statistics and excellent judgment in the choice of argument. She is always ready to speak, and she is happiest in discussion, for she is able to compress a thought into few words, to pick out the sentimental flaw in sentiment and to see the ridiculous side of things.

Miss Shaw is original, quite fearless and there is something very human about her. She is the comedy element of the congress, but her humor is not undignified, and when she is serious there is not a woman in the hall whose speech is so effective.

Charlotte Perkins Stetson is not so human as Miss Shaw, nor so blunt as Miss Anthony. Her comedy is largely face comedy and her tragedy is too serious. Yet she is the most graceful and the most logical speaker in the congress. She knows how to give weight to her words, and her words are worthy of significant utterance. Mannerisms and affectations aside and Mrs. Stetson has not the self-unconsciousness which dignifies every utterance of Miss Anthony and Miss Shaw, and which is the redeeming feature of public speaking for women. Mrs. Stetson is the pleasantest and cleverest speaker of the congress.

Like Miss Anthony and Miss Shaw, she never reads from a paper; her address is delivered in a far-reaching, well-pitched tone; there is not the appearance of effort which detracts from one's pleasure in most women's speaking, and she knows when she has reached the logical end of her subject and when it will be most effective to stop.

If the women of the congress could vote, these three women are the ones on whom they would bestow political honors. The speakers whose addresses are remarkable only by reason of their egotism or their ignorance would no doubt be solicitous office-seekers, but they would not be chosen to represent a body which includes women of intellect, of good taste, of good sense, of brains and of heart.

The Real Susan B. Anthony

Arthur McEwen's Letter, May 25, 1895, 9

Susan B. Anthony is one of the most dignified women I ever met. To the man or woman who has not seen or spoken to Miss Anthony, and who knows her only as the representative of an obnoxious principle, this, of course, sounds like a paradox. But I should recommend an interview with Miss Anthony to those to whom "woman suffragist" means a female who has alienated from herself and her companions the sympathy and the respect of both men and women.

Miss Anthony's manner is courteous, kindly, and refreshingly unaffected. There is not the slightest self-consciousness about her. No thought of a pose. She speaks slowly, but directly. She pauses occasionally to think, but she is too busy and earnest a woman to spend time on the manner of her expression, and she never changes a word or hesitates in the use of it.

I expected to find her hard and pugnacious, the result of a life-long battle; but, I believe, the struggle has broadened instead of narrowed Miss Anthony's sympathies, because her character is too strong and well-poised to be shaken merely by mindless unpopularity. As she sat in a large dark-red arm-chair, dressed in a black gown which was neither extravagantly fashionable nor conspicuously out of date, with large soft sleeves and a certain white daintiness about the throat her fine, strong old face, with its simply arranged white hair, turned toward me, she looked like a woman whom one might love and respect, and I believe the younger women who wait upon her and hover round her at the Congress are more sincere in their protestations and evidences of affection for her than women usually are.

"Will you tell me, Miss Anthony, what good this Woman's Congress does, what it will accomplish?" I asked.

"Nothing, practically. That is, nothing towards giving women the ballot.

But as a sentiment raiser, it will give women something to think about, something to work for."

"It seems to me," I said, cautiously, "that you are better fitted to judge women than any other woman, or man either. You have met so many and so many kinds of them. Now, some of these women at the Congress—"

"Aren't they funny?" Her smile softened the keen, clear-cut face.

"Don't you despair, sometimes," I asked, "when you see the weakness and the dullness in so many women's faces?"

Miss Anthony leaned forward and clasped her thin, knotted hands about her knee.

"There's an old saying that a man will never make a collection of keys, unless there are doors to unlock. The majority of women take things impersonally. Give them an interest in life and they'll make the application. A surrogate judge once told me that he never permitted a widow to shirk the administration of her husband's estate because he knew that she was or would become better fitted to take care of it than any one else. When these women have attended more congresses, when they listen to an address with the feeling of a potential power to alter, or to help the state of affairs the speaker is talking about, that uninterested, helpless look will pass from women's faces. Gladstone[14] said that a political campaign is one of the greatest of educational influences."

"Why hasn't the possession of the ballot, then, done more for men?"

"It has," came an impetuous voice from the door-way. It was the Reverend Anna Shaw, Miss Anthony's staunch "right-bower"; her "bonnet-holder," as she modestly called herself. "Else what has made the difference between the American man and the Russian serf?"

"Talk to Miss Shaw," Miss Anthony said, "while I go up-stairs and get my bonnet. Then we'll go up to the hall together." She left the room with a firm, business-like step, and I faced Miss Shaw.

"You all talk, Miss Shaw, of the benefit the ballot will be to women. How will woman suffrage affect men?"

"It will benefit them as much as it does women. It is impossible to improve woman's condition without improving man's." Miss Shaw speaks quickly and very decidedly.

---

14. William Ewart Gladstone (1809–1898): former prime minister of Great Britain.

"But by giving the ballot to women you only increase the great mass of ignorant voters. You add a few, comparatively, intelligent voters, while the mass of women—"

"I don't agree with you," said Miss Shaw, earnestly. "Statistics"—this stout, gray-haired woman with the youthful face and pleasant voice is great on facts and figures—"statistics prove that for every boy graduated from our schools there are five girls. It is the women who are the intelligent, reading, well-informed, educated class."

"Don't you think," I ventured, timidly, "that the granting of the right to vote to women will forfeit for them the privilege of polite attention from men?"

"In Cheyenne," said Miss Shaw, dryly, "the men treat the women with much greater consideration than they did before women could vote. They want their votes. So they're polite."[15]

"At election time?"

"Yes; and afterwards, too. All men who are not office-holders want to become such at some future time. Why, after all, a man has more respect for a woman with a mind. He'll play with the wax-doll kind."

"And marry them," I added.

"Yes, and marry them," agreed Miss Shaw.

"Then don't you think the change in women will lead to fewer marriages, there being fewer wax dolls to go around?"

"I hope it will. Not one woman in ten is fit to marry nowadays, and not one man in a hundred."

Miss Anthony came down-stairs with her shawl over her arm just then, and we three walked toward the car. Her step was as light and brisk as ours, and when I said to Miss Shaw, "Shall I offer to help Miss Anthony on the car?" she answered, laughingly, "Oh, no; Susan would think we thought she was getting old."

"Miss Anthony," I asked, when the car had started, "if men won't come to the Women's Congresses, how will you influence them in favor of woman suffrage?"

"Women will never influence the average man till women can vote. As it is, men know and women know that a woman's opinion don't count."

---

15. Cheyenne: the capital of Wyoming. In 1869, Wyoming became the first territory to grant women the right to vote.

"But wives have influenced their husbands."

"Never when it was a question of politics. No woman has ever changed her husband's vote."

"But what is the necessity for women's voting? Women may earn their living in any way nowadays. There is no opposition"—

"No opposition!" said Miss Shaw, explosively. "Why, my dear woman, I had to fight my way and earn my living while I was going through college, because my family did not approve of my adopting a profession. They would have nothing to do with me, while if my brother had planned to do as I have done they could not have done too much for him."

"The chief benefit of woman suffrage," said Miss Anthony, speaking slowly, and as if she had not heard the interruption, "will not be for professional women. The woman who wishes to become a minister, a doctor, a lawyer, or a writer will do so nowadays if she has brains enough. But the factory girls, the shop girls, need the ballot. It is the only means by which they can raise themselves, can help themselves. Men will not listen to them now; when they can have a representative to look after their interests, when they can vote, their lives will not be so cheap, their condition will be better, their wages will be equal to men's."

"Don't you think that the female vote will simply follow the male, that a wife will vote as her husband does, that woman suffrage will simply multiply both numerator and denominator, and so not alter the value of the political fraction?"

"No," said Miss Anthony, shaking her head slowly. "A woman will vote as she thinks she ought. She will obey no man's influence in that."

"In Boston," said Miss Shaw, "which is a Democratic and a Catholic city, it was feared that the women's vote in school matters would simply express the opinion of the Catholic priests. I say this," Miss Shaw explained, in her frank, manly way, "without knowing what your religion may be—because it is not a question of religion, it is just a question of politics. Well, there are fewer Democrats and Catholics in Boston's school board now than there were before women could vote on school questions."

"If the sex line should ever be drawn, Miss Anthony, when woman suffrage comes, if the women should outvote the men, do you think the men would abide by the decision?"

Miss Anthony sat thoughtfully looking at me through her gold-rimmed spectacles, and I turned with the question to Miss Shaw.

"You are supposing an insupposable case," decided Miss Shaw, promptly. "There is no reason why men and women should be antagonists."

"But if such a thing were possible," I said to Miss Anthony as the car stopped and we walked toward the church, "do you think men would sustain the majority?"

"Yes; I do."

"You have that much faith in their sense of justice?"

"Yes."

THE REAL NEW WOMAN

Miriam Michelson Likens Her to a Pleasant Dream, Not a Nightmare

San Francisco Call, May 26, 1895, 8

I went to the Woman's Congress expecting to be bored. From what I had heard and seen of the new woman I had come to the conclusion that new womanhood was in so crude a condition that its friends would only be pained by its premature exhibition. I anticipated hearing women "make fools" of themselves. I expected to have my sympathies alienated by hard-faced, hard-voiced, soft-headed women, whose only excuse for addressing an audience is the possession of a tongue and quantities of assurance. I expected to be repelled by the undignified effort a woman must make to be heard in a large hall and I imagined myself straining to catch the speakers' words only to find that they were not worth listening to.

I wasn't wholly disappointed. The women whose names are a pestilence flag to warn healthy-minded people to stay away and whose presence insures the absence of men and women of brains were there. But, after all, the close of the congress finds me with a greater respect for women's abilities, and consequently in a more hopeful frame of mind as to woman suffrage and the effect it will have upon women.

Judged solely by comparison with any similar association of men, the Woman's Congress has been, on the whole, a worthy, interesting, creditable session.

I have seen Miss Shaw set her teeth and hide her open, expressive face behind her programme so that the audience should not see her impatient scorn for some mindless, meddling woman, with neither good taste nor common sense enough to know that she was offending, just as I have seen a politician of tact and brains writhe under the sense of good work undone by the male blunderers and knaves and fools.

There have been sessions of the congress when the great crowd at the church sat or stood and listened to papers and addresses which were uninteresting, badly delivered and altogether purposeless; when the meeting became a dreary kind of commencement day exercises with the only redeeming feature—the youth and beauty and grace of the graduates—left out. But there have been many sessions when women of brains and heart and sense have talked logically, honestly, excellently upon subjects of wide range and universal interest.

The congress has been conducted in a business-like way. A little more experience and less consideration will be necessary, however, before the bores and the busy-bodies can be made to realize their insignificance. A curious feature has been the persistence with which women cling to the idea that poetry is always welcome.

Many of them begin their discussions with "I want to say" and conclude, or hope to conclude, with an appropriate verse. But the president, with laudable insensibility to the flowers of speech, has often spared the audience and economized time. The discussions, however, have shown a degree of practical knowledge, a wide-spread interest and an enthusiasm which are significant of the change in women. Many of the women in the audience spoke ungrammatically, some of them betrayed an hysterical inclination to preach, some of them made short speeches, remarkable only in being utterly foreign to the topic under discussion; but the general effect was to disclose a common-sense point of view, a thoroughness of practice and a surprising activity in affairs.

The reappearance of the superannuated, out-of-date woman suffragists has been both pathetic and ridiculous. These women have been galvanized back into public life by the approaching triumph of the cause, the advocacy of which formerly meant ridicule for them but now means roses for others. They have suffered in the past, and the prospect of future reward brings them back like retired warhorses to the combat, which is a modern one and for which their ideas and their experiences are wholly useless. They wave the bloody shirt of "tyrant man," which the latter-day suffragist laughs at; they are full of awful reminiscence; they are utterly impractical; they are a thorn in the side of the women who respect them for their age and their unavailing work in the past, but dread their effect on the work of the present and the future.

The tone of the congress is very devout. Not only the ministers but most of the other speakers and those in the audience "Thank God!" for something or other. As far as I can judge it is not a particular form of religion the women of the congress cling to; they are quite tolerant, but they insist upon some form of religious belief. To be irreligious in the congress is to be unpopular.

One thing to the credit of the thousands of women who have attended the congress is their appreciation of those who represent the better side of the suffrage question. The favorites of the congress are not those who love to listen to the empty babble of their own voices. It is the women who have something to say, who are fearless and tactful in saying it, who have minds large enough to realize the prejudice and sentiment against them and to make allowances for them.

The applause which greeted Miss Anthony every time she stepped upon the platform was due not only to a sentiment of obligation, but also to respect for her dignity, her good sense, her unpretentious, simple honesty, her quiet unwavering determination, her well-advised counsel.

Miss Shaw has won the women of San Francisco by the charm of her modesty, her kindliness, her keen sense of justice as much as by her wise head, her clever tongue, her sense of humor and her forcible, fluent speech.

Mrs. Stetson, Dr. Shuey, Dr. Maxson, Mrs. McComas, Mrs. Maynard, Mrs. Miller and Mrs. Campbell[16] are among those who have introduced us to the real new woman, who, by the way, is as different from the terrible new woman of our apprehension as a pleasant dream is from a nightmare.

16. Sarah Shuey, Abigail Maxson, Alice Moore McComas, Mila Tupper Maynard, and Caroline Hallowell Miller: suffrage activists who spoke at the congress. Along with Charlotte Perkins Stetson, Helen Campbell edited the *Impress*, the journal of the Pacific Coast Women's Press Association.

Strangling Hands upon a
Nation's Throat

Many Thousands of Native Hawaiians Sign a Protest to the United States Government against Annexation

Will the Great American Republic Aid in Consummating the Infamy Projected by the Dole Government?—

Miriam Michelson Pens a Stirring Appeal on Behalf of the Islanders

San Francisco Call, September 30, 1897, 1–2

On Board Steamship Australia, Sept. 22.

Now that the *Australia* has sailed away out of the harbor of Honolulu, that wonderfully deep rainbow-colored curve of sea and shore and sky—and all that one can see on the horizon is a dim, low cloud, which grows dimmer and dimmer—the memory of the islands is like a dream.

Those great mountains, veiled in tenderest green from cloud-tipped summit to the ocean's emerald edge below, the silver waterfalls tumbling from on high down into the dark blue of the deeper sea, that extravagance of foliage and of flowers, the glory of sunshine on the lava-created hills and the benediction of shade in the dusky, wide ravines, beyond which rises mountain after mountain—it is all like a wonderful transformation scene, where splendor follows splendor till one is satiated with loveliness.

> Where every prospect pleases
> And only man is vile,[17]

---

17. From "From Greenland's Icy Mountains," a hymn by Bishop Reginald Heber (1783–1826).

Quoted the distinguished Congressman who stood beside me on the *Australia's* deck.

I don't know that the honorable gentleman alluded particularly to the Hawaiian Islander, or that mentally he made any distinction between white man and brown. But his quotation is particularly apt in the present instance. For here in Hawaii, the best beloved, the most richly endowed of all Mother Nature's beautiful family, the old, old struggle for Anglo-Saxon supremacy is going on.

The centuries-old tragedy is being repeated upon a stage small comparatively, but with a perfection of gorgeous setting and characters whose classical simplicity gives strength to the impersonation. The only new phase in the old drama is that this time a republic is masquerading in the despot's role. The United States, founded upon the belief that a just government can exist only by the consent of the governed, is calmly making up for the bloody fifth act—preparing to take a nation's life with all the complacent assurance of an old-time stage villain.

For Hawaii has not asked for annexation. There are 100,000 people on the islands. Of these not 3 per cent have declared for annexation. To the natives the loss of nationality is hateful, abhorrent.[18]

It is the old battle—the white man against the brown; might against right; strength against weakness: power and intellect and art against docility, inertia and simplicity.

And the result?

---

18. In 1893, American sugar planters overthrew the Hawaiian monarchy and established a provisional government under the leadership of president of the Republic of Hawaii Sanford Ballard Dole. In response to the United States' continued push for the annexation of Hawaii, 90 percent of the Hawaiian population signed the Hawaiian Patriotic League's Petition against Annexation (also known as the Kuʻe Petition). A Hawaiian delegation and Queen Liliʻuokalani presented the petition to Congress in December 1897, and, in early 1898, the Senate voted against the treaty to annex the islands. On February 15, 1898, the sinking of the battleship *Maine* in Cuba's Havana Harbor further fueled the United States' desire for expansion. The ensuing Spanish-American War (April–August 1898) reinforced the strategic value of Hawaii's mid-Pacific location, and the islands were annexed by joint resolution in July 1898.

"I tell the natives that work for me," said a man suffering from an acute attack of annexation mania to me, "you might as well walk out into the sea and attempt to push back the oncoming waves with your two uplifted hands as to try to prevent what's coming."

"It's purely a question of conquest, I admit," he went on. "We are stronger and we'll win. It's a survival of the fittest."

≈

The strongest memory I have of the islands is connected with the hall of the Salvation Army at Hilo, on the island of Hawaii. It's a crude little place, which holds about 300 people, I should think. The rough, uncovered rafters show above, and the bare walls are relieved only by Scriptural admonitions in English and Hawaiian:

"Boast not thyself of tomorrow."

"Without Christ there is no salvation."

As I entered, the bell on the foreign church, up on one of the beautiful Hilo hills, was striking ten. The place was packed with natives, and outside stood a patient crowd unable to enter. It was a women's meeting, but there were many men present. The women were dressed in Mother Hubbards of calico or cloth and wore sailor hats—white or black. The men were in coats and trousers of American make.

Presently the crowd parted and two women walked in, both very tall, dressed in handsome free-flowing trained gowns of black crepe braided in black. They wore black kid gloves and large hats of black straw with black feathers. The taller of the two—a very queen in dignity and repose—wore nodding red roses in her hat, and about her neck and falling to the waist a long, thick necklace of closely strung, deep-red, coral-like flowers, with delicate ferns interspersed.

This was Mrs. Kuaihelani Campbell, the president of the Women's Hawaiian Patriotic League. Her companion was the secretary of the branch at Hilo.

It was almost pitiful to note the reception of these two leaders—the dumb, almost adoring fondness in the women's eyes; the absorbed, close interest in the men's dark heavy faces.

After the enthusiasm had subsided the minister of the Hawaiian church arose. He is tall, blonde, fair faced, three-quarters white, as they say here.

Clasping his hands in front and looking down over the bowed dark heads before him he made the short opening prayer. He held himself well, his sentences were short and his manner was simple.

There is something wonderfully effective in earnest prayer delivered in an ancient language with which one is unfamiliar. One hears not words, but tones. His feelings, not his reason, are appealed to. Freed of the limiting effects of stereotyped phrases the imagination supplies the sense. Like the Hebrew and the Latin the Hawaiian tongue seems to touch the primitive sources of one's nature, to strip away the complicated armor with which civilization and worldliness have clothed us and to leave the emotions bare for that wonderful instrument, a man's deep voice, to play upon.

The minister closed and a deep murmuring "Amen" from the people followed.

I watched Mrs. Emma Nawahi curiously as she rose to address the people. I have never heard two women talk in public in quite the same way. Would this Hawaiian woman be embarrassed or timid, or self-conscious or assertive?

Not any of these. Her manner had the simple directness that made Charlotte Perkins Stetson, two years ago, the most interesting speaker of the Woman's Congress. But Mrs. Stetson's pose is the most artistic of poses—a pretense of simplicity. This Hawaiian woman's thoughts were of her subject, not of herself. There was an interesting impersonality about her delivery that kept my eyes fastened upon her while the interpreter at my side whispered his translation in short, detached phrases, hesitating now and then for a word, sometimes completing the thought with a gesture.

"We are weak people, we Hawaiians, and have no power unless we stand together," read Mrs. Nawahi, frequently raising her eyes from her paper and at times altogether forgetting it.

"The United States is just—a land of liberty. The people there are the friends, the great friends of the weak. Let us tell them—let us show them that as they love their country and would suffer much before giving it up, so do we love our country, our Hawaii, and pray that they do not take it from us.

"Our one hope is in standing firm—shoulder to shoulder, heart to heart. The voice of the people is the voice of God. Surely that great country across the ocean must hear our cry. By uniting our voices the sound will be carried on so they must hear us.

"In this petition, which we offer for your signature to-day, you, women of Hawaii, have a chance to speak your mind. The men's petition will be sent on by the men's club as soon as the loyal men of Honolulu have signed it. There is nothing underhand, nothing deceitful in our way—our only way—of fighting. Everybody may see and may know of our petition. We have nothing to conceal. We have right on our side. This land is ours—our Hawaii. Say, shall we lose our nationality? Shall we be annexed to the United States?

"Aole loa. Aole loa."

It didn't require the interpreter's word to make me understand the response. One could read negation, determination in every intent, dark face.

" 'Never!' they say," the man beside me muttered. " 'Never!' they say. 'No! No!' They say—"

But the presiding officer, a woman, was introducing Mrs. Campbell to the people. Her large mouth parted in a pleased smile as the men and women stamped and shouted. She spoke only a few words, good-naturedly, hopefully. Once it seemed as though she were taking them all in her confidence, so sincere and soft was her voice as she leaned forward.

"Stand firm, my friends. Love of country means more to you and to me than anything else. Be brave; be strong. Have courage and patience. Our time will come. Sign this petition—those of you who love Hawaii. How many—how many will sign?"

She held up a gloved hand as she spoke, and in a moment the palms of hundreds of hands were turned toward her.

They were eloquent, those deep lined, broad, dark hands, with their short fingers and worn nails. They told of poverty, of work, of contact with the soil they claim. The woman who presided had said a few words to the people, when all at once I saw a thousand curious eyes turned upon me.

"What is it?" I asked the interpreter. "What did she say?"

He laughed. " 'A reporter is here,' she says. She says to the people, 'Tell how you feel. Then the Americans will know. Then they may listen.' "

A remarkable scene followed. One by one men and women rose and in a sentence or two in the rolling, broad voweled Hawaiian made a fervent profession of faith.

"My feeling," declared a tall, broad-shouldered man, whose dark eyes were alight with enthusiasm. "This is my feeling: I love my country and I want to be independent—now and forever."

"And my feeling is the same," cried a stout, bold-faced woman, rising in the middle of the hall. "I love this land. I don't want to be annexed."

"This birthplace of mine I love as the American loves his. Would he wish to be annexed to another, greater land?"

"I am strongly opposed to annexation. How dare the people of the United States rob a people of their independence?"

"I want the American Government to do justice. America helped to dethrone Liliuokalani.[19] She must be restored. Never shall we consent to annexation!"

"My father is American; my mother is pure Hawaiian. It is my mother's land I love. The American nation has been unjust. How could we ever love America?"

"Let them see their injustice and restore the monarchy!" cried an old, old woman, whose dark face framed in its white hair was working pathetically.

"If the great nations would be fair they would not take away our country. Never will I consent to annexation!"

"Tell America I don't want annexation. I want my Queen," said the gentle voice of a woman.

"That speaker is such a good woman," murmured the interpreter. "A good Christian, honest, kind and charitable."

"I am against annexation—myself and all my family."

"I speak for those behind me," shouted a voice from far in the rear. "They cannot come in—they cannot speak. They tell me to say, 'No annexation. Never.'"

"I am Kauhi of Kalaoa. We call it Middle Hilo. Our club has 300 members. They have sent me here. We are all opposed to annexation—all—all!"

He was a young man. His open coat showed his loose dark shirt; his muscular body swayed with excitement. He wore boots that came above his knees. There was a large white handkerchief knotted about his brown throat, and his fine head, with its intelligent eyes, rose from his shoulders with a grace that would have been deerlike were it not for its splendid strength.

"I love my country and oppose annexation," said a heavy-set, gray-haired

---

19. Liliʻuokalani (1838–1917): Queen of Hawaii before the coup by US sugar planters in 1893.

man with a good, clear profile. "We look to America as our friend. Let her not be our enemy!"

"Hekipi, a delegate from Molokai to the league, writes: 'I honestly assert that the great majority of Hawaiians on Molokai are opposed to annexation. They fear that if they become annexed to the United States they will lose their lands. The foreigners will reap all the benefit and the Hawaiians will be placed in a worse position than they are to-day.'"

"I am a mail-carrier. Come with me to my district." A man who was sitting in the first row rose and stretched out an appealing hand. "Come to my district. I will show you 2000 Hawaiians against annexation."

"I stand—we all stand to testify to our love of our country. No flag but the Hawaiian flag. Never the American!"

There was cheering at this, and the heavy, sober, brown faces were all aglow with excited interest.

ﻋﻠﻲ

I sat and watched and listened.

At Honolulu I had asked a prominent white man to give me some idea of the native Hawaiian's character.

"They won't resent anything," he said, contemptuously. "They haven't a grain of ambition. They can't feel even envy. They care for nothing but easy and extremely simple living. They have no perseverance, no backbone. They're unfit."

Yet surely here was no evidence of apathy, of stupid forbearance, of characterless cringing.

These men and women rose quickly one after another, one interrupting the other at times, and then standing expectantly waiting his turn—too simple, too sincere, it seemed to me, to feel self-conscious or to study for a moment about the manner of his speech, so vital was the matter to be delivered.

They stood as all other Hawaiians stand—with straight shoulders splendidly thrown back and head proudly poised. Some held their roughened, patient hands clasped, some bent and looked toward me, as though I were a sort of magical human telephone and phonograph combined.

I might misunderstand a word or two of the interpreted message, but there was no mistaking those earnest, brown faces and beseeching dark eyes, which seemed to try to bridge the distance my ignorance of their language and their slight acquaintance with mine created between us.

I verily believe that even the most virulent of annexationists would have thought these Hawaiians human; almost worthy of consideration.

⸱Ŀ⸱

The people rose now and sang the majestic Hawaiian National Hymn. It was sung fervently, a full, deep chorus of hundreds of voices. The music is beautifully characteristic, with its strong, deep bass chords to which the women's plaintive, uncultivated voices answer. Then there was a benediction, and the people passed out into the muddy street.

As I sat watching them, suddenly I heard a timid voice murmur: "You will tek this from me?"

A girl stood beside my chair, her gentle face with its dark liquid eyes smiling down upon me. She had slipped a rope—a lei, she called it—of gorgeous red and yellow flowers, strung thick and close, over my head.

"But," I protested, "I don't see why. I can't do anything, you know, except repeat what you say."

"It—it is that." She hesitated, and then plunged bravely on with her broken English, she continued: "No one comes to—to ask us. No one listens. No one cares. Your paper will speak for us—us Hawaiians. Our voice will be heard, too. We are poor—you un'stan? And we cannot talk your language ver' well. The white men have ever'thing on their side. But we are right and they are wrong."

⸱Ŀ⸱

"They are not heathens—not cannibals, you see," said a voice behind me as I stepped out upon the veranda of the pretty new hotel at Hilo.

It was Henry West, a half-white, whom I had seen at the meeting.

"Of course not," I answered. "Who said they were."

"Why, a Boston paper—just lately said so. Have you met Mr. Keakolo?"

David Keakolo and I exchanged bows. He is very dark and his hair and mustache are gray. He has a prominent nose and large, dark, expressive eyes. I had noted him particularly at the meeting, for he was the one man present in a dress suit and he spoke often and animatedly. He smiled now, and said, with a profusion of gestures:

"I—am so sorry. I—cannot speak Ingli'. I can un'stan.'"

"Yes," went on Mr. West. "They call us savages—all kinds of names. We are not. We read and write. Yes, more of us—comparing, you know—read and write than in Senator Morgan's own birth State—Alabama, is it? I am so sorry Senator Morgan did not come to Hilo with your party. If he would come here as a judge—if he would hear both sides—we would benefit from it. Your country has wronged us cruelly. Cleveland himself said so. What could we do when the United States soldiers were landed in our streets four years ago? Let the United States right the wrong now—let her not do more wrong."

"Would you prefer the present government to annexation?" I asked.

"The present government cannot last. They know that themselves."

"But in time, supposing the islands are not annexed, don't you think that the natives will become reconciled and—and take the oath of—"

"Never."

And a quick-spoken Hawaiian word and a glance from Keakolo's black eyes emphasized the negative. They turned to leave.

"We are sorry that you are going back so soon," Mr. West said with pathetic courtesy. "We should like to show you the country."

I looked after the two men as they walked down the tree-bordered path with an aching sort of sympathy. They are so weak; their opponents are so strong.

🙖

I had to wait a short time in Mrs. Nawahi's little drawing-room, where I had gone to see Mrs. Campbell. The president of the Women's League, by the way, is the wife of that James Campbell, the wealthy Honolulu planter, who was kidnaped by Oliver Winthrop (now in San Quentin) and held for ransom in San Francisco last year.[20]

---

20. San Quentin refers to San Quentin State Prison in California. James Campbell was an Irish immigrant who became a real estate developer in Hawaii. His wife belonged to the Hawaiian aristocracy. In 1896, Campbell was kidnapped in San Francisco by a con man named Oliver Winthrop.

Every door and window of the room where I sat was curtained freshly in white. The matting floor was brightened by a large square of a checkered pattern, with broad shining plaits. And this is really all I noticed, for Mrs. Campbell entered, and I cared to look at nothing else.

Imagine a very tall woman, a full commanding figure dressed in the sheerest of lace-trimmed white lawn. The wreath of orange-flowers on her black hair and the orange lei about her neck were exquisitely becoming, and the loose gown's graceful flow and full train gave a charming feminine touch to this woman whose sympathies have placed her in so unconventional a position. But Mrs. Campbell is anything but a new woman.

"Do you women expect," I asked her, "to be rewarded for all your work? Do you look forward to being permitted to vote?"

The president of the Women's Patriotic League laughed outright.

"Why, we never thought of that. I am working for my people. That is all. When they are righted, when they are content, I shall be satisfied. You were at the meeting to-day. Did it not interest you? There are such meetings all over the islands. The natives are far apart. It is hard for them to get together. But they all think alike."

Her voice is exquisitely low and full and lazily deep. She speaks slowly, but without a trace of accent. Her manner is gracious and her face is soft, creamy, brown-tinted, with proud lips and languid eyes. She looks Hawaiian, but hers is an idealized type.

"Tell me, does your husband approve of your work?"

"Oh," she answered, smiling, "I could—I would do nothing without his approval."

"Are all families—native families—united on this annexation question?"

"Yes; I think so. Nearly all."

"Suppose a Hawaiian woman's husband in favor of annexation—"

"It is unlikely."

"Well, if it were so, would she continue to work in your league? Could she oppose annexation openly and actively?"

"Oh!" Mrs. Campbell leaned her head upon her large, shapely hand, upon which the diamonds glistened. "Oh, that would be very hard. But—if I were the woman—yes, I should work for my people anyway," said Mrs. Campbell, decidedly and with pretty inconsistence. "You see, they are so poor, so helpless. They need help so badly."

"And are there no native Hawaiians in favor of annexation?"

She shook her head slowly.

"I met a woman at Hana, on the island of Maui. She was."

"Wasn't she in the Government's employ?"

Mrs. Campbell spoke quickly for the first time.

"She was a schoolteacher," I admitted.

"Ah! I thought so. You see, the Government will employ no one who does not swear allegiance. Even the schoolteachers—women, you know—must take the oath. Why, take a private business firm. If a native goes into a store and asks for a clerk's place, if he wants work—no matter what kind—if he will swear to be loyal to this Government (a Government which he hates, which he has had no voice in making, which he hopes to see overthrown) he can get work. If not, he must do without. He cannot get work. He cannot vote. Everything is closed against him. Think of it. Isn't it a great, a wonderful sacrifice by a whole people for the sake of principle?"

"But how long will the natives hold out? How long can they?"

"Forever. Living is easy in Hawaii. No one starves here. The natives will never change."

"How about the exceptions? Do you others resent a man's swearing allegiance?"

"No. It—it isn't quite the same—our feeling for him—as it was before. But they are to be pitied, these poor people, who are given such a hard choice. And besides—" She paused.

"Yes?"

Mrs. Campbell leaned forward now. She had been lying lazily back in the large cane rocking-chair.

"This. In their hearts they do not swear allegiance. In their hearts they are with us. Do you think that the present Government could rely upon the native police if it came to fighting against their own people?"

It wasn't a question. Mrs. Campbell's voice and manner had become almost energetic.

I turned back after I had gone down the stairs and over the long cobble-stone walk, to look back at her. She was standing at the door in her cool, loose white gown, the orange leis on her haughty head and about her shoulders like a gorgeous string of deep flowering topaz; her large, soft brown hands were clasped and her sleepy, dark eyes were lit up in a smiling farewell.

The Portuguese driver was waiting at the gate, and as soon as I was seated in the carriage, he turned around and said:

"Well, what Ma'am think of the country?"

Ma'am thought the country was unspeakably lovely, and she proceeded to expatiate upon its beauties. The boy listened with a patience that was uncomplimentary. Evidently scenic description bored him. He shrugged his shoulders. Every nationality has the trick of some other nation in this mince-pie of peoples.

"Yez—I know," he said at last. "But what ma'am think going to come of the country? I guess they're"—he nodded toward the hotel where some United States Congressmen had been delivering speeches to all Hilo—"I guess they're going to take this country. An' ma'am (he turned squarely around now while the horse plunged along through the muddy town), what ma'am think 'bout these natives? I'm sorry these poor natives. They got no money. They got no land. They can' do nothing. I like see this country belong the natives—it their country. What ma'am think?"

But ma'am had come 2000 miles to find out other people's opinions; not to express her own.

ةلِ

The most interesting native Hawaiian I met on the islands is John Richardson, a lawyer. He came on the Claudine at Wailuku, when the little steamer was on the return trip from Hilo, whither she had gone specially so that Uncle Sam's representatives might see the volcano, the plantations—in short, all the sights, in a short time.

Mr. Richardson is of medium height, heavily built. He is very dark, and his black side whiskers are slightly gray. His eyes meet one squarely, his chin is strong and decided, his English is excellent and his manner is serious and courteous. He is quick at getting the drift of one's questions, and my short talk with him, while we were sailing away from Maui and past Molokai, interested me more than any other interview I had (for business purposes) on the islands.

"I met a man, Mr. Richardson, a native Hawaiian, at Kalului, I think it was. It was something beginning with a "k," anyway. He was in favor of annexation."

"Judge Kalua, a Circuit Judge," Mr. Richardson said, promptly.

"Yes."

"The native Hawaiians who favor annexation are of two classes: Those who are in the Government's employ and dare not do otherwise, and those who have some personal grudge against the former Government; those who expected more than they got. I believe you Americans call them soreheads."

We both laughed at this and then I asked him if he intended to sign the anti-annexation petition.

"Certainly," he answered.

"And how do the lower classes of the natives feel about it?"

"Oh, they're more obstinate than those who are better informed," he said smiling. "They'll never change."

"And do you think your petition will be heeded?"

"It should be. The United States can make no pretense to friendliness for the native Hawaiian, no pretense to honesty or fairness if we are disregarded."

"Of course," I said, "legally the present Government has the right to turn over the republic—"

"The republic! A strange republic where a handful of men are absolute and the great mass of people are disfranchised: where soldiers are on guard before the executive building and the guns stand ready in the basement to be trained upon the people."

"What is the sentiment of the natives on Maui?"

"What is it all over the islands? No native not in the Government employ is reconciled to annexation. And if the United States cared enough to have a secret ballot taken to find out the sentiment of the Hawaiians, not twenty natives would vote for annexation."

At Honolulu I met Mr. James Kaulia, the president of the Hawaiian League. Mr. Kaulia is a thoughtful-looking man, with a brown mustache and very serious, dark eyes. During our interview on the hotel veranda he smiled only once, and that was when he spoke of a man as a "P. G."

"P. G.," I repeated, wondering what in this land of vowels the term might mean. "Yes, P. G.—Provisional Government—you understand? We call those natives who take the oath of allegiance P. G.'s."

"And you people feel bitterly toward the P. G.'s, do you? An American told me that a Hawaiian never resents anything."

Mr. Kaulia's face looked forbidding for a moment.

"I guess—I guess he don't know us. We Hawaiians hate (the word was pronounced with such deliberation as to give it extraordinary emphasis), we hate the P. G.'s when they are—are really in favor of the Government. But there are very few—very few, who are not really with us. Take the police now, who have sworn allegiance, of course. Some of them have signed our petition against annexation. Not the head man, you understand."

"Isn't that rather unwise?"

"Oh, the Government will not find it out."

"But if I should publish the fact?"

"The Government will say it is not true."

"Oh!—Well, tell me, how many Hawaiians, natives, will sign your petition?"

"Thirty thousand, including boys over 15."

"There aren't many more than that in the islands."

"Not one thousand more."

"Will any white men sign?"

"Some. Yes. But of course a white man must expect to suffer in his business, and—and in society, you understand what I mean—if he takes sides against the Government."

"And if the United States annexes despite your petition?"

"Then it will be a seizure. That is all. Here! There are 2800 voters registered for the next election—the end of this month. Of those 2800, 1000, according to the Government's own figures, are what we call the Citizens' Guard; 200 votes more are the soldiers' votes and 1200 more are the Government officials. That leaves only 400 outside votes. You see?"

Mr. Kaulia opened his hands wide. The native Hawaiian has not a very mobile face, but his gestures are as expressive—particularly when his English is not fluent—as a Frenchman's.

"Tell me about your league."

"In every district—all over the islands—there are meetings, one a month. Once a year in November delegates from every district meet here in Honolulu."

"How many signatures have you to your petition?"

"Seven thousand."

"And how long has it been in circulation?"

"Since last Thursday, September 16."

"And are you confident that all natives feel as you do?"

"I am sure. The feeling is the same from Kaena to Hilo."

Which translated means from the Sierras to the sea.

☙

So here's a people pleading for grace at the hands of a great republic. Here's a tiny drop of mercury begging forbearance of the enormous globule that threatens to absorb it.

Poor Hawaii! She seems like a supplicating dusky maiden holding out beseeching hands to a great, swaggering brother nation.

"I believe I'll take your land, Hawaii," blusters the United States, like a big bully.

"I pray you, Brother Jonathan, let me keep it; it is mine."

☙

It has been said that there is no hospitality in these degenerate modern money-making days like that of the white people on these islands. Social life, I am told, is delightful here. Business hours are short. The climate forbids the exercise of and gradually saps one's energy. Men have leisure for social intercourse, and the comparative scarcity of pleasurable occupation in this isolated place induces a readiness to make the most of society—that refuge of the unfortunate leisure class.

Everybody who is anybody in Hawaii knows everybody else. The small white population, cut off from the rest of the world, living in the midst of the most conglomerate assortment of races, controlling the wealth, all official and social positions, with a superfluity of service in the black man or the brown or the yellow (or any combination and all shades of these colors), has evolved a civilization delightfully luxurious, exquisitely refined. Many things are dear in Hawaii, but human labor is not one of them.

Some of the bungalows in and around Honolulu are models of cultured taste, almost perfect specimens of what may be accomplished in the art of living—given a tropical climate and a swarm of inferior human workers.

There are estates here, a traveler tells me, which are rivaled in beauty, luxury and completeness of appliances for bodily comfort only by the homes of the Haytian planters.

The visiting Congressmen from the United States speak delightedly of the gracious hospitality of the people of the islands. They are charmed by the bountiful provisions made for their entertainment, by the generous spirit which anticipates every desire and completes every unspoken wish.

"There isn't a man among them who doesn't consider himself responsible for the weather, for the condition of the roads, for the success of the affair—whatever it may be."

It is all very pretty. There is a charm about life here which soothes the senses and dulls the spirit. It is easy not to think, not to struggle. It must be very pleasant to drift with the tide of bonhomie (especially when rowing against it is so disastrous), to become a member of this small class of cultured, wealthy men and gracious idle women.

In the South before the war, in France before the Revolution, society attained its highest development, of which this island society is an inferior copy in miniature. But this perfection of civilization is a flower—a sort of century plant—that blooms but rarely and for very brief periods. It is a brilliant, marvelously shaped parasite which twines about and kills the plant that nourishes it. It requires conditions which take years to build up, and which, in the very nature of things, cannot endure. For it means the subjugation of the many by the few; it means the enjoyment of the concentrated essence of life's pleasures by a small minority. Material enjoyment, too, is a commodity. The supply is limited. And that a hundred may live as an aristocracy, tens of thousands must be denied pleasure and profit and liberty.

اللہ

One's memory of these beautiful islands depends a great deal upon what side of Hawaiian life one has seen.

If you come to Honolulu for a short visit to a friend, say (and your friend, of course, belongs to the smart set) you will carry back with you the happiest memory, the prettiest picture of the place and the people. You will retain a series of vividly colored impressions of mountains, sea, shaded streets and cool, spacious, charmingly decorated salons. You will not soon forget how beautiful a scene is a great garden of tall tropical trees, covered with drooping sprays of crimson flowers, where the electric-lights look like other flowers of diamonds. The men in white duck and the women in lace-trimmed diaphanous gowns walk about and talk and laugh and listen to the sweet strains of the native music, and the soft evening air is a caress and the plashing of the Southern Sea accompanies it all like the bass chant of a full-toned chorus.

But if you go to the islands as I did—if you see and hear what I did—behind and above this picture you will see another, as if the photographer had taken two impressions on one plate.

It is the face of the native Hawaiian that looks through the enchanting scene—a dark red-brown, sphinx-like face. The large head is set finely upon a strong, full neck. The forehead is broad, with projecting brows. There is an oriental width across the cheek bones, a wide-nostriled, straight nose, a large, thick-lipped determined mouth, that is not loose, and a full, broad chin. The expression is bold, but wistful, and in the dark, somber, well-opened eyes there is a question:

"What are you going to do with ME?"

DARK-SKINNED LION-TAMER IN THE HOUSE OF MYSTERY (EXCERPT)

San Francisco Call, October 10, 1897, 29

O ne day a few years ago when I was on a Sutter-street car the gripman halted at Octavia street. The length of time we waited attracted my attention finally, and I looked up to see who the important personage was for whom that lordly being, a street-car conductor, waits.[21]

I expected to see a beautifully dressed, charming young girl—for even a car conductor is human—or a puffing millionaire, writ all over with the assertion that wealth is privileged, or a cripple, dumbly pleading that misfortune is exempt from the strict letter of streetcar law.

But it was none of these. A spare old negress walked up briskly, but not with undignified haste, entered the car and again the wheels of business turned.

She wore the plainest of black gowns, scant rather in the skirt, a long, large, full immaculate white apron, a green plaid shawl, a large black straw bonnet, tied down over her ears with a broad black silk ribbon, and a white collar at her thin wrinkled throat.

"It's Mammy Pleasant," explained the gripman. "We always wait for her and she pays us well for it."[22]

---

21. The House of Mystery was the San Francisco mansion of millionaire Thomas Fred Bell, located at 1661 Octavia Street. After the death of his father, Thomas Fred Bell Jr. brought a case to court in order to remove his mother from the guardianship of the Bell estate, accusing her of being incompetent and susceptible to the influence of Mary Ellen "Mammy" Pleasant.
22. Mary Ellen "Mammy" Pleasant (1814–1904): San Francisco abolitionist, entrepreneur, and civil rights activist.

When Mammy Pleasant walked into court Wednesday afternoon and was called to the witness-stand a courtroom fiend behind me whispered: "There she comes. She's smarter'n the whole shootin' match."

I'm inclined to believe that no character, however great it may be, is as great as its reputation. This gaunt, tall black woman, the most interesting figure in San Francisco to-day, compels such respect for her mental qualification—leaving out of the question her moral worth or unworth—that reporters have probably been tempted to add to the reputation she has for managing, for controlling, for using the power of the mentally strong over the weak. On the other hand a great lawyer, in closing his argument in the Sharon case, said of Mammy Pleasant:

"This old woman, without whose advice Sarah Althea Hill[23] says she did nothing, wrote nothing, promised nothing, has missed her vocation. If she has strength of character sufficient, not only to influence, but to guide and control such a woman as Sarah Althea Hill Van Amburgh[24] would have been glad to hire her as a lion-tamer."

The dark-skinned lion-tamer walked to the stand. Her face is very, very thin. One can scarcely see her hollow, dark eyes under the shadow of her scoop bonnet. Mammy Pleasant is aging—but not weakening. She walks with a firm, quick step and her voice is full, decided and has less of the negro accent than the voices of many white girls of Alabama or Mississippi or Kentucky.

This old colored woman is as self-possessed as—as Bernhardt.[25] She hasn't a particle of self-consciousness. She is possessed of a simple, natural dignity that makes the stares, the presence of a crowd of strangers utterly indifferent to her.

---

23. Sarah Althea Hill (1850–1937): San Francisco socialite who sued Senator William Sharon for divorce in 1883, claiming that they had been secretly married three years earlier. She later married her lawyer, David Terry, who was killed in 1889.
24. Isaac A. Van Amburgh (1811–1865): an American animal trainer who performed with circuses and was known as the Lion King.
25. Sarah Bernhardt (1844–1923): a famous actress.

She sat up straight in the witness chair and answered questions with a prepossessing readiness. When a long dispute interrupted the course of her testimony she drew up another chair, rested her feet upon its rungs and covered her face with her long, black hands. But it was not to escape the inquisitive gaze of the people in court. It was simply that she was weary.

Her habit of command betrayed itself twice—once when Attorney Schooler asked her what sort of book was missing.

"Bring 'em to me—those books over there," she said, brusquely, "an' I'll show you what it's like."

Later, when she had left the stand and had asked permission to go home, she stopped beside Miss Bell's chair to talk for a moment.

"Give me that chair—you take another," she said to the man who was seated beside Miss Bell.

And evidently it didn't occur to him to demur.

ﻋﻠﻢ

Mammy Pleasant, for all I know, may be the vile, mercenary intriguer her enemies say she is, or she may be possessed of that "great white heart beneath a black skin" of which her friends assure me. But her faults and her virtues must be those of a strong temperament. There is nothing weak, nothing temporizing about her. She is exquisitely loyal. Not even the awful, cumulating misfortunes of Sarah Althea Terry's terribly tragic life could weary the devotion of this tenacious, faithful old black woman.[26] She has been a good friend. I don't doubt that she can be a relentless enemy.

ﻋﻠﻢ

My interview with Mammy Pleasant should rightly be written up under the head, "People I Haven't Met."

If a foreign Prince comes to San Francisco your managing editor, through an influential friend, may arrange a short meeting for you, when only

---

26. Following her husband's death, Sarah Althea (Hill) Terry was committed to an insane asylum. See Miriam Michelson, "Sarah Althea's Mad Babble Comes Weirdly Forth from Her Living Tomb," *Bulletin*, January 22, 1899, 9.

stereotyped questions may be asked. If a famous murderer is to be hanged soon you may talk to him, provided your questions are not too personal or indelicate. If a great lady's daughter is to be married she will grant you an interview, if you will be sufficiently grateful. But tell me, ye gods of the pull, what is the magic string that will open Mammy Pleasant's door and Mammy Pleasant's lips!

I went up the steps at 1661 Octavia street and rang the bell and waited and—no one came.

Again I waited, and again, and presently a pretty-faced lad of about 14 appeared at the door. He was gentle, even smiling, but he was delightfully firm.

All hail to Mammy Pleasant! Any one who can secure service such as this must be a power.

Mrs. Pleasant was very busy. She was engaged. No, he couldn't really take my card up. He wouldn't think of disturbing her.

Did he know when one could see Mrs. Pleasant?

He couldn't say, really.

And Mrs. Bell?

Mrs. Bell was not up. He was sorry.

Evidently not a working woman—Mrs. Bell.

It was 10 o'clock in the morning.

And Miss Marie Bell?

Miss Bell was out of town, lisped the gentle, courteous little liar.

Too bad! and he didn't know when Mrs. Pleasant could see one?

He relented at this—just a shade.

"She might—might happen to see you from the upper window as you are going out and call you back—if you walk very slowly."

I'm ashamed to admit that I walked very, very slowly.

And I'm still more humiliated to confess that she didn't call me back!

اللهُ

I tried again a few days later.

This time an elderly woman admitted me.

I was so surprised at really being on the inside of that charmed door that I could only look about me in silent amaze.

A very, very wide, generous, deep hall, with broad staircase starting half-way back, and—suddenly, from above, a deep, imperious voice:

"Who's the lady? Who's the lady?" it demanded.

I wasn't engaged in any dark, diabolical scheme. But that authoritative voice made me feel as if I were. I haven't felt just that guilty tremor since the first school-teacher I had bade me read from a page that was Greek and Sanscrit and shorthand to me.[27]

"I'm bringing up her card and the letters," said the gentle, timid voice of the woman who had admitted me.

"I can't see anybody. What's your name?"

Up toward the undistinguished darkness I confessed my name and quality, or lack of it.

"You were here the other day."

"Yes," I admitted, like a culprit.

"Well, I can't see you. I'm too busy. I don't want to see anybody. If I want you, I'll send for you."

I laughed aloud at this. It was so unexpected; said so simply, though.

The harsh voice softened almost imperceptibly. It bade me good-by, and repeated not so crossly, "If I want you, I'll send for you!"

رالم

Up to the present time—and THE CALL's about to go to press—I haven't been sent for.

Is it possible that Mammy Pleasant doesn't want me?

---

27. Sanscrit (usually spelled "Sanskrit"): an ancient Indian language.

CHANGING A BAD INDIAN INTO A GOOD ONE

Results Obtained in Educating Lo at the Government Training School, Carson, Nev.

San Francisco Call, April 24, 1898, 25

It takes just one visit to an Indian school to convince one that Uncle Sam doesn't agree with the popular opinion as to the only recognized process of making over a bad Indian into a good one.

This is his recipe, as translated into words from his deeds: "Catch your Indian early: the earlier the better; when he is young and tender. At five years old, or four, or even three, is the time to begin. Wash and clean thoroughly, thoroughly, thoroughly. Season with the best you have of elementary education and simple mechanical training. Then bake slowly, conscientiously, for a dozen years, about basting carefully with healthy, happy surroundings. Serve with a sauce made up of good nature and humane treatment. The result may be recommended."

He allows $167 a year for the maintenance and education of every bronze-faced boy or girl who will leave the familiar, loved discomforts of the wick-iup for the neat iron bedsteads, the cozy sitting rooms of the school; who will forego the delights of broken victuals and cast-off clothes for the simple well cooked food and neat uniform.

There are 150 real Americans at the Indian school at Carson[28] of both sexes, ranging in age from the baby of the school, who is three, to youths of 18, 19 and 20. There are representatives of the Piutes, of the Shoshones

---

28. Stewart Indian School: an Indian boarding school founded in 1890 and located in Carson, Nevada.

and of the Washoes, and to one who knows only the blanket Indian of small Western mining towns it's a pleasing shock and surprise to watch this red-faced colony and note its exemplary behavior, the apparent ease with which it has grown accustomed to the restraint of the buttons and bands civilization has decided upon, the various occupations it pursues, the diligence with which it applies itself to English books and American ideas—and above all, to hear it expressing its opinions in good English with the smallest and not in the least disagreeable accent.

Very human I found these boys and girls at Carson, brimming with good nature, bubbling over with giggles, very much a l'Americaine. These descendants of Indian warriors are the most amenable, the gentlest of pupils, their teachers say. Rarely in some dark breast there lurks the germ of rebellion, the atavistic tendency which cries out against law and order. But, as a rule, it is easier to discipline Lo than his palefaced brother. As for Mlle. Lo, she's copper-colored sweetness personified. During study hours she sits in school demure and neat in her gray uniform with a red ribbon bow at her throat and another tying her dusky braids; but when she isn't studying, when she's sewing or washing dishes or making beds or helping in the kitchen she's attired in the female national dress of shirt waist and skirt, and she's merry and companionable and very interesting. She plays basket-ball, like other co-eds.

"And do you wear bloomers when you play?" I asked a girl of about 14, who sat hemstitching a handkerchief out in the yard, the hot sun beating down upon her uncovered head, with its shining black hair.

"No, no," she answered, vehemently, while a torrent of giggles went up from her companions of all ages about her.

"Why not?" I asked.

But she shook her head and refused to enter into a discussion of the bloomer question. There are two sides to it—the question, not the bloomers— in Mademoiselle Lo's opinion. She is conventionality itself. Bloomers are shocking, masculine, immodest, in her estimation. And you could more easily persuade these young women to forever forswear home and kindred than to don the humiliating objectionable, bifurcated garment.

And her love for home, and her brother's, too, is not a thing to be valued lightly. Uncle Sam himself has had to take this intense filial affection and regard for place into consideration. "Visits of pupils to their homes should be as brief and as infrequent as possible," says one of his rules. These boys and girls never outgrow their fondness for home. It's the strongest feeling they have, probably, now that civilization has robbed them of the opportunities for excitement and adventure the old, wild life held.

No matter what the degree of her learning may be, no matter what she may have acquired of white-face notions of cleanliness and comfort, the Indian girl clings to her early associations. When her squaw mother, trudging out from the nearest point on the railroad to the Indian school, comes to visit Mademoiselle, wrapped in the traditional blanket, a purple handkerchief tied about her walnut, wrinkled, cynical old face, her worn moccasins dusty, her gnarled, knotted hands, worn with scrubbing white women's kitchens, grasping the staff that helps her over the road, her patient bowed head bearing still the burden of the papoose basket, where the youngest of the Los wriggles and stews and sleeps—she is received by her well-dressed, intelligent-faced daughter with open arms, with the fullest of welcomes, with a heart and lips bubbling over with the love terms learned in the old, familiar tongue which she, like others, falls back upon whenever real emotion seizes her.

Here's a lesson to you, Mademoiselle Americaine of the Boarding School, whose little head is turned with crude, false notions of gentility, borrowed from your narrow-headed, full-pursed schoolmate; whom you envy and ape, and for whose sake you are despised and humiliated by the conditions from which you came. An Indian girl can never be educated into disdain for her mother. She can never be taught to be supercilious and superior and affected, and to belittle the filial love and obedience she owes that mother.

The belle of the Indian school at Carson is a young woman of about 17. Like her sisters she clings to the out-of-date bang straight across her forehead. But her eyes are merry, her nose is not ill-shaped, her mouth is distinctly pretty, and her teeth are a dentist's dream.

Ruby can sew. She is as accomplished in this line as a friend of hers is in the culinary art. And anyone who has tasted the kind of coffee she made for us to drink would issue a diploma immediately. The fame of Ruby's sewing has gone abroad, so that in another Indian school where a seamstress is needed she has been offered a position. Uncle Sam pays his employees pretty well. Ruby might receive a monthly salary in addition to her board and her clothes that would mean riches to the simple wants of an Indian girl. But she doesn't dream of accepting. Why? Simply because she couldn't retain the place. She knows that. The acceptance of the offered position means living far from her mother, far from Ormsby County, Nevada.

Every Indian boy or girl who is capable of earning any small sum of money is a contributor to the home budget. The people whose lives have been spent among the younger generation of Indians will point out to you one instance after the other of such unselfishness. Even the small ones, at times, overcome their love of sweets—for which no white-faced spoiled darling has more desire—and refrain from sending into town for the candy a stray dime could buy.

Strange to say, it is the boys who adopt the civilized dress and wear it most easily. The supposed female facility for change of condition does not manifest itself here. Among the girls at the Indian school a graceful figure, a pretty pose, is rare. Mlle. Lo has capped the climax of her conventionality by embracing—or rather by being embraced by—the corset. Perhaps it is this war between two inflexible materials—the Indian disposition and the pattern-making corset—that prevents a harmonious result. But young Lo is distinctly handsome in his gray uniform with its red trappings. He holds himself so well. He is tall, his figure is so straight and looks so strong. His dark face, when it is not of the broad, dull type, has a virile, serious air. His black eyes are keen, and his square set jaws make him look like a soldier. The crack regiment of the army might be formed here, if these young men can fight as well as they look.

"How many of you," I asked a group of the older boys, sitting studying quietly in a room, just before their teacher entered—no trace of that suppressed wicked excitement that pervades the Yankee mice when the cat's away—"How many of you would go to fight Spain if war were declared?"

"I would," answered a fine-looking lad of about 18.

"So would I."

So would every boy in the room, with the exception of one, whose round, dark face was turned squarely upon his fellows, but whose mouth remained closed obstinately. Uncle Sam, you may not count upon him. For some reason—for the youth's intelligent face belies his character, unless there's good reason behind his determination—you have not gained this Indian's good will. There's a grudge against some one or something American that mere clothes and food and shelter will not cure. It would be interesting to know just what injustice or inherited resentment or imagined wrong makes this young fellow differ with his mates.

These boys keep an eye upon the newspapers. They're well informed upon current events. Washington is their hero—at least it is his name that comes from most of them in answer to a demand for the greatest man that ever lived. Of course, this may be school boy prudence or the youthful hypocrisy that seeks to give the answer not in their own minds but supposed to be in that of the questioner. When the subject of woman suffrage was broached to those latter-day savages nearly every boy in the room declared that if the thing lay with him his sisters should vote. But when the question was put to the girls, conservative, demure Mademoiselle Lo cast down her eyes, simpered and declined to commit herself. No doubt she considers voting quite as unladylike, fully as shocking, as the wearing of bloomers.

But education and civilized surroundings have had their effect upon these Indian maidens nevertheless. Only fifty of the one hundred and fifty students at the school are girls. And the reason of this is not a feminine distaste for learning or civilization, but the knowledge gained by experience among the Washoes, the Shoshones and the Piutes that when a girl's mind is enlarged by study, by living on terms of equality with her brothers, by receiving the little attentions and a greater or less degree of deference which civilized man has decreed is woman's due, she is less and less inclined to act out the part which her mother, her mother's mother and generations of red women before her never dreamed of evading. In short, Mahala, civilized, with a good command of English, accustomed to decent clothes, proper food and just treatment, objects to being a drudge.

Jim—like all other Jims of all colors and shades at various epochs of the world's history—finds his squaw not so obedient, not so devoted, not so unquestioningly simple and confiding. As a great historian says, the advance in learning breeds a pessimistic, inquiring spirit. Buckle lauds this spirit, and to it traces all the glory of modern science. But Jim doesn't agree with Buckle, and when Mahala, after leaving the Indian school, pessimistically inquires of her lord why the greater share of the work is hers, and the greater profit is his, Jim becomes disgusted at her want of proper feeling, at her irreverent questioning of precedent, at her iconoclastic desire to destroy the time-honored decrees of the wickiup.

So when there's a question in old Lo's mind as to which, the son or the daughter, is to be yielded into Uncle Sam's keeping for a decade or so, the wise old Indian decides in favor of the boy.

People who have had years of experience in teaching and training Indians declare that the Nevada Indians compare very favorably in intelligence and docility with those in the East. They rank the Piutes first. The Shoshones come next and the Washoes last.

These copper-colored school boys and girls seem altogether happy in their surroundings. The kindergarten, with its circle of dark-faced babies, singing, playing games and marching, is precisely like any other, save that the voices seem a bit unfamiliar, not so shrill, more nasal, deeper pitched; and there is a slight sluggishness of action one doesn't notice in white children. I saw a group of girls chattering and laughing in the washroom, off one of the dormitories—models of neat, small, white-bedded, iron cleanliness—while they washed those round brown faces of theirs and combed the shining, straight black hair. They looked like pretty human brown birds. In the yard just then young Lo was playing marbles. These boys have good football and baseball teams. They were beaten, though, by the Carson boys not long ago. When I asked one of the beaten team for the reason he smiled slyly, and a younger boy volunteered the answer:

"Oh, they didn't dare half try. They were 'fraid of hurting the Carson boys."

Which isn't complimentary, though it may be true, so strong and well-developed are the Indian athletes.

But it isn't all play for these young Americans. Their industrial training is not neglected, and all the work about the school from running the engine to making the rag matting that covers the stairs and halls is done by Lo and his sister. There's a curious case here of a boy who reads and writes backward; who can read ordinary handwriting only when it is held before a looking glass and turned topsy-turvey [sic] as Alice saw it done in looking-glass world. There's genius, too here—John Howe, a Washoe Indian, who possesses a rare faculty of making mechanical drawings. The locomotive he drew from memory, after seeing a train but once or twice in his life, is declared by mechanical engineers absolutely correct in every detail, so quick and accurate are his powers of observation, so great is his love for everything pertaining to machines of all kinds.

They have a natural taste for music and drawing, but the great majority here as elsewhere is hopelessly commonplace. The Indian mind seems unable to advance beyond a certain point. When that point is reached an insurmountable barrier intervenes and forbids further cultivation. Cooks, maids, seamstresses, the girls may become. Those red-brown fingers which have learned to write and to sew so well are hopelessly incapable when it comes to a question of running a typewriter, even. For the boys, too, destiny has ordained only subordinate positions. With a few exceptions, I found a surprising lack of ambition among them. They expect and are content to become farm hands, laborers and kitchen servants.

"It isn't worth while," declared a Carsonite. "What's the use of spending all that money on Indian girls and boys who'd be happier and just as well off out in the campoodies, where they all wind up sooner or later?[29] There's many a white orphan lacks the care those girls and boys get over yonder. And I tell you, nine out of ten of 'em anyway go back to the old life as soon as they're allowed to leave the school. What's the use of teaching 'em to dress and act and talk like white folks when they take to the blanket and the moccasin as soon as they get back to the wickiup?"

The school at Carson is too young yet to answer this question. It hasn't yet sent out a young generation to battle against old habits and inherited tendencies toward savagery. It can point to individual cases, instances of such excellence that one is tempted to idealize. But enough time has not yet passed for the gathering of statistics which will show what proportion of Indian boys and girls "stay put."

Uncle Sam, however, intends that they shall be temporary; they will become unnecessary, he says, "when Indians shall have attained full American citizenship, and with it full and free entrance into the public school systems of the country."

And it's treason to the spirit of American institutions to believe that that time will never come.

---

29. Campoodies: Indian villages.

CHARLOTTE PERKINS STETSON FLAYS HER OWN SEX ALIVE (EXCERPT)

Bulletin, December 11, 1898, 16

C harlotte Perkins Stetson has written a book,[30] a book that will make her many enemies and a few friends; a book that will gain for her numbers of little-minded admirers who will quote her unintelligently, and as many impatient opponents, who will delight in misquoting or half-quoting her.

But it is a book that will provoke discussion, that will be anathematized, that will be admired, that will be everything but overlooked.

"Women and Economics" is the title of Mrs. Stetson's book. In it she has put the thoughts and beliefs she has often expressed in addresses, short articles and in conversations.

That Mrs. Stetson has out-Anthonyed Susan will be no surprise to those here in San Francisco, who have listened to the frank exposition of her extreme radical views on men, women and things—principally on women.

It is the purpose of this book of hers to show that to the financial dependence of woman upon man—a dependence once necessary in the history of the race, but now a detriment to race development—is due nearly all the ills that the world groans and sweats under. In the process of her demonstration Mrs. Stetson shows her clear, logical mind at its best. Hers is a thoughtful, candid book, containing much that is irrelevant, besides an absolutely

---

30. In *Women and Economics: A Study of the Economic Relation Between Men and Women as a Factor in Social Evolution* (1898), Charlotte Perkins (Stetson) Gilman called for the economic independence of women. The book made her a leading figure in the first-wave women's movement.

fearless, passionless, strongly argued discussion of the most vital questions of modern, civilized life, avoiding none, however holy or unholy.

There is a strong, scientific, unemotional tone to the book, a clearness of vision—despite the author's flight on the wings of theory—and a sincerity which demand a respectful hearing, however outraged you may be. And that you will be outraged is a matter of course, for Mrs. Stetson is speaking her mind, her whole mind, without the smallest mental reservation, without the slightest consideration for your hobbies, your prejudices or your deep-seated convictions.

Women—most women—will, at first, welcome Mrs. Stetson with delight in the strength of her weapons, in the good-humored blows she strikes. Then they'll meet one of those unsparing, ironical, epigrammatic sentences which strip pretense from habit, and they'll hate her—as she evidently expects to be hated. The average man, of course, will disapprove—disapprove so strongly, I think, that he'll refuse to read all that Mrs. Stetson has to say.

But on both of these, on man and woman, too, the audacious Charlotte has taken her revenge in advance. Behold, the double indictment, and then say, which of the sexes will most heartily condemn the author of "Women and Economics."

Mrs. Stetson does not believe that women are entitled to financial support from men. She argues that neither maternity nor the fulfilling of the house-keeper's position justifies her in being a non-producer. If being a mother is woman's occupation, the more children she has the more money she is entitled to. Mrs. Stetson goes on to show that the women who are the greatest consumers are childless often or the mothers of few children. Similarly she declares that if the housewife were to receive only what a paid servant would receive for her services, no woman on earth could afford to dress and live as even the middle-class American women do.

Work is good for woman as for man. Work is development. Work is necessary to the perfection of life—female as well as male.

"We are the only animal species in which the female depends on the male for food, the only animal [species] in which the sex relation is also an economical relation," she insists. "The female of genus homo is economically dependent on the male. He is her food supply." And the worst effect of women's being consumers only is not upon women, she declares, but upon man and upon the race. We have been trying, she says, "to make a race with one sex a million years behind the other. • • • In keeping women on this primitive basis of economic life we have kept half humanity tied to the starting post, while the other half ran. • • • Marry any man of a highly developed nation, full of the specialized activities of his race and their accompanying moral qualities to the carefully preserved rudimentary female creature he has so religiously maintained by his side and you have as a result what we all know so well—the human soul in its pitiful, well-meaning efforts, its crosseyed, purblind errors, its baby fits of passion and its beautiful and ceaseless upward impulse through all this wavering."

One thing has saved the world, Mrs. Stetson holds. "Heredity," she says, "has no Salic law."[31] That women have inherited from their fathers some of the qualities developed through experience denied their mothers has been all that has kept this old world half straight. But that men have inherited from their mothers—the innumerable weak and little women, with the aspirations of an affectionate guinea pig—qualities whose persistence is the result of her environment, is the cause of the world's misery—according to Mrs. Stetson.

There is nothing, no institution, no custom so venerated, so well-established as to be secure from Mrs. Stetson's pen. The old-fashioned home, she says, is a "strangling cradle." Our kitchens shall be taken from us. The home of the future is to be kitchenless, and one can imagine her smiling grimly while she follows this with the assertion that she expects an onslaught in the name of "mother's doughnuts."

"The feverish personality of the one-baby household" is also one of the passing institutions. Time will bring a baby kindergarten, she proclaims, to relieve the mother and to better the baby's condition. For women are not a success, Mrs. Stetson says; not as cooks, not as housewives, not as mothers, who lose fifty per cent of their children, "like the codfish." All this, of course, means the non-productive woman.

When women shall work and develop into the equal of man, then shall come Mrs. Stetson's and the world's millennium.

What holds us back is woman—the old woman, to whom, in her childhood was said, "Don't," while to her brother was said, "Do." The author

---

31. Salic law: an early European legal code that prevented men from succession to the throne if they were descended from the monarchy's female line.

ridicules the idea of women choosing professions insuitable [*sic*] to maternity. "Motherhood is not a remote contingency," she says, "but the common duty and the common glory of womanhood. Those mothers who persisted in being acrobats, housebreakers, or sailors before the mast, would probably be extinguished by Nature's unvarying process."[32]

Some of all this the women of San Francisco have heard from Charlotte Perkins Stetson's own lips. During the first Woman's Congress Mrs. Stetson was one of the cleverest speakers that appeared. She was marvelously self-possessed, witty, bright. While she spoke she stood easily, dressed in the simplest of gowns, with one hand behind her and her animated, clear-cut, sharp face held well forward. It is better, though, to read Mrs. Stetson than to listen her. That thin, far-reaching, high-bred voice of hers is a trifle bloodless, after all. Her printed words look more human. Besides, even Mrs. Stetson dares to say in print what she didn't care to give verbal expression to. . . .

---

32. Michelson's quotations from *Women and Economics* are not exact. For instance, in the 1898 text, these lines read: "If women did choose professions unsuitable to maternity, Nature would quietly extinguish them by her unvarying process. Those mothers who persisted in being acrobats, horse-breakers, or sailors before the mast, would probably not produce vigorous and numerous children." See Charlotte Perkins Stetson, *Women and Economics: A Study of the Economic Relation Between Men and Women as a Factor in Social Evolution* (Boston: Small, Maynard, 1898), 246.

Where Waves the Dragon Flag

Bulletin, February 12, 1899, 1

"Kung he fa choy!"[33] said the white woman.

"Happi-Nu-Year!" chirped the small Chinese maiden.

The white woman, holding her gloved hands clasped loosely, swung them back and forth, bowing low toward the Celestial children, who made a flaming spot of color in the dark doorway, from which the steps, black and soft with dirt, lead downward.

The Chinese girl held out a hand, small, narrow, pale, yellow, from the fingers of which depended slender golden chains with flat, beaten gold ornaments attached to the plain gold bands.

"Kung he!" repeated the white woman, proud of the four words she knew. "Fa choy!"

"Thank you. Happi-Nu-Year!" answered the brilliant-hued Oriental fairy, gravely.

For a moment they stood, the white woman with her hands still clasped in proper Oriental style; the small Chinese woman with hers outstretched to shake hands in true American style.

The white woman looked disappointed.

"The trail of the mission is over it all!" she exclaimed, sadly, turning down the alley.

"My! Ain't she silly?" asked the prize scholar in Miss Thayer's class.

The answer is not on record. It was given from a number of tongues and all at once, in the language which the white woman had used in beginning the conversation.

---

33. Traditional Chinese New Year's greeting, translates in English to "Congratulations and be prosperous!"

Across thousands of miles of sea, where west becomes east, there is a very much mothered young Chinese Emperor.[34] He has reigned twenty-five years, I was told last night in Chinatown, though when one has a determined, strong-minded woman for Empress-mother, it's a little difficult to tell just when one's reign begins and ends, and whether one is really reigning after all.

Of course this matter is of no importance to Young China and his radiant sister. To celebrate is the thing. What one is celebrating is a secondary consideration. And if it were the twenty-fifth year of the young Emperor's captivity, ordered by his terrible mamma, instead of his accession to the throne, your long coat, tiny Ah Hong would be just as glowingly purple, your cherry-red silk vest would be as gorgeous, your trousers would be green still as the San Joaquin valley, the red button upon your round black cap would be as fresh, your pink embroidered slippers would be as beautiful and as boxlike as they are today.

And your big sister, Ah Choy, would still wear that stiff gold-embroidered lavender blouse, with the pink and blue wide trousers, which are not curled about her ankles as yours are. Her hair would be waxed and done up in a chic bunch on the side in a net beaded and pearled, and over her shamelessly painted, sweet face—innocent as shameless—the tasseled silver and gold chains would hang from the wide, graceful fillet, flaming with color, while behind would flirt the long, rose-colored ribbons edged with beaded embroidery.

For such is the greed of youth for pleasure.

I have heard it said that even to the all-wise, end-of-the-century white children in the public schools, it is a matter of indifference whose birthday is celebrated, if only a holiday be declared.

---

34. Guangxu Emperor (1871–1908): ninth Chinese emperor of the Qing Dynasty. He ascended to the throne at age four and ruled largely under the influence of Empress Dowager Cixi.

The Chinese babies are Celestial butterflies these days, darting in and out of dark entrances, as graceful as they are unashamed of their finery; small, bowing, gracious tiny Mandarins, decked out as a color worshiper would ornament his idol, glowing in rainbow silks and shining tinsel, smiling with the consciousness which being good to look upon brings with it, in Chinatown as elsewhere, and lighting up the dark, narrow alleys as the flashing dragonflies glorify the black, noisome pool over which they hover.

Here in the doorway of her father's grocery shop stands a miniature Oriental Princess, Ah Git by name. She is just old enough to stammer "Kong-he"—congratulations, and "Fa choy"—good luck. But not a word of English does she understand, though her smiling, black eyes know instantly the significance and contents of the bundle of nuts and candies imported from China that her admirer carries.

This son of the gods is Yet Gee. He is robed in black of the silkiest and softest, embroidered in threads of gold, and his head, which he carries as if he were aware of his divine origin, is crowned with a salmon-tinted cap with a purple button.

Up the street comes Chow Yeong, resplendent in a pea green blouse with pink silk trousers, her head marvelously dressed, her small feet tottering in their white and silver boxes, by the side of Grandpa Chow. She is on her way to make calls this afternoon. She will climb dark, dirty stairs, she will descend into close, ill-smelling basements, she will hobble across cobblestones and slip now and then in the alleys when her foot comes in contact with the wet stones beneath the layers of red and green and yellow paper fragments of firecrackers. But at each place she will be received rapturously—for the Chinese are baby-worshipers on New Year's, if at no other time—and Mrs. Ah Lung and Madame Ah Fook will stuff her with sweet things and present her with "luck money" wrapped in red paper, and Chow, the old grandfather, with the thin, white beard, will bestow largesse similarly upon the babies of the house.

And each of them is a tottering poem in colors; only they ought to have a painted street to walk upon, with a sea of orange gauze for a background.

With the coming of night the baby fireflies disappear. Within a few hours Chinatown's population doubles itself, and the increase is a Caucasian one. The streets are packed with a struggling crowd, that eddies around the Joss houses, the gambling dens, the canopied flower stands, the theatres, the restaurants and the brilliantly lighted "Merchants' Club"—which your guide mentions with a significant smile and a sneer.[35]

Now is the time to cross Sacramento street and travel with one step into the Orient.

You cannot see the dirt for the darkness, and overhead, soft, glowing hexagonal gauze and rounded red Chinese lanterns take the place of stars.

You cannot recognize the Chinaman you know, for he has disappeared. And in his place is a long-limbed Hidalgo with flowing silked skirts, who walks like a prince, who talks like a courtier, and who surrenders himself joyously to the free, glad spirit of the time.[36]

The plaintive street cries, the clatter, smash and bang from the theatres' orchestra, the whining note of the soloist, the lilies, the balloons, the candy stands, the lighted punks, the incense, the riot of color, the pressing, curious crowds, and—thank goodness, the new sewer pipes about to be laid—it is all part of New China.

جمله

"Are your streets in China as narrow as this?" I asked the Chinese gentleman who did the honors with rare courtesy and a quick comprehension of the ludicrous, which is rarer.

We were walking through an alley so dark, so narrow that four people couldn't walk abreast.

"Just half as wide," he answered. "Room for one line to go one way and one the other."

So that it was necessity and not choice that made the Chinaman walk in an unsociable way, one behind the other.

جمله

Up the stairs, through the vestibule with its gorgeous banners, its chandeliers resplendent with prisms and colored lights, though the reception room, where the carved black, teak wood chairs draped in crimson are ranged

---

35. Joss house: Chinese temple.
36. Hidalgo: a Spanish gentleman.

against the wall as for a meeting of Oriental Ambassadors; on through the gilded, painted portal, past the great brass, incense burner, and into the presence of the gloomy Joss himself came Choy Lin.

In all the bravery of her New Year's costume, in all the timidity of her devout Oriental soul, she bowed before the high altar where the perfume of the lilies and the burning sandal wood made the air heavy with sweetness.

She shook hands cordially with herself, and prayed for a moment—for what?

For precisely the same thing the white woman prays for.

For long life—poor little Choy Lin, whose score of years haven't been so very full of happiness! For good luck—which is a vague way of begging for kindness, a sort of blanket prayer that covers all wished-for, or to be wished-for, good things.

Then came the real business of the day. Behind the first great altar and into the sanctuary came Choy. She took two little pieces of bamboo. One she held in her hand musingly for a moment, and then she breathed the word "Fong." Then she held the other tenderly, and called it "Ying."

There was a moment's breathless pause.

Then Choy Lin tossed the two pieces of bamboo into the air.

When they fell the piece she had christened "Ying" was face up.

Choy looked awed.

Then demurely, with her painted porcelain face she crept out, through the halls, and down the stairs and out into the crowd.

"Ah Ying," she was singing to herself, the Chinese version of the old song, "Destiny Meant You For Me."[37]

The Salvation Army's hall was dark. It was not yet time for services, a Chinese captain informed me.

"And do you find the Chinese ready to listen?" I asked him. "Are they really converted?"

---

37. "Destiny Meant You For Me": lyrics from Willard Spenser's 1886 operetta, *The Little Tycoon*.

"Yes," he answered, with important solemnity. "Chinamen worship idols. But they can be saved. I was—four years ago."

"Strange!" I murmured, as we were leaving.

But he overheard.

"No, it is not strange," he answered, with simple dignity.

ﻋﻠﻲ

This is the court of the Palace Hotel[38]—Chinatown's Palace Hotel, facetiously so-called. Its only resemblance to the real thing is in that it has four sides. It is a court, a dark, very dirty one, and it out-smells anything in New China. It is inclosed [sic] on all sides by low, dark dens, containing at least three berths.

Here on New Year's night lies Yuen Sing.

No silken robes of greenish gold for him. No tidy, quiet reception room where the dried watermelon seeds, the candied ginger, the oranges, the great Chinese oranges, the wine and the cigars are provided for the guest. No congratulations or good luck for him. No Chinese child, boy or girl, radiant in colors. No taste of the gambler's greedy joy. No hint of the Celestial dandy's conquests.

None of these is his. But he feels no lack. He has one thing that is all of these in one—his pipe.

The opium smoker's face is a haggard cry of pain. All save his eyes. These— if their eloquence could become audible—would surely quote, "Happiness was born a twin"—my pipe and myself.

"Do you know how much she is worth? She is worth $2,000. That is what it cost to buy her. Her dress must cost $50 more, and the ornaments in her hair that much more."

She is a beautiful creature, this Li Que, in orange and gold and pea-green and purple. And on her graceful, slender little body these colors seem no more to clash than they do in an orchid or in a peacock's tail.

Off the large room where the restaurant proper is, where the gamblers sit, losing and winning in a lordly, impassive way, where the tables are set for

---

38. Palace Hotel: a luxury hotel that opened in San Francisco in 1875.

the banquets later in the evening, there is a long, narrow, grilled apartment, which opens on to the decorated balcony beyond.

Here sits the Pearl of New China, with a face, unpainted, but sweet with the grace of youth and Celestial loveliness. She sips tea from a delicate cup. She smokes tobacco daintily in a short, slender brass pipe. She smiles, and she listens.

"Thy breath is sweet as the lilies," says an ardent, handsome dandy, in garnet silk gown, with pale lavender trousers. He sits at the table beside her. "Thy face is fairer than they. Thy hands is ivory. Thy heart—"

If he doesn't say it, he looks it, which is perhaps more effective.

All the while the musicians play a composition by some Wagnerian Chinese composer. Bang! Smash!! The fiddle whangs. The drum bangs. The cymbals clash. The whining, nasal song of a lesser Pearl of New China fills the interlude. Then over and over again this everlasting Niebelungen Lied [sic][39] of almond-eyed goddesses and bold-faced gods with queues.

༄

Later in the evening at this round table where each place is worth $25, the Oriental men of the world will banquet. Behind each of them will sit a Chinese woman of the world. She will listen to all that is said. She may even drink a bit of wine in the thimble-big glasses, if his Mandarinship in front passes it back to her. But eat in gentlemen's company? Never. It's shocking bad form!

Of course, if one is what my clever guide calls "a sport," he is not limited to one damsel. The greater the "sport" the more damsels in blue or pink or green or purple to trail behind him, like a veritable peacock's train.

༄

We drank our tea in a more modest apartment on the other side, where the table was set with quaint, tiny cups, porcelain spoons and dishes heaped with candied fruits.

---

39. Nibelungenlied ("Song of the Nibelungs"): German epic poem written around 1200.

"In China, of course," said one of the Chinese members of the party, "the number of a man's wives depends upon how many he can support. My mother chose my first wife."

"And did you approve of her taste?"

He laughed.

"Well, when I marry again, I'll choose for myself," he said.

"That was one of the swell places," said my guide, whose English is an idiomatic miracle. We were out again in the close-packed street, beneath a gambling hall, bright with electric lights. "Shall we go to see the tough places now, the real tough places? I used to be a guide, you know, here in China-town, and the American ladies always wanted to see the real tough places."

DOES MATRIMONY DISQUALIFY
WORKING WOMEN? (EXCERPT)

Bulletin, August 13, 1899, 9

W/hen Miss Emily L. Whalley became Mrs. George Beanston[40] at the end of the last school year she uttered a decided negative to the sentiment that

"Man's love is of a man's life a thing apart,
'Tis woman's whole existence."[41]

Mrs. Beanston did not say this to me. In fact, she declined to say anything at all to me, except courteously to decline.

"Do you intend, Mrs. Beanston, to make the disputed point between yourself and the Board of Education ground for a lawsuit?"

"I—I don't intend discussing the matter."

"Shall you continue to hold your position in defiance of them?"

"I have an important engagement across the bay."

"Is it true that you have been advised that the School Directors have no legal right to discharge a teacher for marrying?"

"You must really excuse me. I do not care to speak about this."

Mrs. Beanston has frank, determined blue eyes, the color of her silk shirtwaist; eyes warranted to keep reporters at bay or to challenge a whole Board of School Directors. She carries her brunette head as she wears her long, dark skirt—gracefully and well. She is pretty, and pretty sure of what she wants and doesn't want.

---

40. In June 1899, the San Francisco Board of Education decreed female teachers ineligible to work after marriage. Mrs. Emily Whalley Beanston challenged the rule in court.
41. From "Don Juan" (1818–24) by Lord Byron.

Mrs. George Beanston has committed the high crime and misdemeanor of marrying. In consequence, she is to lose her official head. At least this is what the School Directors say. Mrs. Beanston—by her actions, I hasten to add, nary a word on the subject could pass the discreet young woman's tightly closed lips—by her actions, then, which speak louder than words. Mrs. Beanston shouts defiance to the School Board, declares stoutly that Mrs. Beanston is quite as competent as was Miss Whalley, and, incidentally, raises the question as to whether matrimony disqualifies a woman for work.

Miss Whalley was not the only school teacher who risked decapitation for the sake of a man. But the majority of those who committed matrimony pleaded guilty, resigned their positions in the department and lapsed into what Charlotte Perkins Stetson scornfully calls "economic dependence."[42]

Still Mrs. Beanston is not alone in her contumacious refusal to accept pedagogic death, quickly and painlessly administered at the hands of the School Board, or to [inflict] capital punishment herself upon her wicked married self.

There is a Miss S. Strauss—or rather there was one. She is now Mrs. S. Harband. She is still in the School Department in a way, for she is officially described as absent on leave. When Miss Strauss' leave of absence expires will Mrs. Harband meekly go as the majority of her predecessors have done, or will she follow Mrs. Beanston's example and rebel?

There was once a Miss Letitia Blake. She became Mrs. J. J. Dunne, the wife of the well-known attorney. She has not resigned. Nor has she been discharged. She is merely on the day unassigned list, and till she becomes a regular teacher she may debate within herself the alternative of suicide by resignation or outlawry with Mrs. Beanston.

"Our position is very simple," said one of the executioners; in other words, a member of the School Board. "When a teacher marries, she marries a man who can support her. Or, rather, she ought not to marry if her husband cannot support her. The women who teach are employed by the city, and the city should employ those who need work in preference to those who do not.

---

42. Michelson is referring to Charlotte Perkins (Stetson) Gilman's book *Women and Economics*. See "Charlotte Perkins Stetson Flays Her Own Sex Alive" in this volume.

"Of two women who came to you for work, you could certainly employ one who had no male support—other things, such as its competency, etc., being equal.

"No, we do not uphold celibacy, nor do we discourage matrimony. Some of us feel that a married woman has duties at home that must prevent her doing as good work in the department as she did when she was single. But most of us believe, and we believe the people will be with us in this, that a single woman is entitled to first choice in the distribution of work. And there being an army of unemployed unmarried teachers, the teacher who marries forfeits her position."

No prudent, well-regulated school teacher will sneer at the School Board over her signature. I found teachers, though—some already guilty of matrimony, others perhaps only plotting it—who were altogether impatient of any justification of the Board.

"In the schools to-day," said one, "there are two principals whose wives teach. There are married women whose husband's [sic] salaries are at least twice what is paid the best-paid teacher in the schools. There are unmarried women whose fathers or brothers are better able to support them than a young husband is to support his wife. There are other women who possess in their own right enough to live upon all their days.

"Of course, the Directors insist that they will pass no retroactive measures. And, to be fair, no such measure has been passed by this board. But the woman who wants to help her husband, or who has been supporting a sister or a mother, and who is too proud to transfer the weight of their support to her husband's shoulders is condemned to single blessedness all the days of her life—if the man won't kindly wait till she has taught thirty years and is pensioned. Do you know of any such man?"

Which is a frivolous question unworthy the serious dignity of school-ma'amhood.

I find, though, to my surprise, that the women who are considered furthest "advanced"—if that's the way to compare the measure of new womanhood—disapprove of the Mrs. Beanstons. They have no sympathy with such a position—a position, by the way, which must be very strong or very weak, if discussion of it is so much to be dreaded.

The prominent women of San Francisco are disposed to take the part of the unmarried woman against her married sister.

"Should a married woman work?" I asked a number of them.

"No. Not unless she is compelled to."

"Suppose a woman ambitious, fond of her work, interested in it as a man is in his. Should she be compelled to give up all this upon which so great a part of her life has been spent, merely, because she is now Mrs. Beanston, say, instead of Miss Whalley?"

"Most certainly, if she is keeping some needy single woman out of work. She has her husband's love and strength to comfort her and to lean upon. Should she have that in addition to the independence which some unmarried woman is denied through her greed?"

"Then a woman who chooses the profession of teaching must do so with the idea that her work is merely secondary in her life; that it is a temporary substitute, to be dropped when the right man comes along? And is this the way to get the best teachers, and to secure the best work from them?"

"My dear, matrimony is not a bugaboo. You can't scare women with it. It doesn't frighten them. No clever teacher will be lost, in advance, to the State, on account of this rule. And, there is this on the other hand: What the School Department loses in experienced teachers it will gain in young blood, in freshness, in enthusiasm."

"And does this apply to other departments—to the law, to journalism, to music, to art? And if it does, can you wonder that woman's work cannot be compared to man's?"

"Well—it ought to, but some how, it doesn't. Still everything in this world is secondary to money. There can be no happiness without money. There can be happiness without married women lawyers and journalists and musicians and artists. I still believe the most important thing to be the higher right of the unmarried woman to employment."

"But if employment is to be denied or granted according to need given equal capacity—why should not the principle be extended to men, as well as to women?"

"It is, to some extent. And it would be to a greater extent if the State were the sole employer, and if, for instance, all the teachers in the School Department were men."

"Then you don't agree with Charlotte Perkins Stetson, that he, or rather she, who does not work as men work, should not eat?"

I asked this last question of Mrs. Foltz, the woman lawyer.

"No, I don't agree with Mrs. Stetson," she answered. "I am talking business, plain business. If a man has enough for two he should support his wife. And she ought to, or she should be compelled to give an unmarried woman a chance to earn her living. Odd that it should be a boon—school teaching, the most exacting work in the world.

"No, I don't agree with Mrs. Stetson. I'm talking business. It's all sentiment with her."

Sentiment and Charlotte Perkins Stetson! I don't believe that that cleverest of Western women, who no longer honors us with her presence, has ever before been accused of this.

No, Mrs. George Beanston, married rebel and still teacher in the Hawthorne Primary School, the most liberal of San Francisco women have no sympathy for you.

There is only Mrs. Stetson, to come trumpeting to your rescue, to aid and abet you in your rebellion, to declare that work is woman's—not single woman's and not married woman's—but woman's real right, to insist that woman's dependent condition is the true root of all evil, and to finish by preaching that, "When the mother of the race is free, we shall have a better world, by the easy right of birth and by the calm, slow, friendly forces of social evolution."

Have you read "Women and Economics" Mrs. Beanston? If you're the rebel you seem to be, you'll find that in it which will help you to support the disapproval of a whole dozen of School Directors backed by the best known women in town.

Nevada's Feminine David and Jonathan: A Sketch from Life

Bulletin, October 8, 1899, 9–10

"I will lend you a theme, O poet,
If you would only lend me your pen!
A theme that is worthy the effort
Of the greatest among men.

"No hackneyed tale of a woman's love
For one whose truth's at sea;
No hackneyed tale of a fearful wreck
On the rock inconstancy.

"Nor is it a tale, though rare were such,
Of love like a summer's brook
That bubbles with laughter between the hills
With never an outward look.

"No! The theme I will lend you, O poet,
Is not love of woman for man,
Or man for woman, all such are old;
They began when the race began.

"The theme is richer and rarer.
So rare, you may search the earth
And not find its like in all the tomes
To which though has given birth

"'Tis a woman's love for a woman,
That theme I would have you write.
And now you will grant that a theme so rare
Will invite a poet's might."

—Kate Tupper[43]

These lines are the first part of a poem that was written in praise of "a woman's love for a woman," eleven years before that love came to an end.

It ended in the only way this extraordinary affection could end—by the death of one of the two.

Miss Eliza Cilicia Babcock died in Reno, Nev., a few days ago, and her death has disrupted a unique and very beautiful friendship which has existed for over thirty-five years between herself and Miss Hannah Clapp, librarian of the Nevada State University.[44]

The real poem, though, is in the manner of life which these two women led; in the perfect union, of a kind so rare, between the two, and also in their dealings with their fellow men.

The friendship of Miss Clapp and Miss Babcock is an old story to Nevadans. It is so many years since it began; it has lasted so long, uninterrupted by the smallest ripple of discontent, that cynics have ceased to be surprised and scoffers have ceased to doubt.

Friendship between women is possible. A friendship as pure, as loyal, as lasting as any of the masculine partnerships whose memory the world cherishes and quotes, half in glory to man, half in rebuke to women.

As to the Nevada women who have demonstrated this fact as long as I can remember I have heard their names linked together. For the quaint soul-marriage that existed between the two was consummated before Nevada attained Statehood.

---

43. Kate Tupper Galpin (1855–1906): an American educator who taught at the University of Nevada.
44. Life partners Hannah Clapp (1842–1908) and Eliza Babcock (?–1899) were pioneers in women's and girls' education in Nevada. In 1861, they organized Sierra Seminary in Carson City, Nevada, serving as principal and assistant principal, and later opened the first kindergarten in the state.

There never were two women so unlike as these, who for thirty-five years lived in the same house, occupied the same room, lived absolutely the same life and possessed but one and the same purse.

The older of the two is a woman of masculine mind, with strong, almost rough-hewn features.

The younger was delicate, dainty, short and slight, exquisitely feminine.

The older one, the "man" of this strange, happy family of two, wears her thick, iron-gray hair cut short, her skirts, too, cut short; her boots are strong, thick, "common-sense."

The "wife" of Miss Clapp wore her beautiful soft white hair dressed according to the prevailing style. Her hand was soft and white, tiny and very shapely. Her feet were delicately shod, as such patrician feet should be, in high-heeled, soft boots.

The "man" of the family wears and has always worn a gown absolutely devoid of ornament, serviceable, straight-cut, simple.

The lady of the house dressed herself in soft, feminine fabrics.

No one of all the great number of acquaintances and friends, which Miss Clapp's strong individuality and well-balanced mind have made for her, has seen a jewel on this woman's finger or in her hair or on her breast.

Miss Babcock loved beautiful things and wore them gracefully. For her Miss Clapp had a diamond worth half a thousand dollars set in a ring, which was worn on the first finger like an engagement ring till death broke the compact.

Hannah Clapp loved to work. She was endowed with a good, practical mind, unbounded energy and an original way of looking at things.

Eliza Babcock found pleasure in home-keeping. The domestic triumphs over the holes in stockings, over dust in corners, over refractory recipes for cakes and puddings satisfied her womanly nature.

Hannah Clapp delighted in politics, in business, in playing the man's part with hammer and nails, when occasion demanded and household repairs were needed. She believed strongly in woman's rights.

Nevadans tell of her contemptuous words at a woman's suffrage rally. Her address consisted of only a few words, but they were very expressive.

"When I die," said Hannah Keziah Clapp, sturdily, "no one shall write 'Relict of ——' on my tombstone. As if, even in death, a woman's identity might not be her own!"

I think Miss Babcock approved of woman's suffrage, too—for Miss Clapp.

When Miss Clapp went on a journey it was Miss Babcock who put out her clothes and made up her valise. When the two went together to see any of the multitude of friends their long, strong, faithful life in Nevada entitled them to it was Miss Babcock who set her "man's" hat aright—that hat which never could set quite straight on the short-haired, large, interesting head—and walked out beside Miss Clapp, taking short, ladylike steps.

"I can't seem," said Miss Clapp to a friend the other day when walking down Market street, "I can't seem to keep in step with you. You see—you see," she said, sadly, "all my life I have tried to take short steps so that I could walk comfortably with Miss Babcock."

She succeeded in "walking comfortably with Miss Babcock" through a long life whose years take in the biggest and best part of Nevada's history. And this is how it came about:

Before the Southern Pacific had its rails laid across the continent, before Nevada became a State, before its present metropolis had half a dozen log houses to brag about, before Sharon and Fair, Mackay and Flood had learned their way about the underground city of silver which burrows beneath Virginia City, Hannah Clapp came to Carson City with friends who went to Nevada as to a wild, barren wilderness, where there was money to be made and privations to be endured.

Through a mutual friend she heard of Eliza Babcock, a girl from Maine, then living in Oakland. In a short correspondence between the strangers a partnership was agreed upon. The Maine girl came to Carson, and she and the young pioneer who had been before her started the Sierra Seminary, long before there was a public school in the State.

In these days of higher education, I doubt whether the Sierra Seminary would be accredited. But there isn't a school in the world that holds such a record as this poor, little, pioneer seminary.

For, you see, it was conducted on such unbusiness-like lines. The teachers seemed to think it their affair to comfort and strengthen and uphold and love, as well as to teach. You can't begin to name the prominent men and cultured women in Nevada and California who learned what books and these two women had to teach.

"It was a home," said an important personage down on Montgomery street, yesterday. "They took us into their very hearts. We weren't pupils. We were their own children."

"If you can imagine," said an ex-Nevadan, "how it would feel to come clear across the plain, fresh from college, into a wild, little mining town out in the West. If you can imagine how one's peculiarities and one's little efforts at civilized living were ridiculed. If you can imagine how sensitive and resentful one is when he's young, and how easy it was to get into a fight in young Nevada, then you can understand how I felt when I found myself in jail after a shooting scrape, and Miss Clapp came to me, like the man she is, bailed me out and took me home to nurse my wounds."

"If you were a man," said another man who is a grand-father now, to me, "and drink had taken such a hold on you that there was no resisting; and if a woman, plucky, strong, self-reliant, hauled you up out of the gutter, and took you into her spotless, old-maid's home, and kept you there till you were fit to live as a man, you'd realize how we, who did not go to school at the Sierra Seminary, learned more than Berkeley itself can teach."

Nature intended Miss Babcock for a typical creature of the gentler sex. Yet, so strong was her faith, so unlimited her confidence in the executive, energetic head of the family, that she seconded every plan, no matter how unconventional, that ripened in the head of this woman, who was a new woman before the term was invented.

Witness the building of the fence around the State Capitol at Carson, Nevada—that enduring monument to the business capacity of Miss Babcock's "husband."

It was during Governor Bradley's term that Nevada decided that she could afford to put a high iron fence, mounted on a stone coping, around the Capitol. Plans and specifications were drawn up, and bids were advertised for. The foremost and the richest firms in Nevada and California put in bids, naturally, for the State is a generous employer. When the time came to open the bids, there was one signed H. K. Clapp. It was the lowest one, and it was awarded the contract.

"I never had built a fence, an iron one," chuckled Miss Clapp, when telling the story, "though, since then I have put up wooden ones with my own hands. But I had recently come into possession of information about the cost of iron fencing. I knew that these great contractors would expect to make two or three thousand dollars, at least, out of the contract. A thousand would satisfy me, if I could make that out of it."

She did. She hired men and put them to work. In the morning after she had milked half a dozen cows, and helped her mate and co-worker to put the house in order, they two devoted themselves to their professed work, teaching. After school was over, Miss Babcock turned her attention to domestic affairs. After school Miss Clapp drew on her stout, thick boots, donned a long, warm ulster pulled down over her eyes a small, soft woolen round hat and went off to work.

For two or three hours daily, Carsonites could see this woman contractor—who had never before (and who has not since) undertaken a contract—standing about the Capitol, in all sorts of weather, overseeing her men.

When darkness came and work for the day was over, Contractor Clapp trudged sturdily homeward.

"I think," she would say, musingly, talking over her labors with her wifely confidant, "I think that'll be a pretty good fence."

And it was. It is, in fact; for the personal, conscientious supervision of Builder and Contractor Clapp is to be discovered in that celebrated fence after a lapse of about thirty years.

There was one time when Miss Clapp's unswerving individuality brought her into prominence, not altogether pleasantly. For the protection of these two women living alone in an unsettled mining town, a most savage animal, half bull dog, half blood hound had been bought. Miss Clapp's "Brutus" was the wonder and the terror of the town. He was uncompromisingly fierce, vicious. All day he was chained. At night he was loosed, his hoarse, deep bellow warned shuddering Carsonites for blocks around that Brutus was on guard.

In view of the delight of Carson in the Corbett-Fitzsimmons contest, it will not surprise you to learn that dog fights in the old silvered days of Nevada, were much in vogue. When a new dog came to town, respectfully heralded by human advance agents, a bout was expected. One particular new dog, a regular Jeffries of a dog, had made his first appearance in Carson, and when his admiring press agents bragged about his attainments, it suddenly occurred to a loyal Carsonite to suggest a contest with Brutus.

"Can we have your dog?" said a deputation of sports to Miss Clapp.

"Certainly," responded the obliging woman. "Go out and get him."

They went, but they did not "get him." Brutus nearly tore his chain to fragments trying to get them, and they went off without him.

But there were reporters in those days, too. One of them saw what should have been a story. He wrote up what might have, but what didn't occur, and the pink Police Gazette (whose color, by the way, has been paled by the yellow journals of nowadays) appeared with an account of the flight and a sensational picture of Miss Clapp at the ring side, applauding enthusiastically the upper-cuts and left-hand smashes of her Brutus.

Nothing is more characteristic of the difference in temperament of these two women, so closely united, so far apart in nature, than the way each received this publication. For a moment, Miss Clapp was furiously angry. Then she laughed out with all the enjoyment of one who can see a joke, even upon herself. But the gentle little lady, who loved her, was shocked and horrified. She never quite recovered from the blow to her pride, to her retiring, sensitive disposition. Years afterward, when both had grown gray, Miss Clapp would herself tell the story of her appearance in the Police Gazette. Miss Babcock would shrink and shudder at the thought of it, and then secretly, almost blushingly, this pretty, little old, old maid would bring forth the torn copy and with the ends of her fingers she would expose to a close, discreet friend the awful depravity of pink paper and printers' ink.

Fortune, came to these two in time. When the Centennial was being celebrated in Philadelphia these old maid school ma'ams went abroad, strange countries for to see. Stocks were booming on the Comstock. It was hard to say just what one was worth. These two single women might have been worth $100,000. They might be worth more later. In the meantime, their dividends from "Belcher" alone amounted to over $500 a month. So they traveled. They saw all they wanted to. They visited every place that tempted them. They bought whatever they coveted. They ordered furniture for their home in Carson from the most artistic furnishing houses in the country. And then, slowly, they journeyed back to Nevada—for it never occurred to these two loyal Nevadans to forsake their sagebrush home—to find that the bottom had dropped out of stocks; that their broker had held, instead of selling, and that three twenty-dollar pieces remained of their fortune, after he had been paid and discharged.

So again they set to work, the indefatigable two. Through the influence of one of Nevada's Senators, who has been a close friend of these women for years, Miss Clapp was given a position in the Nevada State University. They removed to Reno, where the university is, and there the health of the weaker one began to fail. But Miss Clapp's salary was a generous one, and the two lived upon it, sharing it as they had shared when they were rich and when they were poorer.

"Let's go to the bank, Duckie," the head of the family would say when pay day came, "and deposit what we can of our salary."

"All right, Miss Clapp," was the reply.

It was always "Miss Clapp"—a queer sort of pedagogical courtesy that remained long after these two were closer than most women who lavish endearing words upon each other. The head of the family, indeed, permitted herself occasional tender, protecting pet names, as a husband might. And so "our" salary was deposited.

Where is the woman married to a man, who has been treated with such financial consideration? In rare cases, he does hand over his wages to you, madam, but the money is his, nevertheless, given in your care only because you are more prudent, less tempted.

The wills of these two were made in each other's favor. Both had relations, who were thought of kindly, but all they had was for each other.

"When I die I shall be cremated," said the strong-minded one.

"When I die, bury me," asked the other, "where your ashes may be laid upon my breast."

The night death came to Miss Babcock. Her protector awakened with the feeling, as she afterward said, that "a mother might have if she is troubled about her baby."

The wife of Miss Clapp was gasping, but she put her arms about the neck of the one who had cherished her so tenderly, so unselfishly, so generously, and clung there with all the strength of her last breath. Her small, stiff white fingers had to be bent back, afterward, that of these two faithful comrades, the living might be separated from the dead.

A MILITARY MATTER IN
BLACK AND WHITE

Bulletin, December 3, 1899, 9

> This article was written at the beginning of the Philippine-
> American War (1899–1902). Spain ceded the Philippines to the
> United States at the end of the Spanish-American War, but Fili-
> pino nationalists continued to fight for independence from the US
> government. The Philippines was to remain an American colony
> until 1946 when it was granted independence according to the
> Treaty of Manila.

66 "Lieutenant Butler?" repeated the sentry. "Which one—black or white?"

He was black himself, but he put the question in such a business-like, impersonal manner as to require a like answer.

It was the black lieutenant, of course, that I wanted to see. Where is the private, white or black, who dares deny the salute to Lieutenant Butler—white? Lieutenant Butler, black, sailed yesterday afternoon for the Philippines. He took with him the knowledge that Uncle Sam's military rules may be interpreted two ways—a white way and a black way.

The white way is uninteresting, for it is the every-day interpretation. The black way is that most radically expressed by a certain white sergeant in the Third Artillery the other day.

"Take that coat off," he shouted to his superior officer (colored), "and I'll salute the straps, but I'll be Alcatrazed if I'll salute you!"[45]

---

45. At the time, Alcatraz was a military prison located on an island off the coast of San Francisco. It later became a federal penitentiary.

A moment later there was a negro lieutenant knocked down by his military inferiors. There was a dishonoring of gilt shoulder-straps, whose significance nearly a hundred thousand men were taught to respect during our last war. And there was a hasty lining-up of two rows of threatening men, one white, the other black, quite as though the war before the last had not put an end to race hatred in America.

"If I report a man for disrespect for neglecting to salute me as his superior officer," said a negro officer out at the Presidio[46] yesterday, "he is brought up before his judges, and so am I. To me they say, 'You are quite right. The offense is plain. It was an open disregard of military regulations.' To him they say, after I am gone, 'Well, of course, there are rules, and their meaning is plain. But I'll admit it's pretty hard luck to have to salute a nigger.'

"I put the blame for this disrespect to the uniform on the white officers. We teach our men to salute the mark of military rank, no matter who wears it. The white officer whose men refuse us the salute is half in sympathy with them himself."

"Yesterday at the Palace Hotel," said the officer whose tent follows, "I happened to be in the court, and, turning, saw a white officer, a surgeon, just beginning, you know, in his profession," he added, with gentle disdain. "I really hadn't had time to recognize the fact that he was an officer, before he turned completely around to avoid saluting me. Doesn't it seem absurd?"

There are colored officers out at the Presidio who will tell you gravely that there is no such thing as disrespect from white military inferior to black superior. These are the same men who decided to hush things up after Lieutenant Butler's encounter with the man who would not salute. They are the same men whose tents faced the quarters of the Fortieth regiment and, separated from them by the scant width of a company street, watched the unmilitary, unmanly maneuvers of those white soldiers, whose ignorance and prejudice were greater than their respect for country and flag. They are the men who saw and felt and breathed insult as long as those tents—now standing empty with canvas draperies looped up like a be-hooped damsel crossing a muddy street—were tenanted. They are the men who think to do away with an uncomfortable fact by the simple, but antiquated, process of denying it.

---

46. The Presidio: a US Army post located in San Francisco.

"This question isn't a new one," said a colored philosopher, who happens to be an officer. "In Jefferson barracks, Missouri, where we were stationed, the thing had finally to be recognized and a test made to enforce discipline."

"Down in Arizona, where I come from," said a negro sergeant, who had just brought a prisoner up to Alcatraz for disobedience and disrespect to a superior, "it's the same way. It's ignorance usually, and the low-class volunteer who makes a personal matter of it."

"And the fact is," said a lieutenant in the Forty-ninth, "the man who happens to be wearing the uniform has nothing to do with the matter. The salute is a mark of respect to a certain rank. It ought not to matter to the man who wears the same uniform I do, who serves the same government that I do, whether that uniform is worn by a white man or a black man or a yellow man, by a man of honor or a scoundrel. And the question of discrimination was not left to the discretion of individuals. It's purely a matter of form, and a military detail."

"You won't understand, will you," interposed Lieutenant Tillman good-naturedly, "that we are deliberately seeking the salute? It makes no difference to a man of sense whether a prejudiced white soldier goes out of his way to make a personal matter out of what is simply a military regulation. We haven't been chasing the salute at all. When a group of men are standing at the head of the street here, I'll not zigzag across in order to relieve them of the painful necessity of saluting. But if these men feel that it humiliates them to salute a colored officer, I'll spare them the salute. Yesterday I overheard two men take a third to task for saluting the rank I wear.

" 'What d'ye mean,' one said, 'by giving that nigger the salute? I'd see him in —— before I'd salute him.'

"Now, I think the common-sense way is the way to treat this thing. Rigidly considered, I should have these men arrested, put in the guardhouse and made to stand trial. That is my right and their fit punishment. But there is no man living, white or black, who will dispute the human necessity of departing at times from the rigid rule. Discretion, good judgment, expediency—whatever you choose to call it—suggests that a man should ignore these things for a time. In ten years, fifteen years it will have passed. I wouldn't make a tragedy of it. It isn't worth while."

"Among the regulars," said a tall, straight, soldierly-looking black fellow with stripes on his sleeve, "we find that a man's too much of a soldier, as a rule, to take up a class war. It's the volunteers, who aren't accustomed to colored officers, who'll say what a white soldier said of me at the Thanksgiving football game.

"'Salute that thing!' he sneered, when his companion stood at attention. 'Touch your cap to that nigger! I'll be —— if I do!'

"Of course there are regulars, officers and men, who'll have urgent business off at a tangent from their line of walk the moment a colored officer appears. And there are those among the white privates who make a distinction between 'swelled-head niggers' and those who are not unduly elated at being above white men.

"But, after all, this is not the serious side of the matter. If a lot of white soldiers are running away from the possibility of being compelled to salute, a colored officer would make a dignified picture, wouldn't he, running after them? The only part of it that a person need consider is the effect it has upon the men. The black private has as much loyalty to his officers as the white man has; often more. If two officers of the Forty-ninth, friends of Butler's, hadn't been at hand to quiet things last week there would have been bloodshed, with whites on one side and blacks on the other. Colored privates are pretty prudent and rather good-natured, and it is the policy of the officers to make as little as possible of the slights no white officer at the Presidio would for one moment overlook. But when you add fighting whisky to the men's knowledge that their regiment's been wronged, there is the danger that'll come from the laxness of the white officers in not seeing to it that their men respect rank in negroes."

"There are only two cures for it," said Tillman. "One is time. The colored commissioned officer is comparatively a new thing. In time men of both colors will become better used to it. The other is war. Down in Cuba, we fought side by side with white men, and came to forget, as they did, that there was any difference between us. We were fighting for the same thing. There were matters so big to be considered that the little points of military etiquette couldn't be thought about.

"Wait till we're in the Philippines. Then even those among us who are inclined to resent every insult of omission and commission will forgive, though they mayn't forget what we've stood in army posts."

If you happen to be of the race that refuses the salute you'll feel rather ashamed while listening to the race that waives it; ashamed that there's anything so small in the army of the greatest of the world's republics at the very dawn of the twentieth century as race hatred; ashamed that Uncle Sam, who is preaching the democratic doctrine of equality to brown-skinned men in the tropics (with the aid of military governors on one side and bullets on the other), doesn't practice it here in San Francisco; ashamed that it isn't military discipline—that red-tape bogey who claims so much and does so little—which has prevented a bloody war between black and white soldiers.

MRS. STETSON IS IN TOWN

Bulletin, December 12, 1899, 1

"Such a review of my book in California does not at all surprise me. I expected that sort of thing, of course, from a San Francisco paper."[47]

The words were spoken in that clear-cut, disdainful tone which Mrs. Stetson uses so effectively; more than that, they were aimed obliquely at the unfortunate reviewer who read Mrs. Stetson's great book last year and wrote what she thought a most appreciative, though necessarily hurried, account of it.

"Mrs. Stetson Flays Her Sex Alive!" quoted the lady. "It was not Mrs. Stetson's intention to flay her sex. The book is essentially a woman's book, written with the kindest feeling toward women, and accepted in that spirit in the East, where I have made many friends through it."

"And enemies?"

"Oh, that, too, was to be expected."

Mrs. Charlotte Perkins Stetson, author of "Women and Economics," lecturer and member of women's congresses, magazine writer and sociological student, is in town.

"No, I am not working," she said at 621 O'Farrell street, where she is visiting Mrs. Cora Morse.[48] "I am resting. I am in San Francisco in an altogether private and personal capacity. I have been lecturing on 'Ethics,' on 'The Child'—on various subjects on my way across, and shall lecture again

---

47. For Michelson's review of Stetson's *Women and Economics*, see "Charlotte Perkins Stetson Flays Her Own Sex Alive" in this volume.
48. Cora Morse was the editor of *The Coming Light*, a progressive monthly magazine published in San Francisco.

when I reach Southern California, where I am going. No, I shall not lecture in San Francisco."

I went to interview Mrs. Stetson this morning and was thoroughly and remorselessly interviewed for all my sins, journalistic and otherwise. Mrs. Stetson interviewed me upon the Zionist movement, upon the pernicious effect of newspaper work, upon any symptoms of personal degeneration I had noticed, upon the probabilities of an obliging, versatile editorial writer being deprived of all journalistic virtue through sheer habitual mental depravity, and led me through a gamut of psychological questions which were cruel because unusual.

But Mrs. Stetson talked herself brilliantly, forcefully and with that ease in expressing subtleties which marks the scientific mind. She sits in unfeminine quiet while she talks, she gestures rarely, and she gives such earnest attention to every subject that one can see the reason of the deep line between her brows.

"The question of having a woman physician at an insane asylum?" she repeated after me. "There is no such question. There might be a question of appointing women school teachers or women reporters or women musicians. There can be no question of the imperative necessity for women physicians where there are insane women."

"Men physicians have claimed that the appointment of women, under the circumstances, is a reflection upon the honor of medical men generally."

"My!" she exclaimed. "Isn't it pathetic to find a class of people so sensitive to attacks upon their honor? When so slight a thing can affect one's honor so seriously, how very, very vulnerable one must be!

"About women's failure to get appointments on school boards, though, it is the ignorance and prejudice of the women teachers of San Francisco that are most to blame. Evidently the teachers here do not know of the excellent record made in the East by women in such positions. Surely the proof of the pudding is in the eating. The placing of themselves on record as opposed to women school directors is significant testimony as to the sort of women who teach in San Francisco.

"Have women advanced in the past five years? How do I know? Have men? Some of them have and some haven't. I know women in the East and in the West who haven't budged an inch. And I know men, too, who are where they were half a dozen years ago or have gone backward.

"The matter of woman's suffrage, which you understand, is only one side of the many-sided question that interests me, has not advanced in Massachusetts, for instance, mainly for the reason that the abuses to which the woman's suffrage agitation called attention, have been remedied. This is the view I took of it in London last year, when I was explaining to some English suffrage women that the very improvement in women's property rights, etc., had served to dull discontent with the present one-sided suffrage arrangement. But, after all, the capacity to see the justice of woman suffrage is not a voluntary capacity. If the little brain cells in a given man's or woman's brain are not arranged in just the proper order, he or she will be against woman suffrage. One must have patience with physical facts. By the way," Mrs. Stetson turned to face her interviewer, "did you write the review of my book?"

I admitted the fact. I thought it better not to deny it, considering that the article named bore my signature.

"Didn't it please you?" I asked.

There was a silence, an uncomfortably long silence. Mrs. Stetson turned in her chair and looked out of the window.

"Well," she said at last, "as I said, I was prepared for that sort of thing from the San Francisco newspapers. I should have paid no attention to it, of course, had any other paper published it. Incidentally, I should not have seen a reporter from any paper but The Bulletin.

"But—no, it did not please me. If one were to make extracts of all the indecent allusions in the Bible, would that give a fair idea of the contents of the Book? You picked out the strongest, hardest things I had said against women to quote. And I maintain—and such papers as the Nation hold the same view—that my book was meant and is accepted by women in the East as thoughtful, earnest work."

STETSON WEDDING

Bulletin, June 24, 1900, 21

The newspapers of San Francisco have at last found a subject upon which they can agree. From each and all of them comes a cackle of unholy glee to mark their satisfaction in the fact of Charlotte Perkins Stetson's marriage.

Charlotte Perkins Stetson has become Charlotte Perkins Stetson Gilman, and the newspaper commentators are as maliciously jubilant over the fact as though this clever woman were the only talented creature that has fallen from the grace of consistency.

I am not an authorized champion of the biggest brained woman since George Eliot[49]—whose marriage, by the way, late in life, to a young nonentity named Cross, was as inexplicable to her friends at Mrs. Stetson's is to her (official) enemies. Mrs. Stetson herself would be first to disown my championship. She and I fell out over my admiration of her book, "Women and Economics," or, rather, over my manner of expressing that admiration.[50]

Nothing, it appears, can shake the invincible poise of this remarkable woman, who writes very bad poetry and such humorous, well balanced prose. It isn't enough that you praise; you must praise intelligently—which means, with Mrs. Stetson, a thorough, staidly-worded realization of the scientific value of her book, with no intrusion of flippant humor; no sensational quoting of forceful, one-sided passages, no italicizing of extraordinary statements that might destroy a symmetrical view of a book which she regards—and justly—as a big part of her life work.

---

49. George Eliot (1819–1880): English novelist.
50. See "Charlotte Perkins Stetson Flays Her Own Sex Alive" and "Mrs. Stetson Is in Town."

Still, though lacking credentials in this particular case, I plead for the new woman, for that last liberty of the other sex—the privilege of making a fool of herself, like the rest of the world. No one in the West knows what sort of man the railer at cook stoves and other insignia of married life has wedded. The jeers of the journalistic critics are at the marriage; not at the husband.

"Mrs. Stetson reviled matrimony; Mrs. Stetson married. Oh, the inconsistency of the cleverest of new women!" This is an epitome of San Francisco's press comment upon the marriage of this well-known woman.

"Mrs. Stetson is inconsistent; Mrs. Stetson is human"—they might better have said. And this would have been no great discovery. For, despite that old grudge which weaker women and most men cherish against a woman-philosopher who could give her husband his freedom and his wish, as Ruskin did with the woman who became Mrs. Millais;[51] despite the reproof without words to jealous, dog-in-the-manger wives and the hurt to marital vanity in the unflattering implication that one woman considers the prize of man's favor not worth battling over with another woman, not worth hazarding dignity and honor, and not necessarily a matter of life and death; despite this, I say, the new woman is very human.

And therefore, fallible.

And therefore, inconsistent.

And apt to express general condemnation of things which she discovers later may be favorably particularized.

"Read Montaigne," advised Emerson.[52] "Read Montaigne. All wisdom lies in Montaigne."[53]

Yet Montaigne was as inconsistent (and manfully admitted his inconsistency) as any latter day woman philosopher.

"'Tis dangerous to trust women," says the one whom the seer of Concord judged the wisest man who has ever lived, "because of their irregular

---

51. John Ruskin (1819–1900): British writer and art critic whose marriage to Euphemia (Effie) Gray was annulled in 1855 so that she could marry artist John Everett Millais.

52. Ralph Waldo Emerson (1803–1882): American writer and Transcendentalist who lived in Concord, Massachusetts. Michelson is likely referring to his essay "Montaigne; or the Skeptic."

53. Michel de Montaigne (1533–1592): French writer and philosopher.

appetites and depraved tastes. They have not sufficient force to choose and embrace that which is most worthy."

And yet Montaigne left that which he himself says is dearer to a man than his own son—his book, "of which I am father and mother both," to a woman to edit and to publish. And that woman's judgment is binding in France to this day. During her life she would not permit a correction or an alteration, and the Frenchman of 1900 docilely reads his Montaigne in the absolute tongue of four centuries ago.[54]

So much for the distinction between what the wisest man wrote and what he did: between the wholesale verdict of guilty his words render and the retail acquittal his acts confess.

Congratulations to you, Mr. and Mrs. Gilman.

---

54. Quotations are Michelson's variations on lines from Montaigne's *Essays*, which were edited and published by Marie de Gournay (1565–1645), a French writer and proto-feminist intellectual.

MIRIAM MICHELSON GOES ON A HATCHET CRUSADE

Accompanies Mrs. Nation at Topeka

Graphic Description of a "Raid" by the Reformer and Her Followers

Bulletin, February 11, 1901, 1–2

Topeka, Kan., Feb. 11—By half-past 6 o'clock this morning Mrs. Carrie Nation[55] had wrecked the Senate Saloon, on Kansas avenue, had been arrested and marched down to the city prison, two blocks distant, and had been booked for joint smashing.[56]

It was bitterly cold in Topeka this morning. The thermometer was ten degrees below zero, the moon was still high, but most of the electric lights and street lamps were out, and the murky, frosty, damp streets, packed high with snow, were deserted.

On the corner of Sixth street and Kansas avenue, where I stood at half-past 5 o'clock, not a soul was in sight. Topeka papers had given 7 o'clock as the time Mrs. Nation would appear upon the street with her hatchet. But Mrs. Nation had said to me the night before, with a smile and a wink, "It'll be before 6 my dear; before 6 o'clock. Right in front of the Topeka Bank. I'll meet you."

---

55. Carrie Nation (1846–1911): temperance activist known for destroying saloons with a hatchet. She became a temperance reformer after her first husband died from alcoholism.

56. Joint: a drinking establishment. Although it was illegal to manufacture or sell alcohol in Kansas as of 1881, joints like the Senate Saloon in Topeka paid monthly fines in order to continue operating.

So in front of the Topeka Bank I stood, wondering how many would come to this freezing rendezvous in the morning's dawn. Not many knew of it—no non-combatant except myself. In a few minutes a man strolled past me—a tall, muscular young Kansan, with a shock of burned fair hair showing beneath the thick woolen cap pulled low over his bearded face. He marched past me, stamping as he walked to keep warm. Presently from another direction another man appeared—gray-bearded, thick-set, muffled like the first—and like the first suspicious and curious.

"Good morning," said the first one, warily. "It's early for a man to be about."

"Ye'es," responded the older man, his eyes turned toward the south, whence came the sound of the snow crunching under some one's feet.

"But I had some business to attend to."

"Oh!" The exclamation came with relief from the first man. The two exchanged a whispered word, and they walked on together.

MRS. NATION MAKES HER APPEARANCE.

These two are part of Mrs. Nation's advance guard men, who are ready to protect her against the violence which her own violence engenders. Down the street came a hurrying little knot of women. In front Mrs. Nation walked alone—taller than the rest—her hatchet clutched beneath her big gray shawl, her bonnet covered with a nubia,[57] her torn and mended black woolen gown—her "smashing gown," as she calls it—flapping in the cold morning wind.

"Oh, Lord, direct me. Oh, Lord, show me the way. I'm trying. I'm trying to do right, oh, Lord," she prayed.

Behind her came Miss Madeline Southard, a slight brunette, whose cheeks were blazing with excitement. With her was Mrs. J. P. White, a little woman, walking sturdily despite the heavy coat she wore. Their heads, too, were muffled in shawls.

As we walked down the avenue toward Fifth street shadowy figures joined us, men ready to battle, if necessary, in this strange crusade; men who were curious, none that were antagonistic or expressed antagonism. "She has been awake since half-past 3," said Miss Southard, as we hurried on. "She

---

57. Nubia may refer to a fabric headpiece draped over Nation's bonnet, which resembled the ancient Egyptian headdress known as a Nubian wig.

has been walking the floor and praying." "Hush, child," said Mrs. Nation, turning. "I am only a handful of mud that God picked up and threw at the unclean shops. Show me the way, Lord."

These three women had walked into town. It is a couple of miles to Clay and Twelfth street, where they live. But the cars do not run in Topeka before 6. So they marched down through the freezing, silent streets on their mission. We turned down Fifth street. It is almost unbelievable, but these women did not know where they were going. They had not determined even among themselves which saloon they would enter. They did not even know exactly where the saloons were, and they stumbled about in the darkness, turning and seeking, followed now by a crowd that had grown larger. We walked nearly a block. Then Mrs. Nation turned suddenly, and all turned and followed her

"Those who say they are my friends hurt me most," she cried, turning from the women and appealing to me. "I don't know the town. Where are the joints? Show me one—"

I reminded Mrs. Nation that she had been in Topeka longer than I had.

"Yes, yes," she murmured, "and I only must say this to them so that they shall not hinder the Lord's work. Good is the road of the Lord. Show me one, I tell you," she cried again to the women who followed.

A Saloon Is Finally Reached.

Her voice was vibrating with the tension, but her step was steady, and her broad, rosy face was composed. We were walking down the avenue now and halted before the closed glass doors of the saloon. Mrs. Nation was just about to push the door open when a young fellow burst from the crowd.

"Don't—don't touch any of those bottles with tubes in. They've got them loaded. And—and don't look through any peepholes," he whispered. And before she could thank him he had turned and had run swiftly down Kansas avenue, disappearing down Fourth street.

She dashed madly in; we followed. No one was in the first room, a very large one, containing four or five billiard tables. Mrs. Nation ran past these, crying "We've come! we've come!" and made straight for the inner door, bursting it open and shouting: "We attack nothing but that which is dangerous to humanity and heaven."

Only the night watchman was on guard. He evidently did not expect Mrs.

Nation's early, informal call. But he leaped upon her now with a yell, trying to wrench the hatchet from her hands.

"Smash, smash!" she kept calling to the women behind her. "Don't—don't wait for me—smash, for God's sake!"

THE WATCHMAN FIRES HIS REVOLVER.

The two men set to work. Crash went the bottles and smash went the glasses on the bar. But a sudden cry from Mrs. Nation brought the men, who had been outrun by the women, into the room.

"She's hurt—she's hurt," cried the women. Mrs. Nation put her hand to her forehead, bruised by her own hatchet. "Sheep" Lytle, the watchman, has some negro blood in his veins, though he looks like a white man. He is short and sturdy. His light eyes wavered for a moment. Then he drew his pistol. In a second, half of the men had run from the room, but these women, excited beyond all fear, hardly knew what he was doing. The report of the pistol—which the man fired into the air—mingled with the smashing of glassware, and the next minute Lytle had turned and escaped through the rear entrance.

"He has taken my hatchet," cried Mrs. Nation. "Here, give me another." She seized Miss Southard's hatchet, and crack, crack, crack went the three mirrors behind the bar.

"When you go to work for God," she cried, "never ask the devil how to do it, but smash, smash, smash!"

She ran about in a frenzy now, destroying two large nickel-in-the-slot machines. She sent them crashing to the floor, the nickels spilling all over, while her hatchet whacked and splintered the machines. "See!" she cried. "Ain't they the devil's own tools?"

A barrel of beer stood over in the corner. The women tipped it over, and Mrs. Nation, lifting her hatchet high in the air, brought it down on the faucet with such vim that she drove it out and the beer spurted in a foamy stream all over her, drenching her from neck to heel.

And then this strange woman, dropping her hatchet and holding out her hands, dripping with beer, burst out laughing. It was a natural laugh, too, but it sounded queer in that place, where the women were strung up to a tension that made their voices rattle in their throats, while the men stood in perplexed and apprehensive silence. "That's the spirit of the jointists," she laughed. "Trying to hurt me."

She Is Again Arrested.

"Mrs. Nation, I'll have to arrest you." She turned to regard the big, good-natured policeman who had just arrived, in a matter-of-fact-way, wiping the beer from her neck and wrists.

"All right, brother, come on," she answered, taking his arm, and together, like an affectionate mother and a strapping young son, they walked down the slippery street to the jail.

The women were jubilant. So was Mrs. Nation. At the jail she saw the officer who had arrested her the day before, and he asked kindly about her and spoke sympathetically.

"The Senate?" mused the sergeant as he wrote Mrs. Nation's name in his book. "It was the Senate, was it? They always are the first to open. This is what they get for it. How old are you, Mrs. Nation?"

"Fifty-four." "What's the charge, officer?" "Disturbing the peace? No! no!" vehemently protested the prisoner. "Just put it joint smashing," said the officer.

Mrs. Nation clapped her hands. "That's the first time I've been booked fairly," she said as the sergeant wrote the novel charge in his book. Then she leaned her arm upon the desk. "Oh, men," she said, her voice trembling for the first time. "I want to show you what an old woman must do, 'cause there ain't no other way. We've got to save you. You won't save yourselves. Oh, save them, oh Lord! This is a beginning surely. Great streams from small devices flow, and oaks from little acorns grow."

She had turned, and she saw two policemen bringing in a drunken old fellow, with a long, white beard and a moist eye, that almost popped out of his head at the sight of her.

"Oh!" she cried, putting out her hands pitifully, the tears in her eyes. "An old grandfather; a poor old grandfather."

"Hullo," began the old man amiably, trying to steady himself against the desk. But the policemen took him away, and Mrs. Nation went to her trial on yesterday's charge.

Old Charge Dismissed Without Trial.

It was the oddest sort of trial—a consistently irregular proceeding, to harmonize with all the rest of this unprecedented affair. The courtroom is a little place. It was crowded by Mrs. Nation's sympathizers. But there was no Judge, no jury, no prosecuting attorney, no lawyer for the defense, no witnesses. The case had merely been dismissed before it was called, without the presence of the prisoner or any one else.

"But I won't have it dismissed!" exclaimed Mrs. Nation. "I have been restrained of my liberty. I have been accused of disturbing the peace, and that is a terrible charge. I won't have it said that I come here disturbing the peace of the people of Topeka. And you might as well speak of my disturbing the peace of mad dogs as of jointists. Where is the Judge? I want the Judge. I'll stay here till he comes."

Court was not in session, but Jud[g]e McGaw,[58] a smooth-faced man who can keep his temper under trying circumstances, came at Mrs. Carrie Nation's bidding to explain to her why her case had been dismissed.

"Oh, there you are, Judge," she exclaimed, going up to him before he had taken his seat. "Now tell me these people ought to know their business. If they had a right to arrest me how can they dismiss the charge against me? I'll have an action against them for false imprisonment. "These policemen," she said, "tell me they're glad of the work I'm doing; tell me I'm doing it for them. Why don't you give me your star, then, and your salary," I ask them. "Or why don't you give it up if you cannot keep the law?"

A RUNNING DEBATE WITH THE JUDGE.

"Mrs. Nation," said the Judge, "the District Attorney advised that the case against you be dismissed. But—"

"Dismissed," he continued evenly. "The charge against you this morning will be tried next Thursday. Till then you are in the custody of the police."

"But why did he advise that the case be dismissed?"

"You'll have to ask him."

"I won't stand any such arrangement. I have been deprived of my liberty. This thing has interfered with my business."

The crowd burst into a laugh, clapping and applauding.

"See here," said Mrs. Nation, looking over her spectacles, shrewdly anticipating the Judge, "you people will make this thing ridiculous if you don't stop it."

---

58. This is likely a reference to Judge C. A. Magaw.

"Although court is not in session, it may not be out of place," the Judge said slowly, "seeing that so many of Mrs. Nation's friends are here, for me to say a few words—"

"Yes, I'll be glad to hear," she interrupted.

"A few words, hardly as an official act, but as a—"

"Friend?" asked Mrs. Nation.

"Yes, as a friend, and in order to make the situation clear and perhaps avert trouble in the future. The law says, Mrs. Nation, that when three or more persons shall proceed together in a violent and tumultuous manner—"

"Now, don't go on like that," she said.

"Don't say violent. There was nothing violent and tumultuous about what we did. You were not there, and—"

"Mrs. Nation, you must keep quiet when I am speaking."

"Let me ask you one question," she pleaded.

Judge Threatened Her Removal.

"No, I don't care to answer any questions, and if you don't keep quiet I shall have the bailiffs take you out of the room."

"That's just what you want." she retorted. "I'll keep quiet."

"As I was saying," the Judge recommenced, his eye upon the typewritten riot law on his desk, "I give this as a piece of advice which it will be well for you to bear in mind, Mrs. Nation. I do not say that you have any intention of breaking the law."

"No, sir; no."

"Or that this law applies to you; I merely wish you to know that when three or more people shall assemble together to do an unlawful act or to do a lawful act unlawfully"—he repeated the phrase—"in a violent—"

"Violent and tumultuous fiddlesticks," snapped Mrs. Nation.

"And shall destroy property or anything by force of violence or in carrying out a threat the law calls that riot."

"Thank you Judge, it don't apply to me at all."

And he left the room, having decided that bail for Mrs. Nation's appearance on Thursday was unnecessary, and permitting her to depart on her own recognizance. She thanked him, but sat calmly for a time reading her letters and receiving congratulations. When she took a check for $10 from an envelope she exclaimed: "I had not a cent when I left Wichita. The

Y.M.C.A. gave me the money for my fare. And yet I have all the money I want."

Before leaving the courtroom she stopped a moment longer to say a last word to the reporters, all of whom she treats as old friends and comrades.

"I want to say that if these young men who write so well knew more about the Word of God they'd succeed better. It mortifies me when I talk to them to have them quote me as saying the 114th Psalm instead of the 144th. The best one among them is not familiar with the Word of God."

Mrs. Nation, Joan of Arc of Temperance Crusade, as Seen by Miriam Michelson (Excerpt)

North American, February 13, 1901, 16

Topeka, Kan., February 12

The most talked about woman in America to-day is Mrs. Carrie Nation, a middle-aged, unromantic, bustling Joan of Arc, who commands an army such as the world has never seen before, such as no man or woman has ever been able to organize—an army of women scattered all over the States, but ready when their leader shall appear to unsheath their one weapon, the homely, domestic hatchet.

"This is one of the greatest warfares," says Kansas Joan, "the world has ever known—not against flesh and blood, but against principalities and powers; against spiritual wickedness in high places. And man's extremity is God's opportunity."

If Mrs. Nation had lived in a country of castes, she, too would have been a peasant, and if her first husband had been a fairly prosperous Kansas farmer, instead of a sot and a weakling, who died in delirium tremens thirty years ago, this woman whose name is on the tongue of all American women, would to-day have been known among her neighbors in Enterprise, in Southern Kansas, as an excellent cook and a big, wholesome housewife with a kindly heart, a jolly laugh and a shrewd, busy tongue.

Where the Nations Live.

The Nations live in Barber county, which touches Oklahoma on the south, with its new conditions and new people. When Mrs. Nation went downtown to do her scanty marketing—for the Nations were poor, very poor, and though tall, old tearful-eyed Mr. Nation may be an attorney-at-law, the humblest laborer in Southern Kansas could make as good a living for his wife as he—when Mrs. Nation went along the principal street of the little town, if she chanced to meet a man who was smoking, she would walk directly up to him, take the cigar or the cigarette from between his astonished lips, and, throwing it aside with an "Oh, how can you smoke the nasty thing!?" or "I really can't bear the smell of it!" pass on her way. There was no malice in the act. It was almost impersonal. She told me that her aversion to tobacco was prenatal. That some one else's fondness for it might be quite as deeply rooted never occurred to her. What she did, she did simply as a matter of course, not to be debated or reasoned over any more than any other impulse which should come to her.

"The impulse was smash, and so was the act," she said in talking about the saloons. "So I suited the action to the word and the word to the action. You must remember that 'diseases desperate grown by desperate appliances are relieved.' "[59]

THE BIBLE AND SHAKESPEARE.

Which manner of expression has become second nature to this peculiar woman. Quotations from Shakespeare come almost as readily from her lips as lines from the Bible. The words of the New Testament, uttered with the utmost reverence and applied in the most rigidly literal way to the common affairs of life, the wisdom of the great poet quoted with a faith in its truth just less than that her Bible inspires—these two rich rivers of expression flow through the country of her speech, vitalizing it, strengthening it, setting it apart from and dignifying the commonplace utterance of a common woman.

Common, not vulgar. Vulgarity is immeasuarably more remote from this woman's manner and words and thought than it is from the minds of many of those who find in her only material to criticise and ridicule. She is of the common people, and so is a better instrument for her purpose than a creature of finer material would be. From the great body of middle-class woman her recruits will come. They will understand her. She understands them.

---

59. Nation is quoting *Hamlet* by William Shakespeare.

When they are brought together her homely ways, her simple, direct mode of speech, her honesty and sincerity, which no one may question—these will be her means of winning followers far more than any claim to inspiration and a heaven-appointed mission can be.

Will the Movement Spread?

Hatchet crusades will hardly become the fashion, although in days when faith was stronger and emotional excitement more contagious the flower of Europe and the chivalry of France could follow an illiterate monk or a dream-mad peasant girl to death and to victory. But it is not beyond the pale of possibilities that this woman may create a sentiment as powerful as the hermit did or Joan herself. Women en masse, women in unusual circumstances and following their emotions, are an unknown quantity. Before long you will see thousands of them in every State in the Union wearing a button bearing the broad, beaming countenance of Mrs. Nation. Special pictures of her have been taken for this purpose, and Carrie Nation buttons and badges will flood the market soon and be a profitable source of revenue for some one.

For whom? That is a question. If once Mrs. Nation's followers shall find the flaw of personal thrift in her, if for a moment they get the impression that she is making capital of her prominence, her influence will melt away like the hopes of the Kansas farmers before the hot winds.

Unspoiled by Publicity.

This woman seemed to me altogether disinterested. I never knew a human being, man or woman, so unspoiled, so unchanged by public attention. Affectation, a pose, it seems to me, would strike her as being as absurd as any outsider might find it in her. Her simplicity, her unsuspicious trust in the good faith of everybody with whom she comes in contact would make her a ready victim for those who wished to capitalize her notoriety, if it were not that she cannot long be deceived. She can be led anywhere by any one she trusts, but the moment she discovers a mercenary purpose behind the ostensible one she will put an end to plans and projects, however well laid and far-reaching.

This at least is my reading of her.

"Do you know," she said to me, "I'd like to give you that little red-letter

Testament of mine. It would do you good. You would read it. And you would say it's the one Mrs. Nation had in the jail with her at Wichita."

This is the sort of naive pleasure Mrs. Nation takes in her present position —a childlike sort of recognition of what she has accomplished. She lives in public these days. She is a mine of copy to the reporters who follow her, for she has not the faintest notion of concealing her thoughts or her plans. She receives each new reporter who comes to her as a personal friend. Everything she has, everything she purposes, is at his disposal.

"Come on, you young men," she called to them in a motherly fashion in the police court at Topeka. "Read these letters. They're public. Just look through them, and if there's any of 'em you want, why take 'em."

She Likes This Reporter.

And she sat there, permitting these strangers to look through her mail, to find an occasional check and hand it to her, to read all the comments encouraging and condemnatory with which she is flooded. "I'm going to introduce you to the reporter I like best, my dear," she said to me. "I don't know his name, but I like him, though I did tell him if he didn't study the Scriptures I wouldn't have anything more to do with him."

The newspaper men reciprocate her kindly feeling. And surely no one would accuse the ordinary reporter of being impressionable or emotional. "I've sort of taken sides on this thing," one of them said to me. "There's more to this woman than you think. I've been trying to write her up squarely, and my paper wouldn't print what I wrote. So I went home and told them what I think about her, and now they're giving me a fairer chance to say what I think. She's such a motherly, kind, good creature. She isn't anything the sort you expected to find. Now, is she?"

I saw a good deal of Mrs. Nation during the time I spent in Topeka. I never once saw her out of temper, except when she received a letter from a woman in California accusing her "who pretend to be inspired" of interpolating words into the psalm whose number the reporters had mistaken. It was that one so often on her tongue. "Blessed be the Lord, my strength, which teacheth my hands to war and my fingers to fight." She turned upon the newspaper men and scolded them roundly, then said that they had humiliated her, and read the letter aloud with emphasis and rebuke, to show them what a serious charge they had caused to be made against her. . . .

She Is Artlessly Effective.

In talking to two or three, in preaching to the most ardent of her disciples in the kitchens of the tremulous Kansas women, her tongue does not falter, and the simple directness and sincerity of her speech are artlessly effective. But, in speaking in public, she will read a whole book of the Bible, if she finds it interesting, ignoring altogether the fact that it is her personality, her experiences which have called her audience together.

The evening that she lectured at Topeka in the great Auditorium she promised her friends faithfully that she would abide by their programme and submit to be introduced conventionally to her audience with all the little recognized formalities. But before they could prevent her, and before she herself could be reminded of her promise, she was upon the platform, waiving all form, acting as her own chairman, inviting various local temperance musical artists to perform—which they did, and very badly—and generally outraging the sense of fitness which the earnest, zealous, but "proper" women of Topeka were trying to live up to. But, though they smile at her weakness, these women—honest, conscientious, good mothers and wives, many of them—never falter in their faith in her. On this particular evening she read nearly all of the Book of Esther, looking up and over her spectacles at her audience to comment occasionally upon the joints and her way of closing them, finishing with a paraphrase like this:

"The Jews—for Jews read women. The women had light and gladness and joy and honor. And in every province, and in every city, whithersoever the King's commandment and his decree came, the women had joy and gladness, a feast and a good day. And many of the people of the land became prohibitionists, for the fear of the women fell upon them."

As Pleased as a Child.

She was as pleased as a child at this effort, and laughed back at her audience, sharing their pleasure. She has an abounding belief in her audience's sympathy with her, and her artlessness is not inartistic, when you consider the sort of people she is to influence, and the kind of work which she hopes to accomplish. A cleverer, more conventional speaker would not be a woman of action, too, as is this grandmotherly Joan of Arc. A more manageable, more presentable reformer would be self-conscious, would be vain, would be self-seeking, perhaps. And the woman who leads women must be free of these qualities, or she will rouse all the dormant envy and jealousy of which feminine human nature is capable.

Her trustfulness disarms criticism. She had seen me but twice when she handed over to me her manuscript, for which she was to receive twenty dollars.

"You send it off for me, will you? Put it in an envelope, and see that it gets off all right. I ain't got any time, and besides I'm in jail," she finished with a laugh.

"Yes, you see that it is all right," said a bearded Kansas farmer, who stood beside her. "You tend to it all right, the way it ought to be, for her."

He spoke with the accent of fond loyalty: as one would speak who takes for granted a common feeling of affection and admiration.

Takes Herself Seriously.

In the little note which Mrs. Nation had inclosed [sic] to her publishers, she asked that the money for it be sent to a given address, "if it be worthy." But although Mrs. Nation has no pose, though she speaks to a thousand people with the unaffected, homely manner, which is natural to her, never consciously recognizing anything out of the common in her position, never feeling a bit abashed at publicity or the presence of strangers, she does take herself seriously.

"Keep it, Mrs. White, keep it," she said the morning after the three women had wrecked the Senate saloon, while she pressed into the little old woman's hand the one hatchet remaining whole after the fray. "Keep it for your grandchildren. And when they grow up, they can say: 'My grandmother was a Home Defender.'"

Mrs. White clasped the hatchet to her breast.

"It's all the Mayor's fault," she said angrily. "He promised to close every saloon in Topeka or resign. Why doesn't he keep his word? If he can't do the one thing, why doesn't he do the other?"

Mrs. Nation laughed. "He's waiting, I guess, till the women make him. The women have to 'tend to most things here in Kansas, it seems."

No Effort at Notoriety.

Mrs. Nation is quite conscious that she is speaking for publication. It is part of her plan, of course, that all she says shall be reported. And yet, a sturdy simplicity, the impression that she gives of being an unsophisticated old woman, unaware of how peculiar is her behavior to conventional eyes, saves the situation. One no more attributes Mrs. Nation's retorts in court to a vain desire to appear "smart," than he sees in her camaraderie with the policemen in the jail anything other than the manner natural to a good-natured, common, old body, who is quite at her ease with this sort of man, and as thoroughly at home among strangers as simplicity is everywhere. The power of publicity which stands behind her is that which compels a Kansas Judge to combat the effect she is trying to produce, while his knowledge of the mixed Kansas sentiment and the inflammable nature of part of the people gives him patience to listen to irrelevant words and countenance irregular proceedings rather than aid in bringing about the appeal to martyrdom which fanatical crusaders court.

"She will be killed!" said one woman fearfully to another, in a cosy little Topeka sitting room.

"Well—let her," answered her visitor, who had just returned from a raid on a "joint," and was relating to her friend all that had occurred. "Let her be killed. If it will advance the cause of temperance and open the eyes of the people of Kansas, let her be killed, or imprisoned, whichever it is to be. 'It is not all of life to live, nor all of death to die.' If prohibition needs a martyr, it shall have one."

When the reporters flocked to the jail upon hearing of the "joint-smashing" and the arrest, they asked Miss Southard, the young woman who took part in it for her name.

"Give your name," said Mrs. Nation, looking into the young woman's eyes with an unspoken command. "Don't you want to give your name?"

"I—I'd hate to have it get into the Kansas City papers," faltered Madeline Southard. "My grandmother lives there and she'd be worried about me."

"Well, other people worry, too," returned her leader. "You don't want to give your name, then?"

GENEROUS AND KIND-HEARTED.

If she had not wanted to, she must have done it, then. Kansas' Joan is generous and kind-hearted. She gave her copy of Thomas à Kempis[60] to a prisoner

---

60. Thomas à Kempis (ca. 1380–1471): author of *The Imitation of Christ*, which is the book referred to here.

in the jail, though she had not finished it, and though she loved it more, she told me, than the red-letter Testament itself. But the woman who elects to follow her, the woman who once pins the badge with the hatchet on her breast, will find that she has enlisted under a captain pitiless to all manifestations of conventionality, of backsliding, of moral cowardice.

Still, though she is as an exacting friend, she is a generous foe. She hesitated when it came to swearing out a warrant for the man who had raised the lump on her forehead with her own hatchet.

"I'll not say, sergeant," she said slowly, "that he meant to strike me. He did not hurt me with the hatchet. Perhaps he didn't mean to. But here's the lump."

Yet, when I suggested some arnica for that bruise,[61] Mrs. Nation's shrewd gray eyes met mine almost with a wink.

"Sh—sh!" she whispered. "I don't want any."

I said to Mrs. Nation's favorite reporter the night I sat watching her making a funny failure of her address in the Auditorium, that he himself must see that a more artistic, more effective Mrs. Nation, considered merely as a means to an end, could be imagined. I had in mind a creature of loftier spirit, a fanatic, but eloquent, and with an inborn sense of artistic values. I was mistaken, of course. The Mrs. Nation I fancied would not be the one who could say, "The Lord said unto me, 'Go to Kiowa (a town in Barber county, near my home) and smash the saloons, and I will stand by you,'" and be believed. She would not be the Mrs. Nation of whom a Kansas woman said to me with a trembling lip, "My husband is not quite ready yet to let me follow her." She would not be the Mrs. Nation who made that one play to the gallery in the close, long view I had of her, which offended me, but delighted her followers, when she exclaimed to the Judge who had once before tried her case, "Faugh, how your breath smells! What bad tobacco you use!" . . .

Brave Enough to Risk Life.

Now, on the whole, I believe even with her lack of eloquence the actual Mrs. Nation is the most effective instrument that could be imagined for the peculiar purpose to which she has devoted herself. She is brave enough to risk her very life, and she is not insensible to the active teachings of martyrdom. She is ready to defy public opinion, yet she realizes the force of sentiment. She is

---

61. Arnica: a herb used to treat bruises.

ready to "smash" a saloon when circumstances seem to require it and when the Lord commands it. Yet she knows that it is not the actual value of what she destroys that will defeat her enemy, the outlaw "jointist," but aroused public sentiment which will sweep him, or fine him—as has already been done in Topeka, in some cases—out of existence.

From my knowledge of the Topeka women who are associated with her, I think there is little likelihood of any "joint-smashing" here in Mrs. Nation's absence. And despite her contention that nowhere on earth is saloon property legally "property," I believe the John Brown[62] of prohibition is too shrewd a crusader to lift her hatchet against bottles of barrels or mirrors or paintings owned by a saloon outside a prohibition State. She will do it, of course, if the Lord should command, but the probabilities are against her receiving such a command.

There is a downtown office which is at the disposal of the crusaders the next time a raid is planned. Mrs. Nation and her small army will not have to walk miles through the snow to reach the field of battle when she returns to Topeka, after she has convinced herself and her audiences that she is not a woman of words, but of actions. She may either fall upon the "jointists" at the head of a small body of flying female infantry, which has passed the night or part of it, on Kansas avenue to be prepared for the attack, however suddenly the order may come, or she may try the efficacy of a cavalry attack, and descending from a closed cab raid one saloon, and be off to another before the police, a whole long block away, can apprehend her.

But till she returns, the reign of the hatchet, temporarily at least, is over. No one can say, though, how long the sentiment which it awakened will go marching on.

---

62. John Brown: a radical abolitionist who believed in violent rebellion against slavery and famously led a raid on Harpers Ferry, Virginia, in 1859. He was found guilty of treason, murder, and inciting an insurrection and was subsequently executed by hanging.

Two Little Slave Girls
Owned in Philadelphia

Bought in Martinique and Brought Here
in Spite of the Law

North American, February 25, 1901, 16

J
ust twenty squares south from Independence Hall[63] Pauline Pariendi, a twentieth-century slave, lives in bondage as complete and hopeless as though a million men had not died thirty-five years ago to wipe out slavery.

This girl slave is 15 years old. She was sold and bought at Saint Pierre, Martinique, and was brought to Philadelphia, about a year and a half ago by her mistress. And she is still a slave, as much the creature of another human being in the third city of the Union as she was in the little French island in the Southern Atlantic.[64]

Alie Campbell, a French Creole[65] of Martinique, bought this bit of black skin, so meagrely filled with human flesh and bones for $25. The bargain was struck fourteen years ago in the "lower city," the negro quarter of Saint Pierre. The two parties to it were I. Pariendi, the uncle of the child, and Alie Campbell; and the bargain still holds, although Mademoiselle Campbell has loaned her slave to her brother, Joseph Campbell, who has a family and can make better use of her.

"Is she yours?" I asked Alie Campbell.

---

63. Independence Hall: Philadelphia building in which the Declaration of Independence and the Constitution were signed.
64. Slavery was abolished in 1865 in the United States and in 1848 in Martinique.
65. A person of French ancestry born in one of France's colonial western territories.

"Yes, She Is Mine."

"Yes, she is mine," she answered. "My brother has a family. I am alone. He needs help, so she stays with him. But she is mine."

At 2110 South Philip street, where the Fifteenth Amendment to the Constitution of the United States is as inoperative as it is in San Francisco's Chinatown,[66] the Campbells live in a typical modern Philadelphia house of brick, with white stone trimmings. An electric bell summons Pauline Pariendi to the door. She could take an electric car a block from the house, and within fifteen minutes she could be walking up the steps of the Public Building—if she had the money and were at liberty to do so.

All the surroundings of the place where this late, black flower of slavery flourishes are up-to-date, civilized, commonplace. Within, though, the occupants are still Creoles of Martinique. They speak only French, despite the Scotch name an adventurous grandfather gave them. They do not know their neighbors, and their neighbors do not know their name. It is the atmosphere of Saint Pierre that you breathe in the poor little dining room; it is the prolific squalor of the negroes and half breeds of Martinique, more than half of whom are illegitimate; it is the country where babes are born in the street and sold cheap as Pauline Pariendi was, that these immigrant island Creoles have brought with them to America.

And it is the law, not of America, not even of Martinique, but of that obscure, intangible, tyrannical power—the custom of the country, the country from which they came—which the Campbells advance in explaining the presence of the little black slave in a Philadelphia house, early in the twentieth century.

Bought and Paid For.

"See, it is like this," says Alie Campbell in the corrupt but not unpleasing French of the island provinces. "In my country every one, no matter how poor, finds some one, a negro, poorer still, to work for him. It is the custom there. Here, if madame is rich, she has servants. If she is poor, she works.

---

66. Fifteenth Amendment: ratified in 1870, this amendment to the US Constitution granted all citizens the right to vote regardless of "race, color, or previous condition of servitude." In the late nineteenth century, San Francisco's Chinatown was a notorious site for sex trafficking.

She keeps her house herself. In Martinique, no. We, my mother, is poor there; but the mother of Pauline, a negress, works for her. She dies, leaving her child, a little thing no longer than my arm, in the streets. Now the child has no father, no mother. I take her. I bring her to America. My brother pays her passage money. And now she works for him, takes care of his child. But she is mine."

"How yours?"

"How?" Alie Campbell repeats the question. She is a slight young woman, dark-eyed and dark-haired, with the high cheek bones and square, oblong cast of countenance that is oddly repeated in Pauline Pariendi's black face. But Manuel Campbell, the one brother who speaks some English, interrupts:

"How? For pay. That's how," he declares, angrily. "That negro belongs to her, my sister. She pay for her to the uncle of Pauline. She keep her, too. No one can take that negro away. Not the President. It is no one's business about that negro. My sister pays for her. She have paper to show for it."

POSSESSION PAPERS UP TO DATE.

But Alie Campbell declined to show the paper within the last few days. This woman has heard of the Fifteenth Amendment. Not long ago she showed a document, written in a patois by a person as illiterate as the uncle of the slave-girl must be, setting forth the fact that for a consideration I. Pariendi, the uncle of Pauline Pariendi, conveys all title to her absolutely to Alie Campbell. Now, since the meaning of the tremendous struggle which shook America before slavery could be abolished has been borne in upon this twentieth century slave-owner, Alie Campbell shows a later document. Unlike the original one it is written in readable, grammatical French, in which Pariendi, suddenly become educated and avuncular, writes a gently-worded epistle to Mademoiselle Campbell, "confiding" to her again his niece, Pauline, and declaring emphatically that in case of the child's attempting to leave her he gives to Alie Campbell the authority to appeal to whomever shall have the right to restrain her.

The idea of restraint in connection with Pauline Pariendi strikes one as altogether incongruous. A gentler creature than this big-eyed, frail, and undersized little slave no one could imagine. She stood before me in the Campbells' dining room, in the presence of the four women and the children for whom she works, as unconscious of her claim to human rights, as simple, docile and ignorant as if she were indeed exposed for sale to me—the remarkable explanation of my visit which Alie Campbell's sister suggested.

Is Not for Sale Again.

"You come from a paper?" she had repeated after me. "Is it that you have seen an advertisement that she is for sale? She is not for sale."

But if she had been, so would this child have stood, removing from her finely-poised head the black scarf she wore, that I might better inspect what might become my property; and then standing there unquestioning, with an animal-like credulity and faith in other people's privileges, in a patient, unreasoning silence.

The Campbells would have you believe that the child understands neither English nor French; that she speaks a patois which would further isolate her, and keep her longer the pitiful legacy which the eighteenth century has left to her more merciful granddaughter, the twentieth.

But, though she speaks an easily-comprehended tongue, and understands the words addressed to her, Pauline Pariendi might just as well be shut in behind the barrier of another language. For it would take greater courage than ever dwelt behind a black skin to answer unconstrainedly the questions put to her in the presence of her masters:

"You are satisfied to stay here?

"You do not care to go back to Martinique?

"You like your home with these people?

"They are good to you?"

And the answer is always the same, "Oui, Madame. Merci, Madame,"[67] in the soft voice of the Creole, with a timid glance from great, shining eyes of astonishment and deprecation.

Work, Work, Always Work.

But one question they would not permit Pauline Pariendi to answer—that concerning the work she had to do.

"No, she does not the work of the house. She cares for the baby; this little one. But she does not the work, and Sunday she goes to Sunday school. She will soon make her communion."

---

67. French for "Yes, Madame. Thank you, Madame."

The neighbors in Philip Street do not concur with this account of benevolent regard for the small black stranger. "That poor little girl!" exclaimed the German woman next door, when pointing out the Campbells' house. "I do not know her name, but my heart bleeds for her. They beat her dreadfully, and she is worked, worked, worked, always worked. She is so puny and thin, and her poor, little black face, with the big, big, eyes, always looking! Ach, it is awful!"

"But they bought her," said a small boy, who was playing with the German woman's son. "Manuel's son says that they can do what they please with her, and the law can't touch them."

No word comes from Pauline Pariendi of this, though. She winds the black shawl about her head again, shivering deprecatingly. And when Madame Campbell appeals to her to endorse what she has said about the Sunday school she says again, "Oui, madame," and resumes her pose of statue-like immobility.

Just as in Slave Days.

"But she gets no pay for her work," I said.

"Pay?"

"The brother to whom Alice Campbell gave her property, or rather loaned it since it is still hers, bent low and interposed a swarthy, excited face. "Pay? And her clothes, then? And her shoes? And what she eats? And the bill for the doctor and the medicine? She is sick. I get the doctor? I pay for it?"

Precisely as they did only thirty-five years ago, and precisely what they said then. And just the same incapacity to understand that, even by providing doctors and medicine for a sick slave, a benevolent slave-owner cannot convince one of his right to own a human being.

Pauline Pariendi is sick. Two winters in Philadelphia have not yet hardened her insufficiently nourished body to the Northern cold. Even in the house, small and stuffy and poorly furnished, she keeps her ragged wraps about her, and feels the chill that only the tropic-born know in being transplanted.

Not the Only One.

And she is not the only child born in Martinique who lives a slave in America. There is another exemption to the emancipation proclamation at 814

Vintner street, where Jeanne Timothy, born in Saint Pierre, of a Chinese father and a negro mother, twelve years ago, lives, the property of H. Delsui.

Alie Campbell, in digressing a moment from the history of Pauline Pariendi, told me yesterday the story of Jeanne Timothy, who came to Philadelphia in care of one of these same Campbell sisters.

"Madame Delsui," explained Mademoiselle Campbell amiably, sitting in the low rocking chair and putting down her sewing, "wished to send a bonne[68] to her son here in Amerique. She had this little girl. She did not need her. Her son had married here, and had a small baby. So she asked my sister to bring the little bonne with her when she came to Philadelphia, and she brought her, to oblige Madame Delsui, on the same ship."

And still to oblige Madame Delsui that thoughtful mother, who continues to provide for the comfort of her son and grandson, though separated from them by thousands of miles of ocean, little Jeanne Timothy lives, a slave, at 814 Vintner street.

I don't know whether it is once more to oblige Madame Delsui that Jeanne Timothy is mercilessly beaten from time to time by Madame Delsui's son. Yet so loving and attentive a mother, so doting a grandparent would doubtless see the necessity for the physical correction of stupid or insubordinate slave bonnes, however childish and small.

THE POLICE INTERFERED.

But Delsui erred, as mere human slave-owners have since first slavery was invented, on the side of thoroughness. He beat Jeanne Timothy till the neighbors revolted and the police interfered. As Marie Campbell's husband put it: "Delsui had trouble with this girl of his. A cop got to interfering and had him up before a Magistrate for licking the kid. But, they did nothing to Delsui and let him go. The kid is his, same as the other is my sister-in-law's. The neighbors is too interfering, and ought to mind their own business."

"Yes" agreed his wife: "Delsui have a paper, same as my sister."

It is from Delsui, too, that the Campbells have learned the way of substituting a paper "confiding" so much animate flesh and bones and capacity to work to the gentle care of a slave-owner for the frank simplicity of the bill of sale, which in some unjust way not quite comprehended by the Campbells

---

68. Bonne: French for housemaid.

has become a source of danger instead of the protection of their rights and property, for which it was originally intended.

Delsui does not care to talk about Pauline Pariendi, and her relation to Alie Campbell. But his own position he feels is impregnable. After he discovered that in addition to the Fifteenth Amendment there is also a bothersome Chinese exclusion act,[69] which concerns itself about Madame Delsui's gracious gift, he wrote to Saint Pierre and received a letter which, he declares, gives him absolute control of Jeanne, the little half-breed bonne.

It is the custom, explains Delsui, in the French West Indies for dark-skinned races to give their children to white people to "bring up." Delsui is "bringing up" Jeanne Timothy, just as Alie Campbell is "bringing up" Pauline Pariendi.

HAVE NO FEAR OF THE LAW.

It would be difficult to make these two little waifs from Martinique understand that they might have a voice in the matter; but after this had been accomplished I rather think they'd prefer staying down to being "brought up" in the Campbell-Delsui way.

As to the women who imported them nothing is further from their minds than a sense of guilt. One of them repeats what Delsui learned—that there are no slaves in America. But she says it as Delsui learned it, under compulsion, and because inquiry about the child has developed a caution that takes the place of knowledge; and to the actual owner of Pauline Pariendi will come a resentful feeling of being persecuted, an intolerable sense of unjust treatment, when our laws, which do not recognize "the custom of the country" from which this soft-voiced Creole mistress of Pauline Pariendi comes, shall interfere between Alie Campbell and the little black girl whom for fourteen years she has considered her property—an asset, in short.

And Madame Delsui, that generous Martinique matron! Imagine what an outrage to the sacred rights of property-owners it would appear to her if the legality of Delsui's magic "paper" should be questioned in a country where it is no longer the fashion for mothers to present little slave nurses to their sons who have become fathers.

---

69. The Chinese Exclusion Act of 1882 restricted Chinese immigration to the United States for ten years.

A CHARACTER STUDY OF
EMMA GOLDMAN

North American, April 11, 1901, 2

"I shall speak in Philadelphia."

Emma Goldman said this to me yesterday. Her hands, a working-woman's hands, were crossed on her knee. She was sitting in a rocking chair in an ordinary little Philadelphia parlor, but her voice, which becomes guttural and strongly accentuated in its Teutonic quality when she speaks earnestly, had nothing of the commonplace in it.[70]

Somehow, I believed her when she said it. There is so much force, as well as sincerity, in this woman's speech that one must find very good reason in one's own mind for differing with her. And when Emma Goldman says she will, a little matter like the "she won't" of the Mayor, the Director of Public Safety[71] and the police force of Philadelphia seems hardly an obstacle worth considering.

"I shall speak in Philadelphia," she repeated, the line between her eyebrows growing more marked as her voice became firmer. "I may have to suffer the consequences, but speak I will. Perhaps the Mayor and Director English will come to their senses. No one would be gladder than I if they come to understand how foolish they have been. But whether they do or not, I shall speak."

"On what subject?"

---

70. In 1901, anarchist Emma Goldman generated a controversy over free speech when the police attempted to keep her from delivering a speech in Philadelphia.

71. The mayor of Philadelphia, Samuel Howell Ashbridge, and the director of public safety, Abraham Lincoln English, denied Goldman permission to speak in Philadelphia.

"The methods of Russia in America," she answered with a smile. "The methods of Russia are of the tenth century; the intellectual development of America is of the twentieth. They don't go very well together, do they?"

SHE IS A CREATURE OF MOODS.

The photograph of Miss Goldman which accompanies this article will not give you an altogether truthful impression of this remarkable woman. To realize her personality you must know that this awful Anarchist is a creature of moods.

When she speaks, when she is interested, when she is delivering an address, the face which on the first page looks sad and rather weary and a bit heavy, is lighted up till it is almost pretty. Miss Goldman would rather face Lieutenant Wood, of the Philadelphia police force, than the camera.

"Newspaper sketches always make me look vulgar," she said, when we were planning her photographs. "I am not vain. I have no reason to be. But I cannot bear to be made to appear vulgar."

Vulgarity is the last characteristic one would think of in connection with Miss Goldman. You must imagine this strong face softened and femininized by its pretty coloring, by a very fair skin, and cheeks and the tip of the chin pink with excitement.

The great, columnlike throat is beautifully white. The hair is a fair brown, and, though the eyebrows and lashes are darker, the small, deepset eyes are a clear gray that looks blue when Miss Goldman's speech becomes emphatic. And this happens pretty often.

"It is my nature to be what I am," she says. "As long as I live I must be a crusader. What I think, what I feel, I must speak. Not for a hundred, not for five hundred years, perhaps, will the principles of anarchy triumph. But what has that to do with it? 'Is it right?' not 'Is it hopeless?' is the touchstone of courage and principle.

"I AM NOT HOPELESS."

"If all the world was at peace and happy, and in one small village there lived a man who was a toiling slave, a woman who was suffering, a child condemned to degrading labor, I could know no rest. It is my temperament to propagate opinions. As a matter of fact, I am not hopeless.

"I see the world improving. I know that fifteen years ago no audience in

America would listen to the doctrines I advocate. I know that today in every town all over the country there is a society formed to disseminate those ideas. I know that when Krapotkin [sic][72] came to America there was but one college in all the country courageous enough, enlightened enough, to listen to him. And today he is besieged by offers for his lectures, offers of $75 and $100 for each address from institutions of learning in every great city of America."

Miss Goldman was born in St. Petersburg, but was educated mainly in Germany. She is a little body, this famous Anarchist, who has roused in the Mayor and the Director of Public Safety and the whole police force a desperate desire to stifle free speech in Philadelphia. She is stout, though, and broad-hipped, a sturdy-looking, quick-moving, intense woman.

"I very well understand," she said with quiet scorn, "why your Mayor and your Director English object to my speaking in Philadelphia. It is not because of my Anarchistic opinions—what do they know of these? They do not know what an Anarchist is. Besides, I have delivered speeches in Philadelphia two months ago, and often I have spoken here.

"But it occurs to your Mayor that he has a very nasty, a very black record. He will do something to show the people that he is not so black as he is painted. He says to them: 'See what it is I am doing for you. See how careful I am of Philadelphia's pure morals. Here comes a shocking woman, an Anarchist, a wretched creature, a bombthrower. See how I stifle her. See how I forbid her speech. Philadelphia shall not be corrupted by her anarchistic doctrines!'

"And as Anarchy is not understood, as it is a bogy to the ordinary so-called respectable community, your Mayor gets the credit of being a very wise, very courageous man, whereas he is only very foolish.

Free Press Is in Danger.

"For he cannot prevent my speaking. It is not Emma Goldman, it is not anarchy, he attacks. It is liberty of speech. Let the newspapers take care. The next thing attacked will be the freedom of the press. For me, I must press this

---

72. Peter Kropotkin (1842–1921): Russian social theorist and leading figure in the anarchist movement.

case. I must see just how far the enlightened public opinion of the independent city of Philadelphia will let its Mayor go.

"Do you realize that Lieutenant Wood, of your police force, came at me with his fist at my breast? I have been treated by this man—an officer, a lieutenant of police—with such brutality and vulgarity as Russia would be ashamed of. I am an impulsive woman. I could control myself only by remembering that there were two young girl students with me just ready for their diplomas. I would face arrest—though I assure you I know the discomfort of prison life—but arrest for them in my company would have hurt their careers. But a brute like that Wood—"

She stretched out her hand, closing her fist and bringing it down upon her knee. We went on talking about herself and her opinions, among other things her opposition to prisons, and her contention that no human being, however degraded, is irredeemable.

"Even Wood—even Lieutenant Wood," she said, hurried by her interest in her subject past the point where her sense of humor usually stands guard, "there is hope even for such a man as that. It is his position that holds him. Let him once break from the fear of losing his little political job; let him cut loose from a corrupt municipal machine that corrupts all who benefit by it, and he can again become a man who dares to think and dares to feel."

There is vigor in this woman's speech. She is utterly fearless, utterly free from restraint. There is no "no thoroughfare" for her mind. She dares to follow wherever conviction leads.

No one who has not heard her deliver an address can conceive of the force there is in this Russian free thinker. No care of the prettinesses of manner or speech can stay her. Her voice may break, her knowledge of English may fail her; but she is more effective than art could possibly make her, more eloquent than the completest elegance of speech could give. She snarls, she sneers, she thunders at her audience, and she is as indifferent to their rage as to their approval.

Has No Faith in the Mob.

"I know the mob," she said, yesterday, "and I do not count upon it—no, not a bit. I looked at the crowd that followed hurrahing for me the other night, and I said in my mind to them, 'You cheer for me, you follow me, but you'd hang me if your mood changed.'

"It is not in the laboring man, the lowest classes, that I find my hope. It is the middle class and the professional people that are being educated to whom theories of life like mine appeal. Just so long as there remain in the world men and women ready to die for principle, there will be hope for mankind. It is from the minority that the strength to uplift the world has always come. In America we are becoming more and more imperialistic. We shall become more like Russia before we become less like her.

"But so far as the spread of anarchy goes, let me tell you that a little political move like this of your Mayor's—yes, or one policeman like Lieutenant Wood—goes further to make Anarchists than all the speeches I have ever delivered. It would have been different if there had been some excuse, if there had been a strike or if the public mind was heated and excited. But as it is, it is your Mayor who is inciting to riot; it is your Lieutenant Wood who appeals to violence. For me, I do not admit that I ever incited men to riot."

But I'll admit for you that what you say is enough to incite them to riot, Emma Goldman. If during a strike, when bitterness and poverty and excitement combine to upset men's reason, a fire brand like yourself were thrown among them the damage done might be incalculable.

If I were a guardian of the peace, I'd rather Johann Most[73] himself would tell the strikers of their wrongs than that a woman like yourself, with your clear intelligence, your impetuous tongue, and your ardent heart, should heap contempt last arbitrament, or encourage them to battle for their rights.

I should fear your influence, Emma Goldman. I should fear your cleverness. I should fear your courage. I should fear your capacity to rouse the sleeping devil in the mob that stirs uneasily when your uncompromising voice rings out.

All of which has nothing to do with the case in point, of course.

Emma Goldman is not a fanatic; nor is she a cruelhearted monster; nor is she a dreamer.

"The man who joins a movement because his stomach is empty," she says in rude epigram, "will leave it as soon as he is better off. We Anarchists want

---

73. Johann Most (1846–1906): German-born editor, orator, and anarchist who immigrated to America and furthered the development of the anarchist movement in the United States. His ideas inspired the young Emma Goldman.

people who think to listen to us—not the people who only feel. Enlightened public opinion will come to know us in time, not as bomb throwers, but as free men and women, who want the world to be free, who hope to teach the people to govern themselves, not to be governed like children by the rod of the law."

"I wonder, Miss Goldman, whether you'd approve of Mrs. Nation?" I asked.[74]

"As a woman who is willing to sacrifice herself for a principle? Yes. As a one-idead reformer, who foolishly expects to make men abstain from drink by smashing saloons—no. And then—I am sorry—I have been unable to convince myself of her sincerity, for she accepts money for what she does."

"And you?"

"I? I am a trained nurse. I support myself by my work. I was to have come here some time ago, but I had an important case which I could not leave.

"Do you suppose I would accept money for my work? Never. It would spoil it all. My traveling expenses, yes; my hotel bill, if I do not stop with friends. But to speak, to work, to propagate the truth I feel—I love that. I could not take money for that."

Does it not occur to you that there's something rather lofty about this point of view—for an Anarchist? As a lecturer, this woman could make more money than half a dozen trained nurses. Her work would be infinitely easier, and, as she says, she loves it. But she loves it too well to make money out of it.

"I am not conceited," she said, "but I am not blind to the fact that I can work, that I can do things. I could make what goodygoody people call an honest living in other ways, but there is no other life than just this for me."

As a property Anarchist, to be used by the Mayor as a bogey, Emma Goldman is not a success. She likes "women to be feminine," she told me. She loves "flowers and pretty things, although I cannot have them, for there are other uses I must put money to."

Worked in a Prison Hospital.

In the car, as we came uptown together she glanced across to a pretty girl, stylishly dressed, and told me how she enjoyed looking at her. As we walked

---

74. See "Miriam Michelson Goes on a Hatchet Crusade" and the excerpt from "Mrs. Nation, Joan of Arc of Temperance Crusade, As Seen by Miriam Michelson."

along the street together she noticed the pretty things in the shop windows and commented upon them impersonally as desirable things for the adornment of other women. When she was imprisoned for a year in New York she served all that time in the prison hospital, and you could not have made the degraded women who learned to adore her believe that she was an Anarchist. She went to Europe last year, because she wanted to study to become a physician. But she is back in America working still at the hardest profession a woman can adopt, and her young brother is going through Columbia College at her expense.

No, if even the Mayor and Director English and Lieutenant Wood were to go to call upon Emma Goldman, the Anarchist, they would find her too human, too kindly, too tolerant, too straightforward and honest and altogether too clever for their purpose.

"Wait, and you will see that I shall speak. It is a small matter, of course, if Emma Goldman is denied the right of speech. But if I am denied that right other Anarchists in this city will also be denied it. For this I must fight. And I will carry it through the courts, and into the prison, if I must, but I will speak before I go back to New York. New York is more cosmopolitan. One can breathe freer there. Philadelphia is narrow, of course. It is the cradle of conventionality. Still, I shall speak here."

I have engaged a seat for Miss Goldman's lecture. I am sure that if the Mayor and the Director of Public Safety and a certain lieutenant of police express a wish to hear it, they can also be accommodated, and they might learn something from this Russian woman of the difference between tenth and twentieth century methods of governing.

Motives of Women Who Commit Theft

North American, May 6, 1902, 8

T he widening of woman's scope as an economic factor has led to a corresponding increase in the variety of her crimes, naturally. When she was a limited, wholly domestic creature, the criminal side of her nature could express itself only in the killing of her lover or her husband, the slandering of her neighbor, preferably by means of anonymous letters or in petty thefts.

With her development as a business entity comes a corresponding versatility, a broadening in prison records, which treat of her. Nowadays women boldly take the initiative in crimes which once they attempted only as subordinates. Today they promote illegitimate enterprises, sell gold bricks of assorted kinds on their own account and even embezzle.

I am not bragging of this. Nor am I responsible for it. I am merely stating it to be the case. I have a theory, though, that the sum of crime is not a varying quantity; that for every innovating penitentiary offense in which the new woman is the pioneer of her sex there would have been a corresponding gain to strengthen the statistics of old womanly crimes had the business world and the professions not been thrown open to women.

Women Are Amateurs in Crime

But, though women have become co-eds in crime, taking all branches in that nefarious institution of learning from experience, where the students shave their heads, wear striped clothing, and dwell studiously apart behind bolts and bars, they still show the mark of the amateur, not only in the cheapness for which they sell their honesty, but in their motives that lead them to do this.

When a man embezzles he leaves behind him a flashing trail of iniquity that serves—if he is wholly unregenerate—as a consolation to himself, if not as a warning to others. Men embezzle to minister to their self-indulgence. Women embezzle to indulge somebody other than themselves. A man who betrays his employer's trust is a thorough rascal, with body and mind corrupted by hypocrisy. But he is, as far as his limitations will let him be, a man of the world. A woman who embezzles is often an unsophisticated mathematician, whose dexterous use of figures is the only evidence of her claim to being a well-balanced business woman. And she is rarely a woman of the world.

Sometimes she is even a saint.

In a little town out in Nevada, one of this sort lived a few years ago. She was a sister of charity, and she actually embezzled the moneys of the convent with which she was connected.

And what did she do with her guilty gains?

Women Steal for Others

She squandered it, not in riotous living, but upon the little girls and boys she taught. To educate her charges properly needed more funds than the convent school had at its disposal. Wherefore Sister Rose stole what she needed to supplement what was given her, spent it on other women's children with the lavishness that accompanies and dissipates illegitimate profits, was found out after a year or two of painstaking falsifying of books, was secretly disgraced and banished, not only from her convent, the only home she had ever known, but from the little boys and girls she had lied and cheated and stolen for.

All women embezzlers are not Sister Roses, unhappily—or happily. But if you will examine the motives for their crimes, you will be struck by the absence of that preliminary dash and splurge, that blaze of malevolent light, which partly reconciles the ordinary male offender to prison oblivion, when discovery finally comes.

In New York, yesterday, a woman was arrested for having padded the pay rolls of her employers till she had gathered in the sum of $130.

And, what did she steal for?

Padded Pay Rolls for a Monument

For a monument, of course. She yearned for a noble stone that might tell to the world, after she was gone, the virtues, the name and the age of her who lay beneath. And even a trusted forewoman's salary doesn't provide for a towering granite column after death.

Of course, no one would steal, if he didn't believe that there was an absolute necessity of having some particular thing without the pain of working for it. The curious thing is to note just what the absolutely essential signifies to different people.

Here in Philadelphia, a woman embezzled not long ago that her dogs might sleep between immaculate, fine linen sheets and have silk attire—so far as they required attire at all—and have their food daintily prepared and properly served.

Stole for Her Friend's Husband

This woman's definition—as she criminally interpreted it—would be altogether incomprehensible to a sister defaulter, who stole to provide another woman's husband with funds to bet on the races, to live soft and well, to have his own little country place—and to be able to put up bail for himself, when the crash came at last, leaving the woman embezzler to lie in prison, in default of it.

No, despite their unquestioned adaptability and the monkey-like quickness with which they learn to imitate men's vices, women sin sadly; not gladly, as their models do. They are still only amateurs, and show the prentice hand whenever they attempt an unfamiliar crime.

As to the motives that lead them to add to the varieties of their sex's infringements of the law—I leave it to any gentleman in stripes who has had his fling at his employer's expense to say whether there's rhyme or reason to them.

3

SHORT FICTION, 1901 TO 1905

INTRODUCTION TO PART 3

The third and final section of *The Superwoman and Other Writings by Miriam Michelson* contains a sampling of short fiction published during the first decade of the twentieth century, the most prolific period in Michelson's career as a fiction writer. With the exception of "In Chy Fong's Restaurant," these stories initially appeared in periodicals. As in all of Michelson's short stories and novels, women play central roles in these pieces, emerging as the texts' most dynamic characters and driving much, if not all, of the action. Even when Michelson's stories conclude with the "happy ending" of heteronormative romance (as in "An Understudy for a Princess") or the death of a tragic female character (as in "Ah Luey's Self"), her writing bucks conventional gender norms. She offers representations of women in power, working women, women of color, and the bonds between women. I selected stories that would reveal the recurring themes of her fiction while showcasing her range as a writer and the arc of her career, capturing her rise to national prominence at a time of significant growth for the American literary marketplace in general and magazine publishing in particular. I also chose these stories with an eye toward classroom use and active pedagogy; all of them gain texture from being paired with pieces of journalism in this collection, and these pairings will allow students to examine the fascinating interplay between fiction and newspaper writing.

Michelson's earliest stories capture the multiethnic diversity of the American West, situating her as a regional writer in the tradition of Twain, Bret Harte, and Jack London. Set in the Hawaiian Islands, "An Understudy for a Princess" pairs well with her article about the anti-annexation movement, "Strangling Hands upon a Nation's Throat," exemplifying how her background as a journalist provided her with material for her imaginative writing. Similarly, both "Ah Luey's Self" and "In Chy Fong's Restaurant" are born from Michelson's experiences as a reporter in San Francisco's Chinatown. With their themes of Orientalism, interracialism, capitalist exploitation, and colonialism, these stories speak to some of the most pressing concerns in the current study of American literature and culture.

The fiction collected here further demonstrates how the arc of Michelson's career was shaped by the commercial demands of the mainstream literary marketplace. It is telling that her breakthrough as a writer came with "In the Bishop's Carriage," which shifts focus to white femininity and away from marginalized women of color. The enthusiastic response of editors and readers to this short story led Michelson to expand it into a full-length novel by the same name. Michelson's spirited and independent white female protagonist was the key to her commercial success: *In the Bishop's Carriage* became a sensational bestseller. Twenty-first-century readers may find that the story has lost some of its daring with time, as female criminals now make regular appearances in literature, film, and television. In the early twentieth century, however, the first-person narrative of a girl-thief, told in a bold, vernacular style, captivated readers, turning the protagonist, Nance Olden, into a pop culture icon who was brought to life on stage and screen by some of the most famous actresses of the day.

Michelson capitalized on the success of "In the Bishop's Carriage" with two magazine serials. In 1904, "Stories of the Nevada Madigans" was serialized in *Century Magazine*; the magazine's publisher, Century Company, subsequently printed the stories in book form under the simplified title *The Madigans*. Michelson's "A Yellow Journalist" series appeared in the *Saturday Evening Post* the following year before being published as a book by D. Appleton and Company. In contrast to the monoracial and monocultural milieu of "In the Bishop's Carriage," these series place unconventional white (or, in the case of the Irish Madigans, white ethnic) female characters against the multiracial backdrop of the American West.

"The Ancestry of Irene" is the second installment in "Stories of the Nevada Madigans," a series of episodic fictions about a family of girls growing up in Virginia City and based on the author's own childhood in the legendary mining town. Written with a juvenile audience in mind, these stories demonstrate Michelson's reach as a writer, while carrying over the themes of female independence and adventurousness that made "In the Bishop's Carriage" a success. As illustrated by the assertive, athletic, and imaginative Irene in "The Ancestry of Irene," these stories contribute to a tradition of literary tomboys spanning from Louisa May Alcott's Jo March to characters such as Laura Ingalls, Pippi Longstocking, Harriet the Spy, and Katniss Everdeen. Just as critics have recently reevaluated Laura Ingalls Wilder's *Little House on the Prairie* series due to its racist portrayals of Native Americans and its erasures of native history and experience, contemporary readers of Michelson's fiction will find themselves troubled by her one-dimensional depictions of Wong, the Madigans' Chinese domestic servant, and the dull-witted "Indian Jim," as well as by Irene's condescending white superiority and act of racial appropriation.[1] As liberating as Michelson's frontier setting may be, freeing the Madigan girls of gender constraints, these aspects of "The Ancestry of Irene" constitute racial blind spots and serve to remind readers that her work needs to be qualified as a *white* feminist intervention.

Along with *The Superwoman*, Michelson's "Yellow Journalist" series is likely to prove the most resonant of Michelson's fictions for contemporary feminist study. In her heroine, Rhoda Massey, a "girl-reporter" for the fictional *San Francisco News*, Michelson offers a compelling representation of a single, ambitious working woman who confronts gender discrimination and sexual harassment on the job but who triumphs despite the odds and uses strategic performances of femininity to her advantage. "The Pencil Will," which focuses on Rhoda's relationship with a black female character named Mammy Sinnott, provides an opportunity to further examine the intersections of gender and race in Michelson's work. The story draws on Michelson's encounters with a real-life woman, the activist and businesswoman Mary Ellen Pleasant (called "Mammy Pleasant" in the press). Read alongside Michelson's newspaper profile of Pleasant in "Dark-Skinned Lion-Tamer in the House of Mystery," "The Pencil Will" offers opportunities to analyze the interplay between representations of white and black working women and between journalism and fiction, as well as the sensationalist discourses and ethical dilemmas engendered by the popularity of the yellow press.

As a complement to the race and gender dynamics of "The Pencil Will," I also include "In Chy Fong's Restaurant," one of the two Chinatown chapters published in the book version of *A Yellow Journalist*, but omitted from the *Saturday Evening Post* series, perhaps due to their risqué content. A narrative of sexual slavery and racial passing, "In Chy Fong's Restaurant" offers a provocative entrée into considerations of the cultural phenomenon of girl stunt reporting and the literary tradition of the Chinatown tale. Like many of Michelson's stories, it uses larger-than-life historical characters as models for characters. The character of Ah Oy, for example, evokes one of the best-known Chinese American women of the era, the prostitute and madam Ah Toy, while Miss McIntosh is based on the Scottish missionary crusader Donaldina Cameron, who ran the Occidental Board Mission Home for Chinese Girls in San Francisco's Chinatown.

This collection concludes with another story from the "Yellow Journalist" series, "The Milpitas Maiden." Published in the *Saturday Evening Post* but excluded for unknown reasons from the book-length edition of *A Yellow Journalist*, this story secures Michelson's place in the canon of suffrage literature. Set at a women's rights convention, the short story will propel readers back to Michelson's earliest assignments for the *San Francisco Call* in 1895, when she covered the Woman's Congress of the Pacific Coast. "The Milpitas Maiden" effectively uses comedy to overturn stereotypical depictions of new womanhood, "lady journalists," and women's rights activists. It is a fitting conclusion to a collection that significantly broadens our understanding of feminist literary history by introducing contemporary readers to Miriam Michelson, a bold-voiced woman writer whose work has much to teach us about American progressivism in the past while remaining relevant to race and gender politics in the present day.

NOTES

1. On Wilder, see, for example, Donna Campbell, "'Wild Men' and Dissenting Voices: Narrative Disruption in *Little House on the Prairie*," *Great Plains Quarterly* 20, no. 2 (2000): 111–22; and Sharon Smulders, "'The Only Good Indian': History, Race, and Representation in Laura Ingalls Wilder's *Little House on the Prairie*," *Children's Literature Association Quarterly* 27, no. 4 (2002): 191–202.

An Understudy for a Princess

Black Cat 70 (July 1901): 1–16

The pepper to the extreme right. A crescent of small, oblong crackers curving in. Still on the right, half of a lemon. Farther toward the centre of the table a line of salt, with a knife laid at right angles. And dominating it all the empty salt cellar, reversed.

The waiter who served Arthur Jerdrum in his London club noted the familiar arrangement with a look of hopeless patience. Jerdrum had just gone out after sitting dreamily over his oysters till it got so late that the weary waiter thought he must have fallen asleep.

In the morning it would be the same, the perplexed waiter told himself. In place of the crackers there would be a bay-line of bread-crumbs, and a cube of sugar would mark the spot where the lemon had been the night before. And at dinner, whether he dined alone, as he usually did, or whether he brought with him a giant Boer whose imperfect speech was all of diamonds and greedy Uitlanders; or a hard-faced Antipodean who held forth on the dry fields of West Australia; or a turbaned, yellow-faced, full-lipped man, with whom he conversed in French; or a fat-faced, prosperous-looking fellow who discussed Nevada mines and Texas cattle—still, after he and his guest had left the table, in front of Jerdrum's place there would be an indenting bay of broken, bent matches, a wine glass standing for the high peak to the right, and the rest of the well-known topographical features carefully, dreamily, smudged-in in cigar ashes on the smooth, white cloth.

Only once had this big young fellow with the burned, blond face and a cosmopolitan lack of nationality in his loose figure and reticent tongue, failed to leave the map behind him. This was when he came into the club with a brown-faced, black-moustached, liquid-eyed Hawaiian, and they talked in an odd, musical, vowel-full language, straight through the courses of which neither partook, both leaving the table suddenly while the waiter was absent. Then Jerdrum was not seen about the club for three days, at the end of which time he came back, and the waiter found a page from a time-table on the Scottish Highlands torn crescent shaped and marked with blue pencil to the right, farther in again, straight across, and then again along the line.

No one would have been more surprised than Jerdrum himself had he known that his habit of thought was being disclosed by the automatic betrayal of his long, strong, nervous fingers. Yet the black man who had served him in Egypt and India, when he was surveying in advance of the railroad; the little French man-of-all-work whose invaluable services had ended in an asylum after they two had been lost on an Arizonan desert; the clever Chinese boy he had picked up in New Zealand—all of these could recall perfectly that same crescent-shaped bay with the familiar landmarks. Black Ali, though, remembered it as having been constructed of uncut, unpolished diamonds. Pierre knew it best as a half-circle of glistening sand, with pieces of string and broken bits of cactus for the landmarks. It dwelt in Ah Sing's retentive memory worked out in rich quartz crystals, with gold nuggets of various sizes to mark the positions from which the London waiter superciliously swept the lemon, the pepper caster and the salt cellar.

Ali made up his mind, after much ostentatious and official thinking, that the plan referred to a highly original and undoubtedly successful scheme for transportation, involving the use of a new and unknown motor.

Pierre smiled knowingly every time he saw the giant Dane absorbed in the work of his fingers. Her room, Pierre said to himself, was marked by the bright bit of red string, her husband's by the cactus thorn. The crescent was the roundabout path her lover must take to get to her—when the time should come.

Ah Sing had decided that it was a plan of the hiding-place of a great treasure. The cheerful little yellow man waited for years, patiently following Jerdrum about the world, expecting confidently that the time and place would come when and where the crescent of powdered quartz and the gold nuggets would reproduce themselves on a gigantic scale, when and where Ah Sing should be regretfully compelled to kill his big young master while he slept, and take possession of the mine himself.

But when Jerdrum sailed from London for Hawaii, he left the indignant

Ah Sing behind him. And when he arrived in San Francisco, in the spring of '98, he had no servant with him.

ع

The Princess knitted her delicate brows. She stood meditating, a card in her hand.

The name was oddly familiar, but when or where she had heard it she could not remember. Arthur Jerdrum! Arthur Jerdrum! How absurd! At the name, the memory of the Islands she had not seen for years grew strong within her. By some strange trick of memory, that odd name seemed associated with the plash of the deep blue summer sea of Honolulu, with the scarlet hibiscus, with the pale, perfumed yellow of the ginger flower, with the waving reflections of tall, graceful cocoanut palms in the still water, with the soft, moist warmth of Hawaii, with all that luxury of tropical island scenery that had surrounded Kaiulani's childhood.

"But, Kaiulani, just how long are you going to stand there while the boy waits?"

It was Lilia's voice that roused the Princess from her reverie.

Kaiulani sighed. "Not a moment longer, Lilia. Father is waiting for me. I cannot see this gentleman. You see him, Lilia. I should remember his name, I know. Tell him—tell him—"

"I'll tell him how sorry you'll be when you hear that he has called in your absence," laughed Lilia. "But, truly, if I were Princess of Hawaii, I'd enjoy seeing everybody that called."

"Well, play princess, dear. Tell this stranger that you are Kaiulani, Princess of Nowhere. He'll not know the difference, and you'll have the pleasure—"

"You might be Queen of Somewhere, if you'd listen just once," answered Lilia, her voice trembling with eagerness. "I'm sure it could be done, Kaiulani. Just say once to the Hawaiians—"

"Lilia, you poor, nonsensical little Lilia, you're the most rabid royalist I ever met. Shall we fight the United States, dear, you and I? Shall we compel the world to see things as we see them?[1] Shall we make ourselves the

---

1. For historical context on the annexation of Hawaii, see "Strangling Hands upon a Nation's Throat."

laughing-stock of the world with another puny rebellion in the so-called Republic of Hawaii, and let our enemies triumph over us even more than they do now? Hush! There comes Mr.—Mr. Jerdrum. I'll slip out this way."

The Princess turned to leave the room. She stopped with her hand upon the bedroom door.

"I know now," she whispered hurriedly. "Jerdrum was half-scientist, half-civil-engineer; he came to the Islands in my uncle Kalakaua's time. He was the only man Liliuokalani ever trusted fully. And this is his son Arthur, my old playmate. Be nice to him. If it weren't for my engagement with father—Sh!"

The Princess closed the door softly behind her and Jerdrum entered from the hall.

"I hardly hoped you would see me," he said, taking the hand Lilia held out. "Our friendship dates back so long ago that I didn't know you'd recognize my name as that of your old playmate."

"So we were playmates?" asked Lilia amused, yet seized by a sudden whim to hear more before she should enlighten this man with the sincere voice and odd blue eyes.

Jerdrum took the chair she indicated. "Yes," he answered, "in Kalakaua's time. You have changed very much since then."

"How?" the girl asked curiously.

"Surely, your Highness—"

Mechanically, Lilia made a disclaiming gesture.

"Isn't it like old times" Jerdrum asked, with his peculiar short laugh. "When we quarrelled, I used to call you 'Your Highness,' and then you wouldn't speak to me."

"But how have I changed?" The coquettish blood of generations of French grandmothers leapt to the cheek of this half-Hawaiian girl. All the woman in her challenged comparison with the beautiful Princess Kaiulani.

Jerdrum drew a small card from his pocket and passed it to her. It was a photograph of a girl of twelve, whose exceeding slenderness and inquiring, large soft eyes reminded one of the ungainly immaturity of a young deer.

Lilia looked long at the picture. She hardly saw the childish features of Kaiulani. Mentally she was putting in place of this youthful face, the graceful, proud head of the Princess as she had just seen it, and for the first time, with the consciousness of Kaiulani's beauty, came an unhappy, a miserable feeling of envy.

"Do you remember the day you gave me this?" Jerdrum asked, amused at her long inspection of the photograph.

"It is so long ago," murmured Lilia, with down-drooped eyes. Something she had never felt before she experienced now when Jerdrum looked admiringly at her.

"And so much has happened since then," he went on. "It may be the influence of a childhood at court, but I have not been able to outgrow old loyalty to your family, Princess."

The words were simple, but the tone touched a chord in Lilia's faithful heart. For the moment, forgetting the part she was playing, the romantic girl put out her hand impulsively to thank him. Jerdrum took the slender little brown hand and raised it to his lips. But this mimic princess had not become accustomed to her royalty. There was something personal to her in the action, fearfully, deliciously personal. The blood suffused her dusky cheeks, and her guilty heart beat so that she hardly heard Jerdrum's words.

"I have wanted to see you to tell you this," he said. "My father took me back to Denmark a few months after you left Honolulu. And then he went to Ceylon and then to South America, and, of course, I went with him. Once when you were in London, not so long ago, I was there, too. I tried to see you, followed you to Scotland, but you had left the week before. I cannot tell you how it seems to me to see you again. You are part of my childhood, Princess. My father is dead—years ago. I have not a tie in the world, and the memory of that happy time in beautiful Hawaii lingers so pleasantly in my mind."

Lilia did not speak. The simplest thing—to tell this man that she had been "playing princess "—seemed now the most impossible. So she waited, drifting helplessly with the tide his conversation took.

He sat and talked as a solitary man will when he meets a sympathetic listener. He told stories of the adventurous life he had led, living over in the young girl's eager interest days of peril and nights of watchfulness. And her presence, her sympathetic silence lent a charm of romance to that which, in living, had at times been merely squalid or wearisome or distasteful.

"But, in the midst of it all, when I heard of the wrong done to you and to Hawaii, Princess—"

"I am not a princess," interrupted Lilia with sudden contempt for the part she was playing.

Jerdrum misunderstood her. And the emotion in the sweet Hawaiian voice brought the words from him that he had not expected to say.

"It is true. You are not a princess, Kaiulani. You have no realm, no royal family, no hope for the future. But you may be Queen. You shall be Queen, if you will only say the word. Listen, only listen patiently to me. I am not a dreamer. I know what I am promising. If you will let me work for you, the greedy Americans will never get possession of Hawaii. The throne shall be restored and you shall grace it, Queen Kaiulani."

It seemed to Lilia that all her senses were merged into one. She could only listen, her unseeing eyes bent upon his strong, long fingers which, straying about the table, had unconsciously shaped the wool escaped from Lilia's workbasket into a semicircle. To the extreme right of this, the silver-topped inkstand had been moved. Farther to the left an indentation was marked by a gay worsted ball. The pearl-topped slender penholder had been placed level, with the paper cutter at right angles, and behind it stood the tiny clock enamelled in forget-me-nots.

"When Liliuokalani was dethroned," he was saying, "had there been but one man near her, one strong, brave man whom she trusted implicitly, the monarchy would never have been lost. If my father had been in Honolulu at that time, Liliuokalani would be reigning there now. But this is all past. The thing is the future. You know, you must know, your advisers must realize, that if the Islands were once again in the possession of the natives, all thought of annexation to the United States would be out of the question. If you will agree, Princess; if you will trust me, if you will only be your own brave self, you shall be seated on the throne, and if for only one hour you are recognized as Queen of Hawaii, on what pretext will a foreign power dare to interfere?"

Lilia had risen. She had altogether forgotten the rôle she was playing. Her ardent nature was fired by Jerdrum's words. She had dreamed of a restoration. She had almost quarrelled with her idolized Princess, whose Scotch father had threatened that he would separate her from Kaiulani, if she did not learn to control the expression of her enthusiastic, uncompromising royalism. To hear her own thoughts, the dream which in her had been derided, uttered by this determined-looking young fellow, whose voice, whose manner of speech was so fervent, so belief-inspiring, transported the girl till she hardly knew what she was doing or saying.

"Oh, if you can do it! If you will—my life, my fortune—oh, what could I do to prove to you—"

Jerdrum caught the fluttering hands she held out to him. "I knew it! I knew it!" he exclaimed. "They told me you were cold. They hinted that you had grown politic, that you valued more the allowance doled out to you by these usurpers than you did your right to the crown. But I never believed it, never! I knew you too well, Kaiulani. The girl who read and studied and played with me—I knew that girl better than others."

And then Jerdrum told his plan. For years he had recognized this scheme of his for Kaiulani's succession to the Hawaiian throne only as a dream, a sort of mental puzzle, an outlet for his imagination. Now that, for the first time, he put into words the details his mind had built up day by day, he saw that what had been first merely exercise for his active brain, food for his adventurous craving for power and action, had become perfected into plausibility, even probability.

Given a group of islands, isolated from the world because of lack of cable facilities, and a small, usurping oligarchy, doomed to fall in time by the weight of its own jealous particles, if no great nation should intervene, and ruling by sheer exercise of military strength an inimical, wronged native race outnumbering the white men twenty to one; given a determined, courageous leadership, money, a just cause, and the legitimate sovereign; given the effective appeal to sympathy and sensibility made by a beautiful maiden Queen, fair in face as her Caucasian father, Hawaiian in instinct and allegiance as her brown mother, refined with European culture, forgiving, gracious and amiable, a stranger to all the local hates and fears, biases and revengeful desires of the petty, bitter civil war, which the old Queen had seemed to embody; given that Queen's abdication in favor of her niece, an abdication of a form that could become substance only after it had been parted with; given all this, and Jerdrum was willing to risk his life in proving his postulates.

"Here is the harbor of Honolulu," he concluded, his eyes suddenly taking note of the work his hands had done unbidden. "Here is Diamond Head, where arms may be smuggled ashore. Here is your place, Princess, at Waikiki, where they shall be delivered. At this point and at this, telephone and telegraph wires shall be cut. Here is the Government Building, of which ten thousand armed Hawaiians shall take possession in a night, almost without bloodshed, for the native police are with us the moment their Queen shall call upon them.

"Before our enemies can communicate with any vessel in the harbor, the monarchy will be re-established and no foreign power may interfere. Then you will make me your minister of war, perhaps, Princess, and after that, if the Kanaka lets the independence of his country slip through his fingers, the white man is welcome to it."

۶ﻟﻪ

LETTER FROM PRINCESS KAIULANI TO
A FRIEND IN SAN FRANCISCO.

MY DEAR PAULIA:

Pardon my neglect. I intended to write you months ago, but, thanks to that tireless small person Lilia, we have been junketing all about the Pacific. I cannot account for Lilia's passion for going about, but, since we have been at the Islands, there is not a town, not a plantation that we have not visited. We have toured the Islands from Lehua to Hilo. You'd laugh at Lilia. She seems to be possessed with a fever for meeting and talking to every native Hawaiian on the Islands. You know how prettily she speaks the language; and how winning a coax she is is evidenced by the fact of my having accompanied her on most of her excursions. The result is—not what you might expect, that the people are in love with her, but that they are mad with loyalty for me! That arch-royalist Lilia infects everybody she meets, it seems to me. She never wearies of singing my praises. She goes about spending her mother's great fortune in doing good in my name. And she appears to he living in some sort of dream which I cannot understand. For, of course, we know, my dear, how hopeless the case is. And yet I find myself—the real sufferer— abstaining from clouding Lilia's hopes, feeling a kind of ridiculous sympathy for the mad little Jacobite[2] who never will learn reason.

---

2. Jacobites: loyalists who continued to support the exiled Stuart King, James II, and his descendants after the Glorious Revolution (1688) in Great Britain.

All this about Lilia has a purpose. I wish you could come down and perhaps look after her a bit. She was always responsive to your control, because of the passionate reverence she has for her dead mother's dearest friend. This madness may be but a fleeting emotional attack, due to the revisiting our old home, which she has not seen for years.

We are to give a great ball a week from to-night. It is Lilia's birthday, and she has begged for possession of my home for one night. You should see the place. That extravagant young person has spent six months' allowance in perfecting arrangements. I never dreamed how eager she is for pleasure. Everybody in town is invited, and on the lawns supper is to be served to the natives, who will come from as far as Kauai. There are to be songs and dances for them, and you'd think it was to be Waikiki's birthday, instead of Lilia's, such gifts she is planning for everybody.

There is something else that I must tell you. I fancy—I need not tell you, Paulia, that to no one else would I tell this—that Lilia has lost her heart down here in Honolulu. It may not be serious as yet, but there is a Mr. Jerdrum, whom oddly I have not met, that Lilia is much interested in. They correspond, I know, and meet occasionally. There could be nothing clandestine about Lilia, and Jerdrum is a gentleman, I'm sure. All my aunt's friends here are devoted to him. But Lilia is the most romantic girl I ever knew. It is such a pity that her father's sudden death provided no guardian for her. She is too young to be mistress of a fortune, and—well, come down, if you can.

> KAIULANI.
> You know—or do you know—that she has
> sold her sugar plantation on Maui?

ᒷᒷ

"Knowest thou, O Kanui, what things these are we carry down to Waikiki all the nights this week and last?"

The old Kanaka looked a moment toward his companion in the stern of the boat. But the night was black and the sea was black, and Hopu's face was hidden.

"Knowest thou, O Kanui," the younger man began again, this time in a whisper, "that my brother Honolii, the runner, sped all one night some weeks ago with a secret message, and that chiefs from all the seven seas were gathered at Hilo when he got there?"

The powerful old Kanaka leaned forward to shift the weight that lay heavy at the bottom of the long boat.

"Knowest thou, O Kanui, the white giant on the schooner yonder who bade us deliver these—these cases at Waikiki. knowest thou that he too was at Hilo that night with the chiefs?"

Kanui bent to his oars. The necklace of ginger flowers about his massive neck rose and fell with the violence of his exertion. Hopu rowed too, his naked brown back bending over the long muffled oars.

"Knowest thou, Kanui," he murmured after a short silence, "that when a chief bade Jeradaruma show his authority, the white man showed before them all the royal feather lei of Kaiulani, and—and Kanui, he showed them, too, the writing of Liliuokalani giving up the throne."

Cautiously the boat drew close to shore. Hopu drew in his oars and Kanui waded out into the water and pulled the boat in. Noiselessly, the long heavy cases were carried up the slope and stored in the basement of the great pavilion. And then, when Hopu turned to walk again down to the water's edge, the silent Kanui fell upon him, gagging and binding him fast; and carefully dragging him over the pavilion's threshold, he closed the door and locked it after him.

"Naught knows Kanui," the old man muttered, shaking his head as he hurried noiselessly down to the boat. "Naught, save that the tongue of Hopu wags too much."

اله

At the door of the small pavilion Lilia Lauzon and Jerdrum stood alone, he looking down upon her with a puzzled frown.

"If—if you regret it all, Princess," he said at last slowly, "there is yet time to go back. No one knows positively anything that could compromise you except the twelve loyal men at the house yonder, who would die rather than betray you. As to myself, I will be blamed for it all, and I can leave on the schooner before anything becomes known."

The girl was so preoccupied with her own thoughts that the bitterness in his voice escaped her.

There was a long silence, and then Lilia spoke.

"Mr. Jerdrum," she said wistfully, "it has all suddenly come to seem so impossible, so fantastic. Be patient with me, and—and reassure me, if you can, for, truly, I could die for the success of it all."

"I swear we will succeed," Jerdrum answered. "Everything is ready. Shall I go over—"

"No, no, I know it all by heart. All day I think of it. All night I dream of it, and always I dream that we have won, and—and that Queen Kaiulani reigns."

"If she will give the word now," Jerdrum answered, his old enthusiasm waking at the thrill in her low voice, "the sun will rise to-morrow on the first day of her reign."

"If—if she will give the word," Lilia repeated dreamily. "If she will—will she? Oh, will she?"

She turned from him and gazed almost prayerfully at the great flower-wreathed pagoda on the east side of the villa, where a sudden illumination of electric lights displayed the queenly, graceful figure of the Princess in her white evening gown, long necklaces of deep yellow flowers about her shoulders, and on her deer-like head a coronal of the same color.

A hoarse shout from hundreds of Hawaiian throats greeted her.

"She is very popular," Jerdrum said, surprised. "Why should the people care so much for Miss Lauzon?"

"Why, indeed," repeated Lilia bitterly. "Why should anybody care for Miss Lauzon? Except me. I care, and now, before we go one step further she must know."

"Why, surely," interrupted Jerdrum, detaining her, "Miss Lauzon must already know. You remember that all my letters were addressed to her, all of our meetings were arranged through her. It was she who—"

"Oh!" Lilia stamped her foot in a fury of hysterical impatience. "You don't understand. Will you wait for me here? I may be gone half an hour. When I come back, it will be decided; then I'll tell you."

She ran swiftly toward the house, leaving Jerdrum looking after the small flying figure, a perplexed frown on his face.

She had not seemed herself this evening, he thought. What potent influence had this tall, imperious Miss Lauzon over the small Princess he meant to serve. Why should she be consulted at such a time as this?

Jerdrum paced up and down in the darkness. To the left the natives were dancing now and singing hulas, the very spirit of action made music. He watched the hurrying dark figures and listened to the strong, sweet voices of the Hawaiian boys, who strummed their instruments and sang, their muscular brown feet moving in sympathy with the motion of the dancers. How well they stood! What strong, fine figures they were! How well they had fought once! How well they would fight again to be released from the tyrannous oligarchy that had despoiled and enslaved them!

From the house strains of civilized hulas, become waltzes and polkas, came to his ears, and between the waving palms Jerdrum caught glimpses of women in evening gowns and men in white duck as well as those in sombre black. The brilliantly lit pagoda was filled now with a crowd of people, white, brown and all intermediate shades, who promenaded or sat and chatted, or passed on toward the ball-room or to the banqueting room beyond. He could not distinguish figures in that crowd, but his eyes flitted from one group to the other, searching for the two girls in whose hands, just for a moment, lay the fate of this small, isolated nation in the South Seas.

Jerdrum stepped back into the small pavilion. He took from his pocket the list of those who had secretly bound themselves to the Princess's cause. One by one, he scanned them, weighing each and every possibility of failure. No, it was all complete. Twelve royalists would remain after all the guests had departed; twelve men who realized that now or never must they regain their country. Before them Kaiulani must assume sovereignty, before these twelve who had sworn to die or conquer her kingdom for her. And each of these twelve could vouch for a thousand.

Restlessly, Jerdrum walked up and down. Now, that the end had come, he felt an odd sort of regret for the companionship—more in thought than in actual presence, for Jerdrum had spent little time at the capital—the companionship which, too, would be at an end. This enthusiastic, generous, brave little co-conspirator would never again meet him on the old footing. As he looked back now upon their exchange of opinions in a few hurried meetings and many long letters, he said to himself that never had there been a revolution planned upon such simple lines; never had there been such exceeding faith, such open-handed generosity on one side, and such assurance of victory on the other. Up to tonight she had been more like a boy, he said to himself, an ardent, reckless, but high-minded lad than—

But just at this point in his reverie the door opened and she stood before him. Her face was white as the gown she wore, but upon either cheek flamed a spot of red, deep as the spicy carnations which were festooned about her shoulders and in her dark hair. She came slowly forward and with her hands clasped tightly, and her soft eyes fixed upon Jerdrum's face, she said piteously:

"Forgive me. Oh, forgive me! Think of all this means to me. Think of what I have lost to-night, and please, please don't you, too, punish me."

"Kaiulani," exclaimed Jerdrum, in alarm, "what has happened? Nothing is lost—"

"Listen," said Lilia. "I am not the Princess. I am Lilia Lauzon. I have deceived you. All this time I have deceived you. Oh, I beg you to believe that it was not my own folly that led me to do it, but my love and my loyalty to her."

For a moment Jerdrum thought either he or she must be mad. His head was swimming. He looked at the pleading little figure before him, and in its place he seemed to see the proudly graceful girl who had appeared a moment in the pagoda.

"You are joking!" he stammered.

Slowly she shook her head.

"You can't be serious!" he exclaimed. "What is it? Has all this strain been too much for you? You are so changed—"

"No, I am not mad. I wish I were," she answered.

"Well!" he exclaimed, "at least she knows—'"

"Oh, yes, she knows everything now," Lilia said, bitterly, sinking into a rustic chair. "She knows it all, and she says she will never forgive me."

"You told her just now—just this evening?"

Lilia looked directly at him. She nodded.

Jerdrum stood looking down upon her. In his face amazement, inexpressible indignation and rage were blended. For a full minute there was silence. Then Jerdrum laughed shortly.

"What a fool you've made of me!" he exclaimed.

She did not answer. She lay back in the chair, her eyes bent on the floor, her hands clasped together in quiet, desperate agony. Her silence enraged him.

"Do you realize what you've done?" he demanded. "What will these men think of me, these men who have put their lives into my hands—and yours? And the money—"

"How dare you!" she said, lifting her eyes suddenly. "The money was my own. And I sold the plantation—the house where my mother died for—for this."

"But the Princess has been in ignorance all this time. All our plans—we have used her name—what must she think!"

"She thinks that I am all your words seem to imply. Oh, well, it makes no difference now. It—it only seems strange that even you should—it is all over. Good-bye."

"You can't go like that," he said, almost roughly, intercepting her before she could reach the door. "You are angry with me. But can't you see how bewildered I am? Can't you understand how strangely I find myself placed? And the Princess—"

"Oh, of course, all your sympathy is for her!" Lilia exclaimed, her eyes blazing now with jealous wrath. "Why can't you pity me? This hurts me worse than it does her—or you. See how little she cares! When you came that day and mistook me for her, it all came to me in a moment how I might serve her in spite of herself. I hoped that if I planned and arranged it all, if I could show her results, I could convince her that she might have the throne merely by reaching out her hand for it. It seemed providential that you supposed I was the Princess, and I—I told you then what a silly thing I am! Remember, when you asked me could we trust Lilia Lauzon, and send letters through her, I said to you, 'She's sentimental, unpractical, nonsensical, people say. But she wouldn't weigh her worthless life one moment in the balance if—if—'"

She stopped, and waited deliberately till she could control her voice.

"And I wouldn't," she went on. "You believe this much? And I did throw myself heart and soul into this. And to-night when I—I told her, she looked at me as though she thought me mad, and she declared that I had done a base, an unwarrantable thing. And it was all for her! Oh, will you not believe it was all for her?"

She was sobbing now and fell back in her chair, a prey to misery.

Jerdrum stood looking at her. But his eyes hardly saw how young and pretty and miserable she was as she lay with a soft, childishly-rounded arm raised to cover her face. His mind was busy planning retreat, not for himself so much as for those others waiting even now for word from him. His odd blue eyes clouded with thought, his fingers strayed restlessly over the rustic table beside him, reproducing again, now that the reality no longer monopolized his mind, that crescent-shaped bay, the bold peak at its entrance, the villa far in, the street, the barracks and the rest—all in the feathery petals of the carnations that had fallen from Lilia's throat.

"Oh, if she had been the Princess!" The regret punctuated the thread of his thought, busy now surmounting one obstacle after another. "There had been something so royal in this girl, so manly, so stanch a comrade, so merrily brave, so daringly devoted, so—"

And all at once Jerdrum's eyes saw the graceful girlish figure, upon which they had looked a moment too long. With one long drawn breath of regret, he swept the map of petals from the table. After all, the thing for which he had toiled, the thing which had monopolized his thought for all these past years was of no consequence. The vitally important thing now was that this girl should look up, should cease to sob, should smile up at him. With every second his distress grew, till his heart seemed aflame with impatient suffering. When he found himself at Lilia's side, stroking the soft brown hair and murmuring words of consolation and endearment, he understood at length what had befallen him.

❦

There is an old Kanaka named Kanui who delivered an extraordinary message in Hawaiian to twelve suspicious Hawaiian gentlemen, standing irresolute at the gates of Kaiulani's villa late one night two years ago and, without waiting for an answer, ran swiftly to the water's edge, whence he rowed a man and woman up the bay to a small schooner, just ready to weigh anchor.

There is another Kanaka named Hopu who believes that he was very drunk for two whole weeks, during which time he imagined that he rowed back and forth every night and all night from Diamond Head to Kaiulani's villa.

There are six of these same Hawaiian gentlemen who do not believe in "praying to death," as did their mothers and fathers. They wish they did, though, for then they might effectively punish a Dane, whom they include in their list of unforgivable foreigners—although they admit that Jerdrum's father was not a missionary.

There are six other Hawaiian gentlemen who believe that a dangerous lunatic named Jerdrum is permitted to live, quite at large, in San Francisco.

There is still a mystery in Hawaiian commercial circles as to the origin of Bamberger's fortune—that Bamberger who sold arms and ammunition, which no one dreamed he possessed, to the Filipinos. Kanui, though, could tell where he got them.

AH LUEY'S SELF

Bulletin, December 22, 1901, 6

A h Luey was a slave girl. At least she fancied she was. What the real slave girl's life is like in Chinatown, Luey knew no more than the slant-eyed, flat-nosed baby she tended.

This slant-eyed, flat-nosed baby was "my lord, Lee Fong" to Luey, as also to his mother, Mrs. Lee, and to his older sisters, called after the American fashion, Mary Lee and Anna Lee. For Mrs. Lee, married according to American rites to an English-speaking Chinese husband, disdained for her daughters the inverted Oriental style of nomenclature. For her son—that was a different matter. My lord, Lee Fong, would live to pray for his ancestors (among whom Mr. Lee expected to be reckoned some distant, unborn day) long after all doubts as to the sincerity of his father's conversion to Christianity had been solved. My lord's sisters not only had no souls of their own to lose, they could not imperil their father's, but a boy's religious belief was a different matter. Mary Lee and Anna Lee might be Christianized to the fullest extent that the mission (which patronized Lee's photograph gallery liberally) desired. They combed their hair in American style—at least Ah Luey did it for them. Their dresses were made with many buttons, bands and ruffles, instead of the comfortable, graceful two-piece garment which even Luey was permitted to wear. And they stamped about in their American shoes til their mother could not tell their footsteps from Ah Luey's own—Ah Luey clattering up and down the uncarpeted, filthy stairs in heavy boots that left her feet to grow to dimensions vilely plebian.

But the cue of my lord, Lee Fong, depended in security from his baby head already shaven, and to every hint from the zealous visitors from the mission Papa Lee returned a bland and smiling lie, varying in its versatility from a simple statement that the boy was ill, and therefore his christening must be longer delayed, to a gentle doubt deprecatingly expressed as to the real benefit to be derived from that latest American importation into Chinatown—the kindergarten.

As for Mrs. Lee, she spoke very little English; but, when the one-sided conversation with her white visitors turned upon the state of my lord, Lee Fong's, soul and his future spiritual welfare, she could be got to understand absolutely nothing. She had had her instructions from Lee, and she obeyed as implicitly as though her skirt were trousers and her shirt waist the old blue blouse she used to wear—obeyed as unquestioningly as Ah Luey herself, whose duty it was, when foreign visitors came, to drag her heavy lord, Lee Fong, to a place of concealment, and there to let him tear her hair and pummel her back and breast to his lordly satisfaction, to bruise and beat and trample upon her, to murder her, if that were necessary to his content—anything so that he should remain hidden till persistent mission seekers for souls should retire, put off again with the old plea that the child was ill.

But my lord, Lee Fong, was not ill. Ah Luey used to wish he would be, so cruelly robust was the child. Though he was four and she was ten, he weighed within ten pounds of what she did, and by the time she had dragged him shrieking and protesting up the narrow, foul, black stairway to the roof, she was so exhausted that all she could do was to lie doggedly before the opening, passively preventing his going down, yet yielding her body a prey to his rarely disputed tyranny.

But compensation came to the slave child. When the baby tired of beating her, he bore her no further ill will. And after he had wreaked his fullest satisfaction upon her, his natural indolent amiability made him content to remain where he was. He had really no objection to the roof. It was the principle of being carried thither without being consulted against which he rebelled.

As for Ah Luey, when she could breathe again, she drank in the elixir of the ideal; for from this dirty, square, flat roof the slave child could see across and up to a neighboring lantern-hung, green-painted small piazza; and there dwelt Ah Luey's Self, as she longed to be—as she expected to be.

The balcony was all decorated with flower-grown lattice work, through an opening in which were visible the cushioned ebony stools, the broad divan, the round low table, with its tiny bowls of tea, its sweetmeats—and Ah Luey's Self.

Ah Luey's Self was older than the slave child: perhaps five or six years older. Her face was a bit of expressionless pale yellow ivory, with a mother-of-pearl transparency and lucency, save where the vivid, painted, pouting lips stained the soft cream-tan of its coloring. Her little hands were close and compactly made as the sheath of a lily, and the slender, cool fingers were tapering and delicate as the lily's golden one, but alive with sensitive flexibility. Her body was a child's still, yet subtly filled and expanded by unchildlike experiences, and about her there hung the indefinable grace and fascination—which is the refinement of repulsion—of soul and body prematurely forced to maturity.

This magnetic attraction the slave child felt to the innermost fiber of her being. At time, when she stood up here, one hand like a dead hand, stiffened in the clutch with which unconsciously she held to the baby's wadded coat, it seemed to her that her very soul had left her body—drawn up and up by that compelling influence to which she turned her hungry, yearning, adoring gaze.

So that when at length she stumbled down the stairs again with my lord, Lee Fong, in response to the far-off, faintly heard screaming command of his mother, her body was numb with longing, and her dazed eyes, looking up through the shock of coarse black hair that fell over her forehead like an animal's mane, had forgotten even the involuntary wince with which nature protects the tender spot in her cleverest, most delicate mechanisms. But the blow that fell, that stained the slave child's cheek and temple and left a bruise that long disfigured her—that blow could not reach Ah Luey's Self. That Self dwelt on high, in a lacquer enclosed shrine, on the flower-hung piazza. And the blood that moistened the dark, dirt-encrusted dun som[3] and dripped to the heavy boots that the slave child wore, she need not even brush away; for in a blouse of silvery blue satin, upon which peacocks were embroidered in silver; in wide blue trousers, whose salmon bands, too, were silver embossed; in silken purple hose and crimson, gold-embroidered shoes, and jeweled bow tow[4] upon her sleek, dark head; with long, pearl earrings and bracelets of jade and silver filigree; and with her sam yun,[5] ornamented with

---

3. Dun som: Chinese for "corduroy."
4. Bow tow: Chinese for "head wrap."
5. Sam yun: Michelson appears to be using this word to refer to a banjo.

precious stones, its strings vibrating under her fingers, Ah Luey's Self, disdainful, calm-eyed, half-toy, half child-woman, all female, stood pictured in the slave child's unawakened, virgin soul—a soul which was an unbroken mirror, and undiscovered lake; too wild, too neglected, too dark and hidden to know reflections, to feel warring impressions.

There was a little song, half prayer, half chant, which Ah Luey's Self used to sing. The slave child had heard it first one afternoon late, when my lord, Lee Fong, had to be dragged up to the roof to escape the Sunday-school teacher, who was on a mission to lure backsliders and recruits to the faith again by promises of Christmas feasting and gifts. Though she dared not sing it, never having heard her own voice above a whisper, the slave child knew the song by heart. Its words ran along in her memory like a little stream that keeps one's feet company.

> "Make me good, O great Teen Hau,[6]
> Make me gentle, chaste and witty.
> Make me all of these or none—
> But O, I pray thee, make me pretty."

This much of it the slave child had known through hearing Ah Luey's Self begin it over and over again in that thin, sweet, little nasal voice of hers, which was more like the plaint of an insect than full-throated human utterance. But the rest of it she never heard—as the singer was always interrupted and called within where the slave child's sight could not reach—till one morning, when the big young policeman on the beat, was called into the house with the little balcony far up. From the roof Luey saw him eject two quarrelsome Chinamen, saw him re-enter on the invitation of the master of the house, and, after a time, saw him emerge upon the little piazza—which seemed all too small for him—where Ah Luey's Self served him and the hideous old Fun Guey with tea. And then, taking the sam yun, the banjo, she sang her little song quite through, the old master of the house lying back upon the divan, a smile on his vile, oily, gross face and a look, half-sneering, half-distrustful in his little black eyes. Indeed, she sang it over and over again and very slowly, while the big young white policemen, laughing

---

6. Teen Hau: Chinese for "Heavenly Queen."

immoderately, repeated the unfamiliar syllables after her, mimicking her reed-like little voice and intonations so aptly that the ivory face of Ah Luey's Self lit up with childish wonder and delight.

And so, down below in the darkness, the slave child heard and learned the rest of it.

> "Make me noble, dread Teen Hau,
> Kind to all, no creature harming,
> Make me patient, generous, faithful,
> But I implore thee, make me charming.

> "Make me shy, and straight, and still,
> Docile, make me, too, and dutiful.
> Make me perfect—if you will,
> But, O, sweet daemon, make me beautiful."

It came to be a prayer to the slave child, all the religion she had; a prayer, which the half-savage little animal only half understood, yet doubted not that it would be answered, when, what there was of her should be some-how merged in Ah Luey's Self. She had never seen herself, had never looked in a glass. Yet feminine intuition in the matter that lies nearest feminine hearts told her that she was uncouth, a black, maltreated, dwarfed creature of another species, it might almost seem, than that ideal Self toward which she looked, and prayed the only supplication she knew.

For though Christmas came nearer, and the number of the Sunday school converts swelled bravely, the guardianship of the slave child's soul was not in demand. Mrs. Lee, who was both feminine and oriental, foresaw the incon-venience of an inquiry into the child's status in the house. And no white visitor saw the wild little drudge, who hurried in and out when she was sent on an errand, and lived for the rest of the time a prey to my lord, Lee Fong's, imperial rule, or cowering in dark corners, whence the call of her mistress evoked her—a tangled-haired, frightened-eyed little monstrosity, who rarely spoke and never laughed or wept.

Yet she longed for the coming of Christmas eve. For, when those late Christian martyrs, the little Lees, in their stiffly-starched up-to-date clothes, had walked off sedately and very self-consciously, accompanied by an uncomfortable Americaned mamma, and a bland (Christian with reservations) papa, to attend the festivities at the church on the hill, the slave child and my lord, Lee Fong, were left alone together.

The baby must have realized the wantonness of the insult that night, for he fought more desperately than ever when Ah Luey dragged him up the stairs. But, toiling like an overladen ant, she got him to the roof. And she lay in an ecstasy of happiness, looking expectantly toward the little balcony where the lighted lanterns swung.

Over the west the spire of the great church shot up into the sky, its resonant, jubilant bells ringing out a peal—the song of triumph of the new faith over the old; the Christian gloria in excelsis pouring out from well-opened, brazen throats over the little transplanted Chinese city that lay below, hugging close its old, old orientalism. It had rained in the morning, but the afternoon and night belonged to that December summer which San Francisco's capricious climate vouchsafes for a day or two to offset the bit of winter in the midst of the last June.

There was a low, battlemented wall about the slippery roof, and my lord, Lee Fong, delighted—when his just anger was appeased—in hanging over this. The strain of holding him back wrenched the slave child's slender arms, but while the baby looked down into the narrow, deep valley of an alley below, she looked up. And suddenly as she looked, the lights on the balcony went out.

A passion of grief surged over the child. She had not caught a glimpse of the vision she adored, and she threw herself, in an agony of disappointment, on the roof, pulling down with her her astonished and indignant lord, Lee Fong. At first the baby's clamor prevented her hearing it, but at length she caught the pale, little nasal melody she knew too well. But it came from below, not from above, and hastily rising and peering over, the slave child saw in the shadow of the narrow alley the tall young white policeman who had sat upon the balcony six weeks before.

> "Make me good, O great Teen Hau,
> Make me gentle, chaste and witty,
> Make me all of these or none—
> But O, I pray thee, make me pretty."

He paused after the first verse, his eyes watching the balcony closely. Then he began to take short, impatient strides up and down, giving a quick glance now and then to the entrance of the alley. At length, in a repressed voice and still carefully imitating the singer's plaintive, reed-like head notes, he began again.

> "Make me noble, dread Teen Hau,
> Kind to all, no creature harming,
> Make me patient, generous, faithful,
> But I implore thee—"

But before he could finish there came an interruption from above. It was the voice of Ah Luey's Self this time, trembling and agitated as though the reed were shaken by a cruel, terrifying wind.

> "Make me shy," she half whispered, half sung,
> "and straight and still,
> Docile make me, too, and dutiful,
> Make me perfect—if you will,
> But O, sweet daemon, make me beautiful."

Then suddenly something whizzed up past the slave child's eager face, and fell lightly upon the balcony. Just then the windows in the tall church on the hill to the right were illuminated, and by their light the slave child saw indistinctly the rope ladder, made fast now, and the slipperless feet of Ah Luey's Self hurrying down.

The slave child did not realize her bereavement—the parting forever with her bright ideal, her future self-embodied, as her warped and stunted imagination had come firmly to believe—till she saw the man below catch Ah Luey's Self in his arms, and run, carrying her to the entrance of the alley, where a carriage waited. She did not know from what the girl was fleeing. Nor could she know that the mission next [to] the church on the hill was to date one more rescue from this mild Christmas eve. She heard the carriage door shut sharply. She felt the black darkness of the loss that came upon her. She was conscious of a sense of intolerable woe and terror, and for the first time in her life let out the strength of her fresh young voice in a shrill scream for Fun Guey.[7]

But before the slave owner could come to the rescue of his property, the carriage sped up the hill, and, leaning far forward to see the last of it, the child lost her balance and fell to the alley below.

She carried my lord, Lee Fong, with her, and the baby was a cripple ever after; a result that his father (who promptly withdrew his entire family from both church and school) attributed to the provoked malevolence of some outraged Kwai.[8]

But the slave child had dashed her brains out upon the iron hydrant, and when old Fun Guey came hurrying out, gesticulating and chattering of his loss, he found the baby screaming with pain and little Ah Luey already dead.

Which was just as well. For, had she lived, she might have realized her ambition.

---

7. "Fun Guey" may also mean "returning home" in Chinese.
8. Kwai: Chinese for "ghost."

In the Bishop's Carriage

Ainslee's 11, no. 3 (1903): 121–29

When the thing was at its hottest, I bolted. Tom, like the darling he is—Yes, you are, old fellow, you're as precious to me as—as you are to the police—if they could only get their hands on you. Well, Tom drew off the crowd, having passed the old gentleman's watch to me, and I made for the women's rooms.

The station was crowded, as it always is in the afternoon, and in a minute I was strolling into the big, square room, saying slowly to myself to keep me steady, "Nancy, you're a college girl—just in from Bryn Mawr to meet your papa.⁹ Just see if your hat's on straight."

I did, going up to the big glass and looking beyond my excited face to the room behind me. There sat the woman who can never nurse her baby except where everybody can see her, in a railroad station. There was the woman who's always hungry, nibbling chocolates out of a box. And the woman fallen asleep, with her hat on the side, and hairpins dropping out of her hair. And the woman who's beside herself with fear that she'll miss her train. And the woman who is taking notes about the other women's rigs. And—

And I didn't like the look of that man with the cap who opened the swinging door a bit and peeped in. The women's waiting-rooms is no place for a man—nor for a girl who's got somebody else's watch inside her waist. Luckily, my back was toward him, but just as the door swung back he might have caught the reflection of my face in a mirror hanging opposite to the big one.

I retreated, going to an inner room where the ladies were having the maid brush their gowns, soiled, from suburban travel and the dirty station.

The deuce is in it the way the women stare. I took off my hat and jacket for a reason to stay there, and hung them up as leisurely as I could.

---

9. Bryn Mawr: a women's college in Pennsylvania founded in 1885.

"Nance," I said under my breath, to the alert-eyed, pug-nosed girl in the mirror, that gave a quick glance about the room as I bent to wash my hands, "women stare 'cause they're women. There's no meaning in their look. If they were men, now, you might twitter."

I smoothed my hair and reached out my hand to get my hat and jacket when—when—

Oh, it was long; long enough to cover you from your chin to your heels. It was a dark, warm red, and it had a high collar of chinchilla that was fairly scrumptious. And just above it the hat hung, a red cloth toque caught up on the side with some of the same fur.

The black maid misunderstood my involuntary gesture. I had all my best duds on, and when a lot of women stare it makes the woman they stare at peacock naturally, and—and—Well, ask Tom what he thinks of my style when I'm on parade. At any rate, it was the maid's fault. She took down the coat and hat and held them for me as though they were mine. What could I do, 'cept just slip into the silk-lined beauty and set the toque on my head? The fool girl that owned them was having another maid mend a tear in her skirt, over in the corner; the little place was crowded. Anyway, I had both the coat and hat on and was out into the big anteroom in a jiffy.

What nearly wrecked me was the cut of that coat. It positively made me shiver with pleasure when I passed and saw myself in that long mirror. My, but I was great! The hang of that coat, the long, incurving sweep in the back, and the high fur collar up to one's nose—even if it is a turned-up nose—oh!

I stayed and looked a bit too long, for just as I was pulling the flaring hat a bit over my face, the doors swung a bit, as an old lady came in, and there behind her was that same curious man's face with the cap above it.

Trapped? Me? Not much! I didn't wait a minute, but threw the doors open with a gesture that might have belonged to the Queen of Spain. I almost ran into his arms. He gave an exclamation. I looked him straight in the eyes, as I hooked the collar close to my throat, and swept past him.

He weakened. That coat was too jolly much for him. It was for me, too. As I ran down the stairs, its influence so worked on me that I didn't know just what Vanderbilt I was.[10]

---

10. The Vanderbilts were one of the wealthiest families in the United States in the nineteenth century, making their money in the shipping and railroad industries.

I got out on the sidewalk all right, and was just about to take a car when the turnstile swung 'round, and there was that same man with the cap. His face was a funny mixture of doubt and determination. But it meant the Correction for me.[11]

"Nance Olden, it's over," I said to myself.[12]

But it wasn't. For it was then that I caught sight of the carriage. It was a fat, low, comfortable, elegant, sober carriage, wide and well-kept, with rubber-tired wheels. And the two heavy horses were fat and elegant and sober, too, and wide and well-kept. I didn't know it was the Bishop's then—I didn't care whose it was. It was empty, and it was mine. I'd rather go to the Correction (being too young to get to the place you're bound for, Tom Dorgan) in it than in the patrol wagon. At any rate, it was all the chance I had.

I slipped in, closing the door sharply behind me. The man on the box—he was wide and well-kept, too, and he was tired waiting, I suppose, for he continued to doze gently, his high coachman's collar up over his ears. I cursed that collar that had prevented his hearing the door close, for then he might have driven off.

But it was great inside; soft and warm, the cushions of dark plum, the seat wide and roomy, a church paper, some notes for the Bishop's next sermon and a copy of "Quo Vadis."[13] I just snuggled down, trust me. I leaned far back and lay low. When I did peek out the window, I saw the man with the brass buttons and the cap turning to go inside again.

Victory! He had lost the scent. Who would look for Nancy Olden in the Bishop's carriage?

Now, you know how early I got up yesterday to catch the train so's Tom and I could come in with the people and be naturally mingling with them? And you remember the dance the night before? I hadn't had more'n three hours' sleep, and the snug warmth of that coach was just nuts to me, after the freezing ride into town. I didn't dare get out for fear of some other man

---

11. The Correction refers to a correctional facility.

12. In the *Ainslee's* version of the story, the character was named Nance Older. Michelson changed the character's name to Nance Olden in the novel version. "Olden" is used here since that is how the character is referred to in popular culture.

13. *Quo Vadis: A Narrative of the Time of Nero* (1895): historical novel by Henryk Sienkiewicz.

in a cap and buttons somewhere on the lookout. I knew they couldn't be on to my hiding place or they'd have nabbed me before this. After a bit I didn't want to get out, I was so warm and comfortable—and elegant. Oh, Tom, you should have seen your Nance in that coat and in the Bishop's carriage!

First thing I knew, I was dreaming you and I were being married, and you had brass buttons all over you, and I had the cloak all right, but it was a wedding dress, and the chinchilla was a wormy sort of orange blossoms, and—and I waked when the handle of the door turned and the Bishop got in.[14]

Asleep? That's what. I'd actually been asleep.

And what did I do now?

That's easy—fell asleep again. There wasn't anything else to do. Not really asleep this time, you know; just, just asleep to be wide awake to any chance there was in it.

The horses had started, and the carriage was halfway across the street before the Bishop noticed me.

He was a little bishop, not big and fat and well-kept like the rig, but short and lean, with a little white beard and the softest eye—and the softest heart—and the softest head—Just listen.

"Lord bless me!" he exclaimed, hurriedly putting on his spectacles, and looking about bewildered.

I was slumbering sweetly in the corner, but I could see between my lashes that he thought he'd jumped into somebody else's team.

The sight of his book and his papers comforted him, though, and before he could make a resolution, I let the jolting of the carriage, as it crossed the car track, throw me gently against him.

"Daddy," I murmured, sleepily, letting my head rest on his little, prim shoulder.

That comforted him, too. Hush your laughing, Tom Dorgan, I mean calling him daddy seemed to kind of take the cuss off the situation.

"My child," he began very gently.

"Oh, daddy," I exclaimed, snuggling down close to him, "you kept me waiting so long I went to sleep. I thought you'd never come."

He put his arm about my shoulders in a fatherly way. You know, I found

---

14. Michelson's title character may be based on Ozi William Whitaker (1830–1911), a missionary bishop in Nevada who later became bishop of Pennsylvania.

out later the Bishop never had had any children. I guess he thought he had one now. Such a simple, dear old soul! Just the same, Tom Dorgan, if he had been my father, I'd never be doing stunts with tipsy men's watches for you; nor if I'd had any father. Now, don't get mad. Think of the Bishop with his gentle, thin old arm about my shoulders, holding me for just a second as though I was his daughter! My, think of it! And me, Nance Olden, with that fat man's watch in my waist and some girl's beautiful long coat and hat on, with the chinchilla on them!

"There's some mistake, my little girl," he said, shaking me gently to wake me up, for I was going to sleep again, he feared.

"Oh, I knew you were kept at the office," I interrupted, quickly. I preferred to be further from the station with that girl's red coat before I got out. "We've missed our train, anyway, haven't we? After this, daddy, dear, let's not take this route. If we'd gone straight through on the one road, we wouldn't have this drive across town every time. I was wondering, before I fell asleep, what in the world I'd do in this big city if you didn't come."

He forgot to withdraw his arm, so occupied he was by my predicament.

"What would you do, my child, if you had—had missed your—your father?"

Wasn't it clumsy of him? He wanted to break it to me gently, and this was the best he could do.

"What would I do?" I gasped indignantly. "Why, daddy, imagine me alone, and—and without money! Why—why, how can you—"

"There! there!" he said, patting me soothingly on the shoulder.

That baby of a Bishop! The very thought of little Nancy Olden out alone in the streets was too much for him.

He had put his free hand into his pocket and he had just taken out a bill and was trying to plan a way to offer it to me and reveal the fact to poor, modest little Nance Olden that he was not her own daddy, when an awful thing happened.

We had got up street as far as the opera house, when we were caught in the jam of carriages in front; the last afternoon opera of the season was just over. I was so busy thinking what would be my next move that I didn't notice much outside—and I didn't want to move, Tom, not a bit. Playing the Bishop's daughter in a trailing coat of red, trimmed with chinchilla, is just your Nancy's graft. But the dear little Bishop gave a jump that almost knocked the roof off the carriage, pulled his arm from behind me and dropped the ten dollar bill he held as though it burned him. It fell in my lap. I jammed it into my coat pocket. Where is it now? Just you wait, Tom Dorgan, and you'll find out.

I followed the Bishop's eyes. His face was scarlet now. Right next to our carriage—mine and the Bishop's—there was another; not quite so fat and heavy and big, but smart, I tell you, with the silver harness jangling and the horses arching their backs under their blue cloth jackets monogrammed in leather. All the same, I couldn't see anything to cause a loving father to let go his onliest daughter in such a hurry, till the old lady inside bent forward again and gave us another look.

Her face told it then. It was a big, smooth face, with accordion-plaited chins. Her hair was white and her nose was curved, and the pearls in her big ears brought out every ugly spot on her face. Her lips were thin, and her neck, hung with diamonds, looked like a bed with bolsters and pillows piled high, and her eyes—Oh, Tom, her eyes! They were little and very gray, and they bored their way straight through the windows—hers and ours—and hit the Bishop plumb in the face.

My, if I could only have laughed! The Bishop, the dear, prim little Bishop in his own carriage, with his arm about a young woman in red and chinchilla, offering her a bank note, and Mrs. Dowager Diamonds, her eyes popping out of her head at the sight, and she one of the lady pillars of his church—oh, Tom! It took all of this to make that poor innocent next to me realize how he looked in her eyes.

But you see it was over in a minute. The carriage wheels were unlocked, and the blue coupé went whirling away, and we in the plum-cushioned carriage followed slowly.

I decided that I'd had enough. Now and here in the middle of all these carriages was a bully good time and place for me to get away. I turned to the Bishop. He was blushing like a boy. I blushed, too. Yes, I did, Tom Dorgan, but it was because I was bursting with laughter.

"Oh, dear!" I exclaimed, in sudden dismay. "You're not my father."

"No—no, my dear, I—I'm not," he stammered, his face purple now with embarrassment. "I was just trying to tell you, you poor little girl, of your mistake and planning a way to help you, when—"

He made a gesture of despair toward the side where the coupé had been.

I covered my face with my hands, and shrinking over into the corner, I cried: "Let me out! Let me out! You're not my father. Oh, let me out!"

"Why, certainly, child. But I'm old enough, surely, to be, and I wish—I wish I were."

"You do!"

The dignity and tenderness and courtesy in his voice sort of sobered me. But all at once I remembered the face of Mrs. Dowager Diamonds, and I understood.

"Oh, because of her," I said, smiling and pointing to the side where the coupé had been.

My, but it was a rotten bad move! I ought to have been strapped for it. Oh, Tom, Tom, it takes more'n a red coat with chinchilla to make a black-hearted thing like me into the girl he thought I was.

He stiffened and sat up like a prim little schoolboy, his soft eyes hurt like a dog's that's been wounded.

I won't tell you what I did then. No, I won't. And you won't understand, but just that minute I cared more for what he thought of me than whether I got to the Correction or anywhere else.

It made us friends in a minute, and when he stopped the carriage to let me out, my hand was still in his. But I wouldn't go. I'd made up my mind to see him out of his part of the scrape, and first thing you know we were driving up toward the Square, if you please, to Mrs. Dowager Diamond's house.

He thought it was his scheme, the poor lamb, to put me in her charge till my lost daddy could send for me. He'd no more idea that I was steering him toward her, that he was doing the only thing possible, the only square thing by his reputation than he had that Nance Olden had been raised by the Cruelty, and then flung herself away on the first handsome Irish boy she met.[15]

That'll do, Tom.

Girls, if you could have seen Mrs. Dowager Diamond's face when she came down the stairs, the Bishop's card in her hand, and into the gorgeous parlor, it'd have been as good as a front seat at the show.

15. Cruelty: Nance ironically uses this shorthand term to refer to the Society for the Prevention of Cruelty to Children (i.e., the orphanage where she was raised).

She was mad, and she was curious, and she was amazed, and she was disarmed; for the very nerve of his bringing me to her staggered her so that she could hardly believe she'd seen what she had.

"My dear Mrs. Ramsay," he began, confused a bit by his remembrance of how her face had looked fifteen minutes before, "I bring to you an unfortunate child, who mistook my carriage for her father's this afternoon at the station. She is a college girl, a stranger in town, and till her father claims her—"

Oh, the baby! the baby! She was stiffening like a rod before his very eyes. How did his words explain his having his arm round the unfortunate child? His conscience was so clean that the dear little man actually overlooked the fact that it wasn't my presence in the carriage, but his conduct there that had excited Mrs. Dowager Diamonds.

And didn't the story sound thin? I tell you, Tom, when it comes to lying to a woman you've got to think up something stronger than it takes to make a man believe in you—if you happen to be female yourself.

I didn't wait for him to finish, but waltzed right in. I danced right up to that side of beef with the diamonds still on it, and flinging my arms about her, turned a coy eye on the Bishop.

"You said your wife was out of town, daddy," I cried gaily. "Have you got another wife besides mummy?"

The poor Bishop! Do you think he tumbled? Not a bit—not a bit. He sat there gasping like a fish, and Mrs. Dowager Diamonds, surprised by my sudden attack, stood bolt upright, about as pleasant to hug as—as you are, Tom, when you're jealous.

The trouble with the Bishop's set is that it's deadly slow. Now, if I had really been the Bishop's daughter—All right, I'll go on.

"Oh, mummy," I went on quickly. You know how I said it, Tom, the way I told you after that last row that Dan Christensen wasn't near so good-looking as you—remember? "Oh, mummy, you don't know how good it feels to get home. Out there at that awful college, studying and studying and studying, sometimes I thought I'd lose my senses. There's a girl out there now suffering from nervous prostration. She worked so hard preparing for the mid-year's. What's her name? I can't think—I can't think, my head's so tired. But it sounds like mine, a lot like mine. Once—I think it was yesterday—I thought it was mine, and I made up my mind suddenly to come right home and bring it with me. But it can't be mine, can it? It can't be my name she's got. It can't be, mummy, say it can't, say it can't!"

Tom, I ought to have gone on the stage. I'll go yet, when you're sent up some day. Yes, I will. You'll be where you can't stop me.

I couldn't see the Bishop, but the dowager—oh, I'd got her. Not so bad an old body, either, if you only take her the right way. First, she was suspicious, and then she was scared. And then, bit by bit, the stiffness melted out of her, her arms came up about me, and there I was, lying all comfy, with the diamonds on her neck boring rosettes in my cheeks, and she was a sniffling over me and patting me and telling me not to get excited, that it was all right, and now I was home mummy would take care of me, she would, that she would.

She did. She got me on to a lounge, soft as—as marshmallows, and she piled one silk pillow after another behind my back.

"Come, dear, let me help you off with your coat," she cooed, bending over me.

"Oh, mummy, it's so cold! Can't I please keep it on?"

To let that coat off me was to give the whole thing away. My rig underneath, though good enough for your girl, Tom, on a holiday, wasn't just what they wear in the Square. And, d'ye know, you'll say it's silly, but I had a conviction that with that coat I should say good-by to the nerve I'd had since I got into the Bishop's carriage; and from there into society. I let her take the hat, though, and I could see by the way she handled it that it was all right; the thing; her kind, you know. Oh, the girl I got it from had good taste, all right.

I closed my eyes for a moment as I lay there and she stood stroking my hair. She must have thought I'd fallen asleep, for she turned to the Bishop, and holding out her hand, she said softly:

"My dear, dear Bishop, you are the best-hearted, the saintliest man on earth. Because you are so beautifully clean-souled yourself, you must pardon me. I am ashamed to say it, but I shall have no rest till I do. When I saw you in the carriage downtown, with that poor, demented child, I thought, for just a moment—oh, can you forgive me? It shows what an evil mind I have. But you, who knows so well what Edward is, what my life has been with him, will see how much reason I have to be suspicious of all men!"

I shook, I laughed so hard. What a corker her Edward must be! See, Tom, poor old Mrs. Dowager up in the Square[16] having the same devil's luck with her man as Molly Elliott down in the Alley[17] has with hers. I wonder if you're all alike. No, for there's the Bishop. He had taken her hand sympathizingly, forgivingly, but his silence made me curious. I knew he wouldn't let the old lady believe for a moment I was luny, if once he could be sure himself that I wasn't. You lie, Tom Dorgan, he wouldn't! Well—But the poor baby, how could he expect to see through a game that had caught the dowager herself? Still, I could hear him walking softly toward me, and I felt him looking keenly down at me long before I opened my eyes.

When I did, you should have seen him jump. Guilty he felt. I could see the blood rush up under his clear, thin old skin, soft as a baby's to find himself caught trying to spy out my secret.

I just looked, big-eyed, up at him. You know; the way Molly's kid does, when he wakes. I looked a long, long time, as though I was puzzled.

"Daddy," I said, slowly, sitting up. "You—you are my daddy, ain't you?"

"Yes—yes, of course." It was the dowager who got between him and me, hinting heavily at him with nods and frowns. But the dear old fellow only got pinker in the effort to look a lie and not say it. Still, he looked relieved. Evidently he thought I was luny all right, but that I had lucid intervals. I heard him whisper something like this to the dowager just before the maid came in with tea for me.

Yes, Tom Dorgan, tea for Nancy Olden off a silver salver, out of a cup like a painted eggshell. My, but that almost floored me! I was afraid I'd give myself dead away with all those little jars and jugs. So I said I wasn't hungry, though, Lord knows, I hadn't had anything to eat since early morning. But the dowager sent the maid away and took the tray herself, operating all the jugs and pots for me, and then tried to feed me the tea. She was about as handy as Molly's little sister is with the baby—but I allowed myself to be coaxed, and drank it down.

Tea, Tom Dorgan. Ever taste tea? If you knew how to behave yourself in polite society, I'd give you a card to my friend, the dowager, up in the Square.

---

16. Rittenhouse Square: a wealthy neighborhood in Philadelphia.
17. Elfreth's Alley: in the nineteenth century, this section of Philadelphia was populated by immigrant families.

How to get away! That was the thing that worried me. I'd just made up my mind to have a lucid interval, when cr-creak, the front door opened, and in walked—

Tom, you're mighty cute—so cute you'll land us both behind bars some day—but you can't guess who came in on our little family party. Yes—oh, yes, you've met him.

Well, the old duffer whose watch was ticking inside my waist that very minute! Yes, sir, the same red-faced, big-necked fellow we'd spied getting full at the little station in the country. Only, he was a bit mellower than when you grabbed his chain. Well, he was Edward.

I almost dropped the cup when I saw him. The dowager took it from me, saying: "There, dear, don't be nervous. It's only—only—"

She got lost. It couldn't be my daddy—the Bishop was that. But it was her husband, so who could it be?

"Evening, Bishop. Hello, Henrietta, back so soon from the opera?" roared Edward, in a big, husky voice. He'd had more since we saw him, but he walked straight as the Bishop himself, and he's a dear, little ramrod. "Ah!"—his eyes lit up at sight of me. "Ah, Miss—Miss—Of course, I've met the young lady, Henrietta, but hang me if I haven't forgotten her name."

"Miss—Miss Murieson," lied the old lady, glibly. "A—a relative."

"Why, mummy!" I said, reproachfully.

"There—there. It's only a joke. Isn't it a joke, Edward?" she demanded, laughing uneasily.

"Joke?" he repeated, with a hearty bellow of laughter. "Best kind of a joke, I call it, to find as pretty a girl right in your own house, eh, Bishop?"

"Why does he call my father Bishop, mummy?"

I couldn't help it. The fun of listening to the dowager lie and knowing the Bishop beside himself with the pain of deception was too much for me. I could see she didn't dare trust her Edward with my sad story.

"Ho! ho! The Bishop—that's good. No, my dear Miss Murieson, if this lady's your mother, why, I must be—at least, I ought to be, your father. As such, I'm going to have all the privileges of a parent—bless me, if I'm not."

I don't suppose he'd have done it if he'd been sober, but there's no telling, when you remember the reputation the dowager had given him. But he'd got no further than to put his arm around me when both the Bishop and the dowager flew to the rescue. My, but they were shocked! I couldn't help wondering what they'd have done if Edward had happened to see the Bishop in the same sort of *tableau* earlier in the afternoon.

But I got a lucid interval just then, and distracted their attention. I stood for a moment, my head bent as though I was thinking deeply.

"I think I'll go now," I said, at length. "I—I don't understand exactly how I got here," I went on, looking from the Bishop to the dowager and back again, "or how I happened to miss my father. I'm ever—so much obliged to you, and if you will give me my hat, I'll take the next train back to college."

"You'll do nothing of the sort," said the dowager, promptly. "My dear, you're a sweet girl that's been studying too hard. You must go to my room and rest—"

"And stay for dinner. Don't you care. Sometimes I don't know how I get here myself." Edward winked, jovially.

Well, I did. While the dowager's back was turned, I gave him the littlest one, in return for his. It made him drunker than ever.

"I think," said the Bishop, grimly, with a significant glance at the dowager, as he turned just then and saw the old cock ogling me, "the young lady is wiser than we. I'll take her to the station—"

The station! Ugh! Not Nance Olden, with the red coat still on.

"Impossible, my dear Bishop," interrupted the dowager. "She can't be permitted to go back on the train alone."

"Why, Miss—Miss Murieson, I'll see you back all the way to the college door. Not at all, not at all. Charmed. First, we'll have dinner—or, first I'll telephone out there and tell 'em you're with us, so that if there's any rule or anything of that sort—"

The telephone! This wretched Edward with half his wits gave me more trouble than the Bishop and the dowager put together. She jumped at the idea, and left the room, only to come back again to whisper to me:

"What name, my dear?"

"What name? What name?" I repeated blankly. What name, indeed. I wonder how "Nance Olden" would have done.

"Don't hurry, dear, don't perplex yourself," she whispered, anxiously, noting my bewilderment. "There's plenty of time, and it makes no difference—not a particle, really."

I put my hand to my head.

"I can't think—I can't think. There's one girl has nervous prostration, and her name's got mixed with mine, and I can't—"

"Hush, hush! Never mind. You shall come and lie down in my room. You'll stay with us to-night, anyway, and we'll have a doctor in, Bishop."

"That's right," assented the Bishop. "I'll go get him myself."

"You—you're not going!" I cried in dismay. It was real. I hated to see him go.

"Nonsense—'phone." It was Edward who went himself to telephone for the doctor, and I saw my time getting short.

But the Bishop had to go, anyway. He looked out at his horses, shivering in front of the house, and the sight hurried him.

"My child," he said, taking my hand, "just let Mrs. Ramsay take care of you to-night. Don't bother about anything, but just rest. I'll see you in the morning," he went on, noticing that I kind of clung to him. Well, I did. "Can't you remember what I said to you in the carriage—that I wished you were my daughter. I wish you were, indeed I do, and that I could take you home with me and keep you, child."

"Then—to-night—if—when you pray—will you pray for me as if I was—your own daughter?"

Tom Dorgan, you think no prayers but a priest's are any good, you bigoted, snickering Catholic! I tell you if some day I cut loose from you and start in over again, it'll be the Bishop's prayers that'll do it.

The dowager and I passed Edward in the hall. He gave me a look behind her back, and I gave him one to match it. Just practice, you know, Tom. A girl can never know when she'll want to be expert in these things.

She made me lie down on a couch while she turned the lamp low, and then left me alone in a big palace of a bedroom filled with things. And I wanted everything I saw. If I could, I'd have lifted everything in sight.

But every minute brought that doctor nearer. Soon as I could be really sure she was gone, I got up and hurrying to the long French windows that opened on the great stone piazza, I unfastened them quietly, and inch by inch I pushed them open.

There within ten feet of me stood Edward. No escape that way. He saw me, and was tiptoeing heavily toward me, when I heard the door click behind me, and in walked the dowager back again.

I flew to her. "I thought I heard some one out there," I said. "It frightened me so that I got up to look. Nobody could be out there, could they?"

She walked to the window and put her head out. Her lips tightened grimly. "No, nobody could be out there," she said, breathing hard, "but you might get nervous just thinking there might be. We'll go to a room upstairs."

And go we did, in spite of all I could plead about feeling well enough now to go alone and all the rest of it. How was I to get out of a second or third-story window?

I began to think about the Correction again as I followed her upstairs, and after she'd left me I just sat waiting for the doctor to come and send me there. I didn't much care, till I remembered the Bishop. I could almost see his face as it would look when he'd be called to testify against me.

No, I couldn't bear that; not without a fight, anyway. It was for him I'd got into this part of the scrape. I'd get out of it so's he shouldn't know how bad a thing a girl can be.

While I lay thinking it over, the same maid that had brought me the tea came in. She was an ugly, thin little thing. If she's a sample of the maids in that house, the lot of them would take the kink out of your pretty hair, Thomas J. Dorgan, Esquire, late of the House of Refuge and soon of Moyamensing.[18] Don't throw things. People in my set, mine and the dowager's, don't.

She had been sent to help me undress, she said, and make myself comfortable. The doctor lived just around the corner and would be in in a minute.

Phew! She wasn't very promising, but she was my only chance. I took her.

"I really don't need any help, thank you, Sarah," I said chipper as a sparrow, and remembering the name the dowager had called her by. "Aunt Henrietta is too fussy, don't you think? Oh, of course, you won't say a word against her. She told me the other day that she'd never had a maid so sensible and quick-witted, too, as her Sarah. Do you know, I've a mind to play a joke on the doctor when he comes? You'll help me, won't you? Oh, I know you will!" Suddenly I remembered the Bishop's bill. I took it out of my pocket. Yep, Tom, that's where it went. I had to choose between giving that skinny maid the biggest tip she ever got in her life—or Nance Olden to the Correction.

You needn't swear, Tom Dorgan. I fancy if I'd got there, you'd got worse.

---

18. Moyamensing: a Philadelphia prison.

No, you bully, you know I wouldn't tell; but the police sort of know how to pair our kind.

In her cap and apron, I let the doctor in and myself out. And I don't regret a thing up there in the Square except that lovely red coat with the high collar and the hat with the fur on it. I'd give—Tom, get me a coat like that and I'll marry you for life.

No, there's one thing I could do better if it was to be done over again. I could make that dear little old Bishop wish harder I'd been his daughter.

What am I mooning about? Oh—nothing. There's the watch—Edward's watch. Take it.

THE ANCESTRY OF IRENE
(STORIES OF THE NEVADA MADIGANS: II)

Century Illustrated Monthly Magazine 68, no. 3 (1904): 421–32

"The Ancestry of Irene" is the second installment in a five-part series called "Stories of the Nevada Madigans." The stories were later published in book form as *The Madigans* (1904) with several new chapters added.

I n her heart Irene was confident that, though among the Madigans, she was not of them.

The color of her hair, the shape of her nose, the tempestuousness of her disposition, the difficulty she experienced in fitting her restless and encroaching nature into what was merely one of a number of jealously frontiered interstices in a large family—all this forbade tame acceptance on her part of so ordinary and humble an origin as Francis Madigan's fatherhood connoted.

"No," she said firmly to herself the day she and Florence were see-sawing in front of the woodshed after school, "he's only just my foster-father; that's all."

How this foster-father—she loved the term, it sounded so delightfully haughty—had obtained possession of one whose birth-right would place her in a station so far above his own, she had not decided. But she was convinced that, although poor and peculiar and incapable of comprehending the temperament and necessities of the nobly born, he was, in his limited way, a worthy fellow. And she had long ago resolved that when her real father came for her, she would bend graciously and forgivingly down from her seat in the carriage, to say good-by to poor old Madigan.

"Thank you very, very much, Mr. Madigan," she would sweetly say, "for all your care. My father, the Count, will never forget what you have done for his only child. As for myself, I promise you that I will have an eye upon your little girls. I am sure his Grace the Duke will gladly do anything for them that I recommend. I am very much interested in little Florence, and shall certainly come for her some day in my golden chariot to take her to my castle for a visit, because she is such a well-behaved child and knew me, in her childish way, for a noble lady in disguise. Cecilia? Which one is that? Oh, the one her sisters call Sissy! She needs disciplining sadly, Mr. Madigan, sadly. Much as he loves me, my father, the Prince, would not care to have me know her—as she is now. But she will improve, if you will be very, very strict with her. Good-by! Good-by, all! No, I shall not forget you. Be good and obey your aunty. Good-by!"

The milk-white steeds would fly down the steep, narrow, unpaved streets. On each side would stand the miners, bowing, hat in hand, hurrahing for the great Emperor and his beautiful daughter—she who had so strangely lived among them under the name of Sprint[19] Madigan. They would speak, realizing now, of certain royal traits they had always noted in her—her haughty spirit that never brooked an insult, her independence, her utter fearlessness, the reckless bravery of a long line of kings, and—and even that very disinclination for study which they had stupidly fancied indicated that Sissy Madigan was her superior! What would Princess Irene want with vulgar fractions, a common denominator, and such low subjects?

"What makes you wrinkle up your nose that way, Sprint?" Florence's voice broke in complainingly on her sister's reverie. She glanced up the incline of the see-saw to the height whence Irene looked down, physically as well as socially, upon her faithful retainer and the straggling little town clinging to the mountain's skirts.

Irene did not answer. She was busy dreaming, and her dreams were of the turned-up-nose variety.

"Don't, Sprint! It makes you look like a—what Sissy just now called you." The smaller sister's eyes fell, as though seeking corroboration from the

---

19. Although Michelson chose "Split" for Irene's nickname, she changed it to "Sprint" at the request of *Century*'s editor who deemed "Split" too "vulgar" and "suggestive." Michelson strongly disagreed with this editorial revision, and in the book version of *The Madigans*, she changed the nickname back to "Split." See Miriam Michelson to Robert Underwood Johnson, April 13, 1904, Century Company records, Manuscripts and Archives Division, New York Public Library, Astor, Lenox, and Tilden Foundations.

middle of the board, where Sissy had been so lately acting as "candlestick"—lately, for the incident had ended (no game being enticing enough to hold these two long in an unnatural state of neutrality) in Sprint's washing Sissy's face vigorously in the snow, and Sissy's calling her elder sister "nothing but an old Indian!" as she ran weeping into the house with the familiar parting threat to get even before bedtime. No Madigan could bear that the sun should set on her wrath; she preferred that all scores should be paid off, so that the slate might be clean for to-morrow's reckonings.

"Fom," said her big sister, slowly, when she was quite ready to speak, "I think you'd better call me 'Irene.' You'd feel gladder about it when I 'm gone."

"Where?" At this minute it was Fom's turn to be dangerously high, and she wriggled to the uttermost end of the plank to counterbalance her sister's weight.

A mysterious smile overspread Irene's face. It became broadly triumphant as she rose presently on the short end of the board, her arms daringly outspread, her toes upturned in front of her, her agile body well balanced, her spirit exulting in the sense of danger without and superiority within.

"When?" asked Florence, with that amiable readiness to consider a question unasked, so becoming to the vassal. "When are you going?"

"To-night—maybe." Her own words startled Irene. She loved to play upon Fom's fears, but she had not really intended committing herself so far. "He may call for me to-night," she added, with qualifying emphasis.

"Who? Not—not—"

"Yes, my father. I must be ready at any time, you know."

Fom looked alarmed. She had heard long ago and in strict confidence about Sprint's lofty parentage. She had even accepted drafts upon her future, rendering services which were unusual in a Madigan fag, with the understanding that when the Princess Sprint should come into her own, she would richly repay.[20] But she had never before heard her speak so positively or set a time when their relationship must cease.

A feeling of utter loneliness came over Sprint's faithful ally. She saw the balance of power in the Madigan oligarchy rudely disturbed. She beheld, in a swift, dread vision, the undisputed supremacy of the party of Sissy. Dismay

---

20. Michelson appears to be using a British meaning of "fag" here, referring to a junior pupil who renders services for a senior pupil.

entered her soul and shook her body, for with the brunette of the twins emotion and action were synonymous. "Oh, don't go, Sprint!" she begged, squirming unhappily at her end of the plank. "Don't go!"

High up in the air, Sprint smiled superbly. There was *noblesse oblige* in that smile; also the strong teasing tincture which no Madigan could resist using, even upon her closest ally.

"Oh, Sprint—o-o-oh, Sprint!" wailed Fom, forgetting in her wriggling misery how close she already was to the end of the plank.

A crash and a bump and a squeal told it to her all at once. She had slid clear off, getting an instantaneous effect of her haughty sister unsupported at a dizzy eminence, before Sprint came bumping down to earth, the see-saw giving that regal head a parting, stunning tap as the long end finally settled down and the short one went up to stay.

It was never in the ethics of Madigan warfare to explain the inexplicable. Florence was on her feet, flying as though for her very life, before Sprint, shaken down from her dreams, quite realized what had happened. And she was still sitting as she had fallen when Jim, the Indian, came for the sawbuck.

Jim limped, his eyes were sore and watery, and it took him two weeks to conquer the Madigan woodpile, which any other Piute in town could have leveled in half the time.

"Him fall, eh?" he asked, dismantling the see-saw with that careful leisureliness that accounted for the Chinaman Wong's contempt for Indians.[21]

"Not him; *her*, Jim."

Sprint possessed a passion for imparting knowledge, of which she had little, and which was hard for her to attain.

Jim grinned.

"She no got little gal like you teach her Inglis," he said, gently apologetic.

"Not she, Jim; *he*. How old is your little girl?" Sprint remembered that a genteel interest in the lower classes is becoming to the well-born.

"He just big like you," Jim responded mournfully, drawing the back of his brown hand across his nose. "But he all gone."

"Dead?" Sprint crossed her legs uneasily as she squatted, and lowered her voice reverently.

---

21. Wong, the family's Chinese domestic servant, was introduced in the first story, "Cecilia the Pharisee."

"He no dead," Jim said, lifting the sawbuck and easing it on his shoulder. "One Washoe squaw steal him—little papoose, nice little papoose. Much white—like you, missy. So white squaw say no sure Injun."

"Jim!"

"Take him down Tluckee valley. Take him 'way. Jim see squaw one day long time 'go—Washoe Lake—shoot ducks. Heap shoot squaw. He die, but he say white Faginia man got papoose."

"Jim!" It was the faintest echo of the first terrified exclamation.

"Come Faginia, look papoose. No find. Chop wood long time. Heap hogady—not much dinner. Nice papoose—white, like you."

Jim paused. He expected sympathy, but he hoped for dinner. When he saw he was to get neither, he hunched his lame hip, scratched his head, balanced the sawbuck, and shuffled away.

Too overcome to move, Sprint sat looking after him. Her father! This, then, was her father! She was dazed, helpless, too overwhelmed even to be unhappy yet.

There came a shrill call for her from Kate, and Sprint, with unaccustomed meekness, staggered obediently to her feet. What was left for her but to be a slave? she said stonily to herself. She was an Indian like—like her father! And Sissy had noticed the resemblance that very afternoon!

"It's the bell, Sprint," explained Kate, who was reading "The Spanish Gypsy" in the low, hall-like library.

She had begun to read it for the reason that no one in her class at school had read it—usually a compelling reason for the eldest of the Madigans; but the poetic beauty, the extravagance of the romance, had whirled the girl away from her pretentious pose, and she was finishing it now because she could not help it; chained to it, it seemed to her, till she should know the end.

"Shall I go?" asked Sprint, humbly.

Kate looked up, too surprised by her sister's docility to do anything but nod. She had anticipated a battle, a ring at the door-bell being the signal for a flying wedge of Madigans tearing through the hall, with inquisitive Irene at its apex—except when she was asked to answer it.

The sisters' eyes met: those of the elder, in her thin, dark, flushed face, hazy with romantic happiness; those of the younger bright with romantic suffering, demanding a share of that felicity which transfigured her senior.

"What're you reading, anyway, Kate?" she asked.

As well tap the bung of a cask and ask what it holds. Kate began chanting:

> " 'Father, your child is ready! She will not
> Forsake her kindred: she will brave all scorn
> Sooner than scorn herself. Let Spaniards all,
> Christians, Jews, Moors, shoot out the lip and say,
> "Lo, the first hero in a tribe of thieves!"
> Is it not written so of them? They, too,
> Were slaves, lost, wandering, sunk beneath a curse,
> Till Moses, Christ, and Mahomet were born,
> Till beings lonely in their greatness lived,
> And lived to save their people.' "

It poured from Kate's lips, the story of the lady Fedalma and her Gipsy father, a stream of winy romance, a sugared impossibility preserved in the very spirits of poetry.

Again the old bell jangled, and again. Kate was glutted, drunk with the sound of the verbal music that had been chorusing behind her lips; while for Irene every word seemed charged with the significance of special revelation. The light seemed to leap from her sister's eyes to kindle a conflagration in her own.

"Read it again—that part—Kate! Read it!" she cried.

And Kate, not a bit loath, turned the page and repeated:

> " 'Lay the young eagle in what nest you will,
> The cry and swoop of eagles overhead
> Vibrate prophetic in its kindred frame,
> And make it spread its wings and poise itself
> For the eagle's flight.' "[22]

---

22. Kate is reading aloud from *The Spanish Gypsy* (1868), a narrative poem by George Eliot. In the poem, a lost gypsy child named Fedalma, raised as Catholic nobility during the Spanish Inquisition, is reunited with her father, chief of the Zincalo people. Abandoning her Catholic identity and her adoptive brother-turned-lover, Fedalma chooses to return to her tribe and pledges to help them recover their lost African homeland.

Sprint breathed again, a full, deep breath of satisfaction. An Indian—she, Sprint Madigan? Perhaps; but an Indian princess, then, with a mission as great, glorious, and impossible as Fedalma's own.

When at last she did turn mechanically to answer the bell, she saw that Sissy had anticipated her and was showing old Professor Trask into the parlor. Ordinarily Irene loved to listen at the door while Sissy's lesson was in progress; for Trask was a nervous, disappointed wreck, whose idea of teaching music seemed to be to make his pupils as much like himself as harried youth can be like worried age. But on this great day the joy of hearing the perfect Sissy rated had not the smallest place in her enemy's thoughts. A poet's words had lifted Irene in an instant from child hell to heaven, had fired her imagination, had rekindled her pride, had given back her dreams.

Reality was not altogether so pleasant, she found, when she went into the kitchen, skirmished with the Chinese cook for Jim's dinner, and went out to the woodpile to give it to him herself.

She did not wait to see him eat it—she was not quite poet enough for that; besides, that impersonal, composite father, her tribe, was calling her.

Pulling on her hood and jacket, with her mittens dangling from a red tape on each side, she flew out and down the long, rickety stairs which a former senator from Nevada had built up the mountain's side, when he planned for his home a magnificent view of the mountains and desert off toward the east.

Sprint did not look at either, though they shone, the one like a billowy moonlit sea, the other like a lake of silver, for the snow that covered them. She half ran, half slid down the hilly street till she came to a box-like miner's cabin, where Jane Cody, the washerwoman, lived with her son. In front of it she halted and called imperiously:

"Jack!"

For this same Jack was her own, her discovery, her possession, who acknowledged her thrall and was proud of it.

But the green shutters over the one window remained fast, and the door tight closed.

"Jack?" There was a suggestion of incredulity in Sprint's voice.

The whistles burst forth in a medley of throaty roars (it was five-o'clock "mining-time"), but the bird-like whistle of Jack was missing.

"Jack Cody!" Sprint stamped her high arctics in the snow.

The door was opened a little, and a round black head was cautiously thrust forth.

"I want you—come!" the Indian princess announced. "And get your sled."

"I can't," replied the head.

"But I want you."

The head wagged dolefully.

"Why not?"

The head hung down.

"Tell me."

The head's negative was sorrowful but determined.

"If you don't tell me I'll—never speak to you again 's long as I live, Jack Cody!"

The head stretched out its long neck and sent an agonized glance toward her.

"Tell me—right now!" she commanded.

"Well—she's took my clothes with her," wailed the head, and jerked itself within, while the door was slammed behind it.

Sprint walked up the stoop.

"Jack," she called, her mouth at the keyhole, "who took 'em? Your mother? Why? But she can't keep you in that way. Never mind. What *have* you got on?"

The door was opened an inch or two, and the head started to look out. But at sight of Sprint so near it withdrew in such turtle-like alarm that she laughed aloud.

"What're you laughing at?" growled the boy.

"What's that you got on?" said she.

"My—my mother's wrapper."

A peal of laughter burst forth from the Indian princess. But it ceased suddenly. For the door was thrown open with such violence that it made Jane Cody's wax flowers shake apprehensively under their glass bell, and a figure stalked out such as might haunt a dream—long, gaunt, awkward, inescapably boyish, yet absurdly feminine, now that the dark calico wrapper flapped at its big, awkward heels and bound and hindered its long legs.

Sprint looked from the heavily shod feet to the round, short-shaven black head, and a premonitory giggle shook her.

"Don't you laugh—don't you dare laugh at me! Don't you, Sprint—will you?" The phrases burst from him, a threat at the beginning, an appeal at the end.

"No," said Sprint, choking a bit; "no, I won't. You don't look very—" she gulped—"very funny, Jack. And it's getting so dark that nobody'd know—really they wouldn't."

"Sure?"

Sprint nodded.

"Get your sled quick, the big, long one, the leg-breaker, and take me down—I'll tell you where. Get it, won't you?"

"In this, this—like this?" Jack faltered.

"It's so important, Jack. Please! It's always you that asks me, remember."

The boy threw his hands out with a gesture that strained the narrow garment he wore almost to bursting. He began to talk, to argue, to plead; then suddenly he turned and ran, a grotesque, long-legged shape, toward the back of the house.

When he whistled, Sprint joined him, and together they plowed their way through the high snow to the beaten-down street beyond. At the top of the hill, Sprint sat down well to the front of the low, rakish-looking leg-breaker. Behind her the boy, hitching up his skirts, threw himself with one knee bent beneath him, and, with a skillful ruddering of the other long, untrousered leg, started the sled.

They had coasted only half a block—Virginia City runs downhill—when they heard the shrill yelp of the Comstock boy on the trail of his prey. As Jack stopped the sled a swift volley of snowballs from a cross-street struck the figure of a tall, timid, stooping man in an old-fashioned cape, such as no Comstock boy had ever seen on anything masculine.

"It's Professor Trask," breathed Irene, keen delight in persecution lending to her aggressive, bright face that savage sharpness of feature which Sissy Madigan called Indian. "Don't you wish you hadn't got that dress on, Jack?" she asked, as the tall, black mark for a good shot still stood hesitating to cross the polished, steep street, down which many sleds had slipped for days past. "You could get him every time, couldn't you?"

Despite the ignoble garment that cramped it, the boy's breast swelled with pride in his lady's approval.

"You could just fire one at him from here, anyway," suggested Irene, adaptable as her sex is to contemporary standards and customs.

"Ye-es," said the boy, hesitating; "but he's such a poor old luny."

Sprint turned her imperial little hooded head questioningly.

"He is—really luny," said the boy, apologetically. "Since his little girl wandered away one day from home and never came back, he gets spells, you know. He was telling ma one day when she went over to do his washing. But—but I will land one on him if you want, Sprint."

But Sprint had suddenly pivoted clear around and sat now facing him, an eager mittened hand staying his hard, skillful, obedient fingers, already making the snowball.

"How—how old would that little girl be, Jack?" she gasped.

"Why, 'bout twelve—thirteen. Why?"

"And what would be the color of her hair?"

"Red, I s'pose, like his; not—not like yours—Sprint," he added shyly, glancing at the brown fire of the curls that escaped from her hood.

But Irene was no longer listening. She was looking over to the other side of the street, where that shrinking, pitiable old figure in its threadbare neatness trembled; not daring to seek safety across the dangerously smooth street, or daring to remain exposed here, where he ducked ridiculously every now and then to avoid the whizzing balls that sang about him.

Irene breathed hard. A coward for a father, a scarecrow, a butt for a gang of miners' boys! This, this was her father! Why, even crippled old Jim, the wood-chopper, seen in retrospect and haloed by copper-colored dreams of romantic rehabilitation—even Jim seemed regrettable.

But she did not hesitate, any more than Fedalma did. She, too, knew a daughter's duty—to a hitherto unknown, just-discovered father. A merely ordinary, everyday parent like Francis Madigan was, as a matter of course, the common enemy, and no self-respecting Madigan would waste the poetry of filial feeling upon any one so realistic.

"You wait for me here, Jack," she said, with unhesitating reliance upon his obedience.

"Where're you going? I thought you were in a hurry to get down to the wickiups."[23]

She did not hear him. She had spun off the sled, and with the sure-footed speed of the hill-child she was crossing the street.

---

23. Wickiup: a small hut used as a dwelling by Native people.

Old Trask, his short-sighted eyes blinking beneath his twitching, bushy red eyebrows, looked down as upon a miracle when a red-mittened hand caught his and he heard a confident voice—the clear voice children use to enlighten the stupidity of adults:

"I'll help you across; take my hand."

"Eh—what?"

He leaned down, failing to recognize her. Children had no identity to him. They were merely brats, he used to say, unless they happened to have some musical aptitude. But he accepted her aid, his battered old hat rocking excitedly upon his high bony forehead, as he ducked and turned and shivered at the oncoming balls. "Bad boys—bad boys!" he ejaculated. "Boys are the devil!"

"Yes," agreed Sprint, craftily. "Girls are best. Your little girl, now—father—" she began softly.

"Eh—what!" he exclaimed. "Who's your father? My respects to him."

"I have no father," she answered softly. A plan had sprung full-born from her quick brain. She would win this erratic father back to memory of his former life and her place in it—somewhat as did one Lucy [*sic*] Manette,[24] a favorite heroine of Sprint's that Sissy had read about and told her of. That would be a fine thing to do—almost as fine, and requiring the center of the stage as much, as rehabilitating the Red Man.

"I have no father," she murmured, "if you won't be mine."

"What? What? No!" Trask was across now and brushing the snowy traces of battle from his queer old cape. "No; I don't want any children. I had one once—a daughter."

Sprint's heart beat fast.

"She was a brat, with the temper of a little fiend, and no ear—absolutely none—for music; played like an elephant."

How terribly confirmatory!

"And what—what became of her?" whispered Sprint.

"She ran away two years ago and—"

"Two years!"

"I said two, didn't I?" demanded the old professor, irascibly.

---

24. In Charles Dickens's novel *A Tale of Two Cities* (1859), the character of Lucie Manette restores life to her father after his long imprisonment in the Bastille.

Disgusted, Sprint turned her back on him. Why, two years ago Sissy had first called her an Indian; how right she had been! Two years ago she, Sprint, was making over all her dolls to Fom. Two years ago she had already discovered Jack Cody's fleet strength, his wonderful aptness at making swift sleds, in which her reckless spirit reveled, his mastership of other boys of his gang, and—her mastery of him.

She turned and beckoned to him. His sweet whistle rang out in answer like a vocal salute, and in a moment she was seated again in front of him, with that deft, tail-like left leg of his steering them down, down over crossstreet, through teams and sleighs and unwary pedestrians; past the miners coming off shift; past the lamplighter making his rounds in the crisp, clear cold of the evening; past the heavy-laden squaws, with their bowed heads, their papooses on their backs, their weary arms bearing home the spoils of a hard day's work, and the sore-eyed yellow dogs trudging, too, wearily and dejectedly at their heels, toward the rest of the wickiup and the acrid warmth of the sage-brush campfire.

In short, swift sentences, as they hurdled over artificially raised obstructions, or slid along the firm-packed snow, or grated on the muddy crossstreets, Princess Sprint told her plan—with reservations. She was not prepared to admit to so humble a worshiper the secret of her birth, but the magnanimous self-sacrifice of a beautiful nature, the heroine concealed beneath a frivolous exterior—these she was willing Jack Cody should suspect and admire.

"We'll lift them up, you and I, Jack. I'm going 'to—to be the angel of a homeless tribe,' or something like that," she quoted, as it grew darker and the sled slowed down a bit, where the slant of the hill-street became gentler and she need not hold on tight. "You'll be their general and I their princess. You'll teach them to be fine soldiers, so that the people in town will be afraid of them and have to give them back their lands—and the mines, too. They're theirs, and they shall have them and be millionaires. And, of course, so will we. We'll own all the stocks and brokers' offices, and after a few years, when they're quite civilized, we'll come up to town to live. We'll take Bob Graves's Castle and—Jack! Ah!"[25]

---

25. Bob Graves's Castle refers to a Virginia City mansion built in 1868 by engineer Robert Graves.

A long scream burst from her. Never in her life had Sprint Madigan screamed like that. For an incredibly fleet instant she actually saw above her head a struggling horse's hoofs. In the next, her calico-wrapped knight had thrown himself and his lady out into the great drifts on the side. Sprint felt the cold fleeciness of new-fallen snow on her face, down her neck, up her sleeves. She was smothered, drowned in it, when with another tug the boy whirled her to her feet, and swaying unsteadily, she looked up into the face of the man whose horses had so nearly crushed her life out.

It was her father—she knew it was. Else why had fate so strangely thrown them together? Yes, this was her true father. No other girl's father could have so handsome a fur coat as that reaching from the tips of this very tall man's ears to his heels. No other could have a sleigh so fine, and silver-belled horses fit for a king. No other could have such bright brown eyes beneath heavy sandy brows, such red, red cheeks, and so long and silver-white a beard which the sun could still betray into confession of its youthful ruddiness. What if he did have, too, a brogue so soft, so wheedling that men had long called him Slippery Uncle Sammy?

Sprint waked with a humiliating start from her lesser, less genteel dreams. Of course this bonanza king driving up from the mine was her real father, and she a bonanza princess, happier, more fortunate than a merely political one; for princesses have to live in Europe, where Madigans cannot see and envy them.

With the mien of one who has come at last into her own, Sprint accepted his invitation to carry her up to town, and, with a facetious twinkle in his eyes that added to his likeness to a stately Santa Claus (though his was not a reputation for benevolence), he lifted her and set her down under the silky fur rugs.

Sprint nestled back in perfect content: at last she was fitly placed.

"Hitch on behind, Jack," she cried patronizingly, and the bonanza king's sleigh went up the hill with its queer freight: queer, for this was that one of them whose strength was subtlety, whose forte was guile, whose left hand knew not the charitable acts of his right—and neither did the right, for that matter.

Thoroughly sophisticated are Comstock children as to the character of the masters of their masters, and Sprint Madigan knew how foreign to this man's nature a lovable action was. All the more, then, she valued the distinction which chance—fate—had made hers. And all the more did a something fierce and lawless and proud in herself leap to recognize the tyrant in him. Kings should be above law, as princesses were, was Sprint's creed; else why be kings and princesses?

"An' where would ye be a-goin' to, down this part o' the world so late?" she heard the unctuous voice above her inquire.

Sprint was silent. That the daughter of a bonanza king should have fancied for a moment that Indian Jim could be her father!

"An' who's the gyurl with ye—the witch ye call Jack?"

"'T isn't a girl." That virility which Sprint's wild nature respected and admired forbade her denying the boy his sex. "It's a boy—Jack—Jack Cody."

King Sammy laughed. His was rich, strong laughter, and men who heard it on C street (they had reached the main thoroughfare now, so fleet were these kingly horses of Sprint's father) knew it—and knew, too, what poor, mean thoughts lay behind it.

"An' this Cody," he said, turning his handsome head to look down at the boy on his sled behind. "Cody—Cody, now," he continued, with royalty's marvelous memory, "your father killed in the Ophir—eh?[26] Time of the fire on the 1800—yes—yes! An' I was goin' to give him a point that very day. Well—well!"

"Ye did!" The boy looked up resentful, and met those smiling, crafty eyes.

"No! An' he sold short? Too bad! Too bad! I thought sure that stock was goin' down. My, the bad man that told me it was! I hope he didn't lose?" he chuckled.

"All we had," said the boy.

"Tut—tut—tut! What a pity! Haven't I always said it's wicked to deal in stocks!" The king shook his sorrowful old head, then turned to the princess beside him. "An' it's out for a ride ye'd be, sweetheartin' on the sly, eh?"

"He's not! I was not!" Sprint's cheeks grew hotter. He was her father, this splendid, handsome king, yet never had she felt for poor Francis Madigan what she felt now for the man beside her.

"What, then?"

"I was going down for—for a reason," she stammered.

---

26. Ophir: a Virginia City mine that was destroyed by a fire in 1875.

"To be sure! To be sure!" chuckled his old Majesty. "An ye've told your father an' mother ye were goin', no doubt."

"No, I—didn't. I—couldn't."

"Coorse not; coorse not, but ye—"

"Let me out!" cried Sprint.

The sneer in his voice had set her aflame. She rose in the sleigh, cast off the furs, and, stamping like a fury, tried to seize the reins.

"Ho! Ho!" The old monarch's bowed broad shoulders shook with laughter as he caught her trembling hands and held them. "What a little spitfire! A divvle of a temper ye've got, my dear. Cody, now, does he like gyurls with such a temper?"

"Will you let me out?" Her voice was hoarse with anger.

"Can't ye wait till we t' a crossin', ye little termagant?"

"No—no!" She tore her hands from him, and, with a quick, lithe leap from the low sleigh, landed, a bit dazed, in the snow banked high on the side of the street.

Uncle Sammy stared after her a moment. Then he remembered the boy behind.

"Hi—there!" he cried, looking over his shoulder as he reached for his whip. "Git!"

But Cody had the street-boy's quickness. All he had to do was to let go the end of rope he held, and the leg-breaker slipped smoothly back, while the king's runnered chariot shot ahead, drawn by the flying horses on whose backs the whip had descended.

"Ugh!" shivered Sprint, as she made her way out of the drift. "It's cold, Jack. Let's run."

Together they hauled the leg-breaker up the hill, parting at the snow-caked, wandering flights of steps, which seemed weary and worn with their endless task of climbing the mountain to Madigan's door.

Irene mounted them quickly. She was cold, and it had grown very dark and late; so late that the lamp shone out from the dining-room, warning her that it must be dangerously near to dinner-time. She had reached the last flight when Sissy came flying out along the porch to meet her.

"Sprint—ssh!" she cautioned, with a friendliness that surprised Sprint, who remembered how well she had washed that round, innocent face in the snow only a few hours ago—the face of Sissy, the unforgiving. "Dinner's ready," she went on, "but father isn't down yet. Go round the back way, and you can get in without his knowing how late you are."

Sprint did not budge. The sight of Sissy had made her a Madigan again, prepared for any emergency the appearance of her arch-enemy might portend. "What are you up to?" she demanded suspiciously.

"Oh!" Sissy turned haughtily on her heel. "If you want to go in and catch it—go."

But Sprint did not want to catch it. Her day's experience had made her content to bear the eccentricities of her humble foster-father, but she was by no means anxious to be the instrument that should provoke a characteristic expression of them.

She slipped around the back way, passing through Wong's big kitchen, the heat and odors of which were grateful messages of cheer to her chilled little body. She flew up-stairs and tore off her wet clothing, and was out in the hall, buttoning hastily as she walked, when the door-bell rang.

In some previous existence Sprint Madigan must have been a most intelligent horse in some metropolitan fire department. It was her instinct still to run at the sound of the bell; every other Madigan, therefore, delighted in preventing that impulse's gratification. But this time Bessie came hurriedly to meet her and even speed her on her errand.

"Quick—it's your father, Sprint!" she cried.

Sprint looked at her. She trusted Bep no more than she did Sissy, whose lieutenant the blonde twin was.

"Oh, you needn't glare at me!" exclaimed Bep, her guilty conscience sensitive to accusation by implication. "Fom told me all you told her about him. She was 'fraid you were coming after her for letting you fall off the see-saw, and she told me the whole thing. She said you expected him to-night—don't you?"

"How—do you know it's—my father that's at the door?" demanded Sprint, all the warier of the enemy because of her acquaintance, with her secret.

"Why!" Bep opened clear, china-blue eyes, as shallow and baffling as bits of porcelain. "Hasn't he been here once for you already, while you were out?"

Sprint turned and ran down the hall. In the minute this took she had lived through a long, heart-breaking, childish regret—regret for the familiar, apprehension of the unknown. It was so warm and snug in this Madigan house; she seemed so to belong there. Why must that unknown parent come to claim her just now, when her spirit was still sorely vexed with the failings of the various fathers she had borne with in one short afternoon!

She got to the top of the staircase that led down to the front door, when she saw that some one had preceded her. It was Madigan, who was on his way down to dinner; poor old Madigan, with his slippered, slow, but positive tread, his straight, assertive back expressing indignation, as it always did when his door-bell was rung. Oh, that familiar old back! Something swelled in Sprint's throat and held her choking, as she grasped the banister and gazed yearningly down upon him. For a moment she had the idea of flying down past him to save him from what was coming. But it was too late; already he had his hand on the door-knob. Did he know who it was for whom he was opening his door? Sprint gasped to herself. Did he anticipate what was coming? Some one ought to tell him—to break it to him—to—

But evidently Sprint herself could not have done this, for in almost the identical moment that Madigan resentfully threw open the door, a stream of water was dashed into his astonished face.

From her point of vantage on the stairway Sprint saw a paralyzed Sissy, the empty pitcher in her guilty hand, the grin of satisfaction frozen on her panic-stricken round face; while, before she fled, her eyes shot one quick, hunted glance over Madigan's dripping head to the joyous enemy above.

And Sprint was joyous. Her explosive laugh pealed out in the second before fear of her father stifled it. So this was how Sissy had planned to get even; so this was the plot behind Bep's baffling blue eyes! And only the accident of Madigan's going to the door had saved Sprint—and confounded her enemy.

Oh, it was so good to be a Madigan! Standing there dry and triumphant, Sprint hugged herself—her very own self—her individuality, which at this minute she would not have changed for anything the world had to offer. To be a Madigan, one's birthright to laugh and do battle with one's peers and win, sometimes through strength, sometimes through guile, sometimes through sheer luck—but to win!

THE PENCIL WILL

Saturday Evening Post 177, no. 35 (1905): 9–11, 40

Each of us reporters had a different name for the long-drawn-out Dilworth trial, and that name was a key to the way we wrote of it. Pert little Frank McGowan called it The War of the Widows. Both the Mrs. Dilworths were widows, but one of them was the sort of woman who will always be known by a man's name, even after death takes it from her.

Bunnell named it A Trial of Temper—poor Mrs. Jim Dilworth's. An undisciplined creature that; a fury, ever ready to make a scene; a scourge to every one whose interests were bound up with hers, and a wrecker of self; but not a shrew, not a nagging woman, and blessed with an open-handed, generous nature and a laugh as hearty and spontaneous as her tears or her temper.

Bliss, of the Mail, always had an allusion to The Sinister Black Hand. He meant the long, scrupulously scoured, knotted hand of black Mammy Sinnott, Mrs. Jim's old nurse, confidant, and, some even said, her evil genius.[27]

As for me, I had had a yearning toward the roasting of Mrs. Muriel Dilworth. I knew just how I should go about it, by dwelling on her perfections—her sweet serenity, the widow's bonnet that crowned and softened her fine, regular features, and her admirable tact and self-control—till every reader should hate her, as I did, for adding these advantages to her social position and her wealth, and so further outclassing her poor, tempestuous, and middle-class sister-in-law.

But Bowman, who knows my weakness, as he does that of everybody under him, got in first.

---

27. Mammy Sinnott was based on the historical figure of Mary Ellen Pleasant. See "Dark-Skinned Lion-Tamer in the House of Mystery."

"No violent and aggressive championing of the under dog this time, Miss Massey," he said, "Wait, wait before you jump on me! I'm as mad as you are. It's a mighty good lay that—partisanship for the lowly and the erring matched against the socially lofty and be-shekeled. You needn't remind your city editor, young woman, that kind hearts are more than coronets to the yellow journal, because there are so many more of 'em. But our respected boss has a wife who's got the society itch, and Mrs. Muriel Dilworth is 'way up in 'G'–as you ought to know if you weren't a rank little Bohemian. So hands off the lady . . . And don't, like a good girl, don't revenge yourself on the paper. If you'll play fair I'll give you leave to get in an occasional blow on the pure and perfect Mrs. Muriel, if you can do it without the umpire's calling foul on you."

So I adopted Baby Jim Dilworth and played him up. In another sense he had already adopted me; came running to me every morning the moment he was brought into the courtroom. Perhaps you think it wasn't a compliment, from a child like that, all gold and pink and blue, a merry bit of human sunshine in his white dresses, that Mammy Sinnott kept immaculate. He was too little yet to be a real boy, but Cochrane, Mrs. Jim's lawyer—Cochrane the vulgar, the sensational, the shrewd and crafty and a bit off-color Cochrane— kept the little one bobbing about the stuffy place for the effect of his presence upon the jury.

Oh, and he was winning, that kid, with his perfectly irresistible assurance of the world's breaking into smiles at sight of him! There wasn't a human being in the courtroom who could resist him—except Mrs. Muriel Dilworth. Why, even Brockinton, her lawyer—old Brockinton, whose fees are five-figured, whose private life's a public scandal, who's a connoisseur of fine things as well as coarse ones, and whose exquisite manners and clothes put to shame the merely Western environment he honors—Brockinton himself mercilessly cross-questioned Mrs. Jim Dilworth with Baby Jim, seated on the table before him, playing with his jeweled repeater.

But—to get back to the newspaper end of it—not one of us reporters had the right name for the case. And we knew it. And everybody in the courtroom knew, too (in spite of Brockinton, Cochrane and the rest, who were ever on tiptoe to anticipate and shut off the smallest allusion to it), that it was the impeccability of dead Albert Dilworth that was on trial; that the widows of the two brothers hated each other with a hatred passing that of mere proponent and contestant of a will; and that the paternity of this same unconscious baby, who went about the courtroom winning hearts, was in question.

"Why is the Dilworth case a moral spectacle, and so deserving of female patronage?" Frankie McGowan scribbled on a pad that he pushed over to me. The courtroom was full of interested women spectators, and Frankie glanced about with a cynical little grin, indicating them.

"Give it up—why?" I wrote.

"Because of its deterrent effect. Phew, but the fate of the transgressor is hard! Look at Mrs. Jim!"

I looked. Brockinton was grilling her on cross-examination. With a perfection of patience, an intonation that was almost an apology for the trouble it might be to her to speak, and a flatteringly courteous assumption of attention to her answers, he was yet able to sting her to a frenzy by the subtle something that underlay his every polite word. She had the look of one who is being baited, who is pushed to the extremest edge of patience. Her full breast, beneath its somewhat too ornate bodice (it looked so, contrasted with Mrs. Muriel's exquisitely simple black), heaved threateningly. Her nicely-booted, small foot was tapping the floor in a nervous crescendo that prophesied storms. The feathers upon her large hat were quivering as the trees in the forest quiver in anticipatory sympathy with the coming tempest. And her face, usually so pale (she had a weak heart, which she overworked, McGowan insisted, playing for sympathy; "coquetting pathologically," Frankie called it)—her face was aflame with wrath.

"At the time, Mrs. Dilworth, that this—this so-called pencil will"— Brockinton held the disputed will delicately between thumb and finger, as one might something not quite clean—"was written, where were you?"

"At my house."

"And Mr. Albert Dilworth—whose last will you say it is—"

"It is!"

The old lawyer bowed. "Mr. Albert Dilworth was—?"

"At my house, too."

"Your husband, Mr. James Dilworth, was present?"

"Mr. Brockinton," she burst forth explosively, "you know very well that my husband was dead six months before that will was written!"

"Ah, pardon me. I see you are correct. I had forgotten the date."

The airy negligence of Brockinton! And yet by this pencil will one-fourth of a half-million-dollar-estate was willed away from his client to the golden-haired boy just now dancing in Mammy Sinnott's arms.

"That isn't true! You had—you do know the date," she cried hysterically.

"Madam!"

The judge turned to her. It was not the first time she had been reproved; but now, as with every other time it had happened, one could see by the quick, angry glance she cast at Mrs. Muriel's discreetly lowered widow's bonnet wherein the bitterness of reproof lay.

"Well," she stammered, trying like a child to justify herself, "it isn't the truth. What kind of a lawyer is he if—"

"One assumes, madam"—her plight and the impossibility of her behaving like an ordinary woman appealed to the judge; his voice was still gentle, though tried—"one assumes that an attorney speaks the truth. In any event, it is not your place to accuse the gentleman. Merely answer his questions."

"I will," she said sullenly, "when there's any sense to them."

The judge lifted his hand. His eyes were angry. I trembled for bad Mrs. Jim in that moment.

"Er—your honor," Brockinton interposed with distinguished grace, "the lady is, of course, quite right. I must apologize. But the—so-called pencil will," he tapped it deprecatingly, gingerly, with his eyeglasses, "is so obvious a forgery—to an attorney, of course—that I have given it too little consideration . . . Mr. Stenographer, be so good as to read the last question."

"I won't answer it," she cried. "I have answered it."

She looked as though she could no longer contain herself. She half rose from her chair as though determined to fall upon her tormentor; but she sat down quickly, both hands at her heart. "The heart pose," McGowan calls it.

"Thank you—thank you!" Brockinton was gracefully oblivious. He waved the shorthand man into silence and waived the quite unnecessary question. "Mrs. Dilworth, kindly tell the court and the jury in what room you were when Mr. Albert Dilworth wrote this—alleged—will."

"I was in my bedroom." Mrs. Dilworth's voice was low, even weak. Was it rage or really heart trouble?

"And he—Mr. Albert Dilworth?"

"Was in the sitting-room beyond."

"An open archway between?"

"An open archway between."

"You say you were ill?"

"I was ill—my baby was a few days old."

"Ah! The little fellow—hold the child up, if you please, Mrs. Sinnott, that the jury may see him." It was Brockinton's ostentatious way of calling Cochrane's attention to the fact that he didn't fear little Jim's influence. "Mrs. Sinnott, if you please . . ."

But Mrs. Sinnott didn't please; it was evident in a moment to us reporters who knew her that Mammy didn't even please to be conscious of Mr. Brockinton's presence, and that she was determined to be deaf to his voice.

Mrs. Jim interposed, a smile in her voice at her nurse's partisanship. It must have been sweet to her—she was so alone, while surrounding and upholding Mrs. Muriel was a group of ultra-respectables, women who were good form personified, good form in morals, in manners, in costume.

"That's the child, Mr. Brockinton," she said with a sneer. "The jury's seen him all right—Baby Jim."

"What—mom?"

It was Jim's clear little trill; the child, hearing his name, had piped out the query. And the woman on the stand smiled back at him responsively, but putting a finger to her lip. I swear she was positively sweet in that minute.

"Look, Frankie, look!" I whispered. "Look at her now, and see if your saintly Mrs. Muriel is half as much a woman!"

But Brockinton had begun again.

"You swear, madam, that you saw Mr. Albert Dilworth write this—ah—will?" There was delicate unbelief in Brockinton's tone.

"No, I don't. I swore that he sat writing something in my sitting-room when—"

"Pardon me . . . With a pencil, Mrs. Dilworth? Mr. Albert Dilworth writing with a pencil?"

It was a strain to put one's credulity to—to fancy that hard-headed, highly respected martinet, Albert Dilworth, doing anything so informal and irregular as making a pencil will.

"I—I couldn't see what he was writing with," she answered resentfully. "He was writing something, and when he finished he came in to me."

"Precisely. And where were you?"

"I have told you," she exclaimed explosively. "I was in bed, in my bedroom."

Mr. Brockinton paused to place his eyeglasses carefully on his nose. It was an old trick of his to postpone and to accentuate a situation; he knew every eye was upon him.

"You say, Mrs. Dilworth, that Mr. Albert Dilworth came into your bedroom, where you lay with your infant, and that he told you of the will he had made?"

"He didn't say 'will.' He said: 'Don't worry about the boy, Belle. I have provided for him.' "[28]

"Did he say why?"

"Why?" The color left her face; she was ghastly pale.

"Why he should provide for another's child?"

She came back at him quick. She was not a cruel woman, though she was almost everything else that a woman wouldn't want to be; but she had suffered too much to let this chance pass.

"He was childless and very lonely," she said slowly. She didn't need to turn her eyes toward the side where Mrs. Muriel sat; a sixth, feminine sense must have made her aware that she had pierced the one vulnerable spot in her enemy's armor.

Brockinton looked at the witness almost admiringly. He had known Mr. Albert Dilworth, the conventional, conservative, cold-blooded banker. Of such depths of sentiment no one had suspected him. He would have smiled himself at the picture Mrs. Jim's words called up. It was nonsense, of course; even the judge passed a discreet hand over his incredulously upturned lips. But she perjured herself like a goose, and then went on, like a woman, to make it thorough.

"He was very, very fond of children," she continued sentimentally. " 'Belle,' he said as he came in from the sitting-room, 'all my married life I have longed for a son; I'll take care of yours now.' "

But retribution came quick, in the very moment of her triumph.

"Mrs. Dilworth"—Brockinton pounced on her, in a flash—"I call your attention to page fifteen of the transcript of your testimony. In that you testify that Mr. Albert Dilworth said to you, 'Don't worry about the boy, Belle. I have provided for him,' and that he said not one word more. *Not one word more!*"

---

28. In the book version, Belle Dilworth's name is changed to Etta Dilworth.

Her eyes flew to her attorney. Cochrane had been doing everything short of shouting to attract her attention, but in her ecstasy of revenge she had forgotten him. It was too late now.

"Madam," persisted Brockinton, "may I ask you to explain the discrepancy?"

She thought for a moment. She was not a stupid woman, but when her emotions were aroused she saw things cloudily.

"If it please the Court—" began Cochrane, sparring for time.

But Brockinton wouldn't have it; he fought, then, earnestly, no play-acting about it. And he won his point.

"I—I was wrong then," Mrs. Jim faltered at last.

"When, pray?"

"The first time. He did say that about being childless."

"Then you deliberately deceived the Court and this jury in a most important particular. Madam, do you know the penalty of perjury?"

"I object!" Cochrane jumped to his feet, dancing with impatience, with apprehension.

He made quite a little speech then, did Cochrane, in his own atrocious style, and Brockinton said never a word in answer—only waited, a bit too politely, for the judge's decision. Then he resumed:

"Mrs. Dilworth, why did you conceal these facts, these remarks of Mr. Albert Dilworth to you?"

For a moment she looked at him warily; then something occurred to her.

"I left that out," she said sweetly, "to spare Mr. Dilworth's widow. I thought it would hurt her."

She was quite right. It would. It did. Mr. Dilworth's widow's bonnet sank as though with a weight, and the lorgnette she was holding to her short-sighted eyes fell with a click.

Brockinton saw the movement out of the corner of his eye; it was the first time his client had flinched.

"Is this the truth this time?" he asked unpleasantly, "or will this, too, be amended later?"

Again her lawyer came to Mrs. Jim's rescue. She needed him; her color was rising, and all the storm signals flew from her flashing eyes.

"And why, Mrs. Dilworth, does your gracious forbearance end now?" Brockinton asked when things were quiet again. "Why do not the same reasons still hold good as to sparing the lady?"

There was a silence, tense and anxious. What would she say? What could she say? Her eyes fell. She bit her lip. She began to speak, then fell silent.

And Brockinton waited, standing, with insulting patience.

"She—she hasn't spared me!" Mrs. Jim blurted out at last. But even on her ears the words fell jangled. "Oh! I—I don't know," she added; "it just happened to come to me!"

Brockinton was silent; just a long, significant second to let the words carry their own weight of venom to the jurors' ears.

"Ah, just a bit of revenge, then," he murmured as though indulgently musing aloud, and then quickly: "Have you told any one of these supplementary remarks of Mr. Albert Dilworth?"

"N—no—it wasn't revenge, Mr. Brockinton."

"Have you not even told Mrs. Sinnott, your confidant?"

"I say it wasn't revenge, Mr. Brockinton," she repeated, blindly stubborn now.

"Mr. Albert Dilworth," Brockinton went on composedly, "had nieces whom he loved—his sister's children. Did he say, Mrs. Dilworth, why he intended to provide for your boy and not for them?"

She set her teeth and merely looked at him, dumb with exasperation.

"Will the stenographer please read the question?" asked Brockinton with superb irrelevance. "I must ask your Honor to instruct the witness to answer the question."

"I will not—I will not!" cried Mrs. Jim, in a fury now, dissatisfaction with herself for putting a weapon in his hands augmenting her rage at her tormentor. "He sha'n't insult me—he sha'n't browbeat me! Mine has been 'gracious forbearance,' and he knows it in spite of his sneers. But he don't appreciate it. It's at an end now. I won't play the game their way any more. I don't care what happens. I'll produce that—"

This far she had fought her way in spite of Cochrane's strenuous objections, the judge's grave commands, and Brockinton's insistently courteous "If the Court please." But the rest of it was inaudible.

Brockinton's "Will the stenographer repeat the last question?" came out of the turmoil like the theme out of a fugue.

But this time Mrs. Jim's face lit up at the sound of it; she hardly waited for the clerk to finish.

"Why shouldn't he provide for my boy," she cried, "instead of those snobbish nieces of his? Why shouldn't he provide for him? Baby Jim Dilworth is his own—"

"Mom—Mom!"

It was the child's voice that stopped her. She looked toward it. Right across from her at the back wall of the courtroom, the tall, old, black Mammy had stationed herself with the boy high in her arms. Beside the gold and pink of his face her gaunt features looked grim and disapproving.

For half a second Mrs. Jim met those hollow black eyes and battled with them.

"—nephew—his own twin brother's child," she concluded lamely, and broke into hysterical tears.

_ℓ_

As we sat waiting in Mrs. Jim Dilworth's little parlor that evening, half a dozen of us reporters, she came storming in, tearing off her gloves and coat as she walked, a creature of temperament, strongly emotional, caught in the cold, steel meshes of the law, and floundering miserably.

"Well, what is it?" she demanded, facing us. We'd interviewed her dozens of times, but never without old Mammy Sinnott's standing guard over her. "You want me to tell what they wouldn't let me tell on the stand. Well, I'm going to. You can have it all—every word of it, the whole lot of you. I don't care if every paper in town is full of it. They've made me desperate now, and they can take the consequences. Here!" She drew a much folded paper from her blouse.

I reached up to take it—I happened to be nearest, and I saw Albert Dilworth's signature on it—when the folding doors opened and old Mammy Sinnott came in.

I watched the change that came over the men's faces. "Checkmate," it said. My own face must have looked enough like theirs to establish a pen-and-ink relationship.

"Ez that yo', honey?" Oh, the sweetness in that old darky's voice! She came forward to take Mrs. Jim's hat and gloves from her, but she stood a moment caressing her hand. "Yo' must be tahed, but won't yo' go in to Jim a minute? He's res'less, thet ol' co't room's mighty bad fer a baby."

Mrs. Jim hesitated, and we held our breath. She knew, and we knew, how much more than solicitude for the child lay behind the old negress' words.

"You'd be furious yourself, Mammy, if you'd been treated as I have!" she cried; but there was uncertainty in her voice.

"Yes, honey. Guess Ah'd jes natchally spill over mahself. But these gemmen will wait for yo', Miss Belle, Ah'm sure."

The men murmured, but Mammy affected not to hear it, and before they could speak she turned to me:

"Yo'll wait, won't yo', miss? Yo' always so fond of Jim; he's got yo' handkerchief thet yo' made into a mouse fo' him in his hand now. He's mighty stuck on yo'."

Bliss loves to write about Mammy Sinnott's hypnotic eye; he had actually run a story that morning in the Mail to the effect that the old black woman had forged the pencil will and hypnotized Mrs. Jim into believing it genuine. It may have been my remembrance of that working suggestively, but I could have sworn there was a special appeal, almost that and a promise besides, in the old woman's cavernous eye as she turned them on me.

"Why, certainly," I said—and I heard Bunnell swear under his breath. "Mrs. Dilworth will see us soon?"

"Oh, co'se—of co'se!" said the old woman soothingly. "Soon he's asleep, eh, Miss Belle? Shall Ah keep the paper till yo' come out?"

Mrs. Jim nodded, put the folded paper into the long, black fingers that closed greedily over it, and left the room.

She faced us then, stern and grim and defiant—Mammy against the lot of us.

"Yo' reporters is jes' another kind of bloodhaound," she snarled. "Yo' ain't got the reason the police has to hunt a man down; yo' don't do it for love or money, but jes' 'cause yo'se haounds an' nothin' else. Yo' kill for the sake of killing; it don' do yo' no good. What's thet woman inside done to yo'? What right yo' got to come snoopin' in hyar tryin' to ferret her secrets out? Ain't it 'nough thet the Co't's against her an' the biggest lawyers in the city bein' paid out her own money—money't ought to be her boy's, anyway—'thout yo' comin' in an' haoundin' her to death? Think shame to yo'selfs—yo' most of any of 'em—yes, yo' they calls Rhody Massey!"

Phew! That was straight from the shoulder!

"Why," I gasped, while the men grinned enjoying, "the truth can't hurt her."

"That's a lie—right thar. Yo' know it can hurt, an' yo' want her to hurt herself. Yo' know she's hot-tempered an' uncareful; she don' mince her words like some that thinks they's so stylish. She jes' come right out, an' yo'—yo' lyin' in wait, the jackal lot of yo', to get hold o' anything! Why don' yo' ask me questions? Ol' Mammy'll give yo' good's yo' send!"

"Mrs. Sinnott," I said in a sweetly casual tone, "won't you kindly tell us the contents of the paper you have in your hand?"

A gleam of humor came into her sunken black eyes.

"Oh, yo's mighty ready, yo' little sass-box! Pity yo' hain't had a ole Mammy t' spank yo' good when yo' was littler!" she growled—but almost tenderly.

But the roar those men set up. They were having the time of their lives. Even Cohen stopped sketching the gaunt old woman in her plain black gown and big white apron to join in the chorus.

It was in the midst of it that she leaned toward me, and I just caught her whisper:

"Git 'em away, chile. For Gawd's sake git 'em away 'fo' Miss Belle comes back! You won't lose . . . When I want yo'"—she spoke aloud now, for the men had stopped laughing to listen—"when I want yo', Rhody Massey, I'll send for yo'."

Oh, the imperiousness in that black woman's voice; it did make me feel like a child!

"That, Miss Massey," sniggered Frank McGowan, "is a delicate mode of intimating that, so far as you're concerned, the audience is over."

I looked at him a minute. But I wasn't hearing him or seeing him. It was Mammy that was pictured in my mind—old Mammy Sinnott, who had never broken a promise (every newspaper man in town knew that) and who never forgot a kindness.

"I guess that's about the size of it, Frankie," I sighed, shrugging my shoulders and walking away.

"You're not giving it up?" he asked, amazed, following me to the door, where Bliss lazily joined us.

But I made no reply, and as we stood for a second talking I saw Mammy, in a swift pantomime, make some agreement with Bunnell. It was done quick as a flash; so quick that I'd have distrusted my own eyes if Bunnell hadn't risen just then and walked out past us.

"I say, what's up?" cried McGowan.

"Nothing's up—Mrs. Jim's down—gone to bed. And I'm not wasting time tackling Mammy Sinnott for a story."

Bunnell turned with a grin and ran down the stairs. I knew that grin; it made me uneasy. And I hesitated for another minute.

"When I want yo', Rhody Massey, I'll send for yo'." The shrewd old negress had read me in a moment.

"Ain't thet plain?"

It was—it had to be. There was a big chance in it, anyway. And I took it.

"Are you coming my way, Frankie?" I asked. "Good night, Mrs. Sinnott."

She nodded curtly at the lot of us standing now out in the hall; closed the door quickly behind us and bolted it.

Something in the action aroused McGowan's suspicions.

"I'm not going," he said. "Think I'll camp out for the night right here."

Bliss lit a cigarette, Enderby, of the Express, took out his pipe and sat down on the steps below him. They were still perched there when I turned up the street.

But I didn't sleep well that night. Bunnell's grin haunted me. I dreamed all night that I was scooped, unmercifully scooped. I saw the Times-Record's first page all broken out in 102-type. And though I knew it was a smashing Dilworth story, I couldn't read a line of it to find out what it was about, for Bunnell's face, with the grin still on it, seemed to be printed life-size behind it all over the page.

I was sick with apprehension when I awoke, so strong was the impression left by that nasty nightmare. I flew to the door and got the Times-Record, and there, sure enough, spread out even blacker and bigger than my worst dreams, and under a screaming headline—MAMMY SINNOTT CONFESSES TO A TIMES-RECORD REPORTER; THE PENCIL WILL IS A FORGERY—was a Dilworth story that would shake the town!

It did. All San Francisco roared—with laughter, for that unconscionable, precious old rascal of a colored woman had confided in four different reporters—differently. She told Bunnell that the will was a forgery and that Mrs. Jim knew it was. She confessed to Bliss—calling him in for the purpose from the landing—that the will was a forgery, but that Mrs. Jim innocently supposed it was genuine. She gave Enderby solemn assurance that the will was genuine and that she had secret evidence corroborating it. And she wisely chose little Frank McGowan for a confidant of a last variation—that the will was a forgery; but that it was a true and faithful copy of a genuine will that had been lost.

Perhaps you think Rhoda Massey didn't hug herself and have the laugh on those bewildered men when, on the stand the next morning, Mammy was questioned about her various interviews, and responded with only a twinkle in the depths of her inscrutable black eyes:

"'Tain't no lie to lie to a newspaper reporter thet gets a livin' by tellin' lies!"

۾

When old Brockinton's sins are forgotten, and the scandals of which he is the hero have passed out of newspaper men's memory (which is tenacious), they'll still tell of the great speech he made in the Dilworth case.

I sat not ten feet from him while he was addressing the jury in the last throes of the great struggle—the case had been on for months—and though I couldn't help seeing through the actor's arts, though I knew his declamatory tricks and was so familiar with the case that I could almost anticipate the points he made—in spite of this he thrilled me. I was shivering with excitement when he turned the thing over to the jury at last and took his seat. I couldn't look at Mrs. Jim; to turn a curious eye upon a thing on the rack, as she was, seemed inhuman. She fainted once during the terrible arraignment. McGowan insisted that it was done for effect, but I caught Mammy Sinnott's eye as she bent over her applying restoratives, and I saw the agonized truth behind it. When the jury retired and the courtroom cleared she was still sitting with her hand on her heart, her face pale and her eyes staring as though in a stupor. She did not notice when little Jim left her side and ran to me, lifting up his arms and crying: "Take—take Jim!"

I looked over at Mammy.

"Let me take him for a while—till she's feeling better," I said.

"Ain't yo' goin' downtown—to yo' work now?" she asked hesitatingly.

I shook my head. And she went gray under her black skin.[29]

"Yo' reckon it'll be soon then—the verdict?"

"Everybody seems to think so."

"Thet means it'll be 'gainst Miss Belle?"

---

29. In the book version of *A Yellow Journalist*, this line was revised to read: "I shook my head, and a grayish pallor seemed to settle like a veil over her black skin."

I tried to evade and to hide my face behind Jim's golden curls, but you couldn't, with those fierce old eyes upon you, tell anything but the truth. The whole courtroom, now that the judge had withdrawn, was humming with it. McGowan was offering odds that the verdict rejecting the pencil will be brought in within half an hour.

"Well, take him, then"—Mammy's voice was hard—"but don' yo' be so sure, miss. An' one thing I tell yo' now—ef they do down Miss Belle this time it'l be 'cause the biggest piece of evidence wasn't put in. Thar! Yo' can say thet in yo' paper fo' me ef yo' want. An yo' can say thet old Mammy Sinnott'll spend every dollar she's got to see her lamb righted, an' no hatched-up business between lawyers'll stop her. . . . No, yo' needn't look at me thet way—I never cheated yo', did I? I tell yo' it's the truth."

"Then prove it, Mrs. Sinnott. Do you think any editor in town will dare to print anything from you now—"

"Oh, won't he? Won't he print thet ef he can git it?"

She pulled a piece of paper from her satchel—and I almost dropped small Jim Dilworth to the floor. It was the paper Mrs. Jim had flaunted in our eyes the night we all went to interview her, and it made me feel now like a little reportorial donkey before whose nose and just out of reach the most tempting wisp of hay is being pulled along.

"Now, look here, Mammy Sinnott—" I began angrily.

"Sh—! Look here yo'self. I'm a-goin' to give it to yo'. I promised myself I would that night yo' got out when I told yo' to. Ef the jury say thet will ain't a true one, yo' havin' this now won't hurt us—fo' we'll fight it out in a higher co't, an' we'll use it nex' time. But ef the jury say the pencil will's truly Albert Dilworth's—"

"It won't, Mrs. Sinnott. It's sure as—"

"Then yo' won't mind promising me, ef the jury decides fo' Miss Belle, yo' won't print this in yo' paper? I'll take yo' wo'd—yo' promise, eh?"

Promise? Who wouldn't promise on a sure thing like that? There, in my shaking hand, was a written acknowledgment of the boy's paternity:

"I commend the child known as Jim Dilworth to my wife Muriel. He is my son."

There it was, in black and white—and not pencil this time—signed Albert Dilworth, and dated scrupulously; the heart of the Dilworth case at last beating in sight of the world!

Mammy watched me grimly.

"I want yo' to say, ef yo' do put it in the paper, thet Mammy Sinnott saw Albert Dilworth write thet paper; thet she told him ef he didn't write it she'd tell that stuck-up wife of his the whole bad story befo' he died; thet she kep' it out o' this here trial to save Miss Belle's name; thet even Cochrane don't know 'bout this paper, but thet ef my lamb don' git his rights through the pencil will he'll git 'em this way, or my name ain't Mammy Sinnott. . . . Mind yo' promise, now!"

She turned back to Mrs. Jim. I danced out into the hall, Jim in my arms. He crowed and clapped his hands, but he wasn't a bit happier than I. Think what a story! Think what a scoop! Think . . .

There was a stir in the hall ahead of me. It was Brockinton, ushering his client into the judge's chambers, from which he and the judge came out immediately to go to luncheon together.

Think what Mrs. Muriel would say to the document I held in my hand! Oh, I must—I simply had to be the first to tell her of it! If the one forlorn chance in a thousand gave Mrs. Jim the victory her secret would be as safe with her proud sister-in-law and rival as with Mammy herself. If the jury brought in the verdict everybody expected Mrs. Muriel would know the story as soon as the News came out, anyway. She must know it now, and from me.

I'd heard the lock click behind Brockinton and the judge, so with Jim still on my arm I hurried back into the courtroom, up behind the judge's seat, and in a minute I had pushed open the other door, and stood in Mrs. Muriel's presence.

It didn't seem like a presence, though. Her widow's bonnet was off, her brown hair was prettily mussed, and her head lay bowed on the desk before her. She was crying—crying just like an ordinary, human woman!

She looked up quickly at the noise Jim made trumpeting through his fists.

"I beg your pardon, Mrs. Dilworth," I said in a rush, "I have just got possession of a document that concerns you deeply, and—"

"You will please excuse me," she said—her voice was still husky with tears; they made it sound strangely soft, very different from the cold, contained one we'd heard from the stand. "On my lawyers' advice I have declined, as I supposed you knew, to speak to anyone connected with the newspapers. If you will see Mr. Brockinton he'll no doubt—"

"Look, Mrs. Dilworth!"

I let Jim slip to the floor and held the paper before her. Mechanically she felt for her lorgnette, but before she could get it her shortsighted eyes had recognized the signature. And then—

Then Mrs. Jim Dilworth came tearing in like a whirlwind.

"You—you give me back that paper! What right have you got to show it to her!" she cried.

She snatched it out of my hand before I could think to hide it, and stormed out again, catching Jim up in a passion that made him hold tight as though the arm he rode was a ship in a typhoon.

I turned, hopeless, to Mrs. Muriel.

"I assure you—" I began.

But she waved apology aside.

"Tell me," she interrupted eagerly, "won't you tell me what was in that paper? It's his signature, my husband's name. I caught only that—my eyes are so wretched. I—I—will you please tell me?"

No, I wouldn't. I couldn't—now. For this wasn't the Mrs. Muriel Dilworth I had been watching week after week in the courtroom, with her unchangeable composure, her pitiless ignoring of the other woman; the Mrs. Muriel who dwelt on cold, inaccessible heights, where humanity's cries couldn't reach her.

"Perhaps, Mrs. Dilworth," I stammered, "this paper may be a forgery, too."

She shook her head. "That was Mr. Dilworth's writing. I know it. I'm positive. . . . Oh!" Suddenly her voice broke, and the tears rolled unhidden down her cheeks. "Do you realize what I am enduring, how I am groping helplessly for the truth?"

At that moment the door opened behind us and the judge walked in.

"They've reached a verdict, ladies. The jury will be in in a moment," he said.

I jumped for the door.

"Miss Massey—please!" It was Mrs. Muriel's voice, appealing, insistent.

"But the jury—"

"What difference does that make?" she cried. "I don't want the money—I want the truth!"

"Here comes Mr. Hewlitt," I put in eagerly. "Mr. Brockinton must have sent him for you."

She wrung her hands. "You cruel girl!"[30]

"All right, then," I capitulated. I spoke in a whisper, for Brockinton's young partner was nearly upon us. "This is what the paper says: 'I commend the child known as Jim Dilworth to my wife, Muriel. He is . . . *not*—my son!'"

I couldn't help it. Up to the instant before I reached the last two words it hadn't occurred to me; but, with that quivering woman standing before me, I fell down like the miserable little coward I am.

When I got to the door of the courtroom I found it so crowded that, instead of making for the reporters' desk, I let the bailiff make way for me to the first empty seat. From where I sat I couldn't hear the words in which the foreman mumbled his verdict, but I caught a glimpse of poor Mrs. Jim's face, white, drawn, incredulous, and agonized, before she fell defeated into Mammy's arms.

It was just then that Mrs. Muriel entered. She passed her lawyers' table and came swiftly toward the spot where Mammy sat chafing Mrs. Jim's hands and holding her heavy head to her breast.

"Belle"—Mrs. Muriel's voice was shaken still, but it was whispered music, and it thrilled with the humility of utter happiness. "Forgive me, Belle. The boy shall have all this and more. He'll be my son as well as yours. Whatever the verdict is—"

"The verdict is already in, Mrs. Dilworth," Hewlitt broke in; he had followed her. "We have won; let me be first to congratulate you."

But she hardly heard him.

"Belle!" she pleaded.

"Go 'way—yo'!" Mammy's eyes blazed furiously up at her. "Yo've half killed her."

Instinctively, Mrs. Muriel fell back before the savage ferocity of the black woman's face. She might have yielded then to the pressure of her lawyer's hand, but suddenly she felt a tug at her dress. It was Jim, lost, forgotten in the excitement of the moment, yet suffering intuitively, feeling and fearing the crisis.

"Take," he cried with a trembling lip, lifting his arms to her—"take Jim!"

---

30. In the book version, Mrs. Dilworth adds, "Has your profession made you utterly heartless?"

She bent down and lifted him, holding his sobbing little body with a tenderness and yet a yielding strength that transfigured her.

Through the crowd Cochrane made his way with a glass of whisky. Mammy put it to Mrs. Jim's blue lips, then let it fall crashing to the floor.

"She's daid, my Gawd! Miss Belle!"

Her black hand crept to Mrs. Jim's heart—then in a second it lifted, knotted and threatening, over Muriel Dilworth's head.

"Yo'—yo'—" the old woman stammered thickly.

But Baby Jim, his blond head curled into the lady's neck, turned his wet, blue eyes wonderingly upon Mammy, and lifting a hand like a dimpled snowflake he touched the black woman's lips with a pleading caress.

That same little tender hand still holds back the real, the awful vengeance Mammy Sinnott might take if she would. It holds me back, too—though the office would fire me in a minute if it suspected, and serve me right, too. But since Mrs. Muriel has legally adopted the boy, what good on earth would be served by wrecking a live woman's faith and dragging a dead woman's name from under the sheltering benefit of the doubt?

IN CHY FONG'S RESTAURANT

Where Miss Massey Meets a Missionary

From *A Yellow Journalist* (New York: D. Appleton, 1905), 100–118

All sorts of queer, disconnected impressions kept coming to me as I sat there in utter silence.

The ear-splitting crash and clang of the Chinese orchestra in the front room, the gaudy, dragon-embroidered hangings to the rear of the restaurant, the gentle twanging of the slave girls' guitars, the teak-wood chairs and tables, the handleless cups, the bizarre, singsong conversation of the men at the banquet table in the next room—even my own satin blouse, upon which peacocks were embroidered in silver, and the absurd, wide trousers of salmon pink, whose bands of purple were embossed in flaming orange, my purple silk hose and crimson, gold-embroidered slippers—all this was unreal to me; as fanciful and impossible as a mad dream.

Reality stood behind it, apart from it, and the strength of its impressions persisted in replacing even the things that my senses recognized.

I could see the *News*'s first page of yesterday, with its screaming headline and my story of the raid on the fan-tan games below it, more clearly, much more clearly than the expressionless ivory face, so near to me, of Ah Oy, the most expensive slave girl in Chinatown, worth $3,000 in white man's money![31]

---

31. "In Chy Fong's Restaurant" first appeared as chapter 5 of *A Yellow Journalist*. In the previous chapter, "The Fascination of Fan-Tan," Rhoda disguised herself as a Chinese boy to investigate an alleged gambling den in the company of a white police officer, Sergeant Wyss, and a male reporter named Forbes, whom her paper had enlisted for her protection. When there are no signs of gambling, Rhoda realizes that Wyss was taking bribes from the highbinders and had warned them in advance of her visit. She returns later, this time accompanied

I could repeat, word for word, the printed statement of Sergeant Wyss, denying the implication of grafting, which was the atmosphere of my story as surely as the faint smell from the opium-smokers' pipes was penetrating every part of Chy Fong's restaurant.

Scraps and phrases of the *News*'s big double-leaded editorial, openly charging Wyss with protecting gambling in Chinatown for a bribe, instead of wiping it out, came to me; and the whole of that last paragraph, accusing him of bad faith, of deliberately tipping off our projected raid, of warning the gamblers in advance, through their spies, who lurked about, when we met at the corner of the alley.

But back of all this there was a still stronger impression, as of a thing one has got by heart.

"No talk.

"No look see.

"No turn head.

"No move.

"No listen.

"No speak.

"No bite lips.

"No move fingers.

"No sit so stlaight. Neck down—so.

"No lift feet when walk—slide—slip—soft.

"All time wait—all time sit still—head down—eyes down—all time wait."

And here I was, "all time waiting," as old Gum Tai, the duenna of the slave girls, had taught me in a long afternoon rehearsal; with my eyes on the floor and my sleek, black head, with its jeweled *bow tow*[32] lowered, my senses dulled by the strong perfume of the narcissi in the *cloisonné* bowls, by the smell of opium, and the dream-like sensation of being apart—all time sitting still, all time waiting; waiting with an Oriental, stupefying patience for bribers and bribed to meet here, as was their custom, and pay the bribe before my very eyes.

---

by an ethnic informant, an elderly Chinese woman named Gum Tai, uncovering not only a game of fan-tan in progress but also a deeper story of graft in Chinatown in which the white police officer was exposed as a criminal.

32. Bow tow: Chinese for "head wrap."

What lifelong rehearsals must these pale, quiet girls' mothers have gone through for centuries and centuries to bring to its perfection that yellow flower of repose that Ah Oy is as she sits idly there with her guitar, ornamented with precious stones, in little hands, closely and compactly made as the sheath of a lily, with nary a twitch of limb nor turn of head, her soft, dull eyes looking straight ahead and down, seeing nothing; and hearing, smelling nothing, one would say, for her ears and delicate nostrils—the color of a softly yellowed magnolia before it falls, overripe, from the tree—seem less like organs of sense than bits of soft but perfect and exotic statuary.

"Look here, Rhoda Massey"—memory, the only faculty which seemed to survive in me the drowsy suspension of my wits, brought McCabe's voice and his words to me as I sat all time waiting—"go slow. Yellow Journalism, and the success you've made of it, are turning your steady little head. You're out-yellowing your master, and when I came on the *News* I held the record. The thing is impossible. You can't play the Chinawoman for a full hour's stretch. You can't fool the Chinamen, much less the slave girls up at Chy Fong's. They're the—"

"But Gum Tai says I can," I had interrupted eagerly. "I'm just saturated with Chinatown, Mr. McCabe. I've taken tea at that restaurant every night this week. I know I can do it—I know I can. Listen to this. Shut your eyes and listen, and say I'm not Ah Oy up at Chy Fong's."

And in a sweet little nasal voice, more like the plaint of an insect than full-throated human utterance, I sang the Chinese of this:

> "Make me good, O great T'in Hau,
> Make me gentle, chaste and witty.
> Make me all of these or none—
> But O, I pray thee, make me pretty!"[33]

"Bully!—encore!" cried McCabe, tapping his blue pencil enthusiastically on the desk.

But I wouldn't sing the other verses. I wanted too much to persuade him while his impression lasted.

---

33. Note that Michelson uses the same song in "Ah Luey's Self."

"See, Mr. McCabe," I began hurriedly, "surely that old Chinawoman knows. I'm to be a Hakka woman, while all the other girls are from Canton. Of course, then, I couldn't understand a word of their dialect, nor they of mine. Gum Tai will tell them all that. So I'll not have to say a word or understand anything. Besides, it's etiquette for a new girl just bought, a novice, not to say anything. And the older girls in slavery ignore her rather contemptuously and critically, much as at our fortnightly dances the *débutante* runs up against the buds of a season or two, and—"

"I won't listen to your wheedling, Rhoda. You've a faculty, carefully and artfully cultivated, I suspect, my lady, of making the melodramatic sound simple and natural, and robbing sensation itself of its off-color. I won't let you try this scheme, I tell you. Am I the News Editor of this paper or am I merely the home secretary for your foreign—very foreign—affairs, you conceited and rampant little yellow journalist?"

I declined to enlighten him, but went on coaxing.

"Do you see a page story, Mr. McCabe," I begged, "with photos of the interior of Chy Fong's, Mr. McCabe? With Sergeant Wyss and Chin Bak You and Yet Kim Gai sketched from a description by Rhoda Massey? With a picture, Mr. McCabe—yes, I'll even let you run a picture of Miss Massey in the costume of a Chinese belle, if only—"

"Get thee behind me, Satan, and let me send for the Lunacy Commission!"

"Please!" I coaxed.

He threw down his pencil and jumped to his feet.

"I won't, I can't, Rhoda. The money's been paid there once and will be again, but I don't dare trust you to fool too much with these yellow devils. If you could have Forbes come along to take care of you; but to send you alone into a den like that—my God, girl, you're clean daft! You've lost your sense of proportion. You don't know the possible from the undoable, and you've forgotten the elementary rules of the game."

"I suppose I have," I said slowly.

"Give it up, Rhoda," he growled tenderly, as I made sorrowfully for the door. (At the office they call me "McCabe's White-headed Boy" since that gambling raid, and it's pleasant to know he hates to refuse me anything.) "We'll think up something else. There's a crisis due in the Lowenthal *ménage à trois* before long. Young Lothal, the son, caught the two—Mrs. L. and Kirby—at the Humming-Bird last night, at supper after the theater. There'd have been a bully row then and there if Mrs. L. hadn't left the place with her stepson. Kirby came over to my table afterward, and I promised him to keep the incident out of the papers. . . . Charming fellow, Jerome Kirby; built for the villain in the play—gay and reckless, handsome and cruel and clever. Just fancy his getting me to—"

I made an impatient movement.

"You mean you're tired waiting for that scandal to ripen?" he asked. "So is the rest of the town. But here's something else that will really come off very soon. The Mission is going to make a star play: they're going to rescue Ah Oy. I'll find out from Miss McIntosh exactly when it is to be, and you can be in on that. It'll be a corking story. But you sha'n't do this other mad thing with my consent. We'll find some other way to trap Wyss . . . but not this. Never with my consent, Miss Rhoda Massey."

"Then without it!" I cried to myself as I shut the door behind me and started for Gum Tai's.

I went over it all again now as I sat "all time waiting" at Chy Fong's. The slave girls were playing pi-gow now—dominoes—gambling silently. It was some comfort to me just to think of McCabe; to feel that outside this opium-scented, Oriental dream a man lived—a big-brained, big-hearted white man, with his fingers playing at the buttons that set the world a-moving, with a head full of knowledge of human nature in all its variety, with a sense of humor that kept him and the rest of us well balanced, and an irresistible strength and originality in his point of view.

And this same man—this far-famed, old McCabe of the *News*—was precisely the newspaper man whose commands I had disregarded, whose advice I had scorned. Oh, if he had only stood in! But to have to set one-self the hardest detail in one's whole newspaper life and to miss McCabe behind one!

I gave a gasp at my own audacity. I wasn't conscious of making any sound, but instantly every eye in the room was turned upon me.

I felt them—those black, ironical, impenetrable Chinese eyes. They made me glow and shiver, and involuntarily I made a motion to get to my feet. I believe I was terrified enough to have scuttled away then and there if at that minute a dominating, high voice, rolling out a chanting string of Chinese, hadn't broken in upon us all. It came from the stairway beyond, and bore—even before its owner followed it—so strong and imperious a suggestion of assertive activity that the whole establishment seemed to respond to it. Chy Fong himself came to the door a moment and sang out an order. Doors were hurriedly closed all over the place. A screen was swiftly stretched across, shutting in our corner that gave on to the high little lacquered, lantern-hung balcony which overlooked the square. And in here a table, upon which chop suey, sweetmeats, tea, and rice wine were already set in fanciful porcelain, was brought and placed in the farther corner, while the waiters flew about like mad.

And Ah Oy daintily touched her long pearl earrings and bracelets of jade and silver filigree with a slender tan finger and a long, pointed nail, sniffing with nervousness just once or twice, as a deer might through distended, dry nostrils.

Yet Kim Gai—the first. I knew him. His walk was a bit more assured, more elegantly pompous, than it had been the other night when we raided the game. In his long mandarin's robe (the New Year must be near) he moved with the dignified roll of a sea-captain aboard his own ship—even though he was smoking a cigar!

I know the smell of a good cigar. McCabe smokes the best in town. (Our respected proprietor, who owns the *News* and Lord knows what besides, facetiously declared to me the other day that he couldn't afford cigars such as his News Editor smokes.) But McCabe's specially imported gold-banded darlings can't be any better than the one this big, young, fine-looking Chinaman removes from his lips to pour out an intoned roar of Chinese which awakens Celestial echoes from his companions.

One of them is Chin Bak You, the fearful old death's-head who presides over the See Yups, the highbinders.[34] It is one of his men, Chow La, who accompanies him—a great, bulky beast of a Chinaman, with a square face framed in the highbinders' locks, with a mouth that's a big, brutal gash, a nose that's obscene, and eyes of black bestiality. (We have his photo in the art room; we keep it to personify the Yellow Peril and that sort of thing.)[35]

All Chinamen look alike, they say, to white men, but these three are strong

---

34. Highbinder: used here to refer to a member of a Chinese-American criminal organization.
35. Yellow Peril: a racist term that expresses white or Western fears of rising Asian power.

types; once seen and their characteristics fitted to them, one isn't likely to forget them.

What I had forgotten in their coming was the panic terror that had seized me. So possessed was I by curiosity now that it was all I could do to remember the old duenna's words:

"No look see—no move—no listen—no turn head—"

No look see—when my eyes were irresistibly drawn, fascinated by the three.

No listen—when, by straining to the utmost, my ears could bring to me only the burden of sound without sense.

Listen? I listened as though all my senses were merged into one. Yet Kim Gai's was the voice that rolled out with a declamatory clearness of utterance; I could almost repeat the syllables after him. Old Chin's grunts and whining, nasal phrases seemed wrung from him as he sat smoking, his dull old eyes like pin points under their wrinkled lids, his everlasting pipe dragging at his misshapen mouth. The hatchet man bellowed out a guttural word now and then; but he ate—ate like a famished beast till, nauseated, I had to bite my painted lips to keep from crying out at him.

I missed my handkerchief then and was putting my sleeve to my lips, when it was twitched suddenly and, looking up, I saw Ah Oy gazing at me in mute astonishment.

I had forgotten—I had forgotten Gum Tai's first and last admonition: to do in Rome what the Romans did. And at just this minute the three other girls were standing about the table.

"Oh, thank—" I began.

But Ah Oy had already taken her place fortunately and, slip-slip, I slid after her.

I had been well trained for this part of it. I knew the slave girls' *rôle* at the banquet—to be mute, to be vacantly smiling and ornamental, like a figure on a fan; and only to accept wine when a guest has had more than is good for him.

I watched Ah Oy take the thimbleful of sam shu—thrice-fired rice wine—from the highbinder's unsteady fingers. I saw her affect to sip a bit and then with disdainful grace spill it upon the floor.

When Yet Kim Gai motioned toward his own cup (he hadn't eaten at all, but drank with a full-throated intemperance that was most un-Chinese),

I was ready. I reached a trembling hand out in front of him, lifted the tiny glass cup to my lips, and—

And let it fall, shattered into bits, upon the floor!

Right opposite me, looking over the screen and straight into mine, was a pair of eyes—gray, American eyes—the eyes of Sergeant George Wyss.

I don't know what happened for a second. If the penalty for it had been his calling out my name and unmasking me upon the spot, I couldn't have done anything other than I did: put my shaking hands up to my face and sob—sob in tearless terror and excitement and—

And satisfaction.

For he had come! He *had* come! It was true, then. The money was to be paid here. What did I care for anything else? The slave girls' horrified hush at my clumsiness and fracture of etiquette; the scolding of the head waiter (I knew the accent, as a dog might, but not the words); the amused laugh of the sergeant as he pushed the screen aside and entered; the good-natured interference in my behalf of Yet Kim Gai, who came to a poor girl's rescue, like the man of the world and gallant he is—his pantomime was unmistakable—it was all nothing to me. My story was coming true—the impossible story, the story that McCabe himself had not dared to tackle!

"*Kung-héi, fát ts'oi!*" The sergeant cried out the New Year's greeting glibly, shaking his own hand cordially in the Chinese style, but refusing the chair a waiter offered.

Old Chin grunted a recognition without removing his pipe. Yet Kim Gai waved his hand in an airy American fashion. Chow La nodded, taking the briefest respite from the business of eating.

"Ah there, Ah Oy!" said the sergeant gayly, putting an arm about her and another impartially around the girl on the other side.

And they tittered, these Chinese belles, and wriggled, complimented by the queer American attention.

In great spirits was Sergeant Wyss, evidently. I watched with satisfaction the quick glances he threw about the place and the flash of intelligence between him and Yet.

It was at a word from the gambler that Ah Oy had taken her queer little guitar and was singing a pale little nasal melody—the inevitable ditty (Wan Hoey translated it for me) whose second verse, put into English, goes:

"Make me noble, dread T'in Hau,
Kind to all, no creature harming,
Make me patient, gen'rous, faithful—
But, I implore thee, make me charming!"

Wyss crooned it with her. He did it better than I could, with a skill that bespoke practice and opportunity. He put out his hand at the end of the verse to pinch my arm, but I reached just then for a cup, and being a merry, easily pleased, gay gentleman of the police, he accepted the girl in the red, gold-embroidered blouse as a substitute.

But everybody was merry by this time—except old Chin. His death's mask never changed a line. His horn-toad's eyes had never a glimmer of light or life.

"Wait, Sachant, I sing for you," cried Yet, taking the guitar from Ah Oy's hand. "Ever hear this—bully song?"

And to my utter amazement he strummed a few familiar bars, and burst jovially into "There'll be a Hot Time in the Old Town To-night!"

A hysterical desire to laugh came upon me. It was so maddeningly funny, so absurd, so crazy a caricature of ourselves in our silliest season! Yet every stolid yellow face about me looked perplexed, or contemptuous, or bored, and only in Wyss's eyes could I read a reflection of that amazed and mocking applause that filled me.

"Great, old boy!" Wyss brought his hand down with a thump on Yet's shoulder. "Eat leisurely," he went on, guying the Chinese method of excusing oneself.

"*Ho hang*—a safe walk to you," answered Yet, entering into the spirit of the translation.

Ho hang—the Chinese good-by! I was still shaking with suppressed laughter, but that sobered me. For, with a parting squeeze to the girl he still held, the sergeant turned on his heel, pushed past the screen, and was gone.

Gone! And not a nickel, not an incriminating word, had passed between them. I couldn't believe my senses. I couldn't realize it. I was frantic with disappointment, and I might have stood there yet, like a gaping idiot, looking after him, if Ah Oy hadn't touched me again significantly, and I turned to see the other girls slipping away.

We were to withdraw, evidently. Gum Tai had told me that when anything of importance was to be discussed, the slave girls were dismissed without ceremony.

I followed Ah Oy dully. I was dazed. I couldn't readjust my mind to so unexpected a result. The sergeant, in the course of his rounds, had looked in a moment at Chy Fong's—not in the open part frequented by Americans, 'tis true. But there he had greeted his Chinese friends, listened to a song of Yet Kim Gai's, and patronizingly hugged a slave girl—not as a man might a woman, but as though she were a child, a doll, or any pretty, non-human, soulless thing that couldn't speak or feel.

And that was all. Positively all!

A fury possessed me as I followed Ah Oy out into the other room. What did I care now for old Gum Tai's instructions and apprehensions and admonitions! Suppose I was discovered? The game was up. And I knew the way out—out this window to the veranda and down into the square. We had arranged that all right.

But fortunately Ah Oy was unsuspicious, or perhaps she was preoccupied and didn't notice the dropping of my *rôle*; for, though I forgot all caution, she seemed hardly conscious of me. She was behaving queerly herself. Even I could see that. If she had been a human being, instead of a passive Chinese doll, I should have said she had something on her mind; for when the other girls sank down into a corner and fell to eating greedily and drinking tea from a tray which had been put there, she gave me one swift, enigmatic glance—imploring, confiding, searching—and passed quickly out upon the veranda.

I, too, slipped out; there was nothing more for me inside. But the narrow little balcony was empty. Evidently Ah Oy's guardianship of me—which shrewd old Gum Tai must have arranged for—was at an end. Now she was looking after herself. What could she be up to, I asked myself.

In spite of my bitter disappointment—I had counted on bagging this story and throwing it triumphantly at McCabe's feet—I stood a minute there, looking out. Evening had come, and the young moon was shining a silver veil down over the hilly town, idealizing its crude, irregular sky line. It poetized the untidy little square and touched a bit of nickel on a cab lamp that glowed in the dusk below. But it concentrated its soft luster upon the wide, wonderful shining bay beyond, where the ferry-boats became floating castles of light and Alcatraz, glorified into outlines only, stood out castellated like an Ehrenbreitstein anchored on the water.[36]

In the reaction of the strain I had been living under, I stretched out my arms toward it all—it was beautiful; it was American; it was Western; it was mine—when clearly down in the street below I heard a whistled melody:

> "Make me shy and straight and still,
> Docile, make me, too, and dutiful;
> Make me perfect—if you will—
> But O, sweet Dæmon, make me beautiful!"

Mechanically I had repeated the words to myself of the last verse to *T'in Hau*, accompanying the whistle below. But I was thinking, thinking hard. A Chinaman might hum that melody, though it was unlikely. A white man might whistle the classic "Hot Time." But only one man I knew would be likely to whistle the slave girl's plaintive little nasal prayer to her goddess.

Down I slipped behind a great potted palm—out here, when Chinese guests have not monopolized the restaurant, white women from the Eastern States come to stand for a moment beneath the huge swinging lanterns and look at Chinatown and the bay from on high.

My heart was thumping an accompaniment, and over and over in my head the words went singing. I could hear someone coming softly up the first flight of steps, and then the second. My finger nails—which had been growing untrimmed for a month, so seriously had I gone in for local color—were digging into my palms. I was trembling, so sure was I, so sure that—

A sergeant's cap!

It appeared above the top step. I was right—I was right, after all!

He passed me so close that I could see the three bars on his sleeve in the light from the window, and when he had gone on in I crouched there a full minute waiting, waiting till I could be calm again.

By the time I'd got to the window (I had taken off the crimson boxes of

---

36. Alcatraz: at the time, Alcatraz was a military fort and prison located on an island off the coast of San Francisco; it later became a federal penitentiary and today is a national landmark and popular tourist attraction. Ehrenbreitstein: a fortress in Germany.

slippers that I might be noiseless) he was seated at the table with the three Chinamen and facing me—Sergeant George Wyss, head of the Chinatown squad, an American police officer bribed by dirty yellow money to betray his trust!

Perhaps you think I didn't make vows to the gods of Yellow Journalism as I stood there. Perhaps you think I didn't compose a dozen different openings for my triumphant entry upon McCabe before I should throw down the booty before him!

I couldn't hear a word, of course, from where I stood, but Yet and the sergeant were having it hot and heavy, evidently. Some dispute as to terms—some reproach for the last raid in which one Rhoda Massey had taken part, perhaps. I could imagine how the clever gambler would score his paid servant for not delivering the goods. I could almost fancy I heard him use the very words. But I did see him at last lift a heavy inverted *cloisonné* bowl from the middle of the table and uncover a pile of twenties—they must have been there the whole evening! I saw both Chin Bak You and Chow La scowling in dispute, and I saw Wyss reach out his strong white hand among all those vile yellow ones, and . . .

And all at once I couldn't see! I couldn't breathe! I couldn't cry out nor hear, except dully. Something had been suddenly thrown over my head, and someone had seized me and was carrying me swiftly down the stairs.

I struggled. I gasped and tried desperately to scream. And somehow I got the idea that my struggles surprised my captor, for he kept murmuring under his breath to me in Chinese, in a tone that I fancied was reassuring. But I was so frantic with fear by now that I distrusted even my own instincts. I would have welcomed Yet Kim Gai himself if I could have brought him there by screaming—but I couldn't scream. And I was still struggling like a cat in a bag when the big Chinaman, reaching the alley below, almost dumped me down into something that quickly moved away.

It was a carriage. I knew that as soon as the door slammed and the horses started. But when I tore at the cloth that covered my head (a woman's hands helping me all the time), and at last sat up, red and furious and terrified—I knew in a moment what had happened to me.

I had been rescued!

Shades of Confucius! I had been "rescued" at the moment when I would have given the earth for one minute more as a slave girl. Yes, rescued, alas!

by the Mission—the good, stupid, angelic Mission, that helps Chinese girls to escape from slavery, and even permits them to pretend to fight against their rescuers, so that in case of failure the unhappy creatures may claim that the effort was an abduction, made against their will and not with their connivance.

I sat up and looked at Miss McIntosh opposite me. She was murmuring the few Chinese words she knew in the most reassuring way. I looked at the dear old respectable Scotchwoman, devoted, tender, brave soul, and I longed to beat her!

"Ah Oy—Ah Oy?" she asked then, doubtfully.

"Ah Oy !" I cried, the words escaping me after hours of silence with the pop of a released piston. "Great Gunnybags, how I wish it was!"

I can see her face yet . . . and it almost consoles me.

ﻋﻠﻰ

McCabe? Oh! he doesn't know yet. I wonder if I'll ever dare to tell him.

Gum Tai? She's safe at sea—sailed on the *China* the next morning.

Sergeant Wyss? They say he's to be our next chief of police. The graft went up higher. And so will he.

Miss McIntosh? She never can understand why I don't write up that story of the slave girls and the Mission, which I told her I was after that night. She thinks me lazy and neglectful of the paper's interests, and incapable, on the whole, of real serious work.

Rhoda Massey? Oh, she's living humble these days, and walking soft! They say at the office just now that the rumor about her getting the big head was all a false alarm. She's a model of amenability, is Rhoda, of conservative good sense and good judgment, and is actually in line for a desk position, I've heard.

But it's 'way down low, that part of it. No man (and only one woman) on the paper would believe it.

The Milpitas Maiden

A Story of Some Women's Rights and Others' Sufferance

Saturday Evening Post 177, no. 52 (1905): 3–5, 16

This story appeared as part of Michelson's "A Yellow Journalist" series in the *Saturday Evening Post*, but, for unknown reasons, was not included in the book version of *A Yellow Journalist* (1905). Because "The Milpitas Maiden" appeared midway through the series, readers of the story would likely be familiar with Michelson's fictional alter ego, "girl reporter" Rhoda Massey, and her ongoing competition with rival male reporters, including her beau, Ted Thompson.

I t was at the big National Woman's Suffrage Convention that she turned up, but not till the third day late in the morning. Enderby, of the Express, was trying to confide something important to me, when Frank McGowan spotted her.

"Get on to the lady journalist, Rhoda," he whispered maliciously as she came up the aisle, self-conscious as only a newspaper woman can be on her first public appearance.

I turned to look at her, and, of course, Cohen and Enderby and the rest turned, too. She was tall and slim: one of those stunning brunettes with cheeks like deep velvet roses and bulging brown eyes, so big and shiny they might have been used for paper-weights.

"My name is Miss Florence Longley," she said primly, after a moment's hesitation, as she sat down in the vacant place beside me—Thompson's place.

"How do you do?" I said, jumping in to do the honors. "I'm Rhoda Massey. This grinning little jackanapes is Frank McGowan of the Press. Mr. Cohen's the Times-Record artist; Mr. Aiken's of the News, my own paper, you know;

Mr. Bliss of the Evening Mail, and Mr. Enderby—Mr. Enderby—" I paused to attract old Enderby's attention.

"Enderby's of the Temperance Twaddler—it's a blue-ribbon paper," interjected McGowan saucily.

"Oh is he? Are you?" She turned to Enderby eagerly.

He looked across at her from out misty eyes. When Enderby's off he finds it hard to take in strange voices and new faces. Poor old Enderby! He never was a journalistic Beau Brummel, but he looked like an untidy little terrier that morning. I found myself wondering what he had done to his clothes. He was grimy with coal-dust.

"I am so glad," Miss Longley went on, her cowlike big eyes resting interestedly upon him. "I didn't know reporters cared for such serious things. In my town they say the reporters are awful wild. And have all the reporters on the Temperance Twaddler signed the pledge, Mr.—Mr.—"

"Enderby," supplied McGowan gravely.

Cohen's shoulders shook with laughter, and Aiken, who was caricaturing stout, florid, untidy Bertha Mayberry Dean, chairman of the convention, stopped to stare at Miss Longley.

"Eh?" grunted Enderby aloud in his bewilderment.

"Sh—sh!" came a warning hiss from the platform where sat Dr. Hester Dalrymple, slim, self-possessed and executive. Her clear, ironical eyes turned reprovingly down upon us and then went quickly back to her rival, Mrs. Dean.

I hastened to take Miss Longley's attention. "What is your paper?" I asked softly.

"The Milpitas Mercury," she answered composedly.

"I beg your pardon?" put in McGowan with suspicious politeness.

"The Milpitas Mercury," she repeated, looking curiously at him. I suppose she wondered whether all city reporters were deaf.

"The Mercury? Oh yes—the New York Mercury or the Chicago evening paper?" whispered Frankie enjoyingly.

"No, the Mil—" she began.

But I wouldn't have it. I wouldn't let that impudent little Frank McGowan make fun of her; not if the Milpitas Mercury were twice the farce it is, and Milpitas itself half as big a village as its nine hundred inhabitants make it.[37]

---

37. Now a city, Milpitas was a small California town located south of San Francisco.

"You're late, Miss Longley," I interrupted, giving Frank a look that ought to have squelched him. "It's only the dreary minutes of the previous meeting they're busy with up there now"—I nodded up at the crowded platform—"but there are some things I can give you. This morning there was a committee meeting from which reporters were excluded. That, of course, we're all out on, unless we can find a leak somewhere. But the regular stuff in here I can give you, if—"

"Oh, no—no, thank you," she said. "I've got it all. A reporter who happened to be standing beside me in the back of the hall told me what to take down. He wanted to arrange for me to go to the big reception to Bertha Mayberry Dean and Dr. Hester Dalrymple this evening—at least, he pretended to. But I knew he was only trying to flirt with me, so I told him that my chaperon—"

"Your—"

"My chaperon, Mrs. Birdsall, couldn't go with us, and then I got up and left him and came here. Why—why—there he is now. Do you suppose he actually has the impudence to follow me?"

I looked down the aisle. There, making his way through the crowd of women, with a mixture of good nature and imperiousness—a manner that's his own and stamps him easily as leader in that guerrilla warfare which reporters wage against the conspiracy of silence—came Ted Thompson.

I gasped. And it took only that second, while I tried to find words, for Frank McGowan to jump in.

"You were quite right, Miss Florence Longley of the Milpitas Mercury," he said gravely—and she never turned a hair at the title—"that is Theodore Gaydog Thompson, the most dangerous man in the profession. Have you heard the story of how—" He paused, delighted at the frightened start she gave. "Well, it's not a subject for mixed company. An unconscionable Lovelace is Thompson, who . . . I was just telling Miss Florence Longley of the Milpitas Mercury about you, Ted," he concluded innocently, as Thompson greeted us all with a comprehensive nod and drew up another chair.

"It's good of you, Frankie," he said. "Miss Longley and I have met," he added with a special nod toward her.

But she lowered her eyelids with the primmest down-drawing of the corners of her mouth, and I turned to her quickly, putting my back between her and Cohen's shaking shoulders.

"You must never believe a word Frank McGowan says, Miss Longley,"

I hurried to tell her. "His reputation for truth and veracity just isn't. He couldn't tell a story straight if he tried, and he never thinks of trying,"

But it wasn't any use—not the least. The ungrateful creature was sitting stiffly impenetrable, as aloof and disapproving as though she saw the mark of the beast on Ted Thompson's puzzled face. After all, when you meet the-villain-still-pursued-her kind of woman, you might just as well let her be insulted—she's determined to be, anyway.

I threw up my hands. I didn't want the boys to guy her, but what could I do? She was simply rippling richness to McGowan, and he led her on with a wicked delight to make a ninny of herself. She showed him her class pins and her engagement ring. She told him that she had never done any newspaper work before, but that the Milpitas Mothers' Club was paying her expenses and her fare to the city that she might write some letters about the convention to the tiny Mercury. She informed him—and anybody else who was within hearing—that her fiancé disapproved of newspaper work, because reporters were so wild and the women who worked on newspapers were such a queer lot and nobodies socially; but that, for her part, she never intended to go on any assignment without her chaperon.

A fiancé and a chaperon! How the deuce could they be of any use on a newspaper, unless you're running the society page? I writhed. The men grinned over their copy—with the exception of Enderby, who was still trying to tell me something mysteriously important—and that little beast, Frank McGowan, fairly chortled; it delighted him so to tease me through her.

I pretended to be deep in conversation with old Enderby. He kept hinting darkly to me—as Enderby always does when he's off the reservation—about a big story he had; or had just missed; or had been basely done out of. You never could tell just which it was with Enderby.

"Never mind, Mr. Enderby," I said consolingly, "the Express wouldn't let you write anything anyway but guff and taffy about the lofty and lovely and intellectual ladies above mentioned."

"Wouldn't it? If those same lovely ladies had got into a lovely row in their secret committee meeting and—"

I jumped. "Not truly?"

He looked at me sorrowfully, nodding his head.

"Miss Massey—Miss Rhoda, look at me," he whispered heavily. "New suit yesterday. Tailor's bill unpaid. Coal-box—big one. I am little—like Napoleon, same height exactly, but slim. I bribed the janitor and in I got; put a piece of coal to keep lid from closing, and—and—" He laid his head down upon the table and grieved silently.

"And what—what, Mr. Enderby?" I shook him gently. Oh to know how much of this was straight stuff! "Tell me what?"

"What?" he asked, lifting his head and wiping his eyes.

"Yes—are you—will you tell me? . . . And—" I helped him along.

"And I went to sleep! Cursed luck! But I know she broke her umbrella—Dean—Bertha Mayberry Dean. Know it pos'tively, 'cause it woke me up. Meeting all over. Cursed luck!" And he fell into bitter revery, abstractedly removing bits of coal from his hair.

He looked very funny, poor, little, old Enderby, but we hadn't time to say anything more, for the convention had got down to work. I put Enderby's story away in the back of my head till noon when the convention adjourned. Then I strolled sweetly up to Miss Adams, Mrs. Dean's secretary, who lunched in the building.

"Miss Adams, might I borrow your umbrella?" I asked wistfully. "So stupid of me to leave mine home."

"Why, I'm sorry, Miss Massey," she answered. "I've already loaned mine to Mrs. Dean. Hers is—" She hesitated.

"Broken?" I suggested innocently.

"Ye—es."

"Too bad! Never mind. Miss Longley's will do for both of us."

And off I danced to join the Milpitas Maiden, whom I had invited to lunch with me. I wished now that I hadn't, I so wanted to work on the umbrella mystery, but I made the best of it. I really tried to talk some sense into her. But when I attempted to give her some points about treating the convention, I was no more successful than Thompson had been. She silently distrusted me. She was in a feverish haze, with all the details of the work crowding upon her—anybody could see that. But, you know, there are two kinds of green reporters—the know-it-all's and the willing workers. The willing ones snap up a suggestion as hungry fish dart after crumbs; the other kind makes it a point of honor to know it all. Miss Longley knew it all.

"Except, don't you know, at night, after I have written my letter and sent it off and I am in bed and it's too late. Then I get the finest ideas! Do you?" she asked me over our tea.

"Why don't you make character studies, contrasting Mrs. Dean and Doctor Dalrymple?" I suggested, all at sea how to help her in spite of herself.

"Thank you. Do you know, by the way, that Mrs. Bertha Mayberry Dean's umbrella and Doctor Dalrym—"

"Oh!"

The exclamation escaped from me before I could suppress it. Was it possible there was a story and she knew it? Could it be that this Milpitas Maiden, as Frankie had christened her, who had stuck to the routine work of the convention with a stupid pertinacity that was exasperating, had dug out a real story, a big thing, a line of which was of more real value to a paper than columns of dreary photographic reporting!

"I beg your pardon?" she said primly.

"I beg yours. What was it you were going to say?"

"I just wanted to know if you'd noticed that Mrs. Dean and Doctor Dalrymple have umbrellas precisely alike, with the very same green-glass tops? I used it in my story this morning. I wanted to be sure to get it in. I think it's such an interesting coincidence, don't you?"

Interesting! I looked at her and I thought of Enderby's story—the bully story of a row between these two leading ladies on the suffrage stage; of their descending from their platform of superhuman purity and charity and "tongue-slinging like a couple of fishwives with a higher education," as Enderby had phrased it.

Only, what did they say? Oh, just what did they say! To be able to quote them word for word in all the unvarnished humanity of their enraged selves! To have a heavy black line of type running clear across my page of the News, just freighted with insult, a feminine slap across the face; and below it, the enjoying cackle betrayed even through its demureness: "Said Mrs. Dean to Doctor Dalrymple." And then photos of the dignified dames in their swellest convention togs—Oh me!

As I sat there opposite the Milpitas Maiden, looking through her into the chances of my getting it, I'd have given the end of my little finger to know just what "said Mrs. Dean to Doctor Dalrymple." I really began to believe that Enderby wasn't romancing. There had been something doing in that committee meeting from which reporters had been excluded. Of course, the committee had leaked, and we all knew what the business was that had called it together, and that Dr. Hester Dalrymple would succeed Mrs. Dean as president for the coming term. But what, oh, what, were the details of all that gorgeous row?

"Shall we go back to the hall?" asked Miss Longley coldly.

"Why—certainly—yes!" I jumped to my feet and called the waiter.

She hardly spoke to me as we crossed the street and got a car. I suppose I had looked suspiciously like Enderby as I sat mooning there; but honestly I had forgotten all about her. In all the sloppy, wet town there was only one thing for me that day—no, two: to get that story and to be terrified for fear that Enderby would tell it to Ted Thompson.

Thompson's absence from the hall, when we got back, was ominous. I'm never very happy when Ted Thompson is out of my sight and there's a big story floating about. But neither was McGowan there. Only Enderby was at the table in the same place where he had sat in the morning, peacefully slumbering, his head fallen upon his blank pile of copy-paper, an unlighted cigar between his lips, and pinned to his lapel a facetious note to me from Frankie McGowan.

> To Rhoda Massey, whom it may concern
> Enderby's devotion to the cause of temperance has exhausted him, as you may notice. Ted has sent in his morning's stuff for him and has gone off on some little lay of his own. I'm booked for the ferry to do the arrival of belated great suffragists. If you'll lend Enderby a hand when he stumbles, perhaps we can keep him on the Express' pay-roll another week. "I throw this out merely as a suggestion," as the ladies modestly say on the platform, but perhaps the Milpitas Maiden will swallow her blue ribbon and stand in.

I looked over at her as she took her seat and, drawing off her gloves tidily, began calmly to copy a long committee report left for us all. Stand in—that lady? I had my doubts.

"I wouldn't bother with that, if I were you," I began cautiously. "None of us wants that stuff. You can take the original if you care for it. Connely, the Associated Press man, will have another."

She looked at me rather doubtfully; evidently generosity only made her suspicious.

"I wonder," I hurried on, "if I could ask a favor of you? It's Enderby, you know. He—he—" I faltered before the bovine brown of her placid eyes. "He sometimes needs help in his work. If I could count on you just to telephone in his stuff! The Express is an evening paper, you know: so's the Mail—we can't ask Bliss to do anything. I'll look after things in here for both of us."

"I don't quite understand," she said. "If he's sick why don't they send some one else to do his work? He—I did think this morning that he looked kind of idiotic."

"Idiotic!" I exclaimed. "Oh, he's worse than idiotic, poor old Enderby!"

As I spoke his name, he waked, smiled at me with sleepy fondness and, pulling his paper toward him, almost immediately began to write.

"Why—why—" began the Milpitas Maiden.

"Sh!" I whispered to her. "He really can't write in that condition. He'll try for a bit, but he'll give it up. Then he'll sit and listen and compose his stuff mentally as he listens. But by two at the latest it ought to be in. All I want, all I'm asking you to do is to go with him to the 'phone in the next room, call up the Express, and say to Halsey—Halsey's the city editor—'This is the Reporters' Room, City Hall,' and—"

"But it isn't, is it?" she remarked.

"What's that got to do with it!" I fumed. "Just go on and say: 'And Enderby's gone out after a big story and left his stuff for me to telephone in. Are you ready?' Then go ahead."

"But is he going out on a big story—what story?"

"Is he?" I exclaimed wrathfully. "Look at him."

He had stopped writing and, holding his head between his hands, sat with his elbows on the table making an effort to concentrate.

"He'll be able to dictate to you and you can work it all right," I told her, "by blaming things on the 'phone, if he's slow."

"But why can he dictate and not write?" she insisted.

I looked at her savagely. I was dancing with eagerness to know where Ted Thompson was, to get to work and then trot out after the real story.

"Because he can," I snapped shortly. "Everybody knows Enderby."

"But why should I help him?" she demanded stiffly.

"Why? Because he can't help himself, and Halsey'll fire him if he falls down."

"You don't mean he—he's—drunk!"

"And disabled," I added with a sigh. "But not disorderly. Why, where—what—"

But she had gathered up her papers and was hurrying over to a table at the extreme left of the stage. Her removal interrupted the flowery speech with which Mrs. Dean was introducing Doctor Dalrymple to the convention, but the Maiden was so eager to get beyond contamination that she wasn't aware of it, the righteous little prig!

"That settles you, Rhoda Massey," I said to myself as I settled back to work. "No crackajack story for you of the squabbles of emancipated ladies. You're up against it. You'll have to see poor old Enderby through, and after that comes the debate between the suffragists and the antis. You've got be in on that. You might fly around at night, but all the big guns of the convention'll be at the reception, and—"

And I saw that beautiful imaginary headline of mine go a-glimmering. But what could I do? If I'd had anything positive to go on I think I might have offered up poor old Enderby; but to let his erratic little bark smash upon the editorial rocks for a mere chance, on a tip that I'd got from himself, too, and after we'd kept him going for three days—I couldn't do it.

"Come on, Mr. Enderby," I said with a sigh when the clock got 'round to two. "Let's go into the reception-room and 'phone it in."

"Rhoda—I love you," he whispered heavily.

"Yes, I know," I said, busily getting my papers together.

Enderby always loves me when he's off ghost-dancing. I'm merely a symptom of the progress of his case.

He followed me pretty steadily across the hall, below the platform and into the quiet little place, where I sat down and took up the 'phone.

"I have lived," said Enderby, leaning heavily upon the table, "for half a century and have met men and women, and have seen the world. But never have I known a being, Miss Massey—Rhoda—dearest Rhoda, who so unites and combines the charms of the intellect with the graces of the heart and person as—"

"Yes, yes—I know. . . . Express?" I called through the 'phone. "Well, give me Mr. Halsey."

"No one but the immortal Shakespeare could conceive a creature so full, so perfect, so rounded," Enderby rambled on. "Tender of heart, clear of head, and with that witchery—"

I had got Halsey on the 'phone. I put up my hand to stop Enderby. He kissed it tenderly. I wanted to box his ears, but unfortunately I'm not left-handed.

"Is this the city ed'tor?" I began naïvely. "I have Mr. Enderby's account of the convention here to telephone to the office. I wouldn't have disturbed you, but Mr. Enderby asked me to tell you that there's a big story developing that . . . What's that? 'Same old gag!' No, it's a new story, he said. No, I can't tell you what it's about. Mr. Enderby? Oh, he left immediately. He said he'd call you up. . . . All right."

I heard Halsey hang up his private 'phone and call for some one in the local room to take down the story, and I made use of that moment to turn to Enderby.

"Now look here, Mr. Enderby—" I began.

"Where else could mortal man look?" he responded with ponderous gallantry. "Sweet Rhoda, oh! journalistic Hypatia, we sit at your feet and—"[38]

I wanted to do my share toward keeping Enderby solid with the Express; the boys expected it of me. They'd done their part. Now it was up to me.

"Get ready now," I commanded, as some reporter on the Express took the line. "I—I couldn't care for a dub, Mr. Enderby. The man who wants me to—like him must earn my admiration. A good, clear introduction now—short but compact, you know, and with a good grasp. . . . All right," I called into the 'phone. "Ready!"

"The present suffrage convention," began Enderby, making a tremendous effort—and I followed him, phrase after phrase—"marks the passing of the old New Woman, the butt of journalistic jokes, a tempting figure for the cartoonist: untidy in dress, violently denunciatory and illogical in speech, a marvel only for that same unflattering reason which Doctor Johnson adduced in the instance of the dog who stands on his hind legs[39] . . . Darling Rhoda,"—he had victoriously completed a sentence and had the impression that his work was done—"we will sail down through the South Seas to the

---

38. A renowned Greek scholar, Hypatia (d. AD 415) was one of the first women to study mathematics, astronomy, and philosophy.

39. Samuel Johnson (1709–1784): an English writer. James Boswell's *The Life of Samuel Johnson, LL.D.* (1791) includes a notorious quotation from Johnson that states, "A woman's preaching is like a dog walking on his hind legs. It is not done well; but you are surprised to find it done at all."

lovely isle of Kauai. There we'll make love and write our book together and, freed from the trammels—"

"Hello—hello!" I was calling into the 'phone, affecting not to hear the Express man's hellos at the other end. "Hello, exchange 801! Why did you cut me off? Yes, you did—oh, is that you? Is that the Express? Wait a minute till I see where I left off. . . . Mr. Enderby," I said in a stern whisper, putting my hand over the mouthpiece, "we shall never write that book together if you don't get your week's wages from the Express. It's payday to-morrow. Come!"

"The new New Woman," he said with a groan—and I parroted it all off into the 'phone—"is a woman of brains, of experience, with a sense of humor and a practical knowledge of life. Her older sister begged for favors, whined about her wrongs and based her claims on purely theoretical grounds. The new New Woman demands rights, not alone because they will benefit herself, but upon the broader ground of benefit to the race. The old—the—the old—Confound the old woman! Rhoda, my soul's one adoration; out of the depths of my heart I swear to you that I have never . . ."

And I had to fake all over again. But I got him to do it. It was short, but it sounded right enough from the Express' standard. He safely contrasted Bertha Mayberry Dean and Dr. Hester Dalrymple, abundantly taffying both without grossly overdoing it, the Express' policy being to ladle out blarney to the convention and strew the flowers of rhetoric with both hands in its pathway.

At the end of it Enderby fell asleep and I telephoned in committee reports, programs and names and that sort of thing to fill up. It was a great half-hour's work. I was right cocky when I looked at my watch and found I was in plenty of time for the debate. I made my way back into the hall—a five-minute recess preceded the debate and the place was noisy with women's voices—at peace with the world.

But my satisfaction lasted just three minutes. Right in front of me, coming down from the platform where he had just been speaking to Mrs. Dean and Doctor Dalrymple, was Ted Thompson. What, oh what had he got from them? He saw me at that minute and made his way to me.

"I've been looking for you," he said. "Where's Enderby? I intended to get back sooner. I hope you didn't take Frankie's note seriously; he's just told me about it—facetious little beggar!"

"But I did. Why not? Enderby's in there asleep"—I nodded back toward the little room. "He's made good for to-day, anyway."

"I don't like it—I don't like it! It isn't fair to you," said Ted irritably. "Enderby's the best fellow on earth, but the best fellow on earth, when he isn't sober, may—"

"Oh, I don't mind Enderby," I interrupted. This big-brother manner of Thompson's made me uncomfortable.

"Did he—does he really—"

"Make love to me? Oh—yes. But I'm used to that."

"Indeed!" he exclaimed with a significant grin. "The whole world, as a matter of course—"

I laughed, and I think we both felt more natural.

"Not at all," I said, following him now as he made way for me to the table; "no, only the tipsy world; and of it only the journalistic part; and of that only the Express staff; and of that only poor old Enderby; and then only—"

"Will you do me a favor?" he asked, placing a chair for me. He has a pretty way of doing things when he's playing lady's man, that busy Ted Thompson!

"What?"

"Let me take the Enderby assignment next time. Oh, I know it's far off— the next bat. But when it comes, wherever I am, whatever I'm doing, let me help him out. You're a good fellow, Rhoda Massey; there isn't anything the boys wouldn't do for you. But next time don't—please."

Now wasn't that nice of Ted Thompson? I half nodded at him—there wasn't time for anything more, for the suffragists up on the stage had fired their first gun, the anti-suffrage batteries were booming out negative thunder—and work was on for the afternoon.

I got my story in by ten and started home from the office. It was a pretty good story and I had that awfully snug, comfortable feeling that's conceit in the other fellow, but merely satisfaction in yourself.

It lasted only till I got in front of the Times-Record office. At first I didn't know what was crumpling the roseleaf of my complacency, and then I remembered Thompson's little talk with those belles of the convention— Mrs. Dean and Doctor Dalrymple.

Perhaps it didn't mean anything, I said to myself as I crossed Market Street. I was tired; conventions take it out of you. But I couldn't, I just couldn't make myself believe it was all right. Of course, I knew we'd all have the story of the row in committee—Enderby had babbled enough of that, and I knew Thompson was on—but fancy the Times-Record getting the details of it and sporting that beautiful headline of mine! Fancy being beat on a woman's convention and by a man! Oh, I just couldn't bear that! Bowman would have a reason for sneering at women if I were to fall down on a detail like this.

I had got home while I was thinking it out, but something in me fought against every step. And even as I undressed and got into bed that same disinclination to consider the incident closed battled in me.

"You're getting fidgety and nervous, Rhoda," I growled to myself. "You'd better take your two weeks off as soon as this convention is over. Don't be silly. Think of what Mrs. Dean said when you sprang that story of the row on her: 'Nothing of the sort ever happened, my dear little girl-reporter. Doctor Dalrymple and myself are bosom friends. Of course, she's got a lot of new-fangled notions, but—don't you believe all you hear. Come in and have a cup of tea when you get tired.'

"And Doctor Dalrymple herself: 'There is not a word of truth in the report of dissension between us. I heartily respect and admire Bertha Mayberry Dean, who's a bit old-fashioned in her methods, but a woman to whom suffragists all over the world are much indebted.'

"Of course, they fibbed like ladies. I know that. But if they fibbed to me they must have done the same to Thompson. Oh, go to sleep, Rhoda Massey!"

But, instead, Rhoda Massey sat up straight in bed. Suddenly a funny thing had struck her—that silly remark of the Milpitas Maiden about the two women's umbrellas. Where had that same Maiden seen the two umbrellas? How could she have known they were alike? When she made her celebrated first appearance, the committee meeting was over and the green-glass top of Mrs. Dean's umbrella had already been smashed to atoms.

I was out of bed by this, ringing for a cab. I dressed myself while it was on the way, telling myself all the time that I was quite as luny as Enderby; that the Milpitas Maiden didn't know anything about this or anything else; and that, even in Milpitas, reporters don't hand over scoops to each other out of sheer goodness of heart.

Of course, it was a forlorn hope, but who wouldn't rather go on a hundred wild-goose chases than miss a real, live story? When the cab got to the door I was downstairs waiting for it. And when we reached her little hotel I climbed the stairs and threw myself at the Maiden's door with a thump that must have terrified her out of her wits.

"Who's there?" I heard her quavering voice cry sleepily.

"Rhoda Massey. Let me in, Miss Longley—I must see you—quick!"

"I—I can't. I'm in bed."

"Of course you are! But let me in, anyway!"

I rattled the door-knob as I spoke and I must have rattled her clear out of bed, for presently she appeared at the door holding it ajar with a two-inch hospitality that touched me. So did the curl-papers about her frightened face.

"What is it?" she gasped. "Is there a fire in Milpitas?"

A fire—in Milpitas! Oh, that finished me! Of course, I was nervous and tired and tense with anxiety, but I just let out a hysterical whoop of laughter at that, and she retreated terrified into the room, where I followed her, apologetically assuring her—in the midst of my interrupting ha-ha-ha's—that so far as I knew the fire department in Milpitas had not been called out. Then wiping my eyes, while she slipped quickly back in bed, I got down to business.

"Have you sent your stuff?" I demanded.

"Ye–es. But I—it isn't very—Oh it's awful h-hard being a reporter and I know the M-Mercury won't like it!" And burying her head in her pillows, there, before my astonished eyes, she sobbed and sobbed.

The poor little ninny! She was half a head taller than I, but I felt like her grandmother just then.

"Oh, come now, brace up!" I cried, patting her on the shoulder. "Why in the world didn't you raise the long yell? I'd have come running. I told you I would."

"B-But," she blubbered, "re-reporters d-don't help each other."

"Don't they? Didn't I help poor old Enderby, and—and aren't you going to help me?"

"You?—Me!" She sat bolt upright.

"If you will. Miss Longley, tell me, how did you know that Mrs. Dean and Doctor Dalrymple had umbrellas just alike?"

"I—I s-saw them," she sniffled, "and I thought it was so interesting. But it didn't s-seem so when I wrote it."

"Never mind that. When did you see them?"

"This morning—why?" she asked uneasily.

"Before you came into the hall, of course?"

She nodded uncertainly.

I looked at her, and as I looked the color suddenly flushed her face crimson. Guilty, she looked. Guilty of what?

It came to me in a flash.

"Miss Longley," I shouted, pouncing upon her, "you stayed in that committee-room when the reporters were sent out!"

"I didn't. I—I—how did you know?"

"That isn't the question," I cried. "How in the world did you manage it so that the women shouldn't know? Oh, I say, you're a deep one! Were you in the coal-box, too?"

"Coal-box? I don't know what you mean. But please—please don't think me deceitful," she said appealingly. "They didn't know I was a reporter. I had never been at the reporter's table, you know. I had no badge. I wasn't sitting with the rest of you and when you all went out I didn't know why. Then when I saw that it was a private meeting I was ashamed to attract attention by getting up to go out, and so—so I just sat there at the desk with the typewriter and then—"

"And you looked so simple and innocuous they thought you some one's secretary? Bully!"

"I don't know," she said sorrowfully.

"And you saw Mrs. Dean bring her umbrella down with a smash on the desk! . . . Oh, I say, Miss Longley, what's all this talk about your story not satisfying the Mercury?"

The tears filled her big eyes again. "I can't help it," she began, "but—"

"Nonsense! With a story like that!" Suddenly the pity of it came over me; a story like that and the Milpitas Maiden to handle it! "Oh, I hope you began it with a smashing paragraph! Direct quotations, wasn't it—the meat of the row banged right in the first paragraph? It isn't any of my business, but— what in the world—"

"I didn't write anything about the—the quarrel," she stammered. "How could I? If I had they would know I was in there and—and—"

"Holy smoke!"

I jumped for a telephone. There wasn't any in the room, so I rushed down the stairs and into the hotel office.

"Give me the News, Central. Rush it!—this is Miss Massey," I cried. "McCabe there? . . . Is that you, Mr. McCabe? Yes, yes! Say, hold the convention page for me. . . . Late? Don't I know? But, please, please, just five minutes. . . . Worth while? Well, just you wait!"

He did, and after storming upstairs and down again, I poured this into his willing ear: "Head it, 'Why Mrs. Dean Smashed Her Umbrella,' and then comes this:

"'*Mrs. Dean*: You're fools, with all your cleverness, you la-de-dah new New Women'

"'*Doctor Dalrymple (swallowing hard, but with insult in her voice)*: Possibly, but at least *we* are clever.'

"'*Mrs. Dean (hotly)*: You mean—'

"'*Doctor Dalrymple*: That it's stupid to persist in an antiquated style of fighting when you only make yourself and us ridiculous. Where is the sense in shrieking at tyrant man when it is evident—'

"'*Mrs. Dean (angrily, at the top of her voice)*: I tell you no fight was ever won on la-de-dah lines. You can't be a philosopher and a prize-fighter, too. It ain't science but muscle that tells. For my part, I believe in hitting hard—'

"'*Doctor Dalrymple (sarcastically)*: Even at windmills.'

"'*Mrs. Dean (furiously, tears of rage in her eyes)*: Doctor Dalrymple, will you have the decency to stop interrupting?' (*Turning her back upon Doctor Hester and addressing the rest of the Committee:*) 'I was going to say that— that we've got to go into this might and main. I repeat, it ain't science but muscle that counts. In the cause of Suffrage and on the platform I'm a heavyweight, I am, and—'

"'*Doctor Dalrymple (quietly)*: You look it.'

"'*Mrs. Dean's umbrella (its head smashing into fragments)*: Swish!!!'"

ﻌﻠ

Perhaps you think that little dialogue didn't look pretty in the News next morning and set the whole convention bobbing! McCabe's a lovely window-dresser, an artist with type, and he just played it up beautifully.

I don't know how it looked in the Milpitas Mercury. I wired it to them at our expense, and my! how it comforted the Maiden.

Bibliography of Works by Miriam Michelson

Books

In the Bishop's Carriage. Indianapolis: Bobbs-Merrill, 1904.

The Madigans. New York: Century, 1904.

A Yellow Journalist. New York: D. Appleton, 1905.

Anthony Overman. New York: Doubleday, Page, 1906.

Michael Thwaites's Wife. New York: Doubleday, Page, 1909.

The Awakening of Zojas. New York: Doubleday, Page, 1910.

The Petticoat King. New York: R. M. McBride, 1929.

The Wonderlode of Silver and Gold. Boston: Stratford, 1934.

Magazine Writing

"A Touch of Civilization." *Black Cat* 3, no. 27 (1897): 39–48.

"A Sagebrush Cicada." *Black Cat* 4, no. 42 (1899): 32–44.

"Poker Jim's Mahala." *Black Cat* 5, no. 52 (1900): 24–27.

"Mancusi and the Diva." *Junior Munsey* 9, no. 6 (1901): 923–32.

"An Understudy for a Princess." *Black Cat* 6, no. 70 (1901): 1–16.

"In the Bishop's Carriage." *Ainslee's* 11, no. 3 (1903): 121–29.

"Count Andre Listened." *Ainslee's* 11, no. 5 (1903): 124–29.

"Fayal, the Unforgiving." *Smart Set* 10, no. 3 (1903): 81–87.

"The Cross-Eyed Saint of Guasapadi." *Black Cat* 8, no. 10 (1903): 1–10.

"Judgment for Defendant." *Smart Set* 11, no. 2 (1903): 79–85.

"The Father of a Full-Back: The Story of Dwight Dettenrider's Greatest Football Game." *Munsey's* 30, no. 3 (1903): 443–47.

"Prince Roseleaf and a Girl from Kansas." *McClure's* 22, no. 4 (1904): 339–50.

"Her Letters from Dakota." *Ainslee's* 13, no. 2 (1904): 50–58.

"Mrs. Walker's Contumacy." *Munsey's* 31, no. 1 (1904): 111–115. Reprinted in *The Spinners' Book of Fiction* as "The Contumacy of Sarah L. Walker" (1907).

"Cecilia the Pharisee." *Century* 68, no. 2 (1904): 192–203.

"The Ancestry of Irene." *Century* 68, no. 3 (1904): 421–32.

"A Pagan and a Puritan." *Century* 68, no. 4 (1904): 639–49.

"A Merry, Merry Zingara." *Century* 68, no. 5 (1904): 720–29.

"A Ready Letter-Writer." *Century* 68, no. 6 (1904): 913–25.

"Mag Haggerty's Knight." *Reader Magazine* 5, no. 1 (1904): 79–85.

"The Mother of the Gracchi." *Ainslee's* 14, no. 5 (1904): 133–39.

"The Pollexfen Story." *Saturday Evening Post* 177, no. 29 (1905): 1–3, 26–27.

"Honors Are Easy." *Saturday Evening Post* 177, no. 33 (1905): 9–11, 23–24.

"The Pencil Will." *Saturday Evening Post* 177, no. 35 (1905): 9–11, 40.

"The Milpitas Maiden." *Saturday Evening Post* 177, no. 52 (1905): 3–5, 16.

"An Old Bachelor of Arts." *Ladies' Home Journal* 22, no. 7 (1905): 7.

"That List of Bassett's." *Saturday Evening Post* 178, no. 9 (1905): 5–7, 21–23.

"Everything in Sight." *Saturday Evening Post* 178, no. 12 (1905): 7–9, 21–22.

"The Ex-City Editors' Club." *Saturday Evening Post* 178, no. 13 (1905): 7–9, 27–29.

"By Soft Persuasion: I—A Conference of the Powers." *Saturday Evening Post* 178, no. 14 (1905): 5–7, 20.

"By Soft Persuasion: II–Some Japanese Prints." *Saturday Evening Post* 178, no. 15 (1905): 10–12, 38–39.

"The Destruction of San Francisco." *Harper's Weekly* 50, no. 2576 (1906): 623–24.

"A Nice Little Thing in Blue." *Woman's Home Companion* (July 1906): 12–13.

"The Greatness of Helena: A Story of an Ambitious College Girl." *Ladies' Home Journal* 23, no. 9 (1906): 9.

"The Darling of a Dowager." *Ainslee's* 18, no. 5 (1906): 1–49.

"Forty Fibs for a Diamond." *Broadway Magazine* (April 1907): 15–21.

"Flower o' Sagebrush." *Ainslee's* 22, no. 1 (1908): 1–36.

"The Superwoman." *Smart Set* 37, no. 4 (1912): 1–48.

"Vice and the Woman's Vote." *Sunset Magazine* 30 (April 1913): 345–48.

"The Terrible Consequences of Clothing with Women Inside of It." *Sunset Magazine* 34 (February 1915): 253–62.

"On the Bridge at Chatelard." *Ainslee's* 36, no. 2 (1915): 19–31.

"The Eternal Beggar: A Frank Study of the Dependent Wife under the Law." *Sunset Magazine* 37 (July 1916): 27–28, 91.

"The Yellow Streak." *Munsey's* 65, no. 2 (1918): 347–55.

"Such a Liar!" *Argosy* 102, no. 2 (1918): 248–53.

"The Country of Two Kings: A Tense Romance." *People's Home Companion* 37, no. 11 and 12 (1922): 11–13, 54–56; 14+.

Plays

"The Ways of Dorothy." *East and West* 1, no. 3 (1900): 69–84.

"The Duchess of Suds" (unpublished, 1911; copyrighted as "Duchess Barbara" in 1907).

"The Curiosity of Kitty Cochraine." *Smart Set* 37, no. 1 (1912): 133–42.

"Amendment No. 5: A Comedy in Three Acts" (copyrighted 1913).

"Bygones." *Smart Set* 51, no. 3 (1917): 81–92.

"Senator Kate: A Four-Act Play" (copyrighted 1921).

Selected Newspaper Writings

"The New Woman Realized: But Miss Matson Doesn't Believe in the New Woman We All Talk About." *Arthur McEwen's Letter*, January 15, 1895, 9.

"Lottie Collins on Woman: She Tells What She Thinks of the New Variety, and Would Like to Vote." *Arthur McEwen's Letter*, January 19, 1895, 5.

"What Say Ye Women to This? Miss Phoebe Couzins on Single Life and an Independent Career." *Arthur McEwen's Letter*, February 9, 1895, 5.

"Viewed by a Woman: Miriam Michelson Gives Her Impression of the Congress." *San Francisco Call*, May 21, 1895, 4.

"Weeds and Flowers: Miriam Michelson Finds Both of Them in the Woman's Congress." *San Francisco Call*, May 24, 1895, 8.

"Cleared the Kitchen: Miriam Michelson Enjoyed the Activities of the Congress Yesterday." *San Francisco Call*, May 25, 1895, 8.

"The Real Susan B. Anthony." *Arthur McEwen's Letter*, May 25, 1895, 9.

"The Real New Woman: Miriam Michelson Likens Her to a Pleasant Dream, Not a Nightmare." *San Francisco Call*, May 26, 1895, 8.

"Strangling Hands upon a Nation's Throat." *San Francisco Call*, September 30, 1897, 1–2.

"Perkins Talks upon Annexation: Miriam Michelson Chats with the California Senator. Not an Interview, Exactly." *San Francisco Call*, October 7, 1897, 3.

"Dark-Skinned Lion-Tamer in the House of Mystery." *San Francisco Call*, October 10, 1897, 29.

"A Threat of Cooly Invasion: Miriam Michelson Talks to Two Congressmen on Annexation." *San Francisco Call*, October 13, 1897, 1.

"Ellen Van Dusen—Woman of Means." *San Francisco Call*, October 23, 1897, 6.

"The Finest Surgery in the World Accessible to the Poor Is in This City." *San Francisco Call*, November 7, 1897, 29.

"Woes of Countess Von Hatzfeldt." *San Francisco Call*, November 13, 1897, 6.

"Psychological Study of the Man Who Killed His Father." *San Francisco Call*, November 14, 1897, 18.

"Young Julian Guinan Given His Freedom: Grand Jury Ignores the Bill against the Slayer of Jones." *San Francisco Call*, November 17, 1897, 1.

"Charlotte Smith's Affliction." *San Francisco Call*, December 2, 1897, 6.

"The Woes of Mr. and Mrs. Walter Ngong Fong." *San Francisco Call*, December 4, 1897, 6.

"The Sins of Children Shall Be Visited upon the Parents." *San Francisco Call*, January 5, 1898, 6.

"What the Noose Said to Durrant." *San Francisco Call*, January 8, 1898, 2.

"Dr. Chapman's Crusade." *San Francisco Call*, January 11, 1898, 6.

"Graveyard Gossip." *San Francisco Call*, January 12, 1898, 6.

"The Conqueror of the Klondike." *San Francisco Call*, January 19, 1898, 6.

"The Penalty of Greatness: The Sad Fate of Dr. Schenk of Vienna, Who Discovered the Secret of Sex." *San Francisco Call*, January 20, 1898, 9.

"Tale of Gold: How the News Started the Biggest Gold Rush in History." *San Francisco Call*, January 23, 1898, 5.

"The Widow Is Blind to Her Shame: Talks Unfeelingly of Her Misdoings of the Past." *San Francisco Call*, January 25, 1898, 8.

"Weeps as He Tells of His Crime: George Clark Says It Could Not Have Been Avoided." *San Francisco Call*, January 25, 1898, 8.

"Clark Held to Answer for Murder: No Evidence Offered in His Defense at the Hearing." *San Francisco Call*, January 29, 1898, 3.

"The Bells of the Mining Fair." *San Francisco Call*, February 5, 1898, 6.

"On the Merry Madness of Gentlemen Who Maltreat Their Wives." *San Francisco Call*, February 8, 1898, 6.

"Genius on the Altar of Mammon: How the Apotheosis of Senator Stanford Was the Martyrdom of Artist Thomas Hill." *San Francisco Call*, February 14, 1898, 7.

"Two Lights of the Turf: Todd Sloan, the Blase [*sic*] Prince of Jockeys, and His Dusky Rival, Modest 'Long-Shot' Conley." *San Francisco Call*, February 14, 1898, 5.

"Gorgioni's Polonaise." *San Francisco Call*, February 19, 1898, 6.

"The Woman Who Did Not Cut Out Her Baby's Tongue." *San Francisco Call*, February 21, 1898, 9.

"No Invalids Need Apply." *San Francisco Call*, February 25, 1898, 6.

"Like a Dumb, Driven Brute: An Italian's Mode of Disciplining a Disobedient Daughter." *San Francisco Call*, February 27, 1898, 30.

"A Rousing Reception to General Booth: The Leader of the Salvation Army Enthusiastically Received by His Followers." *San Francisco Call*, March 1, 1898, 9.

"Rebellious Susie Illinois: She Believes That Taxation without Representation Is Tyranny." *San Francisco Call*, March 2, 1898, 6.

"Where Women Gamble: Poolrooms That Are Run for the Convenience of the Fair Sex." *San Francisco Call*, March 18, 1898, 16.

"Berkeley Girls Beat Sagebrush Maidens 14 to 1." *San Francisco Call*, April 10, 1898, 16.

"Deadlock in the Case of the Finigans: Settlement of the Famous San Rafael Divorce Suit Not Yet in Sight." *San Francisco Call*, April 19, 1898, 4.

"Every One May Help: Those Left Behind Can Be of Service in the War." *San Francisco Call*, April 21, 1898, 5.

"Eager to Begin: San Francisco Is Anxious to Prove Her Patriotism." *San Francisco Call*, April 23, 1898, 7.

"Changing a Bad Indian into a Good One: Results Obtained in Educating Lo at the Government Training School, Carson, Nev." *San Francisco Call*, April 24, 1898, 25.

"Pilar-Morin in Pantomime: Poetry in Acting of Its Own Kind at the Baldwin Theater." *San Francisco Call*, May 10, 1898, 12.

"Pantomime Is Prince." *San Francisco Call*, May 15, 1898, 29.

"Tragedy's Nose Is Out of Joint and Comedy's Lips Have a Pitiful Downward Droop: They're Both Jealous of Melody, and They've Good Reason to Be." *San Francisco Call*, May 22, 1898, 27.

"In the Dramatic Land of Ought-To-Be." *San Francisco Call*, May 29, 1898, 29.

"Hohenstauffen an Acquisition: Clement's Clever Creation at the Columbia." *San Francisco Call*, May 31, 1898, 5.

"The Women in the Betting Ring at the Coursing Matches." *San Francisco Call*, June 5, 1898, 22.

"In the Lower Theatrical Heavens Where Lesser Stars Do Shine." *San Francisco Call*, June 5, 1898, 29.

"Father Bernard and Little Pete: Stevens and Edith Hall a Success." *San Francisco Call*, June 7, 1898, 5.

"Frawley to the Rescue." *San Francisco Call*, June 12, 1898, 29.

"Adolph Sutro Passes Away." *Bulletin*, August 8, 1898, 1–2.

"Poison Is the Weapon Women Use for Murder." *Bulletin*, August 28, 1898, 5.

"Damning Evidence against Mrs. Botkin." *Bulletin*, September 4, 1898, 1–2.

"The Tragedy of the Hapsburgs." *Bulletin*, September 11, 1898, 2.

"Tough Tom of Old Tennessee: Being Descriptive of the Boy Murderer, His

Regiment, and the Conditions Which Brought Him under the Shadow of the Gallows." *Bulletin*, September 18, 1898, 20.

"Belle of Maternity Ward." *Bulletin*, October 9, 1898, 10.

"Dumb Beebe Bean Regains Her Speech: Remarkable Adventures of a Girl in Boy's Clothes Who Was Silent for Five Years." *Bulletin*, October 16, 1898, 1–2.

"A Woman's View of Mayor Phelan at a Mass Meeting." *Bulletin*, November 6, 1898, 9.

"Mayor Phelan Tells the Story of His Victory." *Bulletin*, November 13, 1898, 16.

"Miss Michelson Describes Burning of the Devil." *Bulletin*, November 20, 1898, 10.

"Charlotte Perkins Stetson Flays Her Own Sex Alive." *Bulletin*, December 11, 1898, 16.

"Mrs. Botkin Played Her Part Like a Veteran Actress." *Bulletin*, December 25, 1898, 20.

"Woman's Impression of the Leading Candidates at the State Capital." *Bulletin*, January 8, 1899, 9.

"Sarah Althea's Mad Babble Comes Weirdly Forth from Her Living Tomb." *Bulletin*, January 22, 1899, 9.

"Two Men Claim Choy Lin as Wife: A Chinese Tale That Has in It All the Elements of Another 'First-Born.'" *Bulletin*, January 29, 1899, 16.

"Where Waves the Dragon Flag." *Bulletin*, February 12, 1899, 1.

"Miss Michelson Describes the Tars at the Orpheum." *Bulletin*, February 19, 1899, 1.

"The Jolly Iowa Tars Entertain Mayor Phelan." *Bulletin*, February 26, 1899, 9.

"Nance O'Neill [*sic*] Will Some Day Wear Sarah Bernhardt's Crown." *Bulletin*, March 5, 1899, 9.

"The Legacy of George Boutwell." *Bulletin*, March 12, 1899, 1–2.

"On the Ferryboat with Madame Melba." *Bulletin*, March 12, 1899, 9.

"An Evening Behind the Scenes with Carmen." *Bulletin*, March 19, 1899, 1.

"The Church Is Divided on Prayer for Rain." *Bulletin*, March 26, 1899, 9.

"The Awakening of Zojas." *Bulletin*, March 26, 1899, 17–19.

"Morning Hours Spent in Judge Mogan's Police Court." *Bulletin*, April 2, 1899, 1–2.

"Berkeley Girls Score Another Victory." *Bulletin*, April 9, 1899, 9.

"I. W. Lees Stands Manfully By His Guns." *Bulletin*, April 16, 1899, 16.

"Berkeley Athletes Beat Stanford Boys." *Bulletin*, April 23, 1899, 8.

"The Newsboys' Picnic." *Bulletin*, May 7, 1899, 9–11.

"Nevada's Great Fight for a Governor." *Bulletin*, June 11, 1899, 1–2.

"James J. Jeffries, the King of All Pugilists." *Bulletin*, July 9, 1899, 1.

"Pay Day for the Oregon Boys at the Presidio." *Bulletin*, July 18, 1899, 9.

"Jewell Flint, the Boy Convict, Now a Poet." *Bulletin*, July 30, 1899, 9.

"Does Matrimony Disqualify Working Women?" *Bulletin*, August 13, 1899, 9.

"A Woman's View of the Killing of Jim Franey." *Bulletin*, August 20, 1899, 9.

"Babies and Mothers at the Baby Show." *Bulletin*, September 10, 1899, 8.

"Decorating the Brave Sons of California with Medals of Honor." *Bulletin*, September 17, 1899, 9.

"How 'Esoterics' 'Live the Life' at Applegate, City of Peace." *Bulletin*, October 1, 1899, 9–11.

"Indian Lucy Wants Hite Not His Money." *Bulletin*, October 8, 1899, 9.

"Nevada's Feminine David and Jonathan: A Sketch from Life." *Bulletin*, October 8, 1899, 9–10.

"An Open Letter to Nance O'Neil." *Bulletin*, October 15, 1899, 16.

"Controversy between Junghaendel and Ms. Phebe [*sic*] Hearst." *Bulletin*, October 22, 1899, 9.

"Madam Preston of Preston; or, 'What Fools These Mortal Be.'" *Bulletin*, October 29, 1899, 9.

"Thousands Gather to Hear Phelan Speak." *Bulletin*, November 5, 1899, 9–10.

"Three Women Who Want to Be School Directors." *Bulletin*, November 12, 1899, 1.

"The Man Who Snubbed Queen Victoria." *Bulletin*, November 26, 1899, 9.

"A Military Matter in Black and White." *Bulletin*, December 3, 1899, 9.

"Impressions Formed at the Bohemian Club's Exhibition of Art." *Bulletin*, December 10, 1899, 9.

"The Conversion of Choy Sing and Other Sketches." *Bulletin*, December 24, 1899, 23.

"Amid the Merry Throng of Christmastide Shoppers." *Bulletin*, December 24, 1899, 41.

"If the Socialist Versus Single-Tax Debate Had Taken Place." *Bulletin*, December 31, 1899, 21.

"Crowds of Sympathizers Gather to Cheer the Embattled Boers." *Bulletin*, January 7, 1900, 21.

"Concerning the Willful Barrenness of the State of Nevada." *Bulletin*, January 28, 1900, 1.

"Rivals for Matinee Girls' Affections." *Bulletin*, February 4, 1900, 4.

"Five Minutes on the Stone Fort's Roof at El Caney." *Bulletin*, February 18, 1900, 28.

"A Day Spent with Trained Animals That Seem Almost Human." *Bulletin*, February 25, 1900, 21.

"A Celebrated Case: Done into Doggerel and Set to Unpopular Airs." *Bulletin*, March 11, 1900, 21.

"Cured by a Yoghi, Who Says He Is Queen Victoria's Grandson." *Bulletin*, May 20, 1900, 21.

"Florence Roberts Says 'Sapho' Is Not an Immoral Play." *Bulletin*, June 3, 1900, 21.

"The Terror of Quarantine for an Unsophisticated Chinese Woman." *Bulletin*, June 10, 1900, 21.

"Sweet Love Is Slain." *Bulletin*, June 17, 1900, 21.

"Stetson Wedding, Mike De Young's Letter and Kinyoun Lynching." *Bulletin*, June 24, 1900, 21.

"Woman's Picture of the Trial of a Hazer." *Bulletin*, January 3, 1901, 6.

"Mary S. Anthony's Windmill Battle as Her Sister, Susan B., Might See It." *North American*, January 9, 1901, 9.

"Small Pervert Denies in a Conversational Way That He Tried to Kill His Grandparents." *North American*, January 11, 1901, 16.

"Mrs. Soffel Describes First to the North American the Biddle Tragedy." *North American*, February 3, 1901, 1–2.

"Mrs. Nation to Renew Her Crusade To-day." *North American*, February 4, 1901, 1.

"Mrs. Nation's Faith in Public Opinion," *North American*, February 5, 1901, 5.

"Miriam Michelson Goes on a Hatchet Crusade." *Bulletin*, February 11, 1901, 1–2.

"Mrs. Nation, Joan of Arc of Temperance Crusade, as Seen by Miriam Michelson." *North American*, February 13, 1901, 16.

"Two Little Slave Girls Owned in Philadelphia: Bought in Martinique and Brought Here in Spite of the Law." *North American*, February 25, 1901, 16.

"Easter Fashions Shown in the Rain." *North American*, April 8, 1901, 1.

"Happy Children, with Eggs, Seize White House Grounds." *North American*, April 9, 1901, 1–2.

"A Character Study of Emma Goldman." *North American*, April 11, 1901, 2.

"'Miss Bob White' Great Go with Gods in the Gallery." *North American*, April 16, 1901, 16.

"Betsy Ross and the Old Flag Make Pleasing Stage Picture." *North American*, April 17, 1901, 4.

"Can a Woman Be the Best Friend of Her Husband's Second Wife?" *North American*, April 29, 1901, 8.

"'The Governor's Son' Is Noisy, But Clever." *North American*, April 30, 1901, 5.

"Ballet Alone Saves Weber and Fields: The Vaudevillians Are a Remnant of Prehistoric Type of Stage Artist." *North American*, May 7, 1901, 7.

"Childish Waifs, Victims of Circumstances, Are Rescued from Lives of Sinful Misery." *North American*, May 13, 1901, 16.

"Earl of Yarmouth May Be a Poor Actor on the Stage, But He Was a Fine One While on the Witness Stand." *North American*, May 14, 1901, 2.

"Mothers' Congress Hears Warm Words." *North American*, May 24, 1901, 2.

"Sardou's 'Diplomacy' Revived before an Enthusiastic Philadelphia Audience."
North American, June 15, 1901, 9.

"Man Responsible for Seeming Lack of Charity Woman Has for Woman." *North American*, July 2, 1901, 8.

"'Beaucaire' Is Stage Failure." *North American*, October 20, 1901, 7.

"Mrs. Roosevelt's $300 Idea Upheld: Philadelphia Women Agree Their Wardrobe Need Not Cost More." *North American*, October 23, 1901, 3.

"'Under Two Flags' a Stage Thriller." *North American*, October 23, 1901, 4.

"Astounding Feats in Arithmetic Performed by Jacques Inaudi Are Due to an Abnormal Brain." *North American*, October 25, 1901, 7.

"Name Miss Barrymore's Substitute for Genius." *North American*, October 27, 1901, 2.

"Vaudeville Houses Always Have Something New and Bright for Their Patrons, and Satisfy Demand for Novelty." *North American*, November 3, 1901, 7.

"Is Attack on Philadelphia Manners Refuted by This Street Car Incident?" *North American*, November 5, 1901, 8.

"'Maid Marian,' Sequel to 'Robin Hood,' Is Devoid of Humor and Melody." *North American*, November 5, 1901, 9.

"Decadence of the Bostonians a Sorrowful Thing for Theatre-Goers to Contemplate." *North American*, November 10, 1901, 7.

"Glimmer of Hope in 'The Widow Jones.'" *North American*, November 13, 1901, 2.

"Dreary Comic Operas Make the Gods of the Gallery Sorrowful." *North American*, November 17, 1901, 7.

"Sir Henry Irving's Shylock Is the Same Masterful Characterization as of Old." *North American*, November 19, 1901, 7.

"Twin Dragons of Stageland Have Attacked Ellen Terry." *North American*, November 24, 1901, 7.

"How Hackett's Face Saved the Play, 'Don Caesar's Return.'" *North American*, November 26, 1901, 5.

"Women Take Big Contract in Trying to Purify Politics." *North American*, November 27, 1901, 8.

"Miriam Michelson Advises Young Man Who Sees All the Shows and Wants to Act." *North American*, December 15, 1901, 7.

"Ah Luey's Self." *Bulletin*, December 22, 1901, 6.

"Eternal Femininity Not Altered by College Course." *North American*, December 23, 1901, 8.

"Woman Suffragists Pay Warmest Honors to Their Leader, Miss Susan B. Anthony." *North American*, February 16, 1902, 2.

"Burlesque Needs Only Two Males." *North American*, February 23, 1902, 5.

"'Eben Holden' is Hopelessly Insipid Character, Although the Part Is Acted in Good Faith: Mr. Holland Does His Best with the Material at Hand, Which Is Bad." *North American*, February 25, 1902, 11.

"Diffidence of the Lover in Modern Drama as Seen by Miss Miriam Michelson: Too Many Short Sighted Swains Prove Monotonous as a Regular Theatrical Diet." *North American*, March 2, 1902, 5.

"Mrs. Campbell's Second Mrs. Tanqueray Is Far from a Convincing Character." *North American*, March 4, 1902, 5.

"Sothern's First Act Is Artistic." *North American*, March 5, 1902, 2.

"How a Woman Views the Six-Day Race." *North American*, March 12, 1902, 3.

"Grace George Is a Typical Southerner: 'Under Southern Skies' a True Picture of Dixie Before the War." *North American*, March 12, 1902, 11.

"Pantomime Would Suit Mrs. Campbell." *North American*, March 13, 1902, 7.

"Miss Elsie De Wolfe Is as Impossible as the Part She Plays." *North American*, March 18, 1902, 16.

"Miriam Michelson Tells of the Shortcomings of Elsie De Wolfe as Star." *North American*, March 23, 1902, 7.

"Opera Not Overpoweringly Musical Though It Contains Some Really Good Numbers." *North American*, March 25, 1902, 5.

"One Comic Opera, Miss Michelson Says, Is but the Forerunner of Another." *North American*, March 30, 1902, 7.

"Mrs. Haines Tells Story on the Stand." *North American*, April 1, 1902, 1, 8.

"Mrs. Gilbert Is the Star in 'The Girl and the Judge.'" *North American*, April 1, 1902, 9.

"So-Called Critics, Miss Michelson Says, Are to Blame for Wooden Stars." *North American*, April 6, 1902, 2.

"Miriam Michelson Has a Supposititious Interview with Star of 'My Antoinette': She Also Writes an Open Letter to Janice Meredith, a Favorite of a Year Ago." *North American*, April 13, 1902, 7.

"'Rip Van Winkle' Is Now Out of Date." *North American*, April 15, 1902, 3.

"Miss Miriam Michelson Writes on the Weaknesses of the Theatrically Great." *North American*, April 20, 1902, 7.

"Brownback's Method of Wooing May Lead Some Fair Ones to Similar Conquests." *North American*, April 22, 1902, 8.

"Lingerie Bars to Comedienne's Door: Miss Michelson Breaks in and Secures Supposititious Interview with Marie Cahill." *North American*, April 27, 1902, 7.

"Perverseness of Women Shown in the Case of Mrs. Joseph Prescine, Mother." *North American*, April 28, 1902, 8.

"Actress Impersonation of 'The Unwelcome Mrs. Hatch' the Best Seen Here: She Forgets Herself in the Portrayal of a Most Difficult Character." *North American*, April 29, 1902, 16.

"Miss Michelson in a Suppositious Interview Finds Julia Marlow in Plight." *North American*, May 4, 1902, 7.

"Motives of Women Who Commit Theft." *North American*, May 6, 1902, 8.

"Miss Michelson Compares Slumbering Philadelphia to Other Cities." *North American*, May 11, 1902, 11.

"Army of 30,000 Dunkards Will Gather in General Conference at Harrisburg." *North American*, May 18, 1902, 5.

"Miss Michelson Takes a Peep into the Future of the Musical Comedy." *North American*, May 18, 1902, 11.

"Costumes Should Distinguish the Married from Unmarried Women." *North American*, May 19, 1902, 8.

"Miss Miriam Michelson Makes a Contrast of Some Notable Actors." *North American*, May 25, 1902, 11.

"Mrs. Mason, Disgusted at Human Misery, Starts an 'Old Ladies' Home' for Horses." *North American*, May 31, 1902, 8.

"Theatrical Syndicate Reaped $20,000,000, but the Public Did Not Always Get Its Share of Pleasure: Management That Sits Back and Says, 'What Will You Do about It?' What Was Best and What Was Worst in Season That Is Ended." *North American*, June 1, 1902, 11.

"Miriam Michelson Says Soul Is the Feature Lacking in Mrs. Campbell's Characterizations." *North American*, December 16, 1902, 7.

Archives

The following collections contain materials relevant to Michelson's work, including correspondence.

Bobbs-Merrill MSS, Lilly Library Manuscript Collections, Indiana University, Bloomington.

Century Company Records, Manuscripts and Archives Division, The New York Public Library.

Harvard Theatre Collection, Houghton Library, Harvard University.

Houghton-Mifflin Reader Reports on Manuscripts Submitted for Publication, 1882–1931, Houghton Library, Harvard University.

Joseph T. Goodman Papers, The Bancroft Library, University of California, Berkeley.

Index

Page numbers in *italics* refer to images.

CPSIA information can be obtained
at www.ICGtesting.com
Printed in the USA
FSHW011921230419
57473FS